WOLF'S RECKONING

USA TODAY BESTSELLING AUTHOR
EVE L. MITCHELL

The
Blueridge Hollow
Series Book 1

Wolf's Reckoning

USA TODAY BESTSELLING AUTHOR
Eve L. Mitchell

Foreword

This series takes place in the same world as my Blackridge Peak and Shadowridge Peak series. You don't need to read those first—this series stands completely on its own, and at a timeline similar to Blackridge Peak. However, you might enjoy Blueridge Hollow more if you're already familiar with those stories, since there will be occasional references and cameo appearances. No spoilers though, I promise.

Blackridge Peak and *Shadowridge Peak* are located somewhere in the Rocky Mountains, although their exact positions are intentionally vague.

For *Blueridge Hollow*, I've moved south into the Appalachian range. Once again, geography is loosely drawn on purpose. This isn't about pins on a map—it's about the wolves who live there, the legacy they carry, and the futures they fight for.

Book Description

In Blueridge Hollow, tradition is law—and tradition doesn't bend for daughters.

Rowen was raised to lead: fierce, disciplined, and loyal to the bone. But with her father—the alpha—dying, brutal reality sets in. No matter how skilled she is, no matter how ready, the pack will never accept a female leader.

The Pack Council has a solution. A political mating. Choose a husband. Surrender the title. Smile while they hand her birthright to someone else, and Blueridge Hollow will secure their future.

Then Wolfe returns.

The boy she once rejected is now the man who threatens to upend everything. Wolfe is everything the pack wants in a leader. Dominant, dangerous, and completely outside her control. Worse, her wolf knows him. *Wants* him. And the feeling is anything but one-sided.

Rowen must make an impossible choice:
Fight for a place she was never meant to claim…
Or surrender to a man who could save her pack—and break her in the process.

Some wolves are born to follow.
Rowen was born to *defy*.

Note from the Author

This is an adult paranormal romance set in a traditional pack structure, featuring themes best suited for mature readers. Expect emotionally intense relationships, shifter challenges, and dynamics rooted in dominance, grief, and forced proximity.

As the series progresses, themes of abuse and violence are referenced (though not shown on-page). If you're sensitive to these elements, please proceed with caution.

The central couple's story unfolds over three full-length books—with claws, conflict, and enough chemistry to set the woods on fire.

The mist is rising.
The Hollow remembers.
Tonight, I write in blood and bone.

Chapter 1

Rowen

THE MORNING MIST CLUNG LOW TO THE EARTH, THICK AS wool, twisting around the worn stones of the clearing.

The pack gathered in a semi-circle, quiet, solemn, respectful. I stayed back, half-hidden beneath a drooping pine, watching the Binding unfold.

Kneeling before the druid were two shifters—a girl barely past her first heat and a boy too stiff in his borrowed suit.

Both bowed.

Both allegedly *chosen*.

On paper, an unexpected match. Under the Goddess, a perfect match.

I caught the tremor in the girl's hands as she lifted the iron dagger. Saw the way her breath shuddered out as she carved their names into the old heartwood slab between them. Was it from fear?

Or worse…resignation?

My wolf shifted uneasily under my skin, feeling restless; it felt like it was pacing backward and forward. The true

Binding would take place tonight, under the full moon, where they would perform the rites again, just them, the druid, and the spirits of the pack.

This Binding was for the living. Tonight's would be for the Goddess and the dead.

The moon Binding would be similar to this. Their names would be carved into Heartwood, only this time, it would be the ancient tree that stood in the thickest, most ancient part of the forest.

Their bond would be "sealed in wood and soul." It was said that if it was broken after the rite, doing so risked madness or death.

Or a really messy divorce. I bit back my smile at my thoughts. I watched the two rise shakily to their feet before the druid of the pack.

I'd heard that the girl was caught off guard when her heat hit her. The boy was known to her, and the coupling was consensual, but I questioned if he was her choice; a glance to my left revealed a young male shifter struggling to hide silent tears, which suggested the girl might have chosen differently if she had been able when her heat hit her.

Her family was a proud holder of traditions. The *old* traditions. The ones as ancient as the mountains that sheltered us.

As I watched them embrace their parents, I wondered if this was what we were meant for. Did the Goddess really want us to be bound to each other like this? A partner for life because of an unexpected heat. Bound together from fear, or perhaps surrender? Not through choice.

My gaze wandered over the pack that had gathered here and were now congratulating the two newlyweds. I watched their parents accept the celebratory handshakes and back-slaps. They were smiling, but their lips were thin, their eyes sharp as they watched the boy who cried as he hung back from the crowd.

"You look…contemplative."

I turned to my side, smiling in greeting at Adair as she sidled up beside me. "I didn't expect you here," I told her truthfully.

Adair was younger than I was, but her wisdom and her maturity often made me forget that I was three years her senior. Her short, golden brown hair was thick and a little wild, like she chopped it haphazardly herself one night out of frustration and never looked back. She had more important things to consider than the way she looked.

See? Mature.

Adair shrugged. "I wanted to see for myself that they were willing," she told me, her voice lowered. A wolf's hearing was sharp, but even I had to strain to catch her softly spoken words. "I heard they were together for the full five days of her heat," she murmured.

"Really?" That changed things, and my wolf settled.

Adair nodded. "Yup, their parents were quick to arrange this, because nothing says *you better marry me in the morning* more than five days of unrestrained fucking."

My bark of laughter caused others to turn my way, but I simply met their curious stares. I was used to being subject to the pack's scrutiny. As the alpha's daughter, I had endured their stares, their gossip, and their speculation my entire life.

"Neither of them approached you?" I asked her for clarification. The pack elders respected Adair because she toed the line *just* enough. For the younger pack, she was sometimes seen as the person to go to when you'd screwed up and needed real advice, not lectures.

Or rituals.

"No." She gave me a serene smile, reached out, and patted my hand. "Goddess Luna is happy with these two, I believe." She glanced back at the two newlyweds, who were smiling at each other with joy. "They look happy too."

I watched her as she wandered away, not towards the pack that were gathered but towards our homes.

"The alpha is not with you?"

Once more, I was caught unawares and turned to the speaker. It was the young male who had shed his tears for the couple.

"He is not," I told him. He stood only a few inches taller than I, and up close I wondered about his age. "He blessed the union earlier this morning." I saw the anger spark in his eyes as I spoke. "And the Goddess will bless their union tonight." My voice held a gentle rebuke, and I was glad to see his shoulders straighten.

"Of course, Rowen..." He looked towards the happy couple, and I saw the devastation on his face.

"Her?" I asked him gently. "Or him?"

"Her." His smile was watery when he looked back. "It should have been me."

I inhaled deeply, the smell of earth and pine resin as familiar to me as breathing. "I'm heading back to the hall; do you want to walk with me?"

I watched his eyes widen at the offer, but he quickly recovered and nodded in agreement. As we walked away from the pack, I heard sounds of some of the pack following, but they were far enough away that I could speak quietly to my companion.

"Forgive me, I've misplaced your name."

"Henry."

"Of course. Your mother, Sylvia, bakes the best pumpkin loaf this side of the mountain."

"She'd be honored to hear that, Rowen."

I nudged his side gently. "I prefer to see a smile than see your sorrow, Henry." Looking up at the trees above, I admired the blue sky peeking through. "Were you together?" I asked him carefully, and when he shook his head, I nodded. "Did she know how you felt about her?" Henry gave a sharp nod. "And she…"

"Said we were only friends."

"Ah." Slipping my hands into my pants pockets, we walked on a few more paces. "A female's heat gives little warning." I saw him glance at me, but I carried on. "The first urge is"—I gave a light chuckle—"well, be pleased you never have to experience it."

"Mom says it's painful."

"It is." I recalled my own heats. "It slices through you like a hot knife, everything inside you feels like it's burning, the pain can put even the strongest of us on our knees." I was speaking from experience. I'd been on my knees begging for mercy from the Goddess too many times. "Then the burning changes. It's no longer hurting you, but *consuming* you." I caught his eye, noting his ears reddening as I spoke freely about a shifter's heat. "It needs to be sated or endured." I held his eye. "Do you understand?"

"Yes, Rowen." His head dipped. "But…"

"Once the initial coupling is over, the heat fades, but it

does not disappear," I carried on, ignoring his hesitation, knowing my own misgivings from earlier had been resolved. "What comes after is *choice*."

Henry looked up at me in confusion. "Rowen?"

I stopped and faced him. "Once her initial wave had passed and her body satisfied, she had the choice to leave. She didn't. She rode out her heat with him. She *chose* him." Reaching out, I pushed the fallen lock of hair off his face. "She didn't choose you, Henry. You are her friend, and you need to honor that. Honor our Goddess. Honor your friend's choice."

He nodded, ignoring the lone tear that slipped over and spilled down his cheek. "I know, but it…it hurts."

"It will." We resumed walking. "But in time it will fade, and you can return to being friends." We'd reached the hall, and it was clear this was where our paths would part. "Are you okay?"

Henry forced a smile, and he looked so young and innocent that I wanted to hug him. "You are very wise, Rowen. You honor our pack and our alpha."

My laugh was light. "Well, when I need to remind my father of that, don't be surprised if I call for you."

His grin was a huge improvement, and we both turned when we heard his name called. He turned back to me with an eye roll. "That's my mom. I'd better go. Thank you, Rowen."

I watched him go, then entered the hall. There were few pack members in it, and I moved through them quickly as I made my way to the back chambers, where my father rested. Opening the door to his private quarters, I shouldn't have been surprised to see the druid was already there.

The druid was a staple of the pack, a trusted advisor to the alpha, and they had steered me in the right direction a time or two as well. However, they were also, and I said this with immense respect for them, a creepy bastard.

They sat in their seat, not too close to the alpha but close enough. Their robes were homespun, heavy with charms made of bone, teeth, iron nails, and what looked like raven feathers. The bird feathers changed depending on their mood. I'd never looked too closely at the bones to know if they changed.

Their presence hummed with the quiet power of wind through ancient oaks. Their skin was the color of ivory under the palest moonlight, smooth and almost metallic in the soft light, with a faint scar arcing across one brow—a whisper of past trials.

Their hair was the most startling white. Sculpted into an undercut that exposed the graceful curve of their skull, the sides shaved down to a whisper of stubble, while above, a thick crest of moonlit white swept back in a single, elegant arc. At the nape, those strands cascaded into longer lengths, tumbling in gentle waves down their back, with flecks of pale lavender and dove-gray drifting through the mass. Ever since I was a child, I had been fascinated by the druid's hair.

"Your heat comes soon."

The smile I gave them was not a friendly one, before I turned to my father. "Hi, Dad," I greeted my father, leaning over him to kiss his cheek. "The Binding was nice."

The druid's sniff wasn't quiet. I ignored them, taking a seat beside my father's bedside. He lay still, his arms over the covers, his palms flat against the sheets. His hair was thick and white with age, his skin pale. I didn't remember the last time he'd managed a whole day without needing to rest.

"The pack needs strength." The druid ignored my ignoring of them.

"Can I get you a cup of tea?" I asked my dad.

"Rowen, daughter, you should listen to the druid. They tell me that there may be a strong leader up north, who would be good for the pack. Good bloodlines. It could mean good alliances."

The words slid off me like rain on stone, but inside, the wrongness howled. Leaders. Bloodlines. *Alliances.* A perfect trap just waiting for me to step inside it.

They said *marriage*, I said *cage*.

The druid lifted their staff—a gnarled thing strung with bone and iron—and my father fell silent. "Two wolves, two names, one future," they intoned, their voice low and heavy as a burial stone.

My father nodded with approval. To him, it was just another contract to be sealed under mist and expectation. I made myself stay still. I had been taught stillness as a child —taught how to wear obedience like armor.

But inside, my wolf paced. My wolf wanted to run. Wanted to fight the stillness.

The druid's gaze met mine, one eye gray like mist, the other the deep amber of a wolf's. "Soon you must be ready."

It wasn't a command.

It was a warning.

Soon.

The word throbbed in my blood. Before my father could latch onto it, I stood swiftly. "Were you able to visit the kitchen earlier, Dad?" I asked him, knowing he wouldn't have. "If you haven't, I'll go and ensure our new bonded pair has cake for after their supper."

My dad looked at me with a regretful expression in his gaze. "I'm sorry, I…I wasn't able. And then the—"

I leaned down to kiss his cheek once more. "I'll do it now, Dad. I'll get them to send you a cup of tea and a snack too, hmm?"

He smiled up at me, his gaze softening from alpha to parent. He clasped my hand, the strength all but gone, a reminder that the once unshakable man was fading. "You're a good daughter, Rowen."

I ignored the druid's harrumphing as much as I had since I entered the room. I liked the druid. I respected them. It just seemed that lately, my patience for their comments, sniffs, and harrumphs was running out, and they were grating on my very last nerve.

"I'll be back soon," I promised Dad, and I left before he dismissed me.

I couldn't breathe in that room anymore. The druid would start talking about *Bindings* and *duty* next.

My Binding. *My* duty to the pack.

The druid was not a bad person; on the contrary, they were important to the pack. They were just…*annoying*.

My father was my priority right now. The druid knew that, but still it felt like both of them had a hand around my throat, pressing down on me.

Like tradition itself.

I felt no guilt about leaving them both in my dad's chambers. I visited the kitchen to request a tray be sent to my dad, and then using the back exits to the pack hall, I slipped away, into the trees that offered me a sanctuary from prying eyes. I'd already spoken to the kitchen earlier this morning, and the request for the bonded pair had already been made.

My feet found the trail long before my thoughts did. They knew the way. My black lace-up boots trod lightly on the mossy path until I stopped beside a familiar oak with a deep hollow in its trunk. I tugged them off first—each boot peeling free with a soft "pop"—then stripped away my socks, folding them over the heels. Next came the dark-green, cropped cargo pants, their pockets checked in case I had left anything I shouldn't have unguarded. My black tee, smooth and cool in my hands, followed, and finally, my white tank top, along with my bra. I stacked my clothes neatly inside the tree's cavity, a casual ritual I'd performed countless times before.

My fingers worked through my braid quickly, loosening it until my hair spilled down my back and over my shoulders.

With a sigh of relief, I shifted.

My wolf stretched and then I ran.

Fast and hard, the kind of run that flayed your soul back from your bones. My breath sawed through my chest, my pulse thundered, echoing in rhythm to the grip of soil as my paws thudded over the earth.

Blueridge Hollow opened around me like a secret. Out here, the rules didn't speak. The forest didn't care who my father was or what the druid whispered behind carved doors.

The pines towered over me like ancient sentinels, bark gnarled and thick with moss. Mist curled low across the ground, seeping from the hollows between tree roots, wrapping around my legs like old friends welcoming me home.

Crickets rasped from the underbrush. Something unseen cracked a twig deeper in. A blue jay called once, sharp and lonesome.

And still I ran.

I ran past the iron markers set by wolves long dead. Past the spring that carved through the mountain like a scar and was the source of the Hollow's water. Up and up until the path vanished and the land forgot the touch of man.

Here, the air tasted thinner. Wilder.

The earth smelled of smoke, wet stone, and the sharp tang of something older than even Blueridge Hollow.

I stopped beneath a ridge where the trees fell away into dark ravines, my body panting, tongue lolling, and legs burning.

Above me, the sky was deepening from blue to violet, and the first stars would start to show by the time I returned back to the pack. My head turned as the scent of rain was carried on the wind.

I looked over my shoulder. The Hollow was hidden now, swallowed by the trees below, and the silence all around me felt ominous.

I shifted back to human form, crouched at the edge of the ravine, hair wild and loose, body still feeling the burn of the run, and for a moment—just one—I felt free.

Chapter 2

Rowen

The air tasted wrong.

I'd barely made it back to the pack hall before the scent hit me—my *own* scent. Sharper, heavier, threaded with a *need* I knew too well.

My heat.

Not full-blown, not yet. But close. Close enough the male wolves let their gazes linger too long. Close enough that my skin felt too tight, too hot, like I'd outgrown it during my run.

I didn't detour to my father's rooms; I went to my own rooms and shut myself in. I threw the window open and let in the thick Appalachian air, heavy with mist, moss, and the hint of decay—familiar things. *Safe* things. The slight breeze kissed my skin, and I waited for the pressure in my chest to ease.

It didn't.

I rolled my head from left to right, trying to ease the sudden tension in my neck. This wasn't my first heat—heck, it wasn't even my twelfth. It should've been routine by now. Predictable. *Manageable*.

But nothing about my heats ever felt normal. The ache that simmered in my spine, the pulse that thrummed under my skin. Definitely *not* in the way my instincts had started shifting—searching—without my consent.

As if my inner self knew something I didn't. The wolf inside me began to pace, and I wanted to scold myself for getting worked up early. I'd learned not to shift when my heat was on me.

I would already be on edge when the *gift* from the Goddess hit me, and changing into my wolf form did nothing other than increase the need tenfold.

The pain and suffering of our heat made me wonder if the deity that ruled the shifter race was really a female. Why would a woman choose to inflict the pure discomfort of a heat on a fellow female? The urge, the gnawing *hunger* to be filled by a male when our heat was upon us, was utterly consuming.

Frenzied.

That's what I'd heard one female describe it as once. Her body was fraught with frenzy, and all she could think about was the carnal need to rut. I knew how she felt. Every female shifter knew the need to mate when the heat struck.

Some succumbed to the need. Some did not.

I did not. I had never been with a partner when the heat struck. I was no blushing virgin, but any coupling I had been part of had been when I knew my heat was nowhere near.

In addition to enduring the heat, the Goddess also blessed us with the blood of the moon. Like human women, we bled monthly.

And that wasn't even the worst of it. Goddess Luna made it so that only a male shifter could be alpha. I snorted in contempt. Even the humans allowed their women to rule. To *lead*.

Not shifters. Alphas were male and *only* male.

I closed my eyes against the injustice of our Goddess. The druid had laughed at my observations when I was younger and told me that, because females could not only endure these trials but also *overcome* them, that meant female shifters were the stronger of the race.

It had sounded good for about five minutes and had appeased my ire. Until I learned of a female in our pack who had gone into heat, alone in the forest, and a hunting pack of males had come across her. She was unmated. Unbound to any male. Her heat was on her, and the males were drunk on her scent. I'd been too young to understand it then, but I remember my mother leaving the hall with the wives of my father's betas.

When I was older and knew more about our heat and the need to mate, I realized my mother had gone to check on the female and ensure that, while it was unconventional for a female to take multiple partners during her heat, it had been consensual.

While Luna may have cursed us with this dependency on males, it was still a choice on who we chose to take into our bodies.

We were shifters. Our wolves shaped our personalities, defined who we were, governed our nature, and that nature demanded we *breed*. Survival of the fittest ruled everything. The harsh reality was that, for any species to thrive, there needed to be a species to fight for.

But no matter what, no still meant no.

We could shift our forms from human to wolves, but that did not mean we were animals.

There was *always* a choice.

I sniffed. Well. Unless you were a true mate. Only alphas were blessed with a *true destined* mate. The rest of us picked wisely, but it was said that Luna herself chose the mate of an alpha. A bond so strong neither shifter could resist it. One female meant for one male only. To support. To *serve*.

I thanked the stars that I would never have to endure *that* bond. To be tied to a male like that? With no say in who I would spend my life with? Nope. No thank you.

My father already had gray in his hair when he met my mother, his mate. He'd spent years as alpha of Blueridge Hollow before our Goddess sent my mother his way, years without her and such a short time with her. It was another sign from the Goddess that a pack was blessed. Not only was there an alpha, but there was also an alpha's mate. What more could you want?

A male heir with the alpha gene.

Instead, my father got a daughter.

On the plus side, I had the freedom to fall in love and pick my own husband. I allowed myself the fantasy for a few seconds until reality reared its head.

In truth, I had no freedom to choose. I was as stuck as the true mate. I was an alpha's daughter, and daughters of leaders did not get to choose their partner based on something so weak as *love*.

They chose duty. Pack honor. *Loyalty*. I snorted with contempt. I would like to think that my father would listen to *my* choice, but ultimately, he would decide my husband based on what was best for the pack. On who would serve the pack the best. On what *stranger* to our ways could be molded the easiest by the druid and tolerated easiest by me.

How many like me resented every single bit of the duty we shouldered for the good of the pack? Or was I, as the druid liked to mutter, too strong-willed?

My father was an excellent alpha. Strong. Fierce. Wise. He had taught me everything I knew about pack politics and how to be a good leader. But what neither of us could change was the fact that I was his only child…and packs did not follow a sole female leader. It wasn't our way. Males led in a shifter society because it was the design of the Goddess that an alpha *should* lead every pack.

It was more apparent day by day that my father would be too weak to defend this pack. The sooner I had a husband, a male who would take my father's place, the sooner I would be able to give them my guidance on how to lead this pack.

I knew time was running out.

A knock sounded on my door. Sharp. Deliberate.

I didn't answer. I already knew who it was and what they would want to talk about.

The druid was as obsessed with marrying me off as was my father. Probably more so. I didn't need to answer the door. I didn't need to have the conversation. I already knew what they'd say. What they always said.

"You're the alpha's daughter. You have a duty." Or their other favorite. *"Your marriage could secure Blueridge Hollow's future."* Then they'd talk about strengthening packlands. Alliances. Ensuring bloodlines were preserved.

The druid would try to be subtle. They'd word it in such

a way that made you think it was a choice. But I knew better.

This wasn't even about me. It was about legacy. Territory. Stability. *Duty*.

Blueridge Hollow could not crown a female alpha. But if I secured a good match, a wise match, I could give the druid what they wanted.

A leader they could control. And in time, a husband that I could shape.

I would be the bridge—the bargaining chip. Our traditions here in the Hollow would be preserved. The old ways. The ways that held the spirit of the land in as much reverence as the moon.

Our pack wouldn't need to break tradition. The only thing that would break would be me.

And I still hadn't accepted that. But I would.

For my father. For our way of life. For the pack.

Dad was sitting up in his bed today. He looked healthier; his eyes were bright, his cheeks had a rosy glow, and his smile was quick to grace his face.

I was the only one feeling sour in the room because they would soon revisit their favorite topic: me.

"I came by your rooms last evening," the druid said as he watched me. "You did not answer."

My dad looked up from his bowl of porridge. "Rowen must not have been in," he said quickly. "She would never be so bad-mannered." He beamed at me, and I felt a twinge of guilt.

"I saw her go into her rooms," the druid said with cold certainty.

I shrugged. "And you would have seen that I had been out for a run," I told him. "I was hot and sweaty," I continued, "and needed out of my clothes. As you mentioned yesterday, my heat is coming."

My dad coughed. For shifters, nudity was common. The urge of a female's heat was well known and viewed with either sympathy or envy, depending on how she chose to spend the time. But for some reason, my dad, who had been an alpha of this pack for years, still flushed whenever *I* mentioned my heat. No one else. The druid could talk about my heat all day long, and Dad wouldn't blink. But if I mentioned it? He quickly became uncomfortable.

It was a weapon I didn't mind employing if it meant getting me out of situations like this.

"I knew Rowen wouldn't be rude," Dad said with a smile my way. "She was bathing and probably didn't hear you at the door."

"Of course." The druid fixed me with their hard stare, their mismatched eyes conveying the unspoken *bullshit* that they chose not to voice out loud. "I never considered the possibility."

Because he hadn't heard the pipes running. I knew it. The druid knew it. But Dad didn't question my lie and moved on. My father was indeed a wise alpha.

"Do you wish to know why I was at your door?" the druid asked.

"I imagine it would be to remind me of my need to find a husband." I looked out the window to watch the morning peek through the canopy of trees.

"For the good of the pack." The druid's voice was firm. "There is a Pack Council gathering in a few days."

I turned from the window, heat prickling at the base of my neck. I looked at my dad, who was watching me pensively. "I've never attended Pack Council before." I looked between the two of them. "I stay here while Dad goes. When he goes."

"I won't be attending this Pack Council," my dad said, looking down at his hands. "But I would like for you and my beta Lewis to attend in my place."

"Lewis?" I looked at the druid, who watched me impassively. "Lewis and I are not the best traveling companions, Dad." My glance flicked back to the druid. "Why can't you go?"

The druid sniffed with contempt. "My place is here, with the pack and the land. Pack Council politics are not for me to involve myself with."

Just this *pack's politics.*

"Uh-huh. That's convenient."

"As convenient as you entering a shower as soon as you close your bedroom door."

Well, someone was feeling snarky about being ignored.

"Going to the meeting will let you see the sons who are…free," my dad spoke, taking the conversation back to the point. "There are alphas who don't pass the gene to their sons, and there are many packs that have a pack leader, not an alpha, smaller packs…more malleable."

I didn't comment. I let him and the druid discuss when Lewis and I should leave. I had grown used to being discussed as if I weren't there. It had been happening more and more as his health suffered. I understood his desire to ensure our pack was protected. That *I* was protected.

But the truth stung—they didn't want me to lead a pack. They wanted a symbol. A womb with loyalty.

And the worst part of it was that I *understood* it. Neither my father nor the druid was wrong. Very few packs stayed true to the land and the old ways as we did, preferring to embrace the human world more and let tradition slip through their fingers.

If I didn't find the right husband...then I wouldn't be able to *align* us, and the Hollow would be in danger of its roots, its laws, its very bones being buried in progress.

And yet still, every part of me rebelled at the idea. My wolf didn't want to be chosen like cattle at auction.

She wanted to run.

To bite.

To *decide*.

She wanted something else. *Someone.* And she was growing tired of waiting.

"Do you agree, Rowen?"

I looked up at the druid, who had their stare fixed on me. I knew they knew I hadn't been listening. My upcoming heat was making me cranky and less focused.

"I wasn't listening." I could bullshit with the best, but I also didn't have the energy, and sometimes just owning up and admitting you weren't listening was just as easy.

"Your heat should be passed in a few days, and it is better to leave after that."

Or the alternative was that I traveled in tremendous pain, or worse, tangled in the arms of another. The very thought made me queasy.

"I think if you want Lewis to ever return to this pack, waiting for my heat to pass is best."

My dad chuckled. Lewis was much older than I was, and less likeable, more rigid, and as talkative as a stone. He'd been in my life for *all* of my life, and I don't think he'd ever spoken more than a few sentences to me at a time.

What a fun outing this would be.

"You will be in your rooms tonight." The druid looked over at me.

I almost snapped at him and then thought about how he had said it. It wasn't a question; it was a fact.

My heat would fully be upon me this evening.

Standing, I leaned over and kissed my father's cheek. "I'll get some stuff from the kitchens, check over the meal planning, and ensure the drain from the last storm has been cleared. I'll see you in a few days."

He clasped my hand. "In a few days, daughter. May the Goddess grant you peace."

If the Goddess wanted to grant me peace, she'd allow females to be alphas and wouldn't make us endure a heat. I didn't say that out loud though. Instead, I took my leave and went about my daily chores of ensuring my pack ran smoothly.

Because that's what leaders did.

They led.

Chapter 3

Rowen

My heat had broken sometime in the night.

Three days of pacing, clawing, and sleeplessness passed, and that burning ache that persisted inside me finally vanished as swiftly as it had arrived. Three days of misery left behind what felt like a cracked-open husk of myself.

I hadn't needed a male. Or a promise. Sheer willpower and locked doors had been my "go-to" ever since I endured my first heat with a body that was ready to betray me in every possible way.

I hadn't shifted. Hadn't begged. Hadn't howled.

Not once.

I'd buried the need. The desire. Like always.

But I felt the aftermath in every inch of my skin—sore, hollow, stretched thin. Like something inside me had burned through and hadn't quite regrown.

Still, there was no time for rest. No room for weakness. My father would be waiting to see his beta Lewis and me off for our journey to the Pack Council.

With my hair quickly braided and tied off with a leather

band, I pulled on my boots, grabbed my oversized charcoal-checked jacket with lots of roomy pockets, put it on over my cropped black tank, and pushed the jacket sleeves up to my elbows for maximum reach. After checking that I had everything I needed, I shoved open the door.

As I walked to his rooms, I kept the silent chant in my head. Let them talk about mates and alliances. Let them treat my womb as if it were a bargaining chip.

Let them.

Every time I endured a heat as an unmated shifter, I faced an agony that none of the males of my race would ever know. I wasn't about to bow to anyone now. This was *my* pack, and it would be best if they didn't forget it.

The druid was nowhere to be seen, thankfully, when I reached my father's chambers. Lewis stood off in the corner, his eyes on the pack outside. Dad was up and dressed and looked like he had been out for a run, but he didn't appear better for it. I didn't tell him that though; instead, I forced a wide smile and greeted him with a kiss.

"Hey, enjoy your run?" I noticed that Lewis had a small, compact traveling backpack and frowned. "You packed?" I asked.

He didn't say anything—shocker—but he nodded once. I don't think he disliked me; he was just…quiet. *Reserved,* my father called him. *Thorough.* Meaning he thought over every single thing before committing.

I was all for thinking things through; rash actions had consequences. However, when Lewis was mulling over something, snails crawling backwards would be faster to reach the finish line.

"The morning mist was refreshing," my dad said,

bringing my attention back to him. He reached out and clasped my arm. "Three days," he mused. "You're lucky your heat is so short."

It was a testament to my inner strength that I maintained the smile on my face and kept my thoughts to myself. "Yes, I'm blessed," I murmured.

"Why do you have no pack?" Dad looked me over. "You cannot appear in front of the Pack Council wearing that."

I blinked. Looking down at my cropped top, combat pants, and boots, I glanced back at him. "This is what I always wear."

Dad was scowling. "You need a dress."

"I definitely do *not* need a dress."

Dad glanced at Lewis, who had been watching but had looked away so quickly that I was sure he had pulled an eye muscle. "Beta Lewis, you have daughters...tell my Rowen why she needs to wear a dress."

I fixed my stare on Lewis, one eyebrow raised. *Daring* him to tell me.

"It's a long trek to the Council," Lewis said instead. "Change later."

My eyes narrowed. He hadn't agreed with my father, but he hadn't disagreed either. I sniffed. I admired his diplomacy.

The door to my father's rooms opened, and the druid entered with a small backpack. "Rowen, you left this." He held it out to me, and I almost didn't accept it.

"You packed for me?" I asked him, opening the pack and seeing a change of T-shirts, underwear, and socks, along with a bag I recognized as my toiletry bag. No dresses.

"Pack Council meetings can take two days," the druid

said casually. "I wouldn't want you to worry about your appearance."

They weren't being catty, but I was doubtful they were being sincere. I slung the pack cross-body, the single strap cutting across my chest. Not a full backpack—compact, tough, just big enough to hold what I needed and nothing more.

Lewis jerked his head to the door. That was basically a command to leave. I turned to my dad and reached out to hug him.

"Be gentle, Rowen," he murmured in my ear, low enough the others wouldn't hear. "Watch their actions, their expressions, see beyond the words they speak."

I squeezed him tight. "I will."

"Don't get detained," he warned, louder as he stepped back.

"It was one time," I complained with a roll of my eyes. "And they apologized afterwards."

"Because I tore through their chamber," he reminded me gruffly. "I'm not going to be able to do that again, daughter."

"I'm ten years older and wiser," I said with a wry grin. "I know how not to get caught." With a wink, I left him and the druid both muttering about me being impulsive.

Me impulsive? Once maybe. Six years leading my pack and taking care of the essential things that my father would have deferred to my mother, had sculpted me into a more *responsible* shifter.

I spoke to a lot of the pack as we left. A few reminders to the kitchens for meal requirements, a menu for the upcoming week, even though I was only going to be gone

one, now two, nights, they needed to prep more than just a day in advance.

We were a medium-sized pack, and not all ate together, but it was good to plan ahead and know what stock we needed.

Lewis was my silent companion throughout; he never hurried me, huffed, or gave a pointed look. He knew I was doing as much as possible so my father wouldn't have to.

The druid had assured me they would be on hand in my absence, but all I needed was some sign from the Goddess, and the druid would drop my father's needs for the supposed needs of the land.

Which was how it should be. I knew that. The druid served the pack, not just one member. Yet, I couldn't help but wish they would be a bit more selective about who they served first.

When I was finally at the edges of the packlands, I looked over at Lewis, who was already stripping out of his shirt.

"We're shifting?" I asked him in surprise. We had a pack vehicle, but I wasn't a fan of covering ground on wheels. However, I had assumed we would drive there. Somehow, I imagined the Pack Council was more refined than a bunch of naked shifters turning up.

"Don't plan to walk there on two feet."

Because four feet were faster. Obviously. I looked down at my oversized jacket and my lace-up boots.

Damn it, I would need a bigger pack… I eyed the backpack Lewis had with him.

"You want me to strap it to you?" I asked him, focused

on his pack and wondering if I could sneak my boots in there.

"I got it."

Right. Of course. I pulled my jacket off and quickly shed my clothes. The small pack the druid had given me had room for my pants, top, and underwear. My jacket and boots were an issue. Quickly, I tied the laces of the boots together and looped them around the strap of the pack.

I looked up to see Lewis waiting, his pack open—definitely a man who had daughters. With a grin, I handed over my jacket, and with a sigh, he rolled it, packed it, and then draped the straps out so he could pick it up when he shifted.

He shifted into his brown and black furred wolf. Deftly, he scooped the pack off the ground, and I waited until he had a firm grip before I shifted.

The fluidity of the shift made me stretch out immediately. It was as if all my muscles had been comfortable but not relaxed. They welcomed the leisurely stretch I gave them. My wolf was much smaller than Lewis's. My fur was pale ash with streaks of silver throughout. I had a long black stripe that ran down my back, the color matching my father's wolf. The ash was my mother. The silver was unique to me. The combination allowed me to blend into the shadows at night.

I was the fastest wolf in our pack, a trait I was sure Lewis forgot until I started the run. My boots banged against my chest until I had a firm grip on the upper leather. Looking back, I saw the larger wolf was handling his pack just fine.

We left the Hollow early in the morning, slipping past the iron-bound trail posts before the mist burned off. The

path west ran through forgotten logging cuts and over-
grown switchbacks—no roads, no towns, no scent of
outsiders, just ridgelines and the thick, pulsing breath of the
forest.

By midday, the trees had changed. Denser. Older. The
kind that whispered ancient.

We were in the Smokies now.

We crossed the state line without fanfare—just a river to
ford, a grove to pass through, and then it hit: the deep, wild
silence that lived between Tennessee and the sky.

The shift was subtle at first—a difference in the smell of
the moss, the shape of the ridgelines, the way the air didn't
move the same. But my wolf felt it. Every hair on my arms
lifted in response.

Old mountains.

Older than us.

And it felt like they *knew* we didn't belong.

We moved in single file, keeping to the thickest brush,
claws dulled with dirt and pine sap. No roads. No signs. Not
even animal trails this deep—just the slow, breathless quiet
that lived between shadow and stone.

A crow cried once in the distance, sharp and sudden,
then nothing.

No birdsong.

No wind.

Just the steady beat of our paws on wet ground and the
taste of iron in the air. I saw the way Lewis's ears flicked at
every creak in the trees, every breath of silence too long.

Wolves knew when they were being watched.

And this place was watching.

The trees here grew closer together, bark dark with

moisture and years. The mist didn't rise—it *hung*, like it had been waiting for us to step into it.

Still, despite Lewis's slower pace, we made good time. If we had remained in our human forms, it would have taken us more than a day; however, as wolves, we made it within six hours. Had Lewis not been slowing me down and had I not been carrying my boots, I could have done it in four.

My father's beta nudged my side, and I dropped my boots, and both of us shifted back to our human forms. We may be going to the Pack Council, but they preferred us to attend meetings in our human form so we could all communicate.

I laced my boots up, and Lewis was already holding out my jacket to me. I tied it around my hips. In this heat, there was no way I was going to put it on.

"Welcome to neutral ground," Lewis murmured behind me, voice low. "Let's keep moving."

But it wasn't neutral.

Not really.

Not here.

I could feel the weight of eyes I couldn't name. Not enemies. Not friends.

Something else.

I didn't stop moving. But I let my wolf rise closer to the surface. This wasn't Blueridge Hollow territory anymore.

And whatever lived out here? It didn't give a damn about our laws.

The path down to where the Pack Council was holed up was twisted and just as eerie as the trees that guarded it. Pine needles softened each step, but the silence sharpened everything else—the weight of my thoughts, the clench of my jaw, the low pulse beating at the base of my skull.

There was no wind. No birdsong. Just thick, watching *quiet*.

A warning, if I'd been willing to hear it.

The Pack Council didn't stay put. They moved with the seasons, crossing borders, holding court in the wilds as much as in any hall. There was talk of a permanent chamber somewhere in the Rockies—carved stone, blood-bound, older than memory—but no one saw it unless they were summoned.

The Council preferred the open. Preferred to be seen. Because power that hides is power that fades.

And the Council? They made sure their teeth were always showing.

A large tent had been erected at the center of the ridge clearing, though calling it a "tent" felt like a lie. It looked more like a traveling cathedral, stretched canvas and dark wood supports arching high enough to disappear into the trees. A full marquee meant to impress.

Intimidate.

Around it, smaller tents dotted the slope in clusters— neatly arranged, marked with symbols I didn't recognize at first glance. Most of them carried the crest of their pack. As I took it all in, I saw that even the Northerners had sent representatives.

I slowed as we crested the rise, my breath catching in my throat. This wasn't a routine Council visit.

This was a *gathering*. A summit.

I looked sideways at Lewis. His expression was tight,

unreadable. But his eyes flicked toward the central tent, then back to me.

"Didn't think there'd be this many," I murmured. "And it looks like I am the only female here."

He didn't answer. I didn't expect him to. This was why I never attended these; they were for the males, the leaders of the packs or their seconds-in-command.

I loosened the sleeves of my jacket and slipped it on, suddenly feeling that my black cropped tee was *too* casual for this, seeing too many letting their eyes linger a little longer than was appropriate. Together, Lewis and I headed to the main tent.

Inside, the Pack Council murmured amongst themselves —voices low, reverent, gray as the smoke curling from the fire pit.

No one greeted us. That wasn't how this worked, but I knew I received more stares than I wanted, but I kept my attention straight ahead. Had I been with anyone but Lewis, I would have asked them if I was being paranoid.

I slid onto an empty bench, not near anyone else, and settled in, the wood groaning under Lewis as he got comfortable beside me. I opened the bottle of water that was set in front of me and drank quickly. Lewis had already finished his. We'd each had a rabbit on the way here, but I was grateful for the water.

The Council was already in session. A few seats were empty, which was to be expected. Not all the Council members traveled at the same time, as each member had their own pack to look after in addition to their duties to *all* packs. I noticed that a shaman was present, and tried not to stare at his white eyes. Shamans freaked me out; I'd take a druid any day of the week over a shaman.

I listened as they recited expected reports and discussed matters like territorial boundaries and unpaid debts. A stolen calf from the edge of Riverbend. Nothing urgent. Nothing new from the sounds of it and from the complete boredom of everyone gathered. I settled in for a long day.

I might've let my mind drift, just a little—until I heard my name.

"Daughter of the Hollow."

Not Rowen. Not alpha's daughter. Just the name for those born of the sacred Hollow where my pack territory was. It sounded cold and heavy in this airy space. A signal.

I looked up.

The shaman's eyes met mine, white and unseeing, but I knew he saw me all too well.

"Your heat has come and gone," he said, folding his hands, and I knew I was gaping at him as he declared that to the whole tent. "How long between your cycles?"

What the hell? Lewis nudged me gently, and I turned to glare at him before looking back at the semicircle of males who were all watching me.

"It differs," I croaked out.

The shaman stared at me intently. His head cocked to the side slightly. "Does it?" he mumbled. He turned to the others. "We will not wait long. We should proceed."

Proceed? Proceed with what?

I opened my mouth to ask, but Lewis nudged me a lot harder this time, and I kept my mouth shut.

The shaman turned back to us. "You will have a private audience with us."

I heard Lewis's heavy sigh, and having no idea what was going on, I simply nodded. My dad had sent me here for a reason: to talk to the Pack Council. Well, it seemed they were waiting for me without us having to wait for an audience.

I hadn't expected it right now though, and I watched in stunned awe as visiting pack representatives got up and left.

"Come closer, child," the shaman instructed.

Lewis and I approached the esteemed members of the Council, and I met each of their curious stares with a cool glance of my own.

"Your father is dying."

The simplicity of the statement winded me, and I heard my gasp loud and uncontrolled in the now almost empty hall.

"Our alpha is fighting," Lewis grumbled beside me.

The shaman glanced to his left, and I got the impression Lewis wasn't that happy with the brutality of the announcement any more than I was. The shaman returned to look at me and held up his hand when another Council member went to speak.

"The alpha of Blueridge Hollow is a respected fighter," he said, his tone gentle and respectful. "But the Goddess calls us all home no matter how hard we fight." He was blind, but I felt that we were staring deep into each other's souls. "Your father will join the great hunt soon, child."

Tears threatened to spill, but I stubbornly held my head high. "Do you know when?"

The shaman shook his head. "No, but I think this year's winter will be his last."

The winter that we'd seen or the one to come? I bit my

lip to stop myself from asking. I didn't want to know, because either option was too soon.

"You are a daughter of the moon," the shaman continued. "An only child. Alpha Malric bore no sons."

"It's what *only child* means," I muttered and felt Lewis's not-so-gentle dig of his elbow into my side for the third time that day.

The shaman smiled, not at all upset at my sass. "You've been sent here to look for a husband." He didn't wait for a response. "There has been suitable interest in your pack from those who know your need."

Did they put it out in a flyer?

"Four Winds has offered one of their younger sons. Strong blood. Disciplined. Willing."

"Deep Hollows has renewed their interest," someone else added. "Their alpha has a second son. Single. Unclaimed."

I blinked once, my senses reeling. "This isn't a mating council," I said flatly.

"Everything for you now is a mating council," the shaman spoke smoothly, his voice as light as summer rain. "You carry the Hollow's future in your blood. You are its roots and its bloom. We tend what we must grow."

I stared at him. Was that a… Did he just… "You talk like you mean to *prune* me."

The shaman sighed. "You are not being forced, Rowen." He was so *polished*, considering he looked like he'd been sleeping under the stars in a ditch somewhere. "We are simply providing paths. Options. Ones that keep your pack safe, strong and, above all, sacred." He didn't blink as he spoke to me, and I had the crazy thought that maybe he didn't need to if he was blind. "Your pack holds tight to the old ways, to tradition," the shaman continued. "They place great weight on a child of the alpha born in the ancient depths of the Hollow at the base of their sacred Heartwood." His head cocked slightly. "Old magic there, some would say it should be forgotten magic."

The tent was eerily silent.

I felt like every muscle was drawn too tight, like if I moved too fast, I'd shift and be running before they could stop me. His words wrapped around me like iron chains, reminding me that the freedom to choose was not mine to make.

Lewis spoke for the first time. "We will take these options to Alpha Malric. You'll have his answer when he's made it."

"We will send the prospective spouses to the Hollow for Malric to assess," one of the other Council members murmured.

For Malric to assess. Not me. I'd heard enough.

I left without asking to be excused. I didn't look back.

Chapter 4

Wolfe

THE SCENT OF OLD PINE, MULCH AND COUNCIL BULLSHIT HIT me the second I stepped into the area where the Pack Council had set up camp.

I glanced at my beta, Killian, and he quirked an eyebrow at me with a smirk. Together, we walked into the marquee, and I was sure the scent of shit got worse.

The marquee was too warm. Too quiet. The kind of silence that meant agreements were being made behind veiled words and polite smiles.

Politics. I fucking hated politics.

Killian moved ahead of me, brushing back the tent flap of the inner sanctum. He walked like we'd been expected. It was doubtful. Not this soon.

The central tent wasn't too crowded—not too many, but too many to be packed into one space. Shifters bristling with forced civility and tension so thick I could've sliced it with my claws.

A few heads turned as we entered. Some narrowed their eyes. One tried not to react at all. The rest kept talking like shifters who didn't think we were worth the effort. That wouldn't last.

I looked around as the faint scent of something familiar lingered in the air. I turned to look over my shoulder, but all I saw were males.

"You good?" Killian asked beside me, his voice low.

"Thought I recognized something…" My jaw clenched, but Killian didn't comment as we sat down. Conversation had been stilted since we crossed into the territory. The trees were so thick here that it was impossible to tell who was loitering. Listening.

A stocky wolf with a flat face caught my attention. He was speaking too loudly for someone that forgettable.

"We're following in two days," he was saying, trying to sound bored. Like the very thought of it was beneath him.

I saw the ones listening to him exchange looks; they weren't impressed, but they did seem to "approve," which made me pay closer attention.

He kept talking, voice oily now. I was surprised I couldn't see it oozing out of him. "Best way to let instinct lead, don't you think? The old ways honored. Who needs a fair chance when the bitch just needs rutted?" He smiled, like he'd said something clever.

I stilled.

Killian looked past me. "I hope the *bitch* guts him," he said with a soft snort.

I grunted in agreement. I didn't speak. Didn't move. But the air around me changed. One of the Council members noticed. I saw the way his gaze flicked to me, then to Killian. Assessing. Calculating.

Trying to guess which of us carried the leash.

Killian saw him looking and smiled without showing teeth.

I didn't bother. My attention was on flat face.

"You have competition," one of the other males in his circle said. "I also hear she's got an attitude."

My wolf surged under my skin, pacing, restless. I didn't know who they were talking about, but I knew I didn't like it.

Killian's hand on my wrist stilled me. "Not here," he murmured. "Let them talk. If they're lucky, whoever she is will leave their balls attached." He made a show of looking them up and down. "Might be better for the gene pool if they were removed though."

I grinned.

"Wolfe."

I turned to see a shaman in front of me. Pure white eyes stared right through me. Killian became unnaturally still.

"Shaman," I greeted, conscious of several pairs of eyes on me.

"Walk with me, young one."

It wasn't a request, and I knew better than to refuse. Killian rose with me, and I think we were both appreciative of the fact that the shaman didn't tell him to stay. We didn't speak until the shaman led us to a small enclosure within the marquee, and then through a turn, and we were in his private chamber.

I felt the magic of a shaman, and looking over my shoulder, I could see no barrier, but I knew there would be one. No one would be able to hear what he said to us.

"Your first Pack Council," the shaman said conversationally as he sat down with a sigh that sounded very much like relief.

Killian and I exchanged a look. "Yeah," I answered, watching him closely.

He nodded, his gaze on me. "Were the rites met?"

Killian looked more alert, and I felt my own hackles rise. "They were."

The shaman leaned forward and inhaled deeply, and I didn't need to be told that he was scenting me. "Not all," he murmured. He got to his feet and started shuffling around his room, while Killian and I stood like spare parts, not entirely sure what was going on.

Within minutes, the shaman was mixing herbs and muttering under his breath. He held out a clay cup to me with an obnoxious smelling brew inside it.

"Drink."

My instinct was to tell him to fuck off. My head told me to reach out and take it. Killian leaned forward and sniffed and backed off quickly, grinning.

"Asshole," I grumbled as I took the cup from the shaman. "What is it?" I asked him.

"What you need."

I waited. He didn't say anything else. "That was really enlightening, thanks."

The old shaman smiled. "You want to be enlightened, drink your potion."

"The fact you're openly calling it a *potion* makes me hesitant," I muttered. I drank it in one go. I had to force my body to keep it down. As soon as the liquid touched my tongue, my stomach roiled. My eyes screwed shut as I forced it down my throat, keeping my jaw clenched as my insides shuddered.

I staggered forwards, and it was only Killian grabbing me that kept me on my feet.

What the fuck is wrong with you?

I clutched my friend's arm. "Him." I pointed at the shaman. "What the *fuck* was that?"

The shaman cocked his head, and had I been able to focus properly, I would have seen the considering look he gave Killian. But all I saw through the blurry tears was him watching me.

"Shaman?" Killian asked tentatively. "What… Is he okay?"

The shaman waved the question off and sat back down. "He'll need that bucket," he said, pointing to the floor. "Quickly."

Killian darted forward, letting me go, and I stumbled, and then my entire body curled into itself. I grabbed the bucket and emptied the contents of my stomach. It felt like forever. It was probably less than a minute.

When I was done, I looked up at the shaman to see him holding out a piece of cloth to me. With a shaky hand I took it, wiping my mouth. I hesitated over the glass of water offered, and the shaman laughed.

"Drink. The potion has a strong aftertaste."

"It's called *bile*," I groaned, chugging the water back like I'd been dehydrated for days. "What was it?"

It knocked you on your ass, that's what it was.

"Hardly my ass," I snapped at Killian, who looked at me with wide eyes. "What?" The shaman gave a happy little trill, and I turned back to look at him. "What?"

"Alpha Wolfe, it is an honor to meet you."

I finished the water. "An honor?" I looked at the clay cup. "What do you do to the ones you don't feel honored to meet?"

Can you hear me?

With an exasperated sigh, I rounded on Killian. "You're standing right beside me, of course I can hear you."

"But he didn't speak," the shaman said with a small smile. "Your final block has been overcome, Alpha."

Understanding dawned on me, and I turned to Killian.

Say something, I demanded.

You puked worse than my little brother did after he drank vodka.

"Holy shit." We stared at each other. Killian was wearing a wide smile. "Holy shit," I repeated.

"When you return to your pack, your mindlink to your pack is now open."

Our alpha. Killian looked like he was going to burst with pride.

The shaman watched me, his smile fading. "Your pack deserves you," he told me, his voice smooth and firm. "You are new, but they already welcome you as their alpha. You just needed to accept it. *All* of it."

My eyes flicked to Killian's. "They were grieving the passing of Alpha Lars."

The shaman flicked his wrist again like it was inconsequential. "They endure. Luna does not select rashly."

I didn't say anything; I'd had the conversation too many times about my eligibility as an alpha. Not that anyone really doubted me, but in the beginning, *I* had doubted me. I had a feeling this shaman knew that, so I opted to change the subject. "So…apart from poisoning me, and making me throw up, was there anything else??"

I heard Killian's snort in my head. *Shut it*, I warned him.

"I didn't poison you, just got you to lower that guard you keep so high." The shaman fussed with his herbs and pouches. "Your pack is small," the shaman said, moving on swiftly. "Their history is one that wanders."

It was true. My pack was happier roaming, never in one part of our territory for too long. "We have a permanent hall."

The shaman never commented on that, and I didn't blame him. It seemed we both knew that the word *permanent* was a loose interpretation of the word.

"Why not settle in one place?" the shaman asked. "You are the alpha; you can pick a spot and build in it."

My head cocked to the side as I regarded the shaman. "Is it an issue for the Pack Council that Stonefang Pack moves around their own territory?"

The shaman returned to his herbs and made no further comment.

"Was there anything else?" I asked him, sensing the mood had changed.

"Shaman?" Killian spoke quietly, looking over his shoulder carefully. "Who is the female they were discussing outside?"

The shaman turned his full attention to my companion. "An unmatched female. Daughter of a good alpha, a once-strong alpha." He sighed, sadness overcoming his features. "But the Goddess grows weary of waiting for her alpha to come home."

"He's dying?" Killian asked with a glance at me. His

expression reflected the shaman's sadness. "It is hard to lose the alpha of the pack."

"It is." The shaman was looking at me again. "Worse when there is no alpha to take their place."

My eyes narrowed as I watched him. "No sons?"

"Not one alpha in the whole pack."

Killian and I exchanged a glance. "The beta will become pack leader until a replacement or an alpha is found?" Killian guessed.

"Probably," the shaman answered easily.

It was what they thought would happen in my pack. Lars, the old alpha, had let his beta manage most things in the pack as he got older. A beta was not an alpha and was merely nothing more than a steward. He'd led the pack through lean years and had held it well with grit and duty. But when I came into my alpha power, everything shifted.

"Blood warden?" I asked quietly.

The ghost of a smile graced the shaman's lips. "I thought, in the north, they call them *pack leaders* these days."

"We aren't further north," I reminded him. I looked around as if I could see outside the tent walls. "Blood runs deep in these mountains." I hesitated. "Deeper in some places more than others."

That scent still lingered in the air, and I looked for a vent in the tent wall.

"Blood runs deep," the shaman agreed. "Power runs deeper."

I nodded without commenting. I knew that better than anyone. Alpha Lars had two sons, neither of them alphas. His beta was a good blood warden, but when the pack learned I was an alpha, they had already turned my way.

Wolves didn't follow memories.

They followed dominance.

"No pack leader." The shaman was watching me. "The alpha is hoping to match his only daughter in a fortuitous marriage."

I'd been looking at the walls, wishing I could see beyond to the outside, but my attention snapped back to the shaman.

I heard the scoff, not quite sure it was mine, already shaking my head. "No."

The shaman gave me a serene smile. "The ones who are eager for a match are well—"

"*No.*" I struggled to contain my temper, knowing full well who the unmarried daughter was. "They called her a *bitch*." I looked over at Killian and back at the shaman. "When?"

He seemed to be considering me.

"I asked *when*?" I heard the growl in my voice.

"Wolfe," Killian admonished me, his eyes wide.

"The alpha's time runs out every day," the shaman said, not answering me at all.

I looked down, a humorless curl of my mouth passing for a smile, and back up. "Two days, one of those mutts said." I licked my teeth. "Killian, we're done here."

"Alpha Wolfe, your pack is north. You are here to meet and greet the packs you share a mountain with and to form *alliances*," the shaman reminded me, his voice casual. "Are you sure you want to leave for this?"

I didn't give a damn about alliances in this moment. I cared about what shit she was about to go through. "My pack will survive a few days without me. I'll make alliances along the way." I met his milky white eyes. "I think it's enough that you've seen me, right?"

He didn't say anything, but his upper lip curled into a smile. It was enough for me. I strode out of the room, Killian behind me.

What the fuck is going on? Killian demanded, hot on my heels as I shoved out of the Council tent.

We need to take a detour, I sent back.

A detour where?

I didn't answer. My blood was still boiling, that slick little bastard's voice still echoing in my ears—*bitch*—like she was just meat for sale.

Killian grabbed my arm and yanked me to a stop. "Wolfe. Talk," he growled, "before I knock your teeth out of your skull."

I turned on him, jaw clenched. "Betas are supposed to be obedient."

Killian barked a laugh, sharp and humorless. "Whoever told you that shit was eating 'shrooms. Now fucking talk."

I stared at him, chest heaving, every instinct flaring. The pack bond between us stretched tight—not hostile, but coiled.

"She's the daughter of the Hollow," I said. Seeing his blank look, I explained. "West of here, some packs still hold strong to tradition. Ancient magic, blood magic." I lowered my voice in case anyone was listening. "The Hollow is at the base of the Blue Ridge Mountains, she was born in its most sacred place, and her pack is superstitious enough to think that means something." I took a deep breath. "And the Council just greenlit a damn *matchmaking* for her."

Killian blinked. "Who?"

I scanned the people around us. "*Rowen.* She's not some prize to be chased down and *mounted.* And one of those hungry bastards called her a bitch like she was already his."

Killian's mouth tightened. He didn't like that any more than I did. "Yeah, I heard, not cool."

"Not cool," I muttered. "I need…" What did I need?

Killian clapped my shoulder. "We check it out?"

"Yeah." I swallowed. "We head east." My voice dropped to a growl. "To Blueridge Hollow. We need to make it look like it's routine. We don't let them know why we're there. I just want to check it out, see if this is what she wants. See if the *daughter of the Hollow* wants to be tied to tradition like she once claimed."

Killian looked at me for a long second. Then he beamed at me. "Alpha instincts showing."

I didn't answer. I think it was more hurt pride than instincts, but I kept my doubts to myself.

He grinned, sharp and smug. "Good timing, right? Told you we should have come here."

We left the Pack Council as quickly as we'd come. I was there to be recognized as my pack's alpha. To form alliances with surrounding packs so they knew not to fuck with my territory or my pack. I assumed that I'd done little of that, what with the foul tonic the shaman had given me and the information shared.

We stripped. Killian was built and bulky. He shifted into his warm-brown-furred wolf form as I packed our clothes into a single bag and attached it to a harness that allowed him to carry them. I shifted, allowing my wolf to stretch. My wolf's size was imposing. My fur was a dark charcoal, and my eyes shone like pale silver. I met the gaze of my beta, his cold blue eyes showing me he was ready.

Let's run, I told him. His wave of happiness at hearing me in his mind in his wolf form made my wolf grin, and we set off.

It had been many years since I walked the land of the Hollow, and I wasn't looking forward to returning. I wasn't looking forward to seeing *her.*

But this wasn't about my history with her—or with her pack. This was about doing what was right.

Rowen may be the daughter of the Hollow, but she wasn't a prize to be won. She was a gift the Council had no business offering.

She was a storm in a girl's skin.

Only a fool mistook that for something they could claim.

Once, I'd called her mine. All I wanted to do was make sure she wasn't pressured. That's all. I had no stake in this game.

At least that's what I was telling myself as I ran towards Blueridge Hollow packlands.

Chapter 5

Rowen

I DIDN'T SPEAK AS I CROSSED THE BOUNDARY BACK INTO Blueridge Hollow territory. I barely breathed.

The forest had never felt this quiet before.

Branches shifted overhead, wind dragging through the canopy like the trees were whispering about me. The dirt path under my boots was the same one I'd walked since I was a child, and suddenly it felt foreign. Smaller. Like it was closing in.

As if the Hollow were shrinking to make room for someone else.

I should've been angry. Furious. But all I felt was empty.

They were sending *interested* suitors to try and what? *Date* me? I didn't want to think about the fiasco *that* would be. I knew of one of the prospects, and I remembered too well the crack his jaw had made when I punched it the last time I saw him.

My hands curled into fists at my sides. Let them try. Let them run after me like I was some trembling little thing just waiting to be caught.

They were not alphas. I did not have to bend to their Will.

I'd spent three days locked in my own skin while my heat burned through me like wildfire. I came through it alone. No touch. No comfort. No *male*.

And now the Council was encouraging the idea of turning me into a *reward* for the fastest dog?

No.

Not me. Not a daughter of the Hollow.

Not ever.

The trees thinned as I neared the edge of the ridge where our pack hall sat—stone and wood and iron, carved into the land like it had grown there. Lewis slipped away from my side. Our journey home had been silent.

Voices reached my ears before I stepped into view. Movement. The scent of the pack. I straightened my spine, shoved the ache down where it belonged.

They would not see me tremble. Not now. My pack needed me. I belonged to my pack; I was no one's to give away.

I stepped into the clearing, and the world greeted me like it had been waiting. Pack members milled near the main hall, sparring, hauling wood, or talking in quiet pockets as they discussed their day. Normal. Routine. *Ordinary.* It was as if they didn't know I'd just been served up an ugly version of my future. But they knew; the whole pack was waiting to see who I would wed, who their future leader would be.

Who their future *male* leader would be.

Some looked over as I arrived, pausing in their conversations or tasks. Some offered smiles, one or two more tentative than others.

Adair straightened from where she'd been organizing dried herbs by the steps. She smiled gently as I approached, her eyes kind in a way I wasn't yet ready for.

"You're back sooner than I thought. How was the—"

"It was a farce," I snapped. Too sharp. Too loud. Too much emotion from the one who prided herself on being in control.

Adair blinked, startled. I saw it immediately, the tension in her shoulders, the way her mouth pressed tight.

Damn it. I exhaled softly, not a sigh, just a moment to pull it together. "Sorry," I muttered. "It's been a frustrating day."

Her expression softened again, but the moment was already broken. She nodded and turned back to her work without another word.

I kept walking, knowing my duty to my pack. They wanted me to smile, to be gracious. They wanted the transition from alpha to leader to be a blessing instead of the knife to my heart that it was. The pack was ready for me to walk into the arms of a stranger who'd *earned* me by proving he could outsmart the others. They didn't want a fight between alphas; no one wanted my father to be overcome by the strength of another. Of a stranger.

No, they wanted an *easy* "handover," one with minimal disruption to their lives. And the best way to provide that for my pack was for me to wed someone I could assist in the learning of our pack ways.

The thought made my lip curl. However, my sense of duty and loyalty to my pack forced me to smooth my features into one of calm—the mask my pack was accustomed to seeing—their leader in everything but name.

I would let these imbeciles chase me. I would let them think the alpha's daughter was theirs to win.

They could try. But I wasn't running to be caught...I was running to remind them who the hell I was.

The old hall creaked as I made my way to my father's rooms. The stone was cool beneath my boots. Familiar. It felt good to be home. My dad's scent hit me before I saw him—pine smoke and iron. It used to wrap around the whole Hollow like armor. Now it clung to this one room like a dying ember, fighting to stay alight.

Dad was propped up in the old chair near the fire, a wool blanket draped over his legs, shoulders thinner than they used to be. But his eyes were sharp when they met mine. Always sharp.

"Back so soon," he said with a faint smile.

I nodded. "No point hanging around; they said what they wanted to say."

His mouth twisted. "Sometimes speed isn't always a good thing."

"Tell that to the rabbit that outruns the wolf," I murmured as I sat down opposite him. I saw his face and let out the sigh I'd been holding for too long. "No. You're right, sometimes, speed is not good."

The fire crackled. Dad didn't look away from me, but I could feel the weight of the thing between us—the unspoken truth that had been growing like rot beneath the floorboards.

"They are keen to name your husband," he said quietly.

"They are keen to name my replacement," I corrected, wincing at my sharpness.

Dad gave a low laugh, rough-edged, a little shakier than

it used to be. "You think you can beat them, daughter?" He took a deep breath, his lungs rattling a little with the effort. "You cannot fight them on this."

"I think you're letting it happen."

Silence. Long and brittle.

"I'm dying, Rowen," he said, his voice thin but clear. "And our pack needs a leader, a recognized leader," he said firmly.

"I *am* a leader. The pack recognizes *me*."

He closed his eyes for a moment. Not in pain—in something worse. Regret. "You were always meant for more, my sweet child," he murmured, "but the laws—"

"The laws were written by men who feared daughters."

His eyes snapped open. "Rowen. Don't."

"Why?" My voice cracked like a whip, the simmering fury boiling over. "They'll send them in two days. Wolves who don't know our land, our pack, our *ways*. And one of them will try and *win* me like I'm a prize goat, and they'll call it a *victory*." I leaned forward when my father said nothing. "If you let this happen, you may as well ask them to strike you down, Dad. You're not alpha anymore; you'd be no more than their puppet."

The words landed like gasoline on the fire. My father didn't move. Didn't flinch. But the anger simmered in his eyes as he stared at me. The *alpha* of my pack regarded me.

"You think I don't see the storm coming, Rowen? You think I haven't felt it? Heard the trees quiet. You think *this* is how I choose to die?"

I froze. My pulse spiked, but I said nothing.

"It's coming, daughter," he said. "Change is coming, and you need to accept that our Goddess Luna chooses this.

Whatever male you pick for your husband, this pack will go on, because *you* will be at the helm. A pack leader will be the face of this pack, but you, *you*, Rowen, have the chance to steer them right." He looked at me as if he were trying to make me believe it. It was as if he thought calling it a blessing would somehow gild the cage.

"Steering from the shadows isn't what I want," I said flatly.

"I want you to survive."

The words were soft, but they cracked something in me, because I knew what he meant. He wanted me to live long enough to guide this pack, even if it meant letting someone else wear the title. An alpha could come along, claim this pack, claim a mate, and I would be disposed of, either by death or by the pack. Dad wanted me to live even if it meant pretending I didn't bleed for it.

"I know," I told him, just as softly. "But is it living, Dad? Being someone's pawn?" I stood, my fists clenched at the injustice of it all. "Do you really think this is what the Goddess wants? Does she bless *this*? You think she wants me tied to some Council *pet* because the law says I have to be because I don't have a cock?"

"Rowen—"

"I'd give this pack everything. Every damn piece of myself. I trained harder than anyone else. I fight cleaner. Lead better. And still...I'm not enough. Still, I'm just a *daughter*. A daughter of an alpha, which means I will most likely birth an alpha. That's all I am. A birthing vessel."

Dad watched me, he didn't interrupt, he didn't raise his voice to command me. He waited until I was done. "You are more than enough," he told me gently. "But the law does not change because I want it to. Or because you want it to. This pack follows tradition."

I laughed bitterly. "Or it follows fear dressed as tradition."

"Our Goddess chooses alphas," he reminded me with more bite in his words. "Alphas are *male*." He saw me open my mouth to reply, but held up his hand to stop me. "But a pack *leader* is someone who *leads*, even if it *is* from the shadows." Dad rubbed his forehead tiredly. "This is the hand fate gave you, my daughter; how you choose to play it is up to you."

"I need to unpack." I turned to leave, feeling no less pissed off than before.

"Rowen."

I paused, my back to him.

"I may not live to see how this ends. But I know my daughter. And I know she'll fight to the end before she lets anyone take what's hers."

My throat tightened. I didn't respond. There was nothing left to say, because he was right. I would sacrifice everything I had for this pack. I didn't have to like what that sacrifice looked like. All that mattered was that my pack would survive.

I left him and made my way to my own chambers. We'd always lived in the hall, where our pack could access the alpha easily. My mother passed when I was young, and while I couldn't demand my father stay celibate after her passing, I didn't need to see the females he took to his bedroom the next morning while I got ready for school. I moved into my own rooms when I was fifteen. No longer a child, but not quite an adult either.

A female shifter wasn't considered an adult until we had our first heat. Our heat was the Goddess's way of saying we were mature enough to be women. I never had my first heat until I was nineteen. I wasn't sure what the Goddess was trying to say to *me* when she left it so late for me to *bloom*.

My heats were short, lasting no more than three days at a time, but more frequent than those of some others. The druid, in their unasked-for opinion, believed it was because I chose not to spend my heat on my back with a lover. I grumbled internally at my harshness towards the druid. They hadn't quite been that blunt. But it was what they meant...

I didn't stop until my door was closed, and I leaned against it, letting my mask fall and my shoulders drop, alone at last. No Lewis. No suitors. No Pack Council watching. Just me and solitude.

I pulled off my boots, dropped my jacket behind me, and shed my clothes, heading for the shower. My mother always maintained that you felt better after a nice, long shower, and I was ready to put that to the test today.

By the time I was finished, I was, grudgingly, not as moody. But I knew what would really make me feel better. The window of my bathroom was high, but I'd mastered being able to climb out of it a long time ago, when I used to sneak out and meet a boy.

The boy was long gone, but the escape route from the hall without being seen was still very much in use.

I shimmied out the window, in a sports bra and boy cut shorts. On bare feet, I ignored the trail and pushed deep into the forest. Pine needles bit into the soles of my feet, but I ignored the pain. The air grew cooler in the shadows, thick with moss and decay, and always carrying the lingering scent of rain. My body moved through the trees as if on autopilot, the route as familiar to me as breathing.

In the shower, I had shoved aside the thought of "I'm not enough" and was determined to move on. The thought was not new. It was one I'd lived with since I was old enough to understand what it meant to be born without a claim.

I stopped near a hollowed-out cedar tree, one I used to crawl inside as a child when the world was too loud. I wasn't small enough to fit anymore, but I stood beside it like a ghost revisiting its bones.

Beyond it, just out of sight, was the smooth flat rock I used to spend time on with the boy I used to sneak out and meet, hoping for a stolen kiss, until the day he ran off with much more than a kiss.

The wind shifted, and had I been human, I would have felt the mountain chill a lot more. My head tipped back, and I stared through the canopy to the sky above.

"Luna," I murmured, voice low. "If you're listening—if you still look down on your daughters—tell me. Is this what you wanted for us?"

The sky didn't answer. The forest didn't either.

The silence felt less like peace and more like pressure, like the woods were waiting. Holding their breath.

I took a deep inhale. There was no space for grief, not with the demand of duty clawing under my skin. I needed to shift. Run. Breathe.

I needed to shed this skin of human emotion and let my wolf breathe. I shed my clothes, the tightness in my skin urging me to be faster, and then I let the change take over.

The shift took me hard. It always did when I was too wound up. The shift between forms was fluid, but I felt every crack of bone as my body reshaped into a form that was fire and instinct. I shook my head, my vision sharpening, the color draining to something older, purer. My wolf pawed the ground, silent and fierce, claws buried deep in the earth.

The forest was no longer a place I walked through. It was a place I belonged.

I ran.

Not for distance. Not for speed. Just to *feel* it.

Leaves and low branches tore past me. Bark scratched my flank. My breath came fast and harsh, visible in clouds beneath the canopy as I raced down the ridge path and leapt across the streambed like I had when I was twelve, when the world was simpler and everything still felt possible.

The wind rushed through my fur, and for a moment, I felt weightless. Free of everything.

I didn't stop until my legs began to burn, until the tremble set in from the inside out. Then I slowed. Padded to a stop beneath an old hemlock tree. The air was still. The world was quiet.

Something shifted.

Not in me.

Not in the forest around me.

In the Hollow.

I could feel it.

Something was coming.

Chapter 6

Wolfe

The Hollow didn't welcome me.

It felt like it never had. Not truly.

The air grew heavier the deeper we traveled, the trees watching as we passed beneath their boughs. Judging. Maybe remembering.

I kept my head high, spine straight, as my paws sank into the ground I'd once called home. Killian's brown-furred wolf was at my side, as silent as the woods.

We'd taken our time to get here. I didn't want to look too eager, and I had stopped and met with another pack on our way. Killian had said nothing, which in itself was a miracle, one that I thanked the Goddess for.

We didn't speak as we crossed into pack territory. There wasn't much to say. I thought back over the last few days. The Council's summons had been clear enough; representatives from Stonefang Pack were expected to arrive for negotiations. A "new alliance," they called it. Mutually beneficial.

Politically expedient.

What they meant was to bring the new alpha to the Pack

Council for assessment of his weaknesses. What they didn't mean was to take a look at the potential dumbass with the right bloodline to take Rowen as their wife.

I could still hear their whispers. Their boasts. *Make her compliant. Tame* her.

Fuck that.

My wolf sniffed the air, and I felt my ire rise higher. I hadn't wanted to come back. Not to this place. Nor to the ghosts I'd buried here. But hearing them talk about her in that tent—hearing their boasts tossed around so carelessly—flipped a switch I hadn't realized was still inside me.

Rowen. Daughter of the Hollow.

The girl who had turned away from me without blinking. The one whose words had sliced me like a blade between my ribs, so deep it still felt like I carried the scars.

Alpha Malric was dying. Her pack was fracturing. Now, strangers were circling like vultures around carrion.

Not on my fucking watch.

We broke through the tree line, and Blueridge Hollow packland came into view—rough, stone homes, built into the forest like they'd grown there. The air was thick with the scent of wolves, firewood, and something older.

Something much, much older.

Why is this place so fucking creepy? Killian asked me, his wolf alert for any sign of danger.

Because the pack is creepy.

You serious? he demanded. *I thought you were exaggerating.*

Wait until you meet the druid. Then tell me I'm exaggerating.

If some fucker tries to sacrifice me to Luna or some fucking Hollow *thing, I will haunt you, Wolfe.*

I stifled a laugh. *We need to shift. You remember the plan?*

Your plan sucks, Killian grumbled.

Answer yes or no; do you remember the plan?

Yes, I remember your sucky plan. His wolfish grin made me want to lunge for him and beat his ass.

I shifted, pulling the pack from Killian, and he changed to his human form. Quickly, we dressed in simple jeans and T-shirts. Killian looped the pack over his shoulder and looked at me in confusion when I didn't move.

"What are you doing?" he whispered, his eyes running over me, checking me for injuries or Goddess only knows what.

"I'm preparing," I grumbled back, hating that I needed this moment to collect myself.

Killian looked around. "Preparing for what? They attack, I will rip them in half."

"Calm down, soldier," I murmured. "I just need a second. It's been a long time…"

I was a leader now. An *alpha.* I had my own people to look after; I didn't need to be here to ensure that a woman I hadn't seen in years was okay. She had a pack for that. Hell, she had herself. I was sure that age had only made Rowen even stronger, fiercer, and more independent than when I left.

And yet…here I was. Under the pretense of forming alliances, but really, I was just being a nosy bastard.

With a nod to Killian, I stepped out of the trees, and the two of us joined the trail that would lead to the open ground, visible to all.

I didn't see her as we approached the hall.

But I smelled her.

Not fresh. Not close.

But recent enough to make my jaw clench.

Her scent hit like a punch to the gut—the wild wind and something warm and sharp underneath that smelled of vanilla mixed with orchid. Unmistakably Rowen.

My wolf stirred.

Killian glanced at me. "You good?"

"Fine," I said. My voice was like sandpaper.

He didn't push.

As we crossed the grass, an older shifter approached to greet us. I recognized him and slowed to a stop.

"Wolfe?" Lewis looked me over in surprise. He was Malric's beta and pretty decent. Didn't say much, which is why I'd liked him when I was here. "Is that you?"

I nudged Killian with my elbow. "Lewis, it's been a long time," I greeted him.

He looked between us, a frown line forming on his brow. "We didn't know you were coming…"

Killian stepped forward, just like we'd discussed. "We missed you at the Pack Council," he said smoothly. "My alpha of the Stonefang Pack has sent me to talk alliances with old packs, but we heard the alpha's daughter is to take a husband. He sent me to make enquiries."

Lewis blinked. "Why would an alpha care about Rowen?"

There was no malice in it—just *confusion*. But if she'd been here to hear it, she would've torn him a new one with that sharp tongue of hers.

She'd always been everything they didn't expect her to be.

Calm. Precise. Deadly.

I said nothing. Killian hadn't lied; they just didn't need to know his alpha was standing beside him. Not yet.

"Why would my alpha care?" Killian tilted his head slightly as he assessed the beta in front of him. "Legacy? Bloodline? Tradition? Your alpha's daughter is getting married. That could have consequences. Alliances are sought, so now would be the best time, no?"

Lewis had the grace to look faintly embarrassed, but he gestured for us to follow. "We've had a couple arrive already. I think that the Council wanted to offer a fair opportunity."

Fair. *Sure.* For who?

We approached two wolves lounging near the long table that had been set outside the hall for as long as I could remember. One had the look of someone used to getting what he wanted—smug and bored in equal measure. The other was all sharp angles and ambition, with eyes already tracking us as if we might be competition.

They both reeked of arrogance. One of them was the one who'd called her a bitch.

Killian kept his face neutral. I didn't bother trying.

Lewis introduced us to the other two as he came to a stop at the end of the table. "From Stonefang. Emissaries."

The smug one raised an eyebrow. "Thought Stonefang didn't send boys unless they were ready to run with the big dogs."

"Guess you don't know much about Stonefang," Killian said easily.

I met the dick's gaze and smiled—all teeth, no warmth. He looked away first.

Lewis cleared his throat. "I'll bring you to the druid in a moment." He dipped his head and went into the hall. I watched him go, then turned my attention to the two idiots in front of me.

The druid? Not Malric? Was it really that bad? I looked at the two hopefuls and had to stop myself from shaking my head. Goddess help them, Rowen would eat them both alive.

You're glaring at them, Killan warned. *If you're trying to be subtle, you're failing. Miserably.*

Is my scent masked?

Yeah, no alpha vibes at all. Just the murderous glaring.

I shot him a look.

Yeah, like that. Killian's mouth twitched, and I turned away from him when one of the simpering fools in front of us asked us how our journey was, and Killian answered him smoothly instead of asking him how he thought we got here if not on paws like he did.

I took my time to look around. Not much had changed, but for a pack so closely tied to traditions and the Hollow, that was normal. There were few of the pack that lived so near the hall. Their homes were scattered throughout, hidden, mostly concealed in their surroundings.

Tradition was strong in Blueridge Hollow. A pack that clung to the old ways. Old magic and a reclusive pack, who were deeply distrustful of outsiders. How the Council thought either of these two idiots in front of me would help win over a pack that was led with druid-magic in a heavily protected territory was insane. They still had iron and bone markers to ward off danger at the edges of their territory for fuck's sake.

Malric, Rowen's father, might've been alpha still in name, but everyone here could smell the blood in the water.

My gaze kept sweeping the area, my eyes taking it all in, remembering the pack I left and the one I had now. My attention wasn't on what they were saying; that was Killian's role. My attention was on the scent I'd picked up the moment we arrived.

Still heady. Still wild.

She'd left before we arrived.

Smart.

She was hiding. I could almost see the outrage in her eyes as they greeted her, ready to *woo* her. I was surprised they still had their eyes. I fought back the smirk—yeah, the wildness in Rowen would be fighting this with every fiber of her being. But…but the *daughter*, the *dutiful* daughter whose life revolved around this pack, would go through with this.

For her father.

For her pack.

Not for herself.

Always so ready to sacrifice herself for the fucking pack.

She was escaping them for now, but she wouldn't be able to outrun this forever. And when she returned, she'd see emissaries from a rival pack, and her guard would be up, and she'd be wary and then, and *only* then, could the *true* game begin.

"Wolfe?"

I turned to look at Lewis, who stood just inside the entrance to the hall.

"The druid's ready to greet you."

Are they? I wondered, keeping my thoughts to myself.

Killian didn't look my way as we walked into the hall. The inside smelled like smoke, herbs, and slow decay. I sniffed once as the unpleasant smell enveloped me. It wasn't rot. Or death. It was just the scent of a legacy slipping from its grip. Killian looked undisturbed by it as he looked around, and I kept my thoughts to myself.

We followed Lewis through the narrow stone corridor toward the alpha's quarters, the walls etched with faded runes that meant something once. Maybe they still did—to the right people.

Like the person waiting for us just outside the door to the alpha's rooms.

The druid.

They stood straight, despite their years, wrapped in ash-colored robes, their white hair slicked back from their face and twisted into long locks that fell down their back. Their mismatched eyes didn't catch me off guard; I'd been stared down by their gaze too many times in my youth. But I felt Killian's surprise, though he masked it well. The infinitesimal narrowing of the druid's eyes told me that Killian hadn't masked it well enough.

The druid's presence didn't shout. It watched. Measured.

"Wolfe," they said, voice low and dust-dry. "I'd heard the Stonefang representative was familiar with the Hollow. But still…I did not expect you."

I inclined my head, letting my expression stay neutral. "Just here on behalf of the Stonefang Pack."

"Of course." Their lips twitched—not a smile. A flicker of something older. "And I'm merely the wind."

Killian snorted beside me.

The druid gestured toward the heavy wooden door behind him. "Alpha Malric is weak but aware. You'll be brief." An instruction, not a suggestion.

They opened the door without waiting for a response.

My first impression as I stepped into the rooms of my old alpha was that Alpha Malric looked smaller than I remembered. Shrinking into the frame of a man who used to command mountains. The fire in the hearth was low, but his eyes still burned with the last of what made him alpha.

He coughed once, hard, and waved us forward. "Wolfe?" he rasped. "Didn't expect to see you here."

"Didn't expect to come," I said truthfully. I watched him look me over like I was no more than the boy he remembered.

His eyes narrowed. Coolly calculating. "But you heard about Rowen."

"I did. We're making rounds at various packs. Alliances need to be made now that the Stonefang Pack has a new alpha," I told him. Not one word was an untruth. "But we heard about the Council deciding who gets to make the call on who gets to lead a pack they know nothing about, with your daughter by their side like she's a token in a game of politics, and that, well that, I had to see for myself."

A breath. That pause where pain meets pride. "I didn't want this," Malric said softly. "But a pack is not a pack without a male to lead it."

"Then maybe your pack needs to be reminded what leadership looks like," I snapped before I could stop myself.

Malric didn't bristle at my outburst. He just looked... tired. "Is that what you've come to do, young pup?" he asked with a weary smile. "Remind us?"

I didn't answer.

Because even I wasn't sure yet what I hoped to do when I was here.

I looked away from Malric before I insulted him again. Something that would dishonor what was left of him—or what he'd once tried to be. A father figure to an orphaned boy who didn't yet know his place in the world.

Killian shifted behind me, restless, sensing my tension through the pack bond. The druid, of course, hadn't left the room. They lingered near the door like a shadow cast by the Goddess herself, hands folded in front of them, eyes fixed on nothing and everything at once. Serene.

Malric let out a slow breath, rough and worn. "You're still angry."

I snorted with contempt. I'd been an angry youth, and it seemed he was keen to keep to the past. "Not angry. I'm focused."

"Same thing, sometimes." He didn't say it like a compliment. We held each other's stare for a long moment before a cough from him forced him to break the stare.

How quickly he would fall if challenged for this pack, I mused. Hell, any one of those males out there could beat him right now, and in a pack as stuck in the past as this one, would they care that their new leader was not a born alpha? As long as they had a replacement, I doubted that they would.

I clenched my jaw, sure the druid would use the moment of Malric's weakness to expel us from the room, and I moved a few feet toward the fireplace, heat licking my skin but not doing a damn thing for the chill that had settled in my bones since I smelled her on the wind.

Behind me, I heard Killian clear his throat—a deliberate annoyed sound—and I braced myself for the impact of whatever fuel he was about to throw on the fire.

In true Killian style, he didn't hold back as he turned to look at the druid. "You always hover like that, or is it just when pretty shifters come back from the dead?"

"I never believed Wolfe was dead, though I know that's what he wanted us to believe." The druid turned their head, expression unreadable as they met Killian's look. "I watch where power stirs. It is my role to see."

"Is your role also to decide what a wolf is worth for the sake of your pack?" Killian challenged.

"Rowen's worth is not mine to set," the druid said calmly. "Only to ensure it is honored in accordance with our ways."

Killian snorted with contempt. "Yeah, I've seen what your 'ways' look like. Guess it's easier to bind a powerful shifter than follow them."

The air in the room changed—not colder, not warmer. Just older. The druid now had my full attention as I watched as they stepped closer to my beta. I caught a glint of something beneath their carefully crafted passive mask.

Not a threat.

Something worse.

Conviction.

"She is born of the Hollow," they said evenly. "Alpha blood runs through her veins, but she is not a male, and *all* wolves must bow to the moon." The druid looked at Killian as if he were dirt on the floor. "You'd do well to remember that."

"Funny," I murmured, not giving a single fuck about the slow coiling of ancient power in the room. "I always thought we howled at it."

The druid said nothing.

"I am tired," Malric announced. "It was good of you to come and check on my daughter."

Check on her?

"Stay for supper," he continued. "I won't join you this evening. But you are…welcome. I am sure an alliance may be discussed in later days…perhaps."

A dismissal. I inclined my head and turned to leave, catching Killian's eye, the unspoken warning to say nothing acknowledged when Killian also bowed his head in deference to the dying alpha.

As we left the room, I didn't need to look back to know the druid watched us leave; I felt the pressure of their gaze linger, like a brand between my shoulder blades.

A brand or a knife? Time would tell.

I may have fucked up when I decided to return to the Blueridge Hollow Pack, and that didn't sit well with me. I didn't like surprises and I had a feeling I was in for a big one.

Chapter 7

Rowen

I CAME BACK THROUGH THE LOWER TREE LINE, THE SUN already dipping behind the trees. I'd taken the long route home, looped wide through the creek bed just to avoid what waited for me in the halls.

That feeling of something coming had only grown stronger over the last few days, and I was just permanently on edge now.

I'd taken the long way because, for the first time in my life, I couldn't *breathe* in my pack.

I knew the suitors were coming, I expected it, but I thought that maybe I'd have had more time. A chance to pull my spine straight and square my shoulders. To remember to be sweet and agreeable. Ready to pretend.

It hadn't happened like that. They arrived together with their *companions*. Two males who looked at my pack with opportunity in their eyes and a challenge in their stare. But the challenge wasn't aimed at me; it was at each other. They weren't interested in me or my pack; they were interested in besting *one another*.

Blueridge Hollow Pack may as well not have been there. *I* may as well not have been there. So I took the opportunity they gave me while they fell into a dick-measuring contest, and I went for a run.

I doubted they'd have missed the fact I hadn't returned that night. After all, I wasn't important. I was a means to an end. I was the wife they'd get when they gained a pack. The sobering fact was that they were exactly the same for me, an alliance to ensure my pack survived.

At the end of the day, was I any better than them? Was my father? The druid? Probably not. Which is most likely why I resented them so much, as they forced me to face my own shortcomings and the lengths we would go to, to secure a pack.

I braided my hair as I walked, approaching the pack hall from the forest beyond it. But the second I stepped into the clearing near the hall, I knew something had shifted.

Scents.

Voices.

Strangers.

And—one heartbeat too late—his scent. I stopped dead in my tracks. It wasn't possible. It wasn't him. It couldn't be—

But it *was*. The scent of oakmoss, black pepper, leather, all wrapped in something jagged and unforgiving.

Wolfe.

Blood surged to my ears, too loud to think. I strode across the clearing like it owed me answers, past the fire pit, past the low conversation that paused as I passed. Someone called my name, but I didn't stop.

When I stepped into the hall—into that space—there he

was. His back was turned to me, but I took in his broad shoulders, recognizing the tension crackling through him like a caged beast trapped beneath his skin. His thick black hair kissed the neckline of his simple white tee. His jeans were worn, but he wore them well, showing a sculpted ass, and thighs as thick as my waist. His feet were bare, and my heartbeat picked up. Still wild. Still untamed.

My mouth salivated as I took him in.

The male next to him caught my eye and held mine curiously. Short, really short brown hair, not a buzzcut, more like a rugged, slightly tousled crop. Shoulders so broad and wide he looked like he could bench-press my entire pack. Biceps bulged under a gray T-shirt but not in an obscene way; he was just *built*. And younger than I thought at first glance. Dark blue eyes watched me, and a slow, knowing smile curled across his face.

Wolfe turned.

And just like that, everything I'd shoved down for years since he left tried to claw back up. Those eyes. That jaw. The sheer size of him—like the forest had spat him out whole just to piss me off.

His stormy blue gaze hit me, sharp as a blade, and held. "Rowen," he said it so casually, as if my name belonged in his mouth.

Like the last ten years hadn't happened.

I didn't reply. Didn't blink. Didn't flinch. I just stared back at him like the memory of him hadn't just shattered every wall I'd spent a decade building. My wolf stirred low under my skin, confused but hopeful. Stupid thing. We knew better.

I didn't let him or his companion see my inner turmoil.

Or the spike in my pulse. The way my lungs felt as if I had forgotten how to draw a full breath. No one in this hall needed to see how he affected me.

Especially not him.

So I did what every well-trained alpha's daughter did when the world dropped out from under her feet. I nodded once in acknowledgment and turned my back on him. I didn't speak. I didn't snarl. I walked out of the hall with every inch of dignity I could carry on legs that shook with the shock of seeing him again.

The silence behind me was deafening until I heard the soft, "Rowen, stop."

I closed my eyes as I heard him speak again, but I didn't stop, I didn't answer, I headed to my rooms. Let him choke on it. Let him stew in whatever regret, or duty, or *guilt* that brought him slinking back to the Hollow. He'd lost the right to say my name when he left me. There were no second chances, not here.

I didn't let my mask fall until my door snicked shut behind me, and I slumped against it like I'd just raced for days and never stopped. I staggered to my chair and sank down, my palms flat on the armrests, and let myself *feel* the emotion.

Not all of it. Not the worst of it. Not the depth of it. Just enough to burn the edges off.

Wolfe.

I couldn't believe he was here. After all these years. All the silence. After the rejection and the rebuilding. After *every-thing*. Wolfe *dared* to show up *now* and look at me like I was still *his*.

That wasn't even the worst part. The worst part was my

traitorous wolf *wanted* it. The part of me that lived beneath my skin, that instinctive, primal pulse, had perked up the second we'd recognized his scent in the air. My wolf was eager, tail raised, heart ready to leap.

No. Just…no.

I would not be ruled by biology. I would not be ruled by a man. *Especially* not him.

I rolled the tension out of my neck, my breathing still ragged, my skin still humming like I was ready to shift. I wasn't angry because he was here. I was angry because I wanted to run to him. And I wanted to know *why*.

Why *now*? Did the Council know? Had *they* sent him here? Why did he look at me with those damn eyes that looked like they still remembered every piece of me he left behind?

Fuck.

My head lifted as I heard faint footsteps approach my door. He wouldn't. As they got closer, I realized it wasn't Wolfe. I opened the door just as Adair raised her hand to knock.

"Not one word," I said tightly. "I'm not in the mood."

"Rowen," Adair murmured as she came into my room. "I see you've seen who's here."

I closed the door firmly and turned to see Adair watching me quietly with a look that said she already knew everything.

"Hard to miss him," I muttered.

She smiled. "I noticed." She tilted her head as she sat on my couch. "I also noticed you didn't kill him. Should I be impressed?"

I sniffed dismissively. "It's almost dinner time, bad form to commit murder right before supper."

Adair grinned. "You okay?"

I didn't answer right away, but it wasn't a question I wouldn't be asked multiple times. "No. But I will be." I picked at the leather braided bracelet I wore. "It's Wolfe, he won't stay here long."

She nodded. She didn't offer any sage words of wisdom; she wasn't one for flowery, empty words. Instead, she just settled into the couch, offering me her friendship with her silent support. And somehow, that made me feel steadier.

We sat in silence for a while, long enough for the world to become solid beneath my feet once more and my heartbeat to return to its regular, steady beat.

The pack hall was carved into stone, not built. My father had always said that foundations that couldn't be moved couldn't be broken. I used to think it was wise. Now it just felt like a prison. Strong walls, strong roots, but a prison nonetheless.

Silently, I got to my feet, knowing I had to show my face at supper. Tongues would already be wagging. Adair said nothing as I began to change my clothes.

The measured knock at my door caused my fingers to hesitate as I started to button my shirt, but I finished dressing before I opened it.

The druid stepped inside as if they belonged there, which, in their mind, they probably did. Their robes brushed against the wooden floor, and their hands remained folded in front of them, as always.

"You left the hall abruptly."

I kept my back to them, yanking the shirt off in frustration. Why was I dressing differently? For Wolfe? For my *suitors*? I would not change who I was for a man. I picked up a white tank top, pulled it on, and then put on a loose-fitting, wide-necked gray T-shirt.

"I didn't realize I needed to announce my exits," I answered the druid, noting that Adair had lain back on the couch and looked as if she had gone to sleep. Lucky.

The druid ignored her. "It would be beneficial if you demonstrated your manners in front of your suitors, and possibly potential husband."

My jaw clenched as I shoved my feet into my boots. I'd changed my pants into plain black pants. "*My* suitors? You sure they're not yours?"

"How long will you rage against this, Rowen?" they asked with what sounded an awful lot like disappointment.

I turned to face them, fists clenched at my sides. "You said the Goddess chooses. You believe that, don't you?"

They didn't blink. "I do."

"Then what does it matter if I leave the room they're in? Abruptly or not."

They didn't blink. "Because the Goddess also gave us laws. Laws that keep packs from fracturing. From falling. From becoming prey."

I stepped forward. "So we survive by sacrificing choice? Is that what you're saying?"

"We *survive*," they said calmly, "by doing what must be done. And right now, you are what must be done." They looked around my rooms. "Or do you want change? Your lineage has been in this territory since the very beginning. Do you not think you need to fight for that legacy?"

They knew better than to ask me that. "You know that's not what this is."

"I know *exactly* what this is," they said quietly. "A daughter who wants to lead in a world that only recognizes sons."

I swallowed hard.

"You forget, Rowen," they added, almost gently, "I know you. I know you better than yourself, so does the Goddess, and so does this land. And you know what I see when I look upon the child born at the heart of the Hollow?"

I shook my head, almost afraid of their answer.

"I think you were born to lead anyway."

I couldn't speak. Their praise was unexpected.

They let that hang between us a moment longer, then turned to leave. At the door, they paused. "You need to meet with the suitors. You need to treat them with the respect that they are due…and in turn, you will earn their respect and be seen as a *partner*, not a woman who hides in the woods when life serves her lemons."

"Lemons," I said with a soft chuckle. "I always did make the best lemonade."

The druid dipped their head as they stepped out and closed the door behind them with barely a sound.

Adair sat up and stretched. "They are not always the enemy," she said quietly. "It is easy to forget that sometimes."

I nodded, admonished by both, and rightly so. "You want stew?"

She grinned as she jumped to her feet. "Yes! *And* I heard that there was an extra loaf of pumpkin bread *just* for you, compliments of young Henry." She gave me a sly smile.

"He's young, sure, but I think he may already be over his recent heartbreak."

"Eew!" I gaped at her. "I'm something like ten years older than him!"

"So? Think how *eager* he'll be to learn." She winked at me and then cackled as she dodged the shoe I threw at her.

"Out. No more talking about that." I pushed her out of the door, and between her and the druid, I felt better. Lighter.

That didn't mean that, as I walked into the dining hall, I wasn't holding my breath, apprehensive about meeting Wolfe again or, worse, having to talk to him. But I knew before I'd even looked around, he wasn't here. I shouldn't have relaxed at the realization, but the truth was, I wasn't ready. Not yet.

The hall was busier than normal. It smelled of roasted meat, damp fur, woodsmoke, and the overwhelming scent of home. Of family.

The pack was already eating and talking as I joined them. Adair and I got bowls of stew, and she went to sit with some friends as I slipped into a vacant spot at another of the benches, bumping elbows with the two shifters on either side of me. They both moved eagerly to let me in, pausing in their conversations to make sure I had enough room.

"I'm fine, sorry, I didn't mean to interrupt," I told them both apologetically.

"You interrupted nothing," one of them said. "I'd rather talk to you anyway." They cast a look across the table. "Eric was telling me *again* about the size of his tomatoes."

I laughed along with the others as I looked over at the old shifter with fondness. "What will you do when Marla comes looking for your prized collection for the kitchen store cupboards?"

Eric feigned horror and the table laughed.

"You two have the same fight every year," I said with a shake of my head. "I'm beginning to think this may be your form of flirting," I teased, and the table erupted when the older man blushed. The others jumped in with tips on how to flirt when you're a male in your older years. Eric took it all in good fun and, as my companions settled, he shot me a wink across the table, and I thanked Luna for this small moment of normality.

Laughter spilled over from one end of the long table, and the sound, the *easiness*, eased all my rough edges.

This was my place. Right here, next to my pack, as we ate and discussed our day. The pack didn't stop talking when they saw me; they were comfortable around me, but they would always move to make room for me, include me in their conversations, and listen to what I had to say. They came to me when they needed something resolved or they wanted me to ask the alpha on their behalf.

I didn't need a title for them to see me.

I was passed a hunk of bread from an older hunter Ezra, who was one of our older scouts. He used to carry me on his shoulders when I couldn't keep up with the long treks my father used to send us on to teach me to hunt. His beard was longer now, more gray than brown, but he grinned as he watched me dip my bread in my stew.

"You looked like a hurricane on legs earlier," he said casually. "You good?"

"No," I said, chewing my bread. "But I'm getting there."

He laughed as he picked his tankard up. "Sounds about right."

Further down the table, two young ones were arguing over who got more venison in their stew, and I watched as their mother rolled her eyes and gave them both a spoonful of her own. Someone else further over was singing off-key, and someone else howled in response, making everyone laugh.

This wasn't just a pack. It was a whole damn world. I ate my dinner happily, exchanging smiles, jokes, and small talk with those around me. I leaned into the noise, soaking in the easy, unfiltered warmth. The familiarity. The trust.

"Rowen?"

I looked up to see Henry awkwardly lingering, and I felt the rumble of laughter from Ezra beside me, causing me to *accidentally* elbow him, which only made him laugh louder.

"Hi, Henry." I greeted the young male with a smile as I took a drink of water.

"Mom made you bread," he blurted.

"And it was mighty fine bread," Ezra said with a big smile. "Pumpkin bread with thick butter, yum."

"Delicious," I agreed. "I'll pass my thanks on when I see her."

I was saved from whatever else Henry was about to say when another of the pack called for my attention.

"Rowen?"

"Yes?"

The shifter gestured between himself and his companion beside them. "We're thinking of heading to town in the next couple of days to stock up on supplies. Okay to take three or four with us?"

I swallowed the last of my dinner. "Absolutely," I told them. My attention went back to Henry, who had wandered back to the other table, his shoulders a little more slumped than before. "Take Henry, he's young and strong, and he needs a change of scenery, even for a few days," I added quietly.

The males looked over their shoulders at the young shifter, then back to me, and both nodded. Someone else said that they would join them, and I went to stand when Ezra tugged at the hem of my shirt.

"Nice of you to think of the young one," he murmured. "A break from here would do him good."

"Yes, I think so too," I agreed. I gave his shoulder a warm squeeze as I took my bowl to the kitchens. I discussed the items the cooks needed from town and instructed them to submit their list to the pack members who would make the run.

I went back and sat amongst my pack into the late hours, listening, answering when asked something, and just being part of them.

They didn't need an alpha.

They just needed me.

For the first time in a long time, I slept soundly that night.

Chapter 8

Rowen

I DIDN'T QUESTION THE FACT THAT I HAD A GOOD SLEEP. I didn't question the fact that the very thought of who I might see today should have kept me awake but didn't.

Not really.

As I lay in bed, I listened to the distant sounds of the pack greeting morning—the soft thump of footsteps on stone, the low bark of a laugh that carried through the halls, and the creak of someone opening shutters that caught the breeze.

It was life. Normal.

By dawn, I was on my feet, dressed with a little more care than normal, and pacing my floors as I wondered what the day would hold for me, choosing to stay in the sanctuary of my rooms a little longer.

One of the kitchen workers brought me breakfast, coffee, and a thick slice of pumpkin bread with an equally thick layer of butter. I wasn't hungry, but I could never say no to pumpkin bread. I gobbled it greedily as I eyed the window that would let me sneak out.

But I didn't. I waited. I knew what was expected of me today.

The summons to come to the hall came mid-morning, and I'd changed clothes twice. I opened the door to Lewis, who looked me over, taking in my simple black combat pants and loose gray shirt. My long auburn hair was unbound and loose around my shoulders.

"The alpha's ready for you."

Of course he was. The question that mattered was, am I ready?

The hall had been rearranged. The long tables cleared, chairs spaced with intention, like a damn human job interview.

Three males waited at the far end, flanked by one of our pack elders and the druid. I had the brief thought they were as trapped in this as I was.

There was no sign of Wolfe or his companion. That was a problem I could deal with later, if they were still here. Did anyone know *why* they were here? I pushed thoughts of Wolfe aside as I tried to focus on what was in front of me.

I hadn't met the other shifter, who stood slightly apart from the two I'd already met. He was good-looking, and his face wasn't etched in a permanent sneer like one of the others, but still…he wasn't what I'd imagined my husband to look like.

Tyler, the one I'd punched years earlier stepped forward as I approached. He smiled, all charm and slippery edges. Not much taller than me, golden-haired, oozing the kind of confidence you only earned by never being told no. He extended his hand.

"Rowen, you look beautiful this morning." He beamed at me. His smile was as oily as his charm. "I'm Tyler of the Four Winds Pack."

I took his hand, casting a quick glance at my father. "I've known you for five years, Tyler," I grumbled as I shook it. "Or did my punch to your face years ago knock your memory?"

He didn't smile, but his grip became tighter before he dropped my hand. "I thought a fresh start may be best for both of us."

Shit. He was probably right.

The next male stepped forward, hand extended. "Rowen, I am Scott of the Deep Hollows Pack."

I took his hand. Firm grip. Dry palms. Small beady eyes that flicked over me like he was already assessing the return on his investment. His nose was so flat I wondered who broke it and why his shift to wolf form hadn't healed it at the time.

I gave a polite smile. Neutral.

I turned to the third. Eyebrow raised in question. He really was…pretty. Light golden brown hair, light blue eyes, warm smile. Tall but not as tall as Wol—*others*. His shoulders were broad, and there was a quiet strength about him. He looked comfortable in his skin, and I already suspected he would be my favorite out of the three.

"Rowen," he greeted, his voice light, like him. "My name's Dex, I'm from the Emberfell Pack." He saw my frown and added, "We're small, from up north." He didn't offer his hand, and I liked that about him.

"Rowen," my father spoke. "Be seated."

I took the seat to his right, with Lewis moving to stand behind us both. The druid settled into the seat to my father's left, and a pack elder sat beside me. The three males stood in front of us as if they were lining up in front of a firing squad; only Dex appeared relaxed, while Tyler seemed to regard the situation as beneath him, and Scott looked furious.

An interesting mix.

And I felt…nothing much at all. Huh.

My father indicated for Scott to step forward, and Scott spoke before anyone else. "I think we all know what this is," he said, stiff-backed and puffed-up like a rooster. "This is about politics. Stability. *Alliances*. Blueridge Hollow may be powerful, but without a male to carry it forward—"

"Finish that sentence," I said softly, "and I swear I'll escort you from this territory myself by your own tongue."

His mouth snapped shut, and red bloomed at the tips of his ears.

I didn't blink, didn't say anything else, just turned to my father and the druid. "I'm done with this one."

My father gave a nod. The druid didn't look pleased, but could they actually say they were surprised?

Scott sputtered something under his breath and stalked out of the hall without looking back.

Good.

Dad gestured to Tyler, who had the sense to look hesitant before he stepped forward. He crossed his arms, and I fought the eye roll at the very obviousness of his defensive posture.

"I see playing games won't work with you," he said flatly,

meeting my stare. "You need strength, I've got it. Your pack is disciplined and should stay that way. While Four Winds is my home and one of the oldest in the region, it would be beneficial to come here. I have wolves who are loyal to me, who want to join me, and we would strengthen this pack."

My pack didn't need strengthening. He must have seen the look on my face because he gave a frustrated sigh.

"Rowen, you know me. And I know *you*. I won't coddle you. I'd make sure you didn't have to *try* so hard to be taken seriously—"

I blinked in surprise. "You think I'm not taken seriously?"

That caught him off guard. He opened his mouth, shut it, floundered, and then said, "Well, I'm sure you are, but you need a man. You're not exactly subtle."

I leaned back, studying him. "Neither is a broken jaw. Should it add to your appeal that you have trouble taking no for an answer?"

That got a cough of laughter from Lewis behind me. Even the druid's lips twitched.

Tyler shrugged, unbothered, and stepped back. "My offer stands. Our packs are close, we have history, no matter how jaded, and honestly,"—he looked around the hall— "this pack needs fresh blood."

I didn't answer. He wasn't worth the breath.

Which left Dex.

He didn't rush. He waited for my father to give him the gesture to approach. Dex walked forward with an easy posture, hands tucked in his pockets like he didn't have a care in the world.

"Morning," he greeted us all. "Rowen," he said, a hint of a smile playing on his lips.

"Dex," I replied warily. My wolf watched him cautiously.

"You don't know me," he said easily with a glance back at Tyler. "And I think that may be a good thing." He rubbed his jaw playfully. "Emberfell is a small pack. My dad's alpha, my oldest brother his right-hand man, and my second-oldest brother will be alpha when Dad steps down." He rocked back on his heels. "We're mountain shifters, with stone loyalty, too many sharp rocks and not enough patience to suffer nonsense."

At least he was honest.

He scratched the back of his neck. "I'm not an alpha, but I know how to lead a pack. I'm not here to change things; I'm here because I've heard really good things about the Blueridge Hollow Pack. There's a lot of respect for this pack. And a pack that has respect and holds to the strong values of tradition, I'd like to be a part of that."

I glanced at my dad, who was watching him closely.

"Keep talking," I said before I could think better of it.

Dex nodded. "I can lead, but something tells me so can you, so I'm not asking you to follow me," he said, smiling that lazy smile again. "I could follow you."

I narrowed my eyes, and Dex saw it.

"Pack *leaders*," he emphasized. "Not singular. Let's not watch a good pack get smothered by idiots and their *friends*."

He wasn't just charming, he meant it. And that? That was more dangerous than a pretty speech.

I didn't answer, but I dipped my head, the same way I

would've to a scout bringing a report I didn't want to hear but needed to understand.

He gave me a slight smile but didn't linger, didn't hammer his point home. Just stepped back without posturing and took a stand beside Tyler—who looked like he'd been made to chew glass.

Beside me, the pack elder leaned in, voice low. "That one's different."

"Hmm, I noticed."

Across from me, the druid's brow was furrowed in thought. Calculating. Moving pieces on a board in a game I had agreed to play.

And then my father, sitting in his seat, with his back straight and proud, gave a faint, rasping chuckle.

"Dad?"

His voice was dry, but he looked amused. "Didn't think you'd humor any of them."

"Well…we've not said yes either," I reminded him quickly.

Dad didn't argue, just reached out and squeezed my hand. The elder got up and moved beside the druid. The two of them began murmuring between themselves in that low, secretive way the druid sometimes had. My dad turned to listen, and I let their voices fade as I glanced toward the open doorway…and froze.

Wolfe was there. Leaning in the shadowed arch, shoulder propped against the stone, watching. Listening. His eyes were locked on me like I was the only thing in the room that mattered.

Not jealous.

Not smug.

Just *there*. Unmoving. Unapologetic.

The rest of the room dulled around the edges as our gazes held. He didn't blink. And Goddess help me, my pulse spiked like prey catching scent of a predator it *wanted* to run towards.

I stood abruptly. The druid cut off mid-sentence.

"Rowen? Where are you going?"

I didn't answer. I walked away without ceremony, heading back to my rooms. If Wolfe wanted a front row seat to my humiliation, he could damn well *earn* it.

In my rooms, I pulled off my clothes, tied my hair into a messy bun, and then slipped out the window in just my underwear, and dropped into a crouch.

"I see that some things never change."

Rising cautiously, I watched him. He was propped against the wall, a smirk on his face, eyes roaming over me like he had the right to.

"I don't want your opinion," I told him, facing away from him.

Wolfe snorted. "Tough," he rumbled. "It's never stopped me before." He grinned when I turned and glared at him. "You know I get it," he said, pointing to the high window. "I would need to escape too."

I gave him my best condescending smile. "Because you're weak?"

Wolfe didn't give a shit; he watched me without emotion. "No, because I would also need a moment to drag my fury behind my ribs and cage it where it belonged."

My mouth was dry as I looked at him. I folded my arms across my chest, my eyes guarded, careful, so careful, of him being so close.

"Would you?" I taunted him. "Then tell me how, tell me how you would handle having your worth discussed like an animal at a livestock auction."

Wolfe stepped closer. "I'd rip someone's throat out."

I blinked, thrown by the anger in his tone. "Not helpful," I muttered, breaking the stare.

Wolfe gave a careless shrug. "I didn't say it was advice, just truth."

Silence fell between us like a trap snapping shut. My chest felt tight, and he looked *controlled*. Too controlled.

"Why are you here?" I asked him softly. "Did you hear about this and come to gloat?"

He didn't react, but his head tilted as he considered me. "I didn't know," he answered finally. "About what was being planned for you. The offer to"—he huffed with displeasure —"to *offer* you."

My laugh was sharp and bitter. "Of course you didn't. Because I'm not a person in this, I'm a *strategic* move."

"Haven't you always been? Isn't that what you told me you'd always be? That you *wanted* to be."

The way he was looking at me. The old wounds flared open. Bled. "Not like this," I snapped.

He didn't answer that. I never expected him to.

"I need to move," I told him, my shoulders drooping. "Before they come for me and find me out here." *Alone with you.*

"You mean with me?" he asked, the mockery in his eyes palpable.

"We're older than who we were before," I said quietly.

"Isn't everything?"

"Wolfe." I felt tired, exhausted. "I need to go. Can you just…can you just leave?"

He stepped closer, and I didn't back up. "No."

Wolfe was tall, so much taller than me, I had to tip my head right back to look up at him. I wasn't small; I stood at five nine, but Wolfe towered over me. His dark hair fell over his eyes, eyes the color of the darkening sky before a storm. Sculpted cheekbones, a straight nose, and a sharp jawline with a constant five o'clock shadow, with full lips… Ten years had aged him from a boy to a man.

My palms itched to reach out and run over the taut biceps, smooth across his chest, but I forced myself to remain still. He'd always had the power to affect me. But when you looked like Wolfe, many females would react the same.

"Why are you here?" I asked again. "If not to witness my embarrassment."

"Maybe you should pick the prick with the blond hair; he sounded as conceited as you do."

I stepped back at the venom in his voice. "You've changed."

Wolfe smiled slowly. His whole stance *shifted*, and he looked more like a predator than I'd ever seen in the wild. His eyes danced with wicked amusement as he looked down at me. "You have no idea how much I've changed."

"What would you do?" The whispered question was out before I could still my tongue.

His answer wasn't in words. It was just a look. One long look that made my skin prickle and my tummy turn somersaults. My breathing became shallow, and I saw the flare of interest in his eyes.

Goddess, what the heck was that? I stepped back, squaring my shoulders, fighting the urge to shake my head.

"You shouldn't have come back."

"Maybe not…but the alpha of the Stonefang Pack wants to create alliances." Wolfe hadn't moved, but he broke the stare and looked at the trees beyond us. "And this was once my home."

"You left."

He looked back, eyes unreadable. "You told me to go."

I had. I told him a lot of things. Meant every damn word at the time too. Regretted them a few times too.

"The pack is undergoing change," I said, forcing the words out past the ache. "Your alpha should visit when…" I swallowed. I couldn't finish it. Not with my father's scent still fading from the walls. Not with the weight of goodbye already pressing into my bones.

Wolfe's hand moved before I saw it coming—rough knuckles brushing a tear from my cheek. I flinched. Not from the touch. From the familiarity. From the audacity.

"You're stronger than you know," Wolfe murmured, like that permitted him to be soft. "And smarter than this."

I met his gaze and let the quiet break like glass between us. "I *am* strong," I agreed, and because I could, I lashed out. "I'm not the one who left when they didn't like what they heard," I said. "And I'm not the one hiding behind someone else's crown now."

His jaw flexed. There it was. A crack in the calm. Wolfe stepped back. "Enjoy your run."

He turned to walk away.

This time, I didn't stop myself. "Next time you show up

uninvited," I said coldly, "come as yourself. Not some emissary in borrowed armor."

He didn't turn. Didn't speak. And I didn't watch him go.

Because this wasn't a reunion; it was a *reckoning*. Wolfe had walked into the Blueridge Hollow territory as if he still belonged here.

He didn't.

Not in my home and not in my heart.

Not anymore.

Chapter 9

Wolfe

I WALKED AWAY FROM THE HALL. MY WOLF HUFFED WITH amusement that I was walking *away* from her, but if I went back… Yeah, I couldn't afford to make *that* kind of mistake.

Not again.

Not with her.

Her words echoed behind me like the snap of bone. *"Come as yourself. Not some emissary in borrowed armor."*

She had no idea what she was asking. Of course she didn't. If she knew I wasn't here on anyone's leash or that I hadn't *bowed* to anyone in years, she would choke on her spite.

Still, her words held. Because I *was* pretending to be something I wasn't. Just like *she* was pretending she wasn't the one who carved my heart out and walked away first.

Killian fell into step beside me, quiet at first, but Killian was shit at keeping his opinions to himself. "Is she worth it?"

I shot him a look sharp enough to cut.

Killian shrugged. "Look, I know there's history here; you

walked in here like you have a right to. But what did you expect? A hug?"

"No," I said flatly. "I didn't expect this shitshow either."

Killian scoffed. "You took us here because *this* was exactly what you expected." He looked around and switched to the mindlink. *Seriously, man, why are we here? She doesn't look like someone who needs help, especially* not *from someone she obviously doesn't trust.*

I didn't answer him. Not because I couldn't...I just didn't want to. There was an ache in my body, one I hadn't felt in a long time. Not an ache in my chest, but lower. Deeper. Right at my core. I hadn't felt it since *she* smothered it with logic, pride and a fucking send-off that still echoed in my skull.

And now? She was still spitting fire with my name on her tongue like *I'd* been the one to turn *her* away.

I left this pack because she told me to. Told me she would never be mine, and she never wanted me to be hers. I'd stayed gone because I believed her then. I wasn't as sure that I believed her now.

But I *was* different. I never knew I was an alpha when I left this pack. I'd been young, eighteen, and angry at the world. An alpha came into his power in his early to mid-twenties. I'd been long gone from Blueridge Hollow by then.

I hadn't even known I *was* an alpha; it was Lars, the alpha of the Stonefang Pack, who knew what I was and guided me through my transition to alpha. We'd kept it between us, not letting the pack know at first, and then when he was failing, failing like Malric now was, he'd told his pack he wanted them to accept me as their new alpha when the time came.

They had. The transition was smooth and controlled. I'd inherited a pack like an alpha son would, and there was no resentment from anyone; no one thought I'd earned it without actually *earning* it. I'd served the Stone-fang Pack faithfully; they were my pack, and I *was* their alpha.

Killian gave me a speculative look. "Look, you've told me a little bit about the life you had here, and I know you and her have some history, and…"

"And?" I asked, one eyebrow raised.

"She doesn't know why you came," he said carefully. "You didn't tell her."

"She didn't ask."

"Do you plan to discuss it with her?" Killian probed.

I shook my head. I stopped then, just outside the southern slope, where the trees grew thicker and the curve of the mountain rose in the distance. The scent of the pack drifted in the morning breeze.

"No point," I told him honestly. "She'd never listen. She…" I looked around me. "She can handle herself."

"You took us all the way here to tell me she could handle herself?" Killian looked at me in disbelief. "You serious?" He looked over his shoulder. "You're not going to say anything about what we heard?"

I thought about it. "Nah."

"Nah?" Killian was glaring at me.

"Age only made her fiercer," I said. "I pity the guy she ends up with."

Killian didn't look convinced, but he let it go. "So we make our pack's intent known and go home?"

"Yup. Alliances. This is a pack that's close enough to

Stonefang territory to keep them amiable, let them know the new alpha has no ill intent, and then it's homeward bound."

Killian mulled it over. "Does the alpha really have no ill intent?"

I grinned. "Let's see how we go; it depends on how he's feeling. I've heard he can be a real prick."

Killian laughed. "Praise be to that." We resumed walking. "Their alpha looks frail," he added solemnly. "Do you think he's heard the rumors of the attacks?"

I shook my head. "I doubt it. They've been kept quiet when they shouldn't be. We can discuss it with Alpha Malric and his betas before we leave."

"This pack is prime for attack," Killian murmured. "I've seen no patrols since we've been here."

I nodded. "Before, when I was here, they sent out regular scouting parties, but we didn't come across any on our way here. I wonder if they still do." We'd walked in a slow circle, coming back to the hall. "This territory used to be impossible to cross without meeting a patrol or a scout."

Another thing to check before we leave, I told Killian. *With a dying alpha, she can manipulate whatever pack leader she sees fit, but an alpha or a rogue comes through here? This pack is prime for the taking.*

It's not too far from Stonefang…you could take it.

What the fuck do I need with two packs? I asked him in surprise.

Think about it, you could build an empire. Emperor *Wolfe.*

You're an idiot, I scolded him, fighting the grin, my eyes looking over the packlands that I used to know well and seeing how open they were. The pack was spread out, for one. There may be a pack hall, but the pack was seldom all together. Bone and iron markers did nothing to the living and, if I were being honest, not much for the dead either. Those on the fringes could be attacked and killed before the rest of the pack knew.

There was something off in the air. Not wrong exactly. Just…watchful. Like the forest was holding its breath.

Or waiting for someone to bleed.

I'd grown up here. I came to the pack when I was eight or nine. My parents were killed when I was a babe. My uncle took me in but was killed in a pack war between two old enemies. They hadn't cared what he'd left behind, and his house was reallocated before he was even on the burial pile.

I'd left and didn't look back. An old wolf from the Hollow found me in a ditch, covered from head to toe in mud, trying to blend into the dirt in case he was a rogue. He took me back to Blueridge Hollow, brought me before Alpha Malric, and asked the alpha to give me a place in the pack. He left the next day, and I never saw him again.

But the Hollow had been kind to an orphan. As long as I worked and did odd jobs, I received schooling and had food in my belly. Malric let me stay in the hall, a room off the kitchen, and I was fairly content in the years I spent here.

I had grown up with Rowen and watched her scrape her knuckles raw on pack law while still keeping up the fight. Determined to change tradition, while she clung to those same values as if they were lifeblood.

Not that anyone else noticed. To most of the pack, she didn't look much like a stormbreaker, despite her being all spine and steel, more like someone they indulged because she was the alpha's daughter.

We began spending time together; the alpha didn't approve, but he never spoke against it—not outright. I had been drawn to her fire, her determination, and her willingness to speak out against what she considered wrong.

And then, when it mattered, she'd rejected it all for this pack who still looked over its shoulder to the past instead of the future that would find them all too soon.

I looked up at the Blueridge peaks, listening for the whispers of the mountains to guide me home.

I heard Killian's harrumph beside me, turning to him in question.

Everyone's pretending not to talk about the fact that there are Stonefang emissaries here. Everyone is too busy pretending not to notice, while every single one of them watches us.

They don't trust us, I told him. *Would you?*

We're not the enemy here.

I cast my eye over the few pack who were milling around the far end of the clearing. They weren't scared, not exactly overtly curious, just alert. Like something inside them knew we weren't here for politics. I didn't sense any danger from them, but you could never tell.

"Stay alert," I murmured as we walked back to the hall. "We'll be gone soon."

They'd kept us waiting for two days. In that time, I'd briefly seen Rowen again, but we had said little to each other, probably both recalling the heated words that first afternoon. Other than that, we'd spent time with some of the pack, folks who I'd known before and who were open to allowing Killian and me into their homes.

The pack hall had been where we ate, and I was surprised by how well I could avoid the druid. I could mask my alpha scent effectively, but the druid wasn't paying attention to me the same way his pack might be.

Killian wasn't a big believer in the power of the druid. He was more inclined to listen to shamans than druids, but I knew better than to write off the druid. And a druid sensed power. I knew they would soon realize I was masking myself, so I was keen to avoid them.

Lewis, the alpha's beta, walked over to us where we sat at the fire pit, just the two of us. We'd been out hunting and came back with a big fat doe, which we'd taken straight to the kitchens for hanging, cleaning, and eventually quartering when the carcass had been hung for the appropriate amount of time.

"You want to talk to the alpha?" Lewis asked.

No, we're here just painting our toenails, Killian grumbled.

"We do," I said, shooting Killian a look and receiving a vulgar gesture in return.

"He is frail," Lewis murmured under his breath.

That brought both of us up short. We knew that, we'd seen it, and it was on us that we had not taken into consideration the extent of Malric's frailty.

We followed Lewis through the hall and to the rooms of the alpha. I'd seen Rowen leave earlier with the male Dex. They seemed to be getting on well. I'd wondered how long it would last, but Killian had nudged me, and I'd looked away, clearing my face of the scowl.

The old male hadn't moved from his bed in two days.

But when we walked into his rooms, he was sitting upright. Eyes clear. Spine straight. Like he'd peeled back the curtain on death and told it to fuck off for now.

"Wolfe," Malric greeted me. His voice had a rasp to it that I didn't remember.

"Alpha." I dipped my head in greeting, seeing Killian doing the same.

Malric looked us both over. "Close the door," he told Lewis. "On your way out."

Lewis hesitated, but he left the room, and Killian wordlessly followed. I hadn't asked him to, but he was offering this to my old alpha.

Which was probably a good thing—Killian wasn't known for his tact.

The room was thick with the scent of sage, sickness, and iron. But Malric's gaze was sharp and just a touch of something else, not age…but something ancient lingered in his gaze when he watched me.

"Speak."

"Stonefang Pack has a new alpha. The alpha is keen to let you know that the existing relationship with this pack doesn't change. They are keen to call you allies."

Malric watched me, his face impassive. "What else?"

I didn't waste time. "There are reports of packs falling under attack from a band of rogues." I looked over my shoulder, ensuring the door was closed. "Doesn't matter how *ready* to lead, whoever wins your daughter's attention to take over this pack, they're going to need to be ready to defend it."

Malric watched me intensely; he didn't blink when I told him the news. "How many packs have been attacked?"

"Four, officially. Six, if you count the ones gone quiet."

"Which territories?"

"Southern ridge, eastern timberline, the borderlands. Rogue activity has been noted, not random attacks. Coordinated."

Malric exhaled slowly. "Definitely not random?"

"No," I confirmed. "Someone's moving. Testing walls. Picking off the weak, it looks like, and if Blueridge Hollow loses structure now—"

"Then the whole eastern mountain this side of the Appalachians collapses."

I nodded. "That's my thought."

He leaned back with a wince, pain threading through his expression, but he didn't break eye contact. "And Stonefang Pack is monitoring?"

"We've been watching, sending scouts to the packs who haven't checked in. That's why I think it's more than officially reported."

Malric nodded thoughtfully. "And you came to warn me?" he asked. "And let me know, if we need it, Stonefang Pack will assist?"

I nodded, and when he didn't say anything else, I let the silence stretch.

"You aren't here for my daughter's hand?"

I looked at Malric in surprise. "No. She made her choice about me years ago," I told him candidly. I wasn't sure what Malric knew of my relationship with Rowen when we were younger, but I was sure he'd have put two and two together since then. "But I won't deny the fact that you're—"

"Dying," Malric said bitterly. "At the worst time, it seems."

"Is there a good time to die?" I asked him softly. "The Goddess calls us all to the great hunt eventually."

"My daughter is in danger. My pack is in danger." He looked away from me, his brow furrowed. "This is not the time for old men to be on their deathbeds." He sighed. "But it is what it is. Your alpha is a good one?"

I swallowed. "I believe so."

Malric huffed out a laugh. "You *believe* so?" He gave me a knowing look. "You were always vocal. You wouldn't be with a pack where you *believe* an alpha was good, you'd *know*."

He was right. Lars had been a good alpha. "Alpha Lars was a great alpha," I told him honestly.

Malric accepted that. "He was. He used to drive me insane with his ability to see both sides of an argument, but he was fair. No alpha sons," he added thoughtfully. "His pack has an alpha now?"

"They do."

Malric's eyes narrowed. "Why have you waited for two days?" He held his hand up. "Rogue packs, Lewis could have heard that… Why have *you* waited for two days?"

"We were at the Pack Council, arrived just after Rowen and Lewis left, I think. We heard the…" I sniffed dismissively. "Intendeds talking. Killian and I spoke to the shaman, and during our chat, he told us your pack was vulnerable." I broke eye contact. "It's been years, but I came because your pack, your daughter, could be a target. Whether you or the Council admits it or not, they're out there, circling like vultures. If she chooses wrong, then—"

"It won't just be rogues we have to worry about."

We didn't say anything for a long moment, and I

thought he was struggling with the weight of what I'd revealed.

"She's not ready for this," Malric suddenly announced. "She thinks she is, but…" His head dipped as he looked at his hands. "She's strong, fiercer than I think I ever was," he admitted softly. "But she is not a male." He looked up at me. "More's the pity."

"Or…" I drew in a deep breath. "She's the only one in this pack who is ready."

Malric smiled faintly. "You may be right."

"Where are the patrols? The scouts?" I asked him carefully. "This pack used to be heavily defended. I saw nothing when I crossed."

Malric's shoulders seemed to droop. "My pack is getting old, Wolfe. There are few youths left." I watched as his hand rose and pushed back his white hair. "Very few wish to hold to the old ways anymore. Those who do are too old to patrol as they did." When I said nothing, his look was once more assessing. "And you? Are you ready to fight for a pack that doesn't know you anymore?"

I needed to be careful with my next words. "Stonefang Pack is keen to ally with its neighbors and those slightly beyond. The alpha believes that if the rogues were to face a united front, then they would become less bold. Maybe even move on." I gestured over my shoulder, pointing to the door. "The pack doesn't need to know us to benefit if it means their survival. But…a pack not willing to fight for itself, it's not a good thing, Malric."

His mouth twisted, not quite a smile, and I realized I'd addressed him as an equal. "And Rowen?" he asked.

I looked away. "She'll claw through anyone who gets in her way."

"Even you?"

Especially me. I didn't answer, though, but Malric didn't need me to.

"Which one of them would you pick for her?" he asked instead.

"None of them." It was out before I stopped it. The old alpha laughed out loud, and I looked away ruefully. "Dick move, Alpha," I grumbled, but I felt the smile at his cleverness.

"I never thought she would agree to it," he admitted in a moment of vulnerability. "But then I never thought I would be leaving her like this. The druid is supportive, but…"

"But the druid hears the call of the land more often than not," I finished for him. "They aren't always reliable."

"Agreed," Malric said softly. He pulled himself up in the bed, sitting straighter. "You have given me much to think about. Your candidness is appreciated."

I knew it was a dismissal, and I stood slowly, watching him assess me as I did. "Alpha?"

"You grew strong, Wolfe," he said with admiration. "Your pack is lucky to have you."

"You should rest," I told him.

Malric surprised me when he held his arms out, and, slightly stunned, I moved forward and embraced the old shifter who had, in part, raised me.

I felt him stiffen and knew my mistake as soon as I made it. I'd let my guard down. "Malric—"

"You can't fool me, Wolfe," he said in my ear. "Or should I say, *Alpha* of the Stonefang Pack?"

Chapter 10

Rowen

I'D BEEN MEETING WITH MY PROSPECTIVE MARRIAGE interests for two days.

On the first day, Tyler had brought flowers. Like I was some dainty she-wolf waiting to be courted, not a battle-worn alpha's daughter holding her pack together with grit and willpower.

"They reminded me of you," he said, smug and smiling.

Sharp-thorned and blood-colored? I could've believed that. But these were delicate things. Pale and pretty. I took them with a nod and laid them down on the table before he could say more.

Scott had already left the Hollow after I shut him down, his pride too bruised to linger. Tyler was clearly hoping to win by sheer persistence. And Dex…Dex was different.

He didn't posture. Didn't push. Just watched me the way wolves watched storms—like he respected what I did here.

That made him dangerous.

That also made him interesting.

Which made him a problem.

"You should rest before the next session," the druid had advised earlier, ever the picture of serenity, wrapped in manipulation. "We'll begin the final interviews soon."

Final. Like this was a job. Like I was a position to assign. I'd left the hall before I said something that would earn me another lecture that I wouldn't be able to walk away from.

I needed air.

I needed space.

I needed—

Wolfe.

There. Across the yard, listening to Lewis as he spoke to the shifter Wolfe came with. The one who stuck to his side like a shadow. The one who looked like he would bench-press Tyler and Dex together and not break a sweat. And then beside him...Wolfe stood there like he owned the territory he hadn't set foot on in years. Arms crossed. Brows drawn. Listening more than speaking.

Watching.

Me.

He didn't look away when I caught him. Didn't blink. Didn't move. Like he wanted me to know he saw everything.

Why are you here?

The question had been annoying me for days. Because the truth was...I didn't know. He hadn't declared himself. Hadn't really said much at all. Hadn't tried to sway me or woo me or so much as stepped into my path since that one sharp conversation. He wasn't here for *me*, I knew that... But he hadn't left.

Wolfe wasn't the kind of wolf who lingered without purpose. And whatever he was waiting for, it wasn't romance. I wasn't that stupid; he had no interest in this circus that I was currently hosting.

But was it war?

Vaguely, I was aware that the druid had been talking to me about what to expect tomorrow, and the way Wolfe was watching, I knew he knew that I hadn't heard a word. I made my excuses to the druid and wished I could walk away before Wolfe could smirk. Before he caught me looking at him again.

Let Dex and Tyler hover. Let the druid whisper their advice. Let the pack speculate. I didn't care what they thought of me, thought of this. But I cared what *he* was thinking.

And that pissed me off more than anything.

Returning to my rooms, I retired for the night but didn't sleep much at all. I was dreading what the next day would bring. The next morning, the dread was still lingering, but I managed to get dressed without changing my outfit and acted as I normally would. Did my tasks for the day, ate my meals, joined in conversations. It was just another day, or that was the lie I was telling myself.

We were in the pack hall, separate from my pack, as Tyler and Dex sat across from me. I was pushing the potatoes around on my plate.

Today had been agonizingly slow. I just wanted it to end, and retreat to my rooms and just be alone without the scrutiny.

Dex, to the right. Warm smile. Easy confidence. A quiet offer of understanding in a world built on dominance.

Tyler, to the left. Polished arrogance. A son of an alpha

of a pack with weight and a jawline that probably got him out of more fights than into them.

They both wanted to lead this pack. Maybe they both even wanted me, or the idea of me, anyway.

But my eyes kept drifting to Wolfe and his companion. They sat across the hall, just far enough to be uninvolved. Just close enough for them to watch, if they wanted.

Wolfe wasn't speaking. Wasn't smiling. Wasn't even pretending to eat. He was just *there*. Present. His presence seemed to fill the hall, and I couldn't think with him here.

Every time I laughed at something Dex said or cut off one of Tyler's not-so-subtle jabs, I could feel Wolfe's eyes on me. Judging me and measuring my responses. Like he knew what it cost to keep playing nice.

But there was a look about him, and I kept thinking he wanted me to snap. And I knew I would *if he kept looking at me like that*. So I did the only reasonable thing I could without giving him what he wanted. I stood. "Excuse me."

Both of my companions were at a loss for what to say, and I felt the druid's eyes on me as I walked away from the table. I knew the whole hall was watching, and I *didn't care*. I just needed one minute to myself before I continued with this charade.

I didn't go far—just into the tree line behind the hall where the scent of food faded and the evening swallowed the noise. With my eyes closed, I pressed my forehead against the trunk of a tree, not caring that the rough bark bit into my skin.

I hadn't heard him follow. It didn't matter, not when his presence rolled in behind me like a shadow, making me wonder if I had ever lost the sense of him.

"Not hungry?" he asked, and I heard the laughter in his voice. "You should've stayed; it was just getting interesting."

"*You* should've left," I snapped, refusing to turn around and meet that mocking glare. I knew he was behind me, not close enough to touch, never stupid enough to try.

"Why?" he asked with a light chuckle. "You're like a court jester, but instead of juggling balls, you're juggling potential husbands. It's entertaining."

I turned slowly, every inch of me strung too tight. "This is all a game to you, isn't it?"

"To them, yes."

"Not to you?" I challenged him.

His gaze was steady. Hard. "To me? I've no skin in the game you're playing."

"I'm not playing *games*."

"Really?" he challenged me. "Looks to me like you're pretending to be fragile, and I've never known you to be… *breakable*."

My jaw clenched against the honesty of his scorn, but I'd be damned if I showed him that. "You think you can come back here after all these years and pretend to understand me?"

Wolfe's gaze ran the length of me. "I never stopped understanding you."

I laughed—low, sharp, *furious*. "Do you forget that *you* left this pack?"

"Do you forget that *you* made damn sure that I did?" He was so blunt in the way he said it. No malice. No vulnerability. Just facts. Harsh truths, it was one of his more annoying qualities. We stared at each other across the breadth of space, too close to breathe easily, too far apart to pretend it didn't matter.

Wolfe grinned suddenly, and I hated that I knew it was fake; his eyes were still cold and hostile. "You should get back in there. I can't wait for the conclusion to the little contest you're hosting." He looked like he was fighting back laughter. "Who will you choose, the idiot blond who checks out every female's ass when he thinks you're not looking? Or the one who's putting all his effort into pretending he's laid back and ready to follow *you*, when in reality, he's checked every sentry post at least twice since he's been here. Why would a *follower* need to know how strong your pack's defenses are?"

A rustle in the trees made me break my stare from the male in front of me, only to see his companion lingering.

"Wolfe, are you ready?"

Wolfe nodded, his eyes on me for a moment more. "Enjoy your game, *princess*."

Princess, it used to be his pet name for me, but now he said it with scorn instead. He had once looked at me with something far from scorn, but those days were long behind us now.

"I hate you," I whispered as he walked away.

"I know." His voice carried back as low as mine had been. "You made it very clear what you thought of me."

I knew what he meant. Years ago, we'd been in... Love? Was it love? We'd been young, but I'd never been accused of being foolish. Wolfe was no fool either. I'd been more concerned with what was important, like the pack. Not just *us* in a pack, but the pack dynamics as a whole. Even so, I think he loved me then. Loved me the day he told me of his plan to go to my father and declare his intention that, one day, he would be my husband. Loved me when he told me we could go explore the world as husband and wife. Together. Loved me even when I'd laughed in his face and told him that, while I cared for him deeply, I didn't love him. That I would marry who my father picked for me, for the advantages a good match would bring for the pack. Which benefited my station as the alpha's daughter.

My station.

I told him then that I would marry for the benefit of my pack, not myself. I liked to think I'd grown up since then. I'd had no choice. And look where my haughtiness had gotten me. A dating game with two males who were trying to convince me they'd give me what I wanted, when in reality, they were gaining an entire pack ready to roll over and be delivered to them on a plate.

Much like I was being offered on a platter, like a freshly roasted pig ready to be devoured by the hungry mob.

Maybe I was more of a fool than I realized.

"Well, your flair for the dramatic hasn't gotten better with age," I muttered to myself as I walked back to the hall, knowing that I still had to get through dinner before I could hide in my rooms.

Had I done the right thing all those years ago, rejecting Wolfe? Would I be a happily married woman now? The constant weight of doing what was best for my pack no longer dragging me down?

I'd never expected that he would *leave*. I thought my words would wound, but not so much that he would leave me. I knew not long after he was gone that I'd made a mistake. His leaving had left me empty inside. No one had ever made me feel filled like he had.

I may not have been foolish, but I had learned humility from the arrogance of my youth, a painful lesson indeed.

He had done well for himself; the new alpha of the Stonefang Pack had sent him as an emissary, meaning Wolfe must be a beta to the alpha, which made sense. He was obviously strong; he'd filled out well over the years. Gone was the skinny, lanky boy I once knew. Goddess, if I were honest, everything about him was changed. His looks had only grown more striking, his shoulders broader, his confidence evident in the swagger of his walk. He wasn't the same Wolfe I once knew…except…except that mocking smirk and those thundery blue eyes that saw too much.

Seeing him now, I think I was right to reject him back then. Look at what he'd made for himself. A home somewhere else and a pack he was quick to call his own. Leaving here, leaving *me*, was the best thing for him. I was sure of it.

Or I was sure it was a lie that I could convince myself was true.

The rest of dinner was as agonizing as I'd predicted. Dex and Tyler had both been frustratingly maddening, and I knew I was being irrational.

At one point, I saw Lewis lead Wolfe and his companion through the doors, and they all went to the back of the hall. My father had spoken to him earlier, I knew that, why would he call for him again? I turned my attention back to my suitors, but my mind kept wandering to what my father and Wolfe were discussing.

The druid stood and announced we would reconvene in the morning and bid us goodnight. I stayed a short time with Dex and Tyler, desperate to hurry after the druid, but I had better manners and should probably show them that. That didn't stop the sigh of relief escaping me as I went to my rooms, ready to unwind and shed the mask of interested courtier for the day.

I slowed my walk as I saw the large companion of Wolfe outside my father's rooms. He looked up at my approach, his eyes following me as I got closer, but he said nothing.

"Is there something you need?" I asked him, coming to a stop at my father's door, hand resting protectively on the handle.

"Nope."

I waited, but when it was clear he wasn't going to say anything else, I forced a smile. "We haven't been properly introduced. I'm Rowen."

He nodded once. "I know who you are."

Again, I waited, and so did he, although I didn't think he was keen to continue the conversation. "And your name is?"

He looked away, his jaw tightening. "Does it matter?"

"So your mother never taught you manners?" I snapped. "You are in my home, in my pack, and you should show respect."

He grinned, and it wasn't friendly. "I've not seen anything here that is worthy of my respect except the old alpha in there who is barely hanging on to life as he fights the Goddess's call home."

"It makes sense you'd be friends with Wolfe; he was always a contrary dick too." I grumbled as I pushed the door open to my father's rooms. "Dad? You okay?" I stopped short when I saw the druid standing over my father and Wolfe standing against the wall, his face white and drawn into a frown. "What's going on?"

"Rowen."

The relief that it was my father's voice I heard almost took my legs from me. "Dad?" I hurried over to his bedside, ignoring the man I brushed past to reach him. "What's wrong?"

"Luna is calling," he told me as I took his hand. "It is almost time."

"No."

His smile was weak. "She has sent me the sign I waited for," he told me as he looked past me to Wolfe. "The pack is Wolfe's to lead."

I straightened so sharply I felt something twinge in protest in my spine. "*What?*"

"Wolfe is my chosen successor." My father closed his eyes. "As is witnessed by the Goddess, the druid of my lands, and the heir of my choice."

"As is witnessed by the Goddess and the druid of the land," the druid murmured solemnly.

"*What!*" I demanded again. "This doesn't make sense. Someone, tell me what the hell is happening."

My father mumbled something under his breath, and the druid fussed over him. "If you cause him any more upset, I will ask you to leave," they warned me.

Confused, I turned away and met Wolfe's gaze.

"What did you do?" I took a step forward, not sure if I was going to scream at him or attack.

Wolfe's look of disgust didn't make it better. "I did nothing," he said roughly.

"You tricked him?" I accused wildly. "You *must* have, why would he, why would he *ever* pick you?"

His top lip curled in a sneer as he straightened and took a step towards me. "Watch your tongue, princess."

"Rowen!" The sound of my father's voice made me turn away from the wall of fury in front of me. "Respect my choice. Respect your leader."

"Of course, Father—"

I heard the cold, cruel chuckle behind me. "He wasn't talking about himself."

A shiver of fear trickled down my spine. I turned slowly and looked at Wolfe in front of me. He was smiling, and it wasn't pleasant.

"He means me."

Chapter 11

Wolfe

I DIDN'T MOVE AT FIRST. COULDN'T.

The words were still echoing off the stone walls like war drums.

"Wolfe is my chosen successor."

I wasn't sure what shocked me more—Malric saying it or the druid *agreeing*. I'd expected resistance. Fury. Maybe even a strong curse. But the druid had merely looked at me with their mismatched eyes and…smiled.

When Malric had embraced me, sensing my alpha scent, I had told him I would prefer it if no one knew. He hadn't asked why; he had only told me he needed to rest. I had left him in his room, my head a mess. I'd kept my mask on, let no one see I was off my game. When Lewis came and got me from outside, I'd braced myself for the worst. When I entered Malric's rooms, he had called for the druid right away, and I was sure it was either to have them cast me out or maybe share what I had shared with Malric about the rogues.

To have me declared as his *chosen heir?*

I hadn't even had the power to protest; I had *not* seen this coming. I *had* a pack. A good pack.

When I'd tried to make them listen to that, Malric waved it off, and the druid carried on doing whatever the fuck it was the druid did when an alpha was ready to pass to the great hunt.

Instead of explanations, what I got was silence.

The only light moment in all of this had been seeing Rowen's face. She turned to me, her senses telling her what they said was true, and she'd been very loud in her protest. Thank the Goddess that someone reacted like this was a crazy idea...even if it was her.

She looked at me like I'd just slit her throat and called it mercy.

I couldn't wait in here for a moment longer. I didn't need to hear the druid spin this into a blessing from the land or the Goddess. I stepped out.

Killian immediately fell into step beside me, his silent presence wrapping around me like comfort. We walked out of the hall, into the humid heat of the forest. Away from them all.

He walked with me until I hit the tree line.

"You gonna say something?" he asked, breathing low and tight.

"I... No."

"Want to tell me what happened? Has the alpha passed?"

"Not yet," I growled. "Soon."

"Then why do you look so pissed?"

"I said I didn't want to talk about it," I growled at him.

"And I heard that and thought fuck that, tell me what's

going on." He looked over his shoulder. "She pick one of those assholes?"

My laughter was loud and short. "No. I wish she had."

Killian was frowning. "Right, you tell me now, or I'm going back to ask them."

He would too. Killian had impulse control issues. "Malric named me his successor."

Killian looked as shocked as I felt. "Holy shit…"

"Yup."

He looked over his shoulder again, this time as if he was expecting a pack to show up. "What the fuck?" He looked confused and then angry. "Well, he can fuck off!" Killian declared hotly. "Fuck that and fuck this pack. You are *our* alpha, not this weird fucking place with their creepy druid and fucking stuck-up daughter."

"I know whose alpha I am," I reminded him with a smile. "Stonefang is my pack." I stopped walking. "But Malric named me his successor, in the eyes of the Goddess and the druid, so when he dies, I am likely to be bound, and the power will shift to me."

"No." Killian shook his head stubbornly. "It's not right. He can't hijack you from Stonefang."

"I am still your alpha, but," I reminded him gently, "I don't know how this works." I scrubbed a hand through my hair, pacing under the thick canopy, every nerve burning. "She can't know I am an alpha. Let's keep the pretense, okay?"

"Why?"

I held back my groan. "Because she already thinks I *tricked* her father. If she knows I'm an alpha, she'll think I *took* it from him, by force, and I need time to sort this out." I rubbed my jaw. "I do *not* need her believing this to be a huge conspiracy. She's already on edge."

"She's going to find out eventually…" Killian said dubiously. "I mean, you won't exactly be able to hide it for long."

"I know." I sighed. "Just for a few weeks, okay? This is a fucking mess we didn't need."

Malric had made a move. A *bold* one. Not just naming me, but doing it in front of *her*. In front of the druid. No trial. No vote. Just *me*—the outsider, the exile, the one she told to leave, now being handed *her* pack like some sick joke.

And the worst part? I didn't want it…until I looked at her and realized someone else *would*. Tyler. Dex. Some smiling wolf with sharp teeth and no soul for this land who would make her life miserable. I didn't want the power. But I'd be damned if I let this pack or her drown under someone else's greed.

"Fuck," I muttered, voice shredded with the weight of it.

Killian raised an eyebrow. "That about sums it up." He looked into the canopy of trees above us. "I was only joking earlier," he said to the sky. "I didn't manifest this!"

I stared through the trees, toward the hall I'd just left— toward her. Still inside. Still silent. Probably *seething*.

"She's not going to forgive this," I said to him quietly. "Do you think Luna is punishing me because Stonefang Pack was such an *easy* transition?"

"You had three challenges in one week," Killian drawled.

I shrugged. "But they weren't really serious."

"This is a mess," he said, turning to look back the way we'd come.

"You've got two wannabes back there ready to fight for

this, and you've got *her*." Killian looked pissed off. "Will she accept it?"

"I have no idea." I rolled my head from side to side. "Ugh, I better go back. Fuck."

Killian clasped my shoulder. "It could be worse." When I looked at him, he nodded. "They could expect you to marry her."

"Shut up," I growled in warning. "You've said enough already."

We walked back to the hall. I didn't go looking for the druid. They were already waiting. Seated beneath the ancient ash near the edge of the hall, their robes were dark as crows' wings, hands folded in their lap.

I almost turned back. *Almost.* But I was done walking away from truths I didn't like. I grabbed Killian's arm to stop him from walking away.

The druid didn't rise as we approached; they just looked up, expression unreadable.

"Druid."

"Alpha Malric will soon be gone from this earth." They looked between Killian and me. It was clear from their look that they knew what I'd been hiding. "Your beta?"

"He is." I looked at the druid and knew I had to ask. "Why? Why did you approve it?"

They tilted their head slightly as they studied me, like I was a puzzle they'd already solved but still enjoyed rearranging. "Because the choice is between delay and survival, and I have no fondness for delay."

Killian stepped forward. "That's not an answer."

"No." The druid watched him. "I suppose to you, it isn't."

"He's *our* alpha," Killian snarled. "Find your own."

I almost laughed at his possessiveness, but he was so serious and so right. The druid said nothing, just turned their attention from Killian to me.

I ground my molars. "Do you expect me to play lapdog?"

The druid frowned. "I expect you to lead," they said, calm and sure. "Or at the very least, keep the danger and the ambitious from carving the Hollow into a territory war."

I bit back the taste of bile. "So this was about the land. This wasn't about Rowen."

"It will always concern the daughter born of the Hollow." They finally rose, slow and deliberate, until they stood at their full height. They were shorter, smaller, but no less dangerous.

"She cannot rule in name," they said. "The law is clear. But she can stand behind the wolf strong enough to hold the line—and who is wise enough to let her steer."

"And you think that's me?" I asked, voice low.

"I think," the druid said slowly, "you're the only one the pack won't rebel against. The only one she won't destroy."

I looked away. Just for a second. Because the truth felt too real. I *could* survive her. I'd done it already. Those two others? Wouldn't last a week.

"If you're wrong," I said, "this ends in blood."

The druid smiled at Killian and me. "It always ends in blood."

"You can't tell her," I blurted. "You can't tell her…any of them, what I am. Not yet. Say I'm a leader, fair enough, but you can't tell…them." I meant her; they knew I meant her. "She will think I forced this on him…when he's weak."

I hated the fact that she would think this, but I also knew her too well.

They dipped their head slightly and then went back into the main hall. The fact that the druid didn't defend her or speak up and say she wouldn't, said enough. I didn't follow, but I knew I needed to move. To breathe something that didn't reek of legacy and power plays.

"Want to check out the perimeter with me?" I asked Killian, even though I knew he would.

"Guess I should," he grumbled. "See what I'm working with."

He started to pull off his shirt, stopping when I shook my head. "Let's run it," I told him quietly. "Shift later."

So we ran. Boots on the ground, breath in my throat, tension bleeding out with every footfall pounding against the mountain's skin. The woods of the Hollow hadn't changed much. Still thick. Still ancient. Still whispering secrets to those who knew how to listen.

But the air was…different.

Tighter.

The trees didn't sway; they leaned in, and it almost felt…suffocating. And the wind…the wind didn't smell right.

I slowed at the old boundary line, where the pine just thinned enough to give the world breath. Where Rowen and I used to—

No. Not that memory. Not now. Possibly not ever, not with what was happening now. I knelt, my hand brushing the soil, which was still damp from yesterday's rainfall. That scent again. Wrong. Burnt pine, copper, sweat and underneath it all…rage.

Not the kind that simmers. The kind that festers. A rogue had passed through here. Recently.

Killian sensed the same. He spun slowly, his eyes searching as my jaw clenched.

"Not a Blueridge Hollow wolf. Not a neighbor. Something feral."

Killian was nodding. "The scent's all wrong," he spoke softly. "Wild and not in a fun way."

I rose slowly. Every muscle going still. If I followed the scent, I'd be gone for hours. Maybe days. But if I didn't? I looked back toward the ridge, towards the pack. Towards her.

She was already barely hanging on. I cursed under my breath as I turned to face north. I needed to follow the scent because this wasn't just about me anymore.

I doubted it had been for a long time.

"You need to go back to the pack," I told Killian. "Tell the druid I'm on a trail. Tell Lewis, and Malric if he's still able."

"Fuck off, I'm coming with you."

I shook my head. "No. I need you there, need you to deal with the fallout. You know how to do it," I added with a grin. "You must be an expert in it by now."

Killian looked over his shoulder and then back at me. "Um...me and your little ray of sunshine didn't bond so well."

I fought the urge to laugh. "All the more reason for you to go back, build a solid foundation." I pulled my shirt off. "I'll be a few days at most."

"A few days—"

I'd already shifted and was running north.

Ass move, dickhead.

Killian's beratement was sharp and sour, and I let loose my laugh as my wolf ran fast on the trail of a rogue.

———

THE FURTHER I WENT, the quieter the forest got. No birdsong. No wind. Not even the hum of insects under the bark. Just silence—and the soft crunch of my paws over pine needles as I followed the scent trail like a thread through something ancient.

It was faint, but it lingered. Whoever passed through didn't care about hiding.

That was the first bad sign. The second came when I found the deer.

Its throat was torn out—too messy for a clean kill, too precise for a wild one. The meat left to rot. The eyes pecked by crows, but the rest untouched. A kill made not for hunger…but for practice.

I crouched beside it, fingers ghosting over the edges of the wound. Deep. Jagged. Almost frenzied.

But not random.

The third sign? The claw marks in the tree trunk beside it. Deliberate. Etched too low to be territorial. They were meant to be seen.

A message. Someone was hunting on Blueridge Hollow land—and making damn sure we knew it.

I stood slowly, every part of me shifting into alpha mode. This wasn't a straggler. This wasn't a lone wolf looking for shelter or scraps.

This was a test. Something or someone was probing the pack's defenses.

That pack wasn't ready. Rowen wasn't ready. No matter how much she thought she was.

If I told her now, she'd take it as another move for control. Another move in a game she didn't want to play. But this wasn't a game anymore. This was the sound the forest made when it held its breath before the storm.

I looked north, toward where the trail twisted into thicker woods. More signs. More scent. Taunting me north. *Why?* I turned south. Back toward the Hollow itself. Because if this was a warning shot…the next one would be aimed at the pack, at *her*, and I wasn't about to let anyone else take a piece of Rowen or her pack.

Not while I was breathing. I headed south. My instincts were urging me back to the Hollow, and they'd never failed me before.

By the time I reached the pack's outer wards, the sun was starting to bleed into the trees. Gold through green. Beautiful. Peaceful.

Deceiving.

I came in through the eastern ridge, the same way I used to when I'd sneak around to meet her. Back then, it felt like freedom. Now? It felt like walking into a fire I'd already burned in once. I circled back to where I'd left my clothes and dressed hurriedly.

I saw Killian's influence immediately when I spotted the guards. They stiffened as I approached. One sniffed the air and flinched.

Good. Let them smell it. Let them *feel* it.

Blood. Fear. Rogue.

Killian was already waiting at the edge of the clearing in front of the pack hall, arms crossed and jaw tight. "You went quiet."

"Had a trail."

"Rogue?"

"Worse," I said. "Deliberate."

He didn't ask questions. Just walked beside me as I headed for the hall. "Malric is still holding on," he told me quietly, and I nodded in acknowledgment. I hadn't felt the power shift and had suspected as much, but it was good to have it confirmed.

The door opened before I touched it. Rowen stepped out. She froze when she saw me. Not in fear. In calculation. Her eyes scanned me—boots to jaw, taking in the scent of blood and the sweat still clinging to my skin.

"Where the hell have you been?" she demanded.

"Rogue sign. East ridge."

She blinked. "East ridge? That's pack territory."

"I know," I said. "We've got a breach."

Behind her, I heard voices raised—the druid and *suitors*? They were talking about bonds. About legacy and choosing mates.

While the very pack they sought to control was being sent messages in blood and claw marks.

Turning, I looked at Killian. "Why are they still here?"

"Where else are they supposed to be?" Rowen snapped, her eyes narrowing.

I met her gaze head-on. "I don't give a fuck where they go, so long as they go. *Now.*" I turned back to Killian. "The real fight is on the boundary."

"I tried to ask the druid why they're still here," he

muttered. "She"—his thumb jerked to Rowen—"said, since it's not official that you're pack leader yet, then they should stay."

I turned back to her and saw it, the spark of defiance, the flicker of something dangerous in her stare. Not fear. Not even doubt.

Rebellion.

She moved slightly, her body blocking the door to the hall as she stepped forward. "You have the scent of blood all over you."

"And you're maneuvering a pointless marriage while someone is literally sharpening their claws on your borders."

We stood there a beat too long. Breath short. The distance between us crackling with tension.

Then, from inside, the druid's voice. "Pack Leader Wolfe, if you're finished tracking ghosts, Alpha Malric would like to see you."

She tensed at the title. So did I, but I masked my reaction better, stepping past her as I headed into the hall. Tyler and Dex watched me as I walked past them to Malric's quarters, their scents heavy with confusion, frustration, and even a mix of fear. They'd heard the title too.

This wasn't about hiding who I was or my past, not anymore. This was about a war brewing in the trees. I didn't care who hated me—so long as they listened.

It was time to take control of this pack.

Chapter 12

Rowen

I SHOULD'VE BEEN INSIDE. I SHOULD'VE BEEN IN MY FATHER'S rooms, spine straight, chin high, pretending that all of this was nothing more than a…a formality.

Instead, I was still standing where he had left me. Outside. Still watching the path Wolfe had just appeared from.

He hadn't hesitated. Not once. Not when he said "rogue." Not when he said "breach." Not when the druid called him pack leader, like the title had *always* belonged to him.

I hadn't flinched either. I didn't need to flinch to feel the press of a knife at my throat.

Adair appeared at my side, quiet as always. "Those guys are waiting for you." She rubbed her cheek. "The pack is asking for you too."

Of course they were. Because that's what they did, wasn't it? Ask. Demand. Expect. What they didn't do was *listen.* I hated that I felt so bitter. I hated that I was reacting in this way. I was the alpha's daughter, and I needed to stop thinking about myself and remember who I was. Who I was to my pack.

A leader.

Someone they depended on. If they saw me falling apart, then they would panic and be uneasy. With a deep breath, I squeezed Adair's hand, turned around, and walked back inside the hall.

Dex and Tyler were hovering, but I had no energy for them right now. Yes, I had told Wolfe's beta—Killian, his name was—that the two of them were staying, but I'd been foolish. There was no need for them to stay. Seeing Wolfe walk out of the woods, the scent of him surrounding me, I felt silly for not seeing his natural leadership. It was evident in the way he walked; no wonder my dad had picked him over the others.

A quick glance around the hall told me Wolfe and his friend had already gone to my father's rooms. I hurried to catch up. I slipped inside, no one looking my way, as I made my way to my father's bedside.

That was new.

I was used to being scrutinized and watched. Wolfe didn't even pause as he spoke. He was at the map on the wall that my father had of our packlands, one hand planted on the edge as he pointed to the border.

"I caught the scent here," he said to no one and every-one. "This is your marked territory. They'd killed without feeding, claw marks on the trunks, sending a message."

Lewis looked at my father before speaking. "Could've been a stray?"

"No," Wolfe said, glancing at him and then at Dad.

"This was a trained soldier; they knew what they were doing."

Killian nodded. "The kill was deliberately vicious. The prey was not the deer it took down." His gaze swept the room, landing on me briefly, dismissing me just as quickly.

"And you followed them, alone. Why?" The druid hovered near my father, but their attention was wholly on Wolfe.

"The scent was strong. I thought I would be able to catch up to them." Wolfe shrugged. "The more I followed, the more I knew I was being led on a chase."

"You've seen this before?" my dad asked him.

Wolfe looked towards Killian before answering my father. "Yeah, we've seen this before."

The druid gave a soft, agreeable hum—just enough for my father to nod in agreement to whatever they said through the mindlink. Every alpha could communicate with their pack through a mindlink. Another gift from the Goddess.

Lewis asked a question, and I heard murmurs around me as Wolfe answered. I watched my dad as he watched them all. He looked paler, his face more drawn, with blue-tinged circles under his eyes. The voices faded as I looked him over, seeing how much he had deteriorated as they spoke of borders, territory, security, and marriage.

Wait, what?

I refocused on the conversation and saw that they were all looking at me. "What?"

The druid frowned at me. "What of your decision, Rowen?" they asked me firmly.

I blinked. "My decision?"

"Your husband?" they asked, and it was not said unkindly, though it did make my skin prickle. "Surely the danger to the pack makes it more urgent for you to choose."

I would *not* look at Wolfe.

But then I realized that I could feel his eyes on me from where he stood across the room in my peripheral vision, feel him pulling at me like a string ready to snap.

"I need time," I said.

The druid was unimpressed. "You've had time."

I met their gaze, teeth clenched. "Then you can give me more." I looked at my dad and saw the sorrow in his eyes. "Two more days."

The room was quiet. The druid cleared their throat, already preparing a lecture, I had no doubt.

But Wolfe spoke first. "If she needs two more days," he said, "she gets two days."

The room was still, utterly silent. I almost breathed a sigh of relief until I met his gaze and saw the blue mocking gaze.

"As pack leader, I will honor the request."

The statement felt like a slap, right across my face. I didn't speak. I couldn't. I looked at my dad, and he was practically *beaming* with pride as he looked at Wolfe.

The truth hit harder than anything else. Wolfe hadn't *taken* the title of pack leader. He was *using* it. Using it for *me*. I didn't know whether to be grateful or enraged. So I did what I had been doing a lot lately. I nodded once, sharp and clean, and then I walked out. Because if I didn't, I was going to say something that I couldn't take back and he knew it.

I didn't go far.

Just outside the hall, down the low steps, around the bend toward the overlook where the pines opened just wide enough to show the ridge beyond, where I waited for him.

Two days. That's what I asked for. That's what I was granted. Not because the druid listened. Because *he* spoke. And worse, because the druid nodded.

"You're welcome," came the voice behind me.

I didn't turn.

"You think I owe you now?" I asked him.

"No. I think you're used to fighting alone. And it's making you see enemies where there aren't any."

That got to me. I spun on him, fists clenched, heat in my throat. "You think you're not my enemy?"

Wolfe didn't flinch. "I didn't take anything from you, Rowen. You were never allowed to claim it."

"And you were?" I snapped. "You've been gone for years, and now you come back and they hand you this pack like it's…like it's nothing."

"It's not nothing," he said. "It's survival."

"I didn't ask for your protection."

"No," he said, stepping closer. "You asked for two days. I gave them to you. Don't confuse that with submission."

I hated how calm he sounded. How steady. Like he was a pack leader now, and not just some ghost from my past.

"You're not doing this for the pack," I said, voice low. "You're doing it for yourself."

"Your father named me his heir—trust me, I didn't see that coming either." His jaw twitched. "You think I wanted this?"

"I think you wanted me on my knees."

His eyes flashed. Just for a second. "That's not the way I remember it."

Goddess. That smirk.

That infuriating, perfect *smirk*.

"You arrogant, self-righteous—"

He stepped into my space. Not touching. But close enough that I could feel it—his wolf straining at the seams of his control.

"You want a fight, Rowen?" he said. "Fine. But fight the others. Fight the wannabe husbands. Fight the ones who would turn your strength into a political pawn." He leaned in, voice rough and quiet, his lips so close to mine I could feel the warmth of his breath. "But don't waste your rage on the only one here who actually sees you."

Silence stretched. Hot. Tight. Tearing at the edges of everything I hadn't said.

"I don't need you to see me," I whispered. "I don't want you looking at me at all."

His eyes danced with amusement and something else, something dangerous. "You need to learn to lie better, princess."

He held my gaze a second longer, then turned and walked away, leaving me breathless, furious...and more undone than I'd ever admit.

This was getting me nowhere. Ever since I'd left this pack for the damn Pack Council meeting, I hadn't been right. Not felt right in my own body. I had wanted to lead my people, control what happened, and ever since I spoke to that shaman, I hadn't felt in control.

This was not who I was.

Honestly, I didn't recognize myself right now. Who

was this person sniffling in the corner, all "woe is me." *Not* me. I was stronger than this. I closed my eyes for a moment, centering myself. I could do this. So the pack would have a new leader, a *sanctioned* leader, picked by my father himself.

A new leader for my pack.

I let out a low breath as my brain finally caught up with what I'd missed.

What the hell did I need a husband for now? Wolfe would be the pack leader, this pack would be his, and I would…what? Marry a male I had no interest in whatsoever, who wouldn't even be an advisor to the new leader?

I started to smile. *Wolfe* would be the pack leader. *I* didn't have to marry anyone. I was free.

I felt the weight leave my shoulders at the realization and tipped my head back to the sky. I could stop the pretense, I could be myself again and, hoping Luna didn't judge me, maybe even be who I wanted to be.

Wolfe had a pack. He would need to leave the other pack. Or maybe…maybe he wanted to spend time between the two? Which meant…I needed to be nicer to Wolfe. Ugh, the idea was repulsive. But if I wanted him to trust that I knew what was best for my pack, then I needed to show him that I could lead. I needed to show him that he could be away from Blueridge Hollow and it would be left in good hands.

My hands.

And my first course of action was to send my two suitors home.

I found Dex and Tyler near the practice ring, half-dressed and smug, like their *performances* meant something.

Like I hadn't already seen what they were made of—which was barely much of anything.

Tyler spotted me first. His smirk sharpened like I was already his. "Back from playing politics with your…allies?"

Dex said nothing. Just watched me. Too still. Too smart. The echo of what Wolfe had said about him still lingered in my ears, and I'd been watching him closely.

I didn't smile. I didn't bother softening the steel in my voice. "I asked for two days to decide which of you would be best suited here. Then I realized I didn't need two days."

"To decide?" Tyler asked, circling me, measuring me up. "Or to pretend like it's not already decided?"

"I don't pretend," I said, turning to face him full-on. "And you should stop assuming."

He stepped closer. Just a hair. "You forget who I am, Rowen?"

"No," I said coolly. "I remember exactly who you are. That's the problem."

He blinked.

Dex chuckled softly. "Damn."

"Still interested in leading my pack?" I asked Dex.

His gaze met mine. Steady. Unflinching. "Interested in serving it. The leading part comes later."

Better answer. Still not enough. Neither of them was right for this pack. I knew it before and I was certain of it now. Now that I knew there was no desperate need to fulfill a place that could never be filled.

I took a step back and folded my arms. "You both think this is about strength. About bloodlines. About conquest. But it's not."

"It's about legacy," Tyler snapped.

"No," I said. "It's about *my* people. *My* land. My father's bones and my mother's silence and every wolf in this Hollow who deserves to know their next leader sees them as more than leverage."

Tyler scoffed. "Sounds like you've already made your choice."

"I have."

Then I looked at Dex. "I don't need a husband beside me to know what's best for my pack. I choose neither of you." I saw the surprise in his eyes and the flash of fury before he quickly masked it.

I left them there. Let them chew on it. Let them second-guess everything they thought they knew about the shifters of the Hollow. We deserved their respect as a pack.

I wasn't picking a husband. Not like this. Not now. I was choosing *myself*. I was reminded to be the wolf I had always been. The one who wouldn't break when I stood at the front of the line and refused to kneel. The fact it was Wolfe who reminded me of that was not important. I was sure I'd have gotten there eventually. Best not to dwell on it.

Now I just had to make sure my dad and the druid accepted it. I doubted Wolfe would care one way or the other. I didn't examine the bitter taste in my mouth at that realization.

I entered my father's chambers quietly, grateful to see him still awake. The candles were dimmed, the fire low, and the druid was gone. For once, it was just him and me.

He was lying on his side, facing the window, looking smaller than I ever remembered. "Rowen," he greeted me. "It's been quite the day," he rasped, without turning.

I moved to the chair beside the bed and sat, not

answering right away. Just watching the slow rise and fall of his chest. Listening to the crackle of the hearth. Letting the weight of the day settle between us.

"I couldn't stomach it," I said finally. "Pretending like I had a say in marriage when we all know I don't."

He smiled faintly. "That's never stopped you before."

"No," I murmured. "But I thought maybe it wouldn't matter this time if I chose myself. Chose myself over a suitor."

He turned his head, eyes finding mine. *Goddess, he looked tired.*

"It does matter," he said. "It matters more than our pack will ever admit. They think control is strength. But you… you make them feel seen, Rowen. That's why they follow you."

I didn't want to cry. I'd done enough of that lately. But hearing him say it—like he still believed I was *meant* to lead, even when everything around us said I couldn't—cracked something open in my chest.

"I'm tired of fighting ghosts," I whispered. "Tradition. Expectations. Males who think they're owed me."

His hand, veined and cool, reached for mine. "Then stop fighting them. Start *leading* anyway."

"Why, Dad? I can't be alpha. I can't even be pack leader."

"No," he said, voice rough. "But you can be the heart of this Hollow. You already are." Silence stretched, soft this time. The kind that didn't need to be filled. After a moment, he added, "Wolfe will be a good leader for this pack."

"Probably," I agreed quietly.

"Does that scare you?"

"Yes," I admitted. "Because he sees me. And if I fall apart or mess up, he'll see that too."

Malric gave a soft, low laugh that caught in his chest. "Then don't fall apart yet. Not until you've finished terrifying those suitors and reminding your pack why they will follow you."

I smiled, even though my throat hurt. "I'll try." I plucked at a thread on my dark combat pants. "I told Dex and Tyler I wasn't picking either of them."

He squeezed my hand once, then let go. "That's my girl."

I watched him as he lay there. "You knew I was never picking them?" I asked quietly, disbelief in my voice.

Dad snorted. "I'd have disowned you if you had."

"The druid?"

My dad squinted as he thought about it. "Think you might need to ask them to forgive you. They'll get over it though."

I should have felt relief. I didn't. I felt irrationally angry. "What was the *point* of this charade if you didn't want me to go through with this?"

Dad closed his eyes as he spoke. "To remind your pack what lengths you would go to, to protect it."

It was a diabolical plan. Or was it brilliant? I wasn't sure.

"Let me get this right," I said slowly. "All this was a *ruse* to show the pack that I would *sacrifice* myself, my happiness, for them if I needed to?"

Dad opened one eye to look at me. "Demonstrating your commitment to your people is a full-time job. Never forget it."

"I wore a dress," I blurted, still pissed off with what I was beginning to understand.

Dad smiled as he closed his eyes again. "Even after all these years, you even surprised me with that level of commitment."

I sat back in the chair, staring at him in shock. Maybe fury. *Definitely* mixed emotions.

"That's the most monstrous thing you've ever done to me."

He choked out a laugh. "Just wait for my next trick," he murmured with glee.

I leaned forward in my seat, anxiety stirring in my belly. "Dad? What are you planning?"

Chapter 13

Wolfe

"Tell me you didn't see that coming," Killian said beside me as we left the overlook.

"I saw it."

"You looked like you wanted to drag her off by her hair."

I didn't answer because I had wanted to.

Rowen, standing in the middle of the training field and dismissing two potential husbands as if they were nothing, really pissed me off—that it took her so long to do it. Even though they had been handpicked by the Pack Council, maybe her father, and every law this region still clings to… and she'd told them all to fuck off.

She looked every bit the leader they said she couldn't be.

I hated that I felt *proud* when she did it. I hated how much I wanted to rip that control out of her hands and make her submit.

To *me*.

"She's doing it her way," Killian muttered, watching me from the corner of his eye. "You going to let that slide?"

"I'm not the alpha of this pack yet," I said flatly. "She's not mine to rein in."

But even I didn't believe that.

Not really.

Because she *had* been mine. Still was. Only different circumstances now. But that didn't stop the way her scent hit the back of my throat when she passed. The way her voice cut through a room like she was born to be followed. The way her wolf still reacted to mine, even now.

But none of that mattered.

Because she didn't trust me, and I sure as shit didn't trust her.

I wasn't the boy I'd been when I left the Hollow. Back then, I'd bled for a different kind of power. Now, I bled for my pack, not bloodlines. If she thought I came back to play politics or stand in the shadows while she decided who got to keep this pack? She didn't know me at all.

"She's testing you," Killian said. "Waiting to see if you bite."

"I don't bite," I said. "I take."

I looked toward the Hollow again, toward the heart of the land that was calling her name.

Not mine. Not yet. I needed to claim this land if I was going to lead it. I did not doubt that Rowen would be trying to lead it too. But if she thought I'd stay out of her way? She didn't know me as well as she thought.

"They haven't left," Killian murmured. "And I'm bored."

I shared a grin with him. "Then let's move these fuckers out of here."

Killian rolled his head on his shoulders. "I was *so* hoping you'd say that, Wolfe." He rolled his shoulders back, loosening up.

"We remind them of where they are, scare them, don't scar them, Kill," I murmured as we walked back to the pack hall. I saw his pout. "I didn't say don't make them bleed if they push it."

He gave me a wicked grin. "Today is going to be a beautiful day after all."

The two potentials were still at the training area, neither training, leaning too casually against the far post, talking to two Hollow males as if they belonged there. Both looked a mix of annoyed and sulky. They resembled pups who had been told they couldn't have any more ice cream. It made me want to punch them harder, but I knew I couldn't be splitting my knuckles on anyone's face today. I glanced at Killian, grinning to myself because I knew I couldn't say the same for him.

The pack's training ground was smaller than I remembered. Over the years, whenever I thought about it, I always imagined it to be bigger. More ferocious. The sense of violence and *strength*, but now standing here, it was just a small patch of grass with a makeshift fighting ring marked out on the land and, from the looks of it, barely used.

I looked around, wondering if it had changed or if I had. I knew I had, but either my memory was playing tricks on me or I had romanticized it into something it wasn't. I'd done a lot of that when I was younger, before I knew it was better to look forward instead of back. Before I had a pack of shifters who relied on me, who needed me to lead and protect them.

I didn't need to introduce myself as we got closer. Both

of the males looked up and moved closer together. Was it defiance? Or self-defense? I suspected the latter.

I was already the trouble they sensed was coming.

Voices hushed. Heads turned. One of the pack elders slowly rose from his chair, as if instinctively about to bow before his mind caught up.

Killian walked beside me, quiet but steady.

I didn't slow down as I crossed the grass. I stopped just before the fighting ring and pulled one of the chairs over— Malric's chair. The one always reserved for the alpha.

I sat in it.

Conversations came to a complete stop. The move wasn't subtle, nor was it meant to be.

"You think this is smart?" Killian asked under his breath.

"No," I said. "It's necessary."

Tyler pushed away from the post, eyes narrowing. "You lost, Stonefang?"

I looked at him. Let the silence hang. "Wrong question," I said. "Try again."

Dex didn't say anything, but he looked at me differently now. Not like a rival. More like a wolf deciding whether to run or not.

A few of the pack glanced toward the pack hall, expecting someone, probably Rowen, to storm out—to stop me. She didn't. Because even if she was watching, deep down, she knew. This wasn't about disrespect; it was about order.

"This pack is vulnerable," I said to those gathered around, voice steady and calm. "Your alpha is ready to join the Goddess. Your borders are compromised. The Pack

Council is more focused on wedding proposals than preparing for war."

I let that hang.

Tyler shifted. "You think sitting in a chair makes you a leader?"

"I think anyone who lets this place fall apart while they measure their dicks for a dowry doesn't deserve to be here."

Tyler's growl started in his throat, but I was already on my feet, the chair tipping back slightly. Power surged through every limb.

I stepped toward him.

"You want to lead in Blueridge Hollow?" I asked. "Then *take* it."

It was so quiet, I was certain everyone was holding their breath.

Tyler's jaw clenched. His eyes darted to Killian, then back to me. He didn't move or even flinch.

That's all I needed to see. "I didn't think so." I turned my head slightly to look at Dex. "You?"

The male shifter looked me over, a sneer curling his top lip. "You want to bully me, *Wolfe?*"

I smiled, showing all my teeth, with no humor. "Bully you?" I kept my gaze fixed on him. "I'm asking if you want to challenge for the position of pack leader. That's why you're here, isn't it?"

"I came for Rowen."

The fuck you did.

I didn't say that to him, though; instead, I laughed out loud—harshly and full of contempt. Killian was like stone beside me, but I knew he was ready for anything.

I moved around them slowly and carefully. Circling

them, watching their spines stiffen as I looked them over. Assessed them.

"You may have come for the daughter of the alpha," I said clearly, making sure the whole pack heard. "But neither of you is leaving with her." I moved back in front of them. Tyler kept his gaze lowered with his back straight, but the scent of fear made my nose twitch. Dex held my gaze, but he couldn't hide the scent of apprehension.

Weak. Both of them. Neither deserved her—or even the time she'd already given them.

"She rejected you both," I said, feeling Killian take a step back. "So tell me…" I moved closer, just slightly. "Why the fuck are you still here?"

Dex's eyes flicked to Killian before settling back on me. "I want to speak to the alpha before I leave."

"Denied." I saw his shock before I spoke again. "Alpha Malric knows his daughter's decision and supports it. There's nothing for you here." I flicked my fingers in a shooing gesture as I looked at them. A gesture of mockery, and they knew it. "Both of you, fuck off back to where you came from."

Tyler's head jerked up, his arrogance getting the better of him. "You have no right to talk to us like that! I am an *alpha's* son!"

"And *I* will be the one leading this pack. Get the fuck out of this territory. Now. I won't ask so nicely again."

Dex snorted dismissively. "This is your idea of *asking*?"

Killian stepped forward. He didn't need to posture or pose. He simply moved, and both of the pricks moved back simultaneously. "You want to see what happens when he *isn't* asking?"

I don't know which one I want to punch first, he grumbled through the mindlink.

I knew exactly what he meant. *I want to pick that snot-nosed fucker up and use him to hit the other one.*

Killian couldn't hide his huff of amusement, and both of the idiots took another step back, mistaking his amusement for intent.

"Fuck me," I snarled in disgust. "Look at you both cowering together. Neither of you ever deserved to breathe the same air as her," I sneered. "Neither of you are fit to lead a pack. Especially not this one. Get out of my sight, and make sure you are *both* gone before dusk."

Movement to the left caught my eye, and I turned my head to see Rowen watching, her hands curled into fists at her side, but she was quiet. Watching and internally raging against the way I was handling it, no doubt, but she was keeping quiet.

I winked at her and saw a flash of anger in her eyes. Yeah, she was pissed. Good. I was tired of watching her second-guess herself.

With a final glance at the pack that watched silently, I walked away from the training ground.

Killian followed, grinning like the bastard he was. "So subtle," he murmured with amusement.

I didn't smile. This wasn't about subtlety; it was about sending a message. The game had changed. And anyone still playing by old rules? They were already too late.

"It's time to lead this pack," I murmured to him. "And that takes us to our next stop."

The druid's quarters were tucked at the edge of the pack's inner circle, half-hidden beneath an outcrop of moss-covered stone and old bone charms. The kind of place that felt more sacred than it had any right to. Their quarters adhered to the old ways—a tent made of hide and canvas that could be dismantled and moved anywhere. Nothing permanent on the land, because *we* weren't permanent on the land.

Killian paused at the entrance. "You sure?"

"I don't need to knock." I pushed the hide flap aside and stepped into the shadows.

The scent of sage and iron filled the space. A low fire burned in the hearth, casting flickering light across the tent walls. Shelves lined with jars, roots, and dried herbs. It smelled like a memory that was always out of reach. Like something older than law.

The druid was already waiting. Of course. They stood by the fire, robes loose, eyes dark with knowledge they didn't share. "You made quite a scene."

"A scene?" I didn't blink. "I made a statement."

"A hostile one."

"No. A protective one."

They turned to face me fully. "You sat in Malric's chair."

"And no one stopped me."

Silence. Then they spoke. "You're not being sympathetic, Wolfe."

"I'm not trying to be." I moved closer. "This pack is in flux. You know it. I know it. The rogues roaming this territory know it. You're losing control."

The druid didn't flinch. "Control is an illusion. Stability is not."

"And you really believe that marrying Rowen to some half-trained show dog brings stability?"

Their jaw clenched. "The old ways demand structure. An alpha. A bonded pair, if possible. That is how it's always been."

"And look where that's gotten you."

They looked at me sharply. "You question Luna's wisdom?"

"I question your interpretation of it." I leaned in, voice low. "You've tried to twist tradition into a bond. And you know me, druid, I'm not a wolf that wears a collar."

They took a step back, just a breath. Just enough to acknowledge they felt the pressure of my presence.

"You want to rule here?" they asked me, eyes narrowing on my face. "You do," they said with something that was almost surprise.

I laughed quietly and darkly. "I already do. You're just too proud to admit it."

Another pause. The fire crackled.

The druid looked between us, their expression deliberately blank. "You're dangerous, Wolfe."

"No, I'm really not," I said. "But I *am* necessary."

The druid studied me, and I allowed them to. Let them see me—the raw certainty in my stance, the weight of my dominance pressing against the air like a coming tempest.

Finally, they spoke. Quiet. Controlled. "The pack won't follow you if you destroy everything that came before."

I stepped to the doorway, hand resting on the frame. "Then maybe it's time for all of the pack to decide what traditions are worth keeping," I said. "And what needs to burn."

I left with Killian following me out.

"Not one I'd make an enemy of," he murmured as we

walked, casting a glance back to make sure we were far enough away not to be overheard.

"The druid is not my enemy," I told him. "But I refuse to let them be an obstacle."

"How does this work?" Killian asked as he looked around at a scattered pack. "You lead both packs, I get it, but how?" He shook his head. "The packs are too far apart for this to be easy."

I knew that. "No one said it was going to be easy." I kept my eyes on Rowen's chestnut brown hair as she talked to her father's beta, Lewis. She looked determined, and that could only mean trouble. For *me*. "Speaking of things not being easy," I muttered when I saw her glance across the grass and see me.

"Too late to duck?" Killian mumbled.

"Way too late."

Rowen cut off from Lewis mid-sentence. She didn't rush —no, that wasn't her way. She walked directly toward me as if the ground had already submitted beneath her boots.

Killian eased back a step, smart enough to recognize a battlefield when he saw one. I held my ground, arms crossed, spine straight.

She stopped a few feet away. Her mouth was tight. Her eyes sharper than any blade I'd ever dodged.

"You enjoyed that, didn't you?" she said.

"You'll have to be more specific."

She scoffed. "Taking the chair. Lording over them like you've already claimed Blueridge Hollow."

I pretended to frown. "Did I look uncertain?"

She stepped closer. "No," she spat. "You looked *smug*."

"Smug?" I looked her over. Her dark green combat pants, black laced-up boots, and a cropped black T-shirt that clung to her chest. She looked prepared to fight. "If I looked *smug*, maybe it's because no one stopped me."

Her breath caught for a split second—just long enough for me to see it. That flicker. That wild part of her wolf that didn't know whether to challenge me or run.

That's right. Let her feel it too.

"This is not a game," she hissed, voice low.

"No, it's not," I agreed. "But if it were, I play to win." My gaze drifted over her body more slowly. "You know that better than anyone."

That got her—just a flash of teeth. No smile, just a warning. Reminding me that she could bite. "I'm not some conquest."

"I never said you were."

"Then stop acting like you've already claimed me." Furious deep green eyes, the color of moss, glared at me.

I leaned in. Close enough for her scent to hit like a sucker punch to the ribs.

"I'm not here to *claim* you, Rowen," I said, voice rough. "You rejected all your prospects," I added, hearing her sharp intake of breath at the reminder I had once been one of them. "Your father passed this pack to me, and I will look after it as he asked me to." I leaned back. "You're only interested in the pack. Right?"

She didn't move. Didn't blink. But her pulse kicked hard in her throat, and fuck me if it didn't do something to mine. She stepped back first. Not far. Just enough to reclaim space.

But I'd felt the shift, and I knew she did too.

Rowen looked between us, her temper flaring.

"You forget yourself," she whispered furiously. "Our alpha is dying. This pack is getting ready to grieve. They don't need you rubbing it in their faces." She took a deep breath, fighting back the tears that threatened to spill as she spoke of her father's failing health, and I felt a stab of guilt. "Show compassion, Wolfe," she said softly. "If not for me, for the pack you'll lead very soon."

She didn't say anything else as she turned and walked away, and I didn't try to stop her.

No need to. That pulse at her throat? The flicker in her eyes when I moved closer? I'd gotten under her skin—and she hated it.

Fine. Let her hate me. That was simpler. Easier. Love made wolves stupid. Rage made them honest.

Killian let out a slow breath beside me. "You're really leaning into the villain arc, huh?"

"They don't need a hero right now, neither does she."

"Yeah? What does she need?"

"She needs someone willing to make the hard call. Someone who doesn't flinch when blood spills."

"She's not flinching either," he said, nodding toward where she'd gone.

"No," I agreed. "That's why it's going to get worse before it gets better."

Because I hadn't come here to oversee a transfer of power. I hadn't come here to play politics with men who didn't deserve to lead a den of rats, let alone a pack. I was here because something was coming. I'd seen it in the shadows at the edge of our territories. I'd smelled it in the broken bones of prey that rogues sent as a warning.

And I knew—knew—that when it hit, this pack needed more than tradition. It needed someone who didn't give a damn about playing nice.

Rowen thought she was still fighting me. She hadn't realized we were already fighting on the same side.

Just not for the same future.

Chapter 14

Rowen

I wasn't avoiding him.

I told myself that again as I shut the door to my rooms with a little more force than necessary. The wood creaked in protest but didn't splinter. Shame. I needed something to break besides my own composure. Wolfe was playing a game I hadn't agreed to—and somehow, I was already losing.

He hadn't challenged my father. He hadn't demanded the title. Hadn't even thrown a single punch or issued a single command in open forum.

And yet…he was everywhere.

He'd walked into Blueridge Hollow and taken up space like he'd never left. Spoken to my father like a son returning from exile. Paced our borders like they were already his.

And the worst part? No one stopped him. Not the suitors. Not the pack. Not even the druid.

Not me either.

They were watching him the same way they'd once watched my dad—like he might just have the answers. Like maybe, finally, someone strong enough had come to carry the weight of this place.

I should've been angry.

I *was* angry.

But underneath that? I was scared. Not of Wolfe. Not exactly. But what it meant if the Hollow started bending for him. Of what it meant if they already had.

I dropped into the chair near my window and stared out at the pine-slicked slope beyond the ridge. Mist moved low across the ground like a second skin, clinging to every root and stone.

This land was mine. *Mine.* I was born to it. I'd bled for it. Sacrificed more than Wolfe could understand, just to be seen, let alone respected. And now he strolls in with his big dick energy and wry smile, and suddenly everyone's forgotten that I've been holding this pack together by the bones of my back?

I wanted to scream.

Instead, I closed my eyes and whispered to the silence: "What is your angle, Wolfe?"

Because there was one, there always was. The question wasn't whether he was playing the game. The question was how many pieces he'd already moved without anyone noticing. And whether I had the guts to flip the board while he crowned himself leader.

I couldn't ignore the pang of guilt; my father had made him heir, and all Wolfe had done was accept it.

After my "talk" to myself this morning, I went and did the same thing again. I had hidden and wallowed, which was stupid. Wolfe didn't expect me to hide; in fairness, Wolfe didn't expect *anything* of me except to be the reminder of why he left this pack in the first place.

When I thought about it, was there any wonder he was hostile? He *had* loved me when we were younger, no matter how much I tried to deny it, and I told him I chose my pack over him. I had hurt him. I knew it then, as much as I knew it now.

The irony that he had ended up coming back and would be the one to *inherit* this pack was not lost on me. Karma really was a malicious bitch. I could have saved myself years of fighting against a system if I had listened to my heart instead of my head ten years ago.

But then I'd have been his wife, and while I had loved him then, I think we'd both changed too much to be nostalgic about the past. He was most definitely not the male that I knew. He was harder, more ruthless, still saying *fuck you* to anyone and everyone, but now he had the power behind it.

Not just the temper.

With a sigh, I brushed my hair, braided it, and decided to go visit with my dad; he still hadn't told me the plan he was scheming, and the unknown was still making me wary. I toyed with my hairbrush. Maybe a run first. I could spend longer with Dad if I let my wolf out first.

I grinned as I ran my fingers through my hair, loosening it, then shed my clothes and slipped out the window. I was in my wolf form before my paws hit the ground. I ran free over the Hollow and headed to my favorite bluff on the ridge. The wind in my fur, the soil of my packlands beneath my claws, the scent of freedom on the air.

It was the perfect run. I felt more like myself than I had in weeks.

I should've known something was coming.

On my return, my wolf padded contentedly over the ground that I knew better than anyone else. However, there was an underlying current of unease as I returned to my packlands. The air was too still, the conversations too quiet, and the pack was sparse.

When Adair found me, I was in the northern clearing, pacing the line where the training fields met the old woods, an unknown scent tickling my nose.

"They're asking for you."

I shifted back into human form. "Who?" I didn't stop scenting the air. "Is it important?"

"It's not who you think," she said carefully. "It's your father."

That was different.

Ten minutes later, I was dressed and back in my father's room. Lewis and the druid were already there, and—of course—Wolfe and his shadow, Killian.

I didn't look at the druid as I entered. I could feel their gaze like a noose around my neck. Dad was sitting up, his face pale but sharper than it had been in days. That alone set every alarm bell ringing.

"You called for me?"

He gestured for me to come closer. "Sit, daughter."

The air felt *full*. Tense. "I'd rather stand."

"Fine." His sigh was old and heavy. "Then listen." He cast a shrewd look at me. "With an *open* mind."

My whole body felt coiled too tightly. I chanced a look at Wolfe and saw he looked as closed off as I felt. What the hell was going on this time?

The druid moved first, stepping into the space between us like the harbinger they always pretended not to be.

"There's a proposition Alpha Malric wants you both to consider," they said. "To secure the pack. To quiet the Pack Council. To preserve the Hollow's legacy."

I knew what was coming before they said it. Hell, I *felt* it in my bones.

"A marriage bond," the druid said. "Between you and Wolfe."

No one spoke. Not even the shadows. Wolfe didn't move. He didn't speak. He didn't *need* to.

My heart thudded once. Then again. Louder this time. Rage crawled up my spine. "Is this a joke?"

"It's a solution," the druid replied evenly. "A way to ensure power stays in the Hollow. With *two* proven leaders. With Luna's blessing."

I looked at my father in a mixture of surprise and horror. "*This* is your *trick*?"

He didn't meet my eyes. "I think it's a very good idea." He didn't look up. "You said it yourself: all anyone is interested in, outside of this pack, is your womb, for the alpha you *could* birth."

I blinked back the sudden sting of tears as my father laid my personal issues out for everyone to hear.

"If you marry Wolfe," my father continued, "it removes you from scrutiny. You will be protected by a strong leader through marriage. Your pack, *our* pack, will be that step closer to being what we all want it to be. Secure."

Wolfe still hadn't said a word. He was standing with his

arms crossed, gaze sharp, jaw tight—watching me like I was a storm cloud with teeth.

"Nothing is official," the druid added. "It's simply an option that Alpha Malric would like you to consider."

"No," I said. "It's not an *option*, it's insanity."

Wolfe's mouth twitched. Just slightly.

I turned on him. "You could speak up any time."

He raised a brow. "You're doing plenty of speaking for both of us."

"Then say it. *Say* this isn't what you want." I could hear the plea in my voice, and I didn't care.

He watched me and then finally shrugged. "What I want doesn't matter."

"Liar."

He held my gaze. "I want peace. Stability. Safety for the pack. If this gives them that—"

"You think *us* married gives them *stability*? You and I, as husband and wife, is the last thing that this pack needs!" My eyes narrowed on his. "Or is this just another of your power plays?"

"I don't need to make a *power* play," he said sharply. "I *am* going to be the leader of this pack. I already have all the power here, and this pack will be mine." He didn't even have the grace to look at my dad, who lay there silently. "I think," he said carefully, with a nod to my father, "that this pack needs *unity*. And if you weren't so busy sharpening your pride into a weapon, you'd see it too." He looked at Killian, whose features were carefully blank, but he winced when his companion looked his way. "This is the first time I'm hearing this too," Wolfe added with a sigh. He gave my dad a rueful glance. "Not sure I agree with the method, but desperate times, I guess…"

"So…what you're saying, what you expect *me* to believe, is that you have no part in this lunacy?" I asked, the venom in my voice clear for everyone to hear.

"As much as it must disappoint you, princess, the idea of being your husband soured for me a long time ago." He gave me a vicious grin. "I'd rather stick my dick into a nest of vipers than sleep next to you."

Someone coughed to cover a laugh, and I had a sneaky suspicion it was one of *my* pack. *Not* Killian, but *Lewis*. I glared at them both anyway. When I looked back at Wolfe, he was looking at me, and he was *entertained*.

The bastard was laughing at me.

I wanted to hit him. Really hard. Hit all of them. I wanted to *burn it all down*. I wanted to scream at them all, mostly my dad, for this crazy idea, but I couldn't be the only one in the room losing it. It would only prove to them that I was an emotional female, and I had fought that stereotype all my life.

"It won't work," I told them flatly.

"Not with that attitude," Killian mumbled, and I envisioned my claws in his throat.

I suppressed my sigh. "It won't work because I can't *fake* this. I can't…" I struggled to speak. "I can't fake a relationship." I refused to look at any of them. "Especially with *him*."

Wolfe laughed. He *laughed*. "Who the fuck cares? No one *cares* if you're happy, princess. You were ready to marry one of those other idiots. The only difference in marrying me is that I'm not an idiot, and you already know me." His smile was sin as he looked me over. "And you know me *very* well."

"He's right," Dad said softly. "This marriage, if you both agree, protects you from those who only want you for what you can give them. Wolfe doesn't need you for anything." The harsh reality was bitter to swallow as my father continued. "If he agrees to this, he does you a favor, and he grants me peace as I leave this earth."

"Peace?" I asked, tears threatening to spill.

My dad reached for me, and I took his hand. "How could I leave you alone, knowing no one was there to protect you, daughter?"

I couldn't speak, my head bowed, a tear brushing over. "That's a really shit guilt trip there, Dad," I mumbled. "Emotional blackmail will win you no favors."

I heard his raspy chuckle, and I took a moment to compose myself. When I lifted my head, I met Wolfe's stare. He was completely closed off. Unemotional. Stoic. Ready to do whatever he needed to secure his pack.

Like a true leader. Fuck.

The urge to hit him was still strong. Instead, I said, "I'll consider it." I turned and walked out before any of them could see how hard it was to breathe.

I found Adair near the fire pit at the edge of the training grounds. She was sitting on the edge of one of the stone benches, legs folded, gaze on the embers like they were whispering secrets only she could hear.

She didn't look up when I dropped beside her. "Let me guess," she said. "You're not here for warmth."

"No," I muttered. "I'm here to stop myself from clawing someone's face off."

She hummed. "So, the usual."

I exhaled as I stared into the fire. "They want me to marry him."

Adair didn't flinch. Didn't gasp. Just stirred the fire with a stick, sending a small burst of sparks into the night. "I figured."

I looked at her. "You *figured?*"

"You think I didn't see the way the druid was circling? The way your father's eyes light up when Wolfe walks into the room?"

I dragged a hand down my face. "It's not a solution. It's a trap."

"Maybe," she said softly. "But it's a trap with an easy escape hatch. You know Wolfe, you used to *like* him a lot more than you seem to remember."

I barked a laugh. "You think this is funny?"

"No," she said, finally turning to face me. "I think it's tragic. Because you've wanted to lead this pack your whole damn life—and now that the path is *actually* in front of you, you're too busy snarling at the wolf beside you to see it, no pun intended."

I tensed. "He's not beside me. He's ahead." I had a moment of clarity. "I think he always was."

Adair shook her head. "Not always. Not when you were younger. Not when he left."

I said nothing.

She pressed on. "Rowen…what do you want? Not the pack. Not the politics. You."

"I want my father's pack to continue."

"That's not what I asked."

My throat tightened. "I want to choose."

"Then choose," she said. "But don't confuse freedom with fear."

I stared into the fire again. Let the silence stretch. Then I whispered, "What if choosing him means losing myself?" I took a deep breath. "It's what I was fighting against with the other two, and now…how is this *different*? If anything, it's *worse*. I know him. He's…he's, ugh, it's *him*. He hates me for what I did to him."

Adair's voice was quiet. Steady. "Then you don't choose *him*. You choose Blueridge Hollow. You choose your pack, just like you were prepared to do. If he's worth anything at all…he'll choose them too."

I looked at her in surprise. "You think he'll say no?"

Adair smiled, her eyes dancing with mischief. "He has *options*," she reminded me. "He's potentially got someone at his pack."

I lost some of my anger. She was right. He could already be involved with someone, he could bring them here, and then they could be the pack leader's wife, which would be even worse than me being the pack leader's wife.

My head dropped into my hands. Somehow, my father's *trick* was far more complicated than the prospect of marrying Tyler or Dex could ever be.

I had no idea what I was going to do, and worse, I had no idea what Wolfe would do. I could see the benefits for me, but how did Wolfe benefit?

Adair let the silence stretch, only the fire crackling between us. Finally, her soft voice penetrated the night's air, "That's the part you're not used to, isn't it?"

I lifted my head, brow furrowed. "What?"

"Not knowing what someone else wants." She shrugged,

like it was obvious. "You're used to controlling the pieces. Steering the ship. Making sure everything and everyone lines up so you can carry the whole damn pack on your back without dropping a single one."

I frowned. "That's what being a leader is."

"No," she said gently. "That's what being alone is."

I stared at her. At the flames. At the flicker of ash spiraling into the night sky.

"What if he says yes," I whispered, "but he means no?"

Adair reached over and rested her fingers on my wrist. "Then you'll know. You're not blind, Rowen. And Wolfe isn't a coward. If he agrees to this...it won't be with his teeth gritted and his heart elsewhere."

I wanted to believe her.

I wanted to believe *anything* right now, other than the gnawing fear that I was one move away from losing everything I'd fought for.

Because maybe Wolfe didn't need this marriage.

But *I* did.

Not for power. Not for status. But because this might be the only way I could stay in the Hollow and protect it on *my* terms. And if he was willing to give up a pack to help me do that? Goddess help me. I didn't know if I could hate him for it...or be grateful. Either way, I'd owe him.

And I didn't like owing anyone.

Especially not him.

Chapter 15

Wolfe

The woods were quieter here.

Less feral than Stonefang's territory, but not soft. Blueridge Hollow had always worn its strength differently—coiled, patient, hidden beneath moss and silence.

Like her.

Killian had stayed behind. Too many words in the air between us. Too many opinions I didn't want to hear. I needed quiet. I needed to think. I crouched near the old creek bed, watching water slip over rock, faster in the dark than it ever looked in daylight.

What the hell was happening here? I came here to talk about alliances for my pack. *My* Stonefang Pack. Along the way, I'd gotten involved with the stupid situation of Rowen's marriage prospects, and now…I wasn't a *prospect*, no, I was the fucking solution?

Rowen had been fighting battles all her life. Most of the time, no one else recognized them, but still, she fought. She fought so damn hard for this pack, and they worshipped her for it.

And me? I was about to become her next fight, but the pack…I don't think they'd appreciate her fighting *me* when they learned what I was. Their alpha.

Shit.

I tipped my head back and looked up at the darkening sky. "Is this what you wanted, Luna?" I asked quietly. "Something's at play here, and even I can't put all of the blame at the druid's feet," I grumbled. "What are you brewing, Goddess?"

They wanted a marriage, which was essentially just another term for a political alliance.

A wedded bond.

I knew what it meant. Knew what it could cost me. The Goddess didn't always give a second chance. If I married Rowen, and Luna had someone else in mind for me? An actual *fated mate*, what happened then?

Was it just too bad?

You didn't double-dip with fate. I rubbed my forehead. I should've said no outright. Should've stood in that room with her father and the druid and all their smug little hopes and shut it down cold. I could have a destined mate out there, a mate who *wanted* me. I should have said no to their insane idea.

But I hadn't.

Because somewhere deep in my bones, I'd known this was coming the second I scented her again. Rowen wasn't a pawn to be offered; she was the damn chessboard. If I truly wanted to protect this pack, I needed to take the seat at the table that couldn't be taken away. Not by the Pack Council. Not by the druid. Not even by her. I needed to be their alpha and let them accept me as that. But Rowen…she would never accept me as pack leader or alpha. She would always resent the fact I'd lied about what I was.

I inhaled, slow and deep, letting the air burn down to the bottom of my lungs. Well, as she had learned over the last few months, one shifter did not make a pack, unless they were the alpha.

This was out of her hands now. Luna and Malric had come up with a plan, and it was one I needed to take control of.

This was about control. It always had been.

Control was the spine of every pack, the silent law that kept blood from spilling on the wrong side of the border. You didn't become an alpha without knowing what it meant to carry that weight. Not just the decisions, not just the consequences—the pack themselves.

Their fears. Their hungers. Their trust.

Without control, a pack fractured. With it, they thrived. They obeyed. They survived. And Rowen? She was every-thing a pack feared in a leader. Female. Fierce. Unbound. The druid saw it. So probably did the Pack Council, and I realized today, so did her father. Even if he wanted it to be different for her, the fact was, it just wasn't.

She wasn't unstable—she was *unclaimed*. And in the eyes of tradition, that made her dangerous.

Blueridge Hollow was teetering. Between the pressures from the Pack Council and the hovering rogues and every old law whispering that a woman couldn't lead—this place needed a name that meant power.

Mine did. *Wolfe*. Alpha of the Stonefang Pack. Soon to be Alpha of Blueridge Hollow.

An alpha that they *knew*. A leader they would openly

recognize…and if I was being honest, recognize with a sigh of relief. If tying myself to Rowen was what it took to keep this pack from bleeding out? Why would I not do it?

A marriage bond wasn't romance. It was a strategy. Strategy, I knew. Strategy, I could do. With teeth bared, head high, and not a single heartbeat of hesitation. Because control wasn't just what I wielded. It was what I was—as an alpha.

"Hey."

I looked up and saw her hovering near the edge of the brush she'd just come through.

"You always were quiet on your feet," I murmured as I straightened. Her hair was loose around her shoulders, falling down past her breasts. A simple black tank top, black pants, and her boots. She looked ready for whatever life threw at her. I wondered when she stopped recognizing that.

Rowen didn't look me in the eyes as she said, "I'm sorry."

I hadn't expected that. "Why?" I asked her, knowing I sounded as suspicious as I was.

Rowen smiled as she looked away, pushing her hair over her shoulder. "Because they suggested a marriage to a woman you don't want, and despite that, I know you're out here considering it." She took a deep breath. "Do you…" She cleared her throat. "Do you have someone at home?"

"I have a whole pack of someones."

Rowen gave me a flat stare. "You know what I mean. Don't be a dick." I widened my eyes and feigned shock, and I saw her fight the smile. "Do you have a…female at your other pack?"

"We have a healthy mix of male and female," I told her with a straight face.

"Oh, for fuck's sake, Wolfe, do you have a partner? A lover?" She saw me about to speak. "I mean, a woman you are in a relationship with!"

I considered playing with her some more, but the look in her eye made me think she might throttle me, and I wasn't in the mood to play fight with her. "No."

Rowen swallowed, licking her bottom lip as she looked away. "And there's no…"

"I haven't found someone to spend my life with yet."

Rowen nodded, eyes on the ground. "Yet…"

I sighed out my frustration. "What do you want me to say, Rowen?"

She looked up at me sharply. "I want you to say it. If we agree to this…this insanity—you think about what you're letting go."

My body stilled. Cold. Controlled. "Letting go?"

Her mouth twisted. "I won't tolerate infidelity."

"You won't tolerate it?" I huffed a laugh. Bitter. Ugly. "What if I don't care? Or what if I want a harem of women at my beck and call?"

She didn't miss a beat. "Well, you already told them where you'd rather stick your dick, but I think a *harem* might be ambitious, even for you."

I moved.

Two steps, no warning, all dominance. She flinched, startled—but didn't run. Just backed up as I approached, spine hitting the rough bark of the pine behind her. Her breath caught, but she didn't break eye contact. Brave, foolish girl.

I leaned in, voice like velvet soaked in venom. "Are you disappointed I said I didn't want to fuck you, princess?"

Her breath hitched. Just once. Then she lifted her chin. "Not at all. But you saying it out loud now makes it sound like you're trying to convince yourself."

Goddess, she was fire. Every word she threw at me only lit the fuse shorter.

I stared down at her, jaw tight. "Careful," I warned, voice low. "You don't want to bait something you're not ready to handle."

"I've been handling wolves like you my entire life."

"Not like me."

Her pulse jumped at her throat. Her scent shifted—heat and fury, stubborn and sweet—and I nearly cursed.

"I've *handled* you before, remember?"

It was a taunt. A reminder of the past, and it made my blood boil. Not because she was right. But because I was close to proving her wrong.

My knuckles brushed across her cheekbone, and she looked up at me, eyes wide. "You're going to regret that, princess." I stepped back. "I accept your terms: if I'm fucking someone, I'm only fucking you." I smirked when I saw her eyes widen at what she'd basically demanded. "Same for you, princess. It's me inside you or no one." I let that settle for a second. She was still looking at me in a mix of confusion and wariness. "Tell your father and the druid I accept."

Rowen gaped at me. "Wh-what?"

"We'll be married in the morning," I told her as I walked away. "Wear a dress. You turn up in combat pants,

I'll strip you naked and have you on your knees begging for my forgiveness."

"*What?*" I heard her shriek. "Wolfe!" I heard her hit something. "I'm not wearing a fucking dress, asshole!" she shouted behind me.

I didn't reply, just left her with the sound of my laughter.

I was still smirking by the time I made it past the pack-lands' outer ring. Her voice had echoed after me—loud, pissed off, gloriously unfiltered. Goddess, I wanted to bottle it.

"I'm not wearing a fucking dress!" Yeah, she would because she didn't know me well enough anymore to know if I was bluffing. I knew one thing as I heard her rage behind me, she'd show up burning.

That's all I needed. Not her compliance. Not her sweetness, if she had any left. Just her presence.

Because tomorrow morning, the pack would wake up and see what strength looked like. They'd see Rowen standing next to me, not because she was claimed—but because she had *chosen*. And whether she wore silk or steel, it wouldn't matter.

The choice would still be hers. But the power? That would be *mine*.

I didn't go back to my rooms. Couldn't settle tonight, I knew that. The pack hall walls were too small, the silence too heavy. Instead, I walked the border—circling the perimeter like a wolf with a bone-deep itch. Reminding myself that this wasn't about her. It wasn't about me, either.

This was about stability. Packs didn't thrive under uncertainty. They followed the strongest one in the room—and I'd just made damn sure that was me. Even if it meant tying myself to a woman who wanted to rip my throat out.

A flicker of movement caught my eye. A young Hollow wolf darted between trees, probably doing patrol. He saw me and paused. Nodded once. Kept going.

That was new. Respect. Acceptance. I wasn't sure I liked how much I needed it tonight.

I hadn't come here to be a savior. But now that everything had changed, I wasn't interested in saving everyone, only the ones smart enough to stand behind me when the shit hit. It *was* coming. The rogue pack, if that's what they were. The unrest. The whispers between packs.

This marriage was a distraction. But it was also a shield. A symbol for the pack that needed that.

If Rowen wanted to test me? Fine. Because when she finally stepped up beside me, dress or not—I wanted her wild. I wanted her *angry* because it's the wolves who fight the hardest that lead the longest.

And I was done playing nice.

I woke early. It wasn't because I was excited—hell no—but because my wolf wouldn't shut the fuck up. It kept pacing. Snarling. Restless, like we were about to walk into battle, not a bonding ceremony. But considering my wife-to-be was Rowen, maybe there wasn't a difference. Because standing next to Rowen in front of her pack wasn't a wedding.

It was a fucking challenge.

One I had to win. This wasn't about tradition or vows or some twisted fairy-tale redemption arc.

This was politics. This was control. This was about standing beside a woman, who right now hated that I existed, and making damn sure she regretted turning me away that day.

I wanted to say this wasn't the eighteen-year-old boy in me getting a slight taste of revenge, that I wasn't that petty…but maybe a *little* bit of me was that petty.

I wasn't proud of the feeling, but I also wouldn't dwell on it.

Today, I needed to look the part. Killian had said his piece—it hadn't been complimentary—and then left me to find clothes fitting of an alpha.

I dressed precisely, all in black. No frills. Just borrowed clothes. Black pants and a black shirt that was a little too tight around the neck, so I had to keep the top two buttons undone if I wanted to breathe.

By the time I stepped into the clearing, the pack were gathered. Not in rows. Not in reverence. Just…watching. Weighing.

Judging.

I could feel Killian behind me. Still. Focused. He didn't need to say anything—I already knew what he was thinking. *We shouldn't be here.* Maybe he was right. But I was here because someone had to keep this pack from destruction.

Malric stood beside the druid. I hadn't expected him to make it, but then, why would he not? She was his only child after all. I admired the strength of the alpha, knowing how much it would cost him to bring himself here. To give the blessing.

He saw me looking and dipped his head slightly, but he

couldn't hide the sheen of sweat on his brow or the worry in his eyes as he looked at me.

Seemed Killian wasn't the only one wondering if this was a huge mistake, and then I felt it.

Not a sound. Not a scent.

But her.

I didn't turn right away. I waited. Measured. Controlled the snap of my wolf behind my teeth because I couldn't afford to lose control.

When I looked up, Rowen stood across the clearing, walking toward me like she was on her way to an execution.

Not hers. *Mine.*

She was dressed in something dark—blood-red or maybe rust-brown, I couldn't tell—but the silky fabric clung to her like a weapon. Every curve was on show, and I instantly hated her choice of dress, knowing that's *exactly* why she picked it. She didn't offer a smile. There was no softness. Just tension in her shoulders and fire in her eyes. Her hair was loose and free, the morning sun catching the red in her hair as if she were wearing a fiery crown.

She stopped in front of me, and I didn't speak. Neither did she.

That silence dragged for one beat too long.

"Last chance, princess?" I said to her, quiet, low. "There's still time to run."

Her mouth curled, not in amusement but in disgust. "Run? Is this a fight, Wolfe?"

"No," I grunted. "You're not dressed for a fight."

"I'm *always* dressed for a fight."

Goddess, send me patience.

I let my eyes rake over her, just to provoke her, and watched the flush rise high on her cheeks. "You look—"

"If you say *beautiful*, I will knee you in the dick in front of the entire pack."

My smirk was slow, calculated. "I was going to say *dangerous*. But now I'm thinking *delusional*."

She didn't flinch. "Keep pushing, Wolfe. You'll find out just how dangerous I am."

The druid cleared their throat behind us. I didn't move. Neither did she.

This wasn't a normal Binding. It was a declaration of war—with rings instead of blades—and we were both ready to bleed for it.

The druid stepped between us, face carved from ancient stone, voice calm as a winter storm. "This is not a wedding."

No shit.

"This is a pact. A bond not forged in love, but in necessity. In duty. In power."

The gathered shifters were silent. Watching. Judging. Always fucking judging. Rowen stood to my left, still as a statue, jaw clenched so tight I could practically hear her teeth grinding.

"This is how peace is kept," the druid continued. "Two leaders. One vow."

I didn't look at her. Her presence was a second skin—abrasive, electric, unavoidable.

The druid turned to me. "Wolfe, do you accept the bond offered, not in heart, but in loyalty? Will you protect this pack as your own, as a natural born *leader*?" I saw the glint in their eye as they avoided saying *alpha*. "Will you accept its daughter as she stands beside you as your equal?"

I spoke without hesitation. "Sure."

The druid glared a borehole in my head, no doubt displeased with the casualness of my answer, but what were they going to do? Ask me to leave? With a dissatisfied sniff, they turned to her.

"Rowen, daughter of the Hollow. Do you accept the bond offered, not in surrender, but in unity? Will you stand beside this leader and have this bond blessed by Luna?"

Her chin lifted. "I will stand beside him," she said. "I will *not* follow behind him."

I didn't hide my smirk. Not a yes. Not a no.

The druid hesitated, frustration at our disobedience riding their scent, but they nodded once. "Accepted."

I almost laughed. Of course it was.

We stepped forward—one pace, side by side. The druid raised a blade, ceremonial, curved like a fang. They sliced across both our palms, swift and shallow, and held them out.

Rowen didn't hesitate. Neither did I. Our blood met in the bowl. Smoke curled from the surface like it recognized the storm brewing between us. The wind picked up and swept through the trees. A chorus of murmurs rose behind us—some in celebration, some in warning.

She still didn't look at me.

I didn't look away. "You can drop the scowl," I muttered under the howl of the wind. "You survived it."

"For now," she replied, voice flat.

The druid lifted the bowl high. "It is done. Let Blueridge Hollow endure."

I turned to face the crowd. My pack. My challenge. But my thoughts were already ahead—on the aftermath, the fallout, the fury still brewing in the woman beside me.

Because this Binding wasn't over; it had only just begun.

Chapter 16

Rowen

I WOULD'VE RATHER BEEN BLEEDING IN THE WOODS THAN sitting here with a silver plate in front of me, flanked by shifters who now thought I belonged to him.

The feast wasn't about food. It was about power plays. It was about who sat where, who chewed first, who lifted their cup, and who didn't. Everything had meaning. Everything was performance.

And right now, I was the star of the show.

The roasted meat came from a kill made by Wolfe—out of respect, supposedly, for the "new bond." But I knew better. It was a test. Another tradition the elders insisted on keeping.

The newly bonded pair eats first. Same plate. Same bite. To show the pack that trust existed. That unity was more than words.

I picked up the carved iron fork and felt Wolfe's eyes on me. The silence was suffocating. It stretched too long, as if the entire hall was waiting for one of us to flinch.

It wouldn't be me.

I speared a piece of meat, lifted it, and held it out to him. His gaze flicked from the fork to my face, unreadable as ever, and for a heartbeat, I thought he might refuse. Instead, he leaned in—slow, deliberate—and took the bite from the fork, teeth brushing against metal.

The room exhaled.

He didn't break eye contact as he chewed. Bastard probably thought this counted as foreplay.

"Your turn, *princess*," he murmured when he swallowed.

I snatched the fork back before he could say anything else, took a bite without flinching, and forced myself to swallow even though my throat felt like it was packed with gravel.

Killian made a quiet comment to one of the pack sentries. Something about the flavor. I didn't hear it. My pulse was a steady drum in my ears.

A warm hand covered mine, and the fork was taken from me. Wolfe lightly stabbed a piece of meat with a thick strip of fat clinging to it. Wolfe seemed to remember that I hated the taste of soft fat in my human form. The fucker didn't hide the glee in his eyes as he held it out to me.

"For you, my *wedded mate*."

I hate you.

Even though I didn't speak out loud, the sly, victorious smile he gave me let me know he knew exactly what I was thinking. To anyone watching, we looked composed. Civil. Maybe even compatible.

But inside? I was seething. I leaned forward, my hands in fists, when he playfully pulled the fork back a bit, but I snatched at the meat. The thick white fat lay heavy on my tongue, and I swallowed the piece whole, hoping to the

Goddess that I wouldn't choke, or throw up, as I resisted the urge to down my cup of water.

Wolfe drew back, his low chuckle grating on my nerves. He sat beside me like he owned the damn chair. Like he belonged here. Like he hadn't just inserted himself into this pack.

Across the room, I saw Adair watching me. She smiled at me, and I forced myself to be steady. Calm. I could do this.

I lifted my cup. "To Blueridge Hollow," I said clearly.

The hall answered in a low rumble, voices overlapping. I didn't look at Wolfe again. If I did, I was afraid the rage might turn into something worse. Something hotter. Something *hungrier*. I wasn't ready for that. I would never be ready for that.

Instead, I watched my pack as they celebrated the Binding of two shifters they knew. My father sat at the other end of the table. I'd looked over at him more than once, and as the feast progressed, I wasn't sure if the table or the chair was the only thing holding him up. Lewis hovered nearby, not quite ready to grab him, but close.

The scraping of a chair against wood made me look his way again. Alpha Malric stood on legs that were too shaky.

"Today is a day of significance," my father said, voice low but resonant, a grave smile tugging at his mouth. "The pack celebrates not just a bond, but a beginning." He paused, his breath hitching like it cost him something. "My daughter—*your* daughter of the Hollow—has been joined in union with a strong leader. One raised by this land. One known to us. Once lost to distance, now returned."

He turned toward Wolfe.

"Wolfe, of the Stonefang Pack, is no longer a guest in the Hollow. As declared by me, witnessed by our druid, and blessed beneath Luna's gaze—Wolfe is now the leader of Blueridge Hollow."

The silence that followed was thick. Sacred. But I couldn't breathe. *He had declared it to everyone.* My heart was racing, and I saw all of them looking at Wolfe in…*admiration.* A few with surprise, but all of them, *all* of them, looked *pleased.*

Then my father brought their attention back to him, voice steady and steeped in memory. "By claw and vow, by blood and stone—so it is bound."

The murmur ran through the hall. "By claw and vow, by blood and stone—so it is bound."

I jerked when a hand landed on my shoulder. I looked up to see the druid. "It is time."

On legs that felt like lead, I rose from the table and followed the druid from the hall. I knew Wolfe was only a few feet behind me, and laughter and calls of goodwill followed him. Followed *him.* All that followed me was silence.

He fell into step beside me as we walked. But he kept his words to himself, and I was grateful. I was scared, I was barely hanging on, and our union, no matter the political *convenience* of it, still had to have the night ceremony.

The forest at night was quiet in that way that wasn't quiet at all. Crickets. Wind through leaves. The slow creak of old branches bearing ancient secrets. The kind of quiet that felt…watched.

I stood barefoot in the ritual circle, toes sunk into the mossy earth, a shiver running up my spine that had nothing to do with the cool wind.

Wolfe stood across from me. Arms folded. Eyes sharp. Still in his ceremonial black. He hadn't said a word since the feast.

I didn't blame him. This wasn't a moment for words.

The druid circled the stone altar between us, an iron bowl filled with ash in one hand and a polished antler blade in the other. The blade had been carved with runes so old I couldn't read them—but my blood knew them. My wolf stirred as the wind shifted, as the scent of old magic tickled the back of my throat. The Heartwood tree loomed over us as we stood in the most ancient, most sacred part of our territory.

"Tonight," the druid intoned, "we mark the bond between you—as protectors of a shared people."

My skin crawled. This wasn't just theater. This was legacy. The druid dipped the blade in the ash and approached me first.

"Do you accept the burden of this bond?" they asked. "Do you swear to this union not for power, but for the good of the Hollow?"

I swallowed, the weight of it pressing down. My pulse thrummed in my jaw. "Always."

The druid stepped close, pressed the edge of the blade against my skin—just under my collarbone—and drew the mark. It stung. Sharp. Hot. The ash burned into the shallow cut, a sigil drawn in blood and soil and vow. I could shift one hundred times or more, and this mark would never change.

Then they turned to him.

"Do you accept the burden of this bond? Do you swear to protect this land as your own; does the Hollow have your heart?"

Silence.

For one tense breath, I thought he might say no. That he'd laugh. Walk away. Burn it all down.

Wolfe looked past the druid, blue eyes dark in the night. I dared not speak, but I felt he was waiting for something.

"Wolfe?" the druid probed.

Wolfe looked past me, to the trees, to the sky above. He waited for a long moment. "Yes," he said.

The druid moved forward to mark him the same way— his throat tensed, but he didn't move.

"Not there," Wolfe said gruffly. He quickly unbuttoned his shirt, dropping it to the ground, and half-turned, giving the druid his shoulder. "Mark me there."

The druid hesitated for just a moment and then did as commanded. I watched as the ash pulsed faintly on Wolfe's skin. I wondered if it burned less than mine.

"Luna sees you," the druid whispered to him. "She accepts your bond…whether you accept it, remains to be seen."

They stepped back and raised the empty bowl to the stars.

Just like that, it was done. No fanfare. No magic explosion. Just a scar that would burn for a full moon cycle and a promise neither of us had wanted to make. We would not carve our names into the Heartwood as others did; we weren't paired for that, and I doubted that the druid would allow a false marking on such an ancient rite.

I turned to leave. Wolfe grabbed my wrist. The touch was light. But it stopped me cold.

"We're bound now," he said, voice low.

"We are, by blood and politics," I shot back, seeing the druid had already left.

A flicker of something—amusement? anger?—twisted his mouth. "You don't think the Goddess knows what she's doing?"

I stepped closer, chin high. "I don't think she cares what I want."

"Then we've finally got something in common." He gave the Heartwood a wary glance. "Try to stop fighting me," he said quietly, his gaze still on the tree.

I almost said something clever, hurtful, but this was so much more than us. "I'll try."

Wolfe looked back at me and shook his head. He knew I didn't mean it. He'd never been a fool. The resentment fell back into place between us—familiar, comforting, danger-ous. We turned away from each other in the same breath.

The trees swallowed us again as we made our way back to the pack. Somewhere, above the clouds, I swore I heard the wind laugh. As we stepped out of the trees, both of us slowed at the sight in front of us.

"Goddess, they are bringing out *all* the old traditions tonight," I grumbled, and I heard Wolfe's snort of agree-ment as he surveyed the scene in front of us.

The flames roared high, their crackle and snap the only voice that seemed to matter tonight.

The bonfire rite wasn't about pomp or speeches. It was about showing Luna our strength. About proving to the pack—and the land itself—that the bond forged today could withstand both fire and fury. It was an old tradition that I hadn't seen adhered to in many years. I wasn't happy it was being resurrected tonight.

I was going to yell at my father so bad.

Wolfe and I stood at the edge of the clearing, the heat from the blaze warming our faces, licking at our skin. All around us, the pack gathered in loose, watchful circles. Some stood with arms crossed, while others sat cross-legged in the dirt, silent as the dead. More weaved through the pack in their wolf form. A few of the younger ones leaned forward like this was a story passed down and they didn't want to miss a word.

The druid stood beside the fire, hood lowered now, their face shadowed and lined with wisdom and knowing.

"Step forward," they called.

We did. Together.

Wolfe's shoulder brushed mine, and I told myself I didn't feel anything. Not the heat of him. Not the strength of his presence. Not the way my wolf stirred like it remembered him from another life.

The druid extended another carved wooden bowl, smoke curling from its contents—embers, herbs, and a single drop of both our blood. Where the hell they got it from, I would never know.

"Add to the flame," they instructed.

I reached in first, preparing myself for the burn. Instead, it felt more like powder, and I pinched a bit of the mixture between my fingers and cast it into the fire. Sparks danced upward like a thousand fireflies released all at once.

Wolfe followed.

The fire roared higher, a howl of approval rising with it —not from the druid, but from the pack. I looked around and saw it on their faces. They weren't just watching. They were accepting.

They were *excited*.

The druid raised their arms. "By flame and fang, the bond is seen."

Then came the part I'd forgotten about.

The *dance*.

Another ancient ritual. The rite demanded movement— some ancient, instinctive rhythm that predated even words. It was intended to demonstrate balance, power, and trust between newly formed pairs.

I turned to Wolfe. I shouldn't have been surprised that he was already waiting, still shirtless. "Try to keep up, princess," he murmured as he saw my surprise.

"Just…shut up."

The smirk he gave me was feral as he moved towards me.

Around the fire, we circled—each step deliberate, each motion mirrored and challenged. Not graceful. Not beautiful. Powerful. I lunged; he parried. He advanced; I twisted. A dance or a fight, I don't think we cared. Our shadows stretched and merged in the firelight, our bodies caught in some ancient memory that lived in our bones. The pack howled again as we fought each other in the dance.

This was not mating.

This was not affection.

This was war dressed as ritual.

And Goddess help me—I felt *alive*. When it ended, I was panting, sweat clinging to my spine. Wolfe stood across from me, chest rising and falling like mine.

His eyes held mine. "I thought you said you wouldn't fight me," he said.

"I lied," I whispered.

He laughed outright, and the fire between us crackled, as if Luna herself approved.

Pack came to talk to us, separating us unintentionally, and I seized the opportunity to leave. I didn't walk away so much as vanish. One second, I was standing with my pack, letting their cheers, their howls, their approval wash over me like smoke—and the next, I was slipping between the trees, the weight of the night too much for even my wolf to carry.

The forest beyond the Hollow pulsed with life, crickets and wind and the occasional rustle of something wilder. But it was quiet enough. Dark enough. I could breathe here.

I pressed my palm against a pine trunk, grounding myself. The bark bit into my skin, but I didn't mind. At least it felt real. So much of tonight had felt like theater—rituals and vows and fire-bright gazes watching my every breath. But this? This solitude? This was mine.

Or it would've been…if he hadn't followed me. I didn't look back. I felt him.

That wolf-strong energy curling around the edges of my senses, brushing up against my spine like it had a right to be there.

"Didn't anyone teach you it's rude to stalk your wife?" I asked, not turning.

Wolfe's voice came low and sharp behind me. "Didn't anyone teach you not to run from your husband after a ceremony meant to unify a pack?"

I turned then. Slowly. Deliberately. "You want unity?" I asked. "Then start by letting me breathe."

He stepped into the clearing, moonlight catching the edges of him—jaw tense, hair wild, chest rising, and his bare skin was far too distracting.

"I gave you two days. You remember that?"

"I remember you used them to maneuver yourself into my pack," I snapped.

"I used them to give you a choice. You just didn't like the choices."

We stared at each other across a few feet of moss and dirt, but it may as well have been an ocean.

"Is this how it'll be?" I asked, voice low. "Us arguing?"

"I don't know. I think," Wolfe said, stepping closer, "that you're terrified of this *marriage* because you know it changes everything."

"I know it changes nothing," I hissed. "You're still an outsider who showed up and let everyone believe you're here to save us."

His mouth curved. Not a smile. A weapon. "Your father manipulated this to his advantage. I was only here to talk about an alliance between packs."

That stopped me. Goddess help me—I didn't know what to believe. "Then why?" I asked, softer now. "*Why* agree to this marriage?"

His gaze locked with mine. No softness there. Just iron and fire. "Because if someone's going to stand beside you, it should be the only one who can *actually* stand beside you. Not some prick who only wants to use you."

My breath caught, and in the silence that followed, I felt my wolf lean forward. Curious. Unafraid. Not ready to give in. But maybe…ready to listen.

Wolfe stepped back. "I have two packs that will need me going forward," he said quietly. "Two packs, that I will serve. There are rogues out there, or…something out there, that we need to be ready to fight." He looked me over. "I have enough fights; do you have to be one of them?"

My throat felt dry as the weight of his honesty settled around us. "No."

He nodded. "Good. Let's not make this any harder than it already is."

Approaching footsteps made both of us turn. I didn't say anything when Wolfe stepped in front of me, like he wanted to protect me.

Killian looked at him first, and then, with a gentleness I hadn't seen in him before, he turned to me. "Rowen, come. It's your father."

Chapter 17

Rowen

The Hollow was too still.

Not quiet.

Still.

Like the whole mountain was holding its breath, waiting to see if the world would shift without him in it.

My father was gone.

The concept felt foreign in my mind, like something borrowed. Like if I spoke them aloud, they'd steal the last of him from the air.

I stood outside my father's rooms, still wearing the dress from the night before, though it smelled of smoke and sweat and reminded me of the bond I hadn't wanted but received anyway. Wolfe hadn't spoken to me since Killian found us.

Because when Killian found me in the trees, eyes gentle in a way they'd never been before, he hadn't needed to say what he came to say. With the way he had looked at me, I knew that my father would take his last breath soon.

He passed to join the great hunt about an hour ago.

The Hollow had lost its heartbeat.

The mourning walk wasn't optional. It was part of the old ways. A tradition as old as the stones that marked the pack's burial grounds. We walked from the place he died to the highest ridge—alone—so the Goddess could hear our grief and carry it on the wind.

So the mountain would remember.

I needed to change. I pushed the door open to my rooms, dropping the dress behind me as I walked to my closet. My fingers paused on the hanger of my pants. With a low sigh, I pushed them back, my eyes going to the furthest item in my closet. A simple white cotton sleeveless dress. It had a floral appliqué around the hem, but other than that, it was unadorned.

Plain. Simple. Unlike my grief.

I took it from the hanger and pulled it over my head. It was loose and comfortable and...*I didn't care what I wore because my dad had died*. With a shaky breath, I pushed that thought aside. That was not how a leader reacted. My pack would need me. I brushed my hair quickly, ran a wet cloth over my face and arms, wondering if I shouldn't have taken a shower, and then left my rooms before I found an excuse to stay.

The pack hall was empty. Outside, the path was already cleared. Someone—likely the druid or Adair—had laid the markers. Small iron rings embedded in the dirt. Symbols of protection. Of passing. Seeing them made me falter, but I knew I had to keep going.

I didn't cry.

Not because I wasn't broken. But because tears weren't how we mourned here. Blueridge Hollow grieved in ritual. In silence.

Each step was a memory. A wound pressed into the earth beneath my bare feet as I *remembered*.

The time he taught me to track by scent, before my first shift. The way his voice cracked with pride when I bested him for the first time while we sparred. The sound of his laugh when I told him I'd rather marry a rock than marry Tyler. The way he called me little storm when I was younger, like he knew I would never be anything soft. The look in his eyes when he told me Wolfe had left the pack, and was there anything I needed to tell him? I never said a word, and he never pressed. But he knew. I knew he knew. Even at seventeen, I was choosing pack first…like he'd taught me.

The pack followed behind but far enough that I couldn't hear them. This was my walk. You walked alone, and the pack walked alone behind you. One long progression of silence and solitude.

When I reached the ridge, high above the Hollow, wind howling like something half-wild and half-divine—I knelt. I placed my palm on the stone. Spoke his name and let the mountain take it.

I couldn't move. I couldn't make myself get up. My palm pressed harder into the stone, and I fought back the tears. This was not the place to cry. This was not the place to break. Everyone was waiting for their turn. I could not break down. Not here. Not now.

The stone was still warm beneath my palm. As if it remembered him. As if it also refused to let him go just yet.

I didn't move.

The wind picked up around me, pulling at my hair,

tugging at the hem of my dress. I wasn't cold, but I was shivering anyway.

This was where I was supposed to stand. This was where the alpha's bloodline knelt in farewell. But I was just a daughter here, a daughter in mourning. I still felt like that little girl clutching her father's hand the first time he showed her the ridge and told her, *"This is where we come to speak to the dead."*

I pressed my forehead to the stone. "I'm not ready," I whispered, feeling tears spill over. "Not like this. Not without you."

The breeze shifted, and without turning, I knew he was there. Wolfe didn't speak. Didn't come closer. I could hear him breathing, though. That steady, quiet cadence. Calm. Present.

Watching me crack—but not offering pity.

I hated him a little for it. I needed it more than I could admit. "You're not supposed to be here," I whispered.

"I'm not," he agreed.

He was behind me, a step or two away, not too close, but close enough that the air quivered between us.

"You were supposed to stay back and wait your turn."

"I don't follow instructions well," he said quietly. "Ask anyone."

I didn't smile.

Couldn't.

"Rowen…you can't stay here," he said, voice low so only I could hear over the wind.

I shook my head. "I need to."

"You need to breathe," he murmured. "And stand."

I closed my eyes, the weight of everything I'd lost pressing harder. "They're watching me."

"They always will," he said. "But you decide what they see."

I opened my eyes again. The wind was stronger now, tearing through the trees like it knew something had broken loose.

"I don't want to be strong today," I admitted, my lips barely moving, feeling another tear roll down my cheek.

"You don't have to want it," Wolfe said quietly. "You just have to stand, princess."

Princess. Goddess, I hated that name. It made me sound spoiled. *Weak.* I was not weak.

I rose into a sitting position. Slow. Controlled. Bones aching from restraint.

I looked at him through blurred vision. The mountain gave nothing without effort—no shelter, no comfort. Only height. Only space to fall.

Wolfe stepped closer and extended his hand, palm up, fingers open. No command. No claim. Just an invitation.

My heart thundered. To reach for him would be to admit I needed help. *His* help.

But the pack below needed their alpha's daughter on her feet, and I knew in this moment that I couldn't rise without him. I closed my fingers around his. His grip was firm, steady, solid as the mountain itself. He didn't pull me up. He let me haul myself to standing.

For a long moment, we simply faced the wind together, the home of the pack far below us, out of sight. Here, it was just the two of us and the memory of what was lost.

When I found my voice, it was just above a whisper. "Thank you, but I shouldn't lean on you."

He didn't turn to look at me. He stepped slightly closer, still subtle, still respectful of my space. "Leaning's okay," he said. "You're already standing, Rowen."

I inhaled, lungs burning, even as they trembled, but I straightened even more. Wolfe lingered a moment, and then he just turned and walked the few steps back to where he had been, ready to say his own goodbye.

The wind carried away my last tears, and when I turned to face the Hollow again, I knew I could fall apart later. But not today. Not on the ridge. Not in front of the dead.

With a deep breath, I left the ridge and began the long descent. I took the long way down, as was my right, knowing that there would be many behind me on the ridge who would get back to the pack hall long before me.

But I didn't care—this I was allowed to do. I also knew I wouldn't be alone in taking this route; some would need the longer journey to reflect and remember before the final ceremony.

The pack hall came into view through the thinning trees. I hadn't realized how far I'd gone until the ridge was behind me and the wind shifted. The scent of my pack hit next— pine and earth and mourning smoke. They were gathered. Waiting.

I hated that I had to walk into it like a leader instead of a grieving daughter.

I crossed the edge of the clearing, my spine straight, my face blank. The moment I stepped back into view, voices hushed. Pack stilled. They tracked my every move. They'd seen me walk that path alone.

Now they wanted to see if I'd *stand*.

The druid stepped forward first.

Their robes were heavy with dew, hem darkened from the damp earth. Their expression was unreadable, carved from centuries of ritual. But their eyes—those always held truth. Old truth. Deep truth.

"You walked the mourning path," they said softly. "Now the Hollow must mark the passing."

I gave a sharp nod. "I'm ready."

They lifted a hand, pulling ash from a pouch and smearing it across my brow, then touching my sternum. "Blood to mourn. Ash to lead."

The words echoed through the gathered pack. They bowed their heads in unison, not to me, but to the rite. To the old ways.

I turned to step back, but someone else stepped forward. A slender form. Familiar. *Henry*.

He looked nervous, big brown eyes too wide for a face still shedding childhood. But as he looked at me now, with his chin lifted, I paused. "Alpha Malric said you'd protect us."

My throat tightened. "He said that?"

He nodded. "Alpha Malric told me that once. That if anything ever happened to him…we'd still be safe. Because you'd be here. And you never lie, Rowen. So we believe you."

That affected me more than the stone on the ridge. Not because it hurt. Because it *healed*. I reached out to him, brushing a leaf off his sleeve. "You believe in me, Henry?"

He nodded again. "We all do. Even the ones pretending they aren't watching right now."

I almost laughed. Almost cried. Instead, I stood and faced the pack. "Let them watch," I whispered to him and saw his smile. "I will not fail you."

Then I turned and walked back toward the pack hall—not as a grieving daughter.

But as the storm my father raised.

I didn't expect him to be waiting. But there he was. Wolfe stood just beyond the threshold of the hall, arms crossed, posture easy—but I knew better. He was watching everything. *Everyone*. And right now, me most of all.

His eyes flicked to the ash across my brow. The smear over my heart. The mark at my neck from last night's rite. His expression didn't change, but something in him shifted. I felt it like a tremor in my ribs.

"You took the long way back," he said quietly.

I stopped a few paces from him. "It felt like the right thing to do."

He nodded as he watched the pack gather. "It is a sad day for us all." He didn't look at me as he spoke. "I meant what I said, two packs, I *will* serve them both."

"I believe you," I murmured. "You are allowing us to follow the old traditions. I…" I exhaled. "I know that your other pack is more…modern."

Wolfe huffed out a laugh. "I follow tradition when tradition calls for it." He looked around. "This is the only way to do the walk of mourning."

"You did this for the alpha of Stonefang?" I asked, almost surprised that he would.

Wolfe looked at me, his gaze unreadable. "Alpha Lars was an alpha worthy of the same respect shown here to your father."

"I…" I gave him an apologetic grimace. "I didn't mean to imply he wasn't…sorry."

Wolfe squinted at me. "An apology? From the great daughter of the Hollow?" He smirked, but it was almost playful. "I know today is an exception; I won't tell anyone."

I punched his shoulder.

"And she's back in the room," he murmured with a small grin.

Asshole. But I felt better—*double asshole.*

Before either of us could speak again, the druid appeared behind me, stepping from the shadows like they'd always been there.

"It's time," they said. "The Hollow must see it sealed."

Wolfe's jaw tightened, but he nodded. Curiously, I followed the druid without a word, Wolfe a silent presence beside me. Neither told me to leave.

We walked to the hallowed ground, where I'd stood only the night before, getting an ash mark carved into my skin. Like then, a fire was already burning, but this time it was to celebrate the end of something, not the beginning.

A pyre—not for a body, but for a legacy.

The druid stepped into the glow of the flames and raised their arms. The smoke curled around us like the mountain was exhaling.

"By the Goddess Luna's will and the Hollow's law," the druid intoned, "we bear witness to the passing of one leader and to the binding of the next."

They turned to Wolfe. "The ash marks grief, but it also binds memory to duty. The flame consumes the past, but it also lights the path ahead."

They reached into their satchel and withdrew a shard of

blackened pine—charred wood from a long-dead tree at the heart of the Hollow.

"This is your mark," they told me. "The final rite of mourning. You carry it until the next death…or until you no longer need reminding." They pressed the shard into my palm, and it burned—hot, sharp, a bite of pain that grounded me more than any speech ever could.

When I opened my fist, seeing only ash, the druid nodded.

"Then it is done," they said. "You are no longer *just* the alpha's daughter." They turned toward the fire. "You are the flame that follows."

The ash still pulsed in my hand, warmth radiating through my skin like a second heartbeat. The druid's words hung in the air, thick with the weight of history, as the fire snapped and hissed behind us.

But they weren't finished.

They turned slowly, robes catching the orange light, and faced Wolfe. He hadn't moved—broad, still, unblinking. He watched the druid like a predator, unsure whether to trust the hand being extended.

The druid tilted their head. "And you, *Wolfe*."

The tone of their words struck like a bell. *What was that undercurrent?*

Wolfe didn't flinch, but I saw it in the way his shoulders were squared. The way the firelight flickered in his eyes.

"You returned not as a claimant, but as a servant," the druid said. "You did not demand to lead the Hollow. You earned the right to take it. Through action. Through defense. Through sacrifice." They stepped forward. "Our laws are clear. The Hollow requires a leader. Not just by bloodline, but by Luna's will. And the Goddess, it seems, has chosen her leader for this pack."

I saw Wolfe's jaw twitch when the druid said *seems*.

The druid reached into their robes once more, producing a band of old, weathered leather stitched with silver thread and marked with a carved emblem I recognized instantly—the Blueridge Hollow crest.

"This was your father's," the druid said, speaking to me, but their eyes never left Wolfe. "Passed to him by his father. It does not sit on blood alone. It rests on the one who leads."

They extended it to Wolfe. A challenge in offering's clothing. Wolfe didn't hesitate. He stepped forward and took it in silence. The leather disappeared into his grip like it had belonged there all along.

"Then let the Hollow witness," the druid called, voice rising. "Alpha Malric is gone. His flame has passed. And in its wake stands Wolfe of Blueridge Hollow. By the rite of bond, the right of might, and the will of the Goddess Luna —so it is spoken, so it is bound."

A low, collective howl rose behind us, causing me to jump. I hadn't known they were there. Pack members tucked in the shadows, spread throughout the woods, answering the call.

It wasn't celebration. It was *allegiance*.

My pulse thundered in my throat. Wolfe turned his head toward me, looking at the gathered pack, the firelight turning his eyes gold.

We stood side by side, and I knew Blueridge Hollow would never be the same.

Chapter 18

Wolfe

THE LEATHER BAND WAS STILL IN MY HAND. OLD, WORN, BUT heavy in a way no strip of hide should be. It smelled of smoke.

Of history.

Of blood.

I didn't wear it. Not yet. Not until I decided where to place it—arm, wrist, *throat*. Like a noose perhaps.

Rowen didn't look my way again. She hadn't since the druid named me leader. She just stood in the flickering glow of the pyre, silent and unreadable, like her soul had gone into the smoke with her father's name.

I didn't blame her.

But I wasn't going to carry her mourning too.

I was the alpha now. Theirs. Even though they didn't know it, and I had no time for sentiment.

The druid had stepped back into the shadows, disappearing as easily as they'd appeared. The fire behind me roared higher, wind catching the flames like the Goddess was hungry tonight.

Let her feed.

Killian appeared at my shoulder without a word. He didn't congratulate me. Didn't offer sympathy. Just stood there, like a goddamn pillar—stone-faced, dependable, and waiting.

"What's the first move?" he asked quietly as he watched the pack.

I looked out over the ridge. The trees. The Hollow. The pack gathered. My pack now.

The power of the alpha had come as Malric took his last breath. I'd been in his rooms, not too close that anyone saw the power shift, thank the Goddess. It hadn't slammed into me like it did when Lars passed; it had been more like a deep inhale after being underwater for too long. Killian had noticed the way my body stilled as I accepted the gift Malric gave me.

"They think I'll play along," I murmured, my voice kept low as I watched Rowen move among them, accepting their words and love as we stood back. "They think I came to marry the girl and keep the traditions warm."

Killian snorted. "You're terrible at warm."

"They need to learn that fast," I said. "This isn't the old world anymore. I'm not the same as when I left, and I'm not their ghost king, raised from the ashes to nod and bow to anyone either." I finally looked down at the leather. The stitching. The weight. "No." I looked up. "I came here because something's wrong in these mountains. Packs are being hit. Borders tested. Shifters going missing." I clenched the band in my fist. "And this pack—they're not ready to defend themselves or this land they cherish so much."

"This pack? Your pack now." Killian tilted his head. "You planning to fix their *readiness*?"

I met his gaze. "I already started."

He grinned as we walked away. Behind us, the howls were still echoing through the trees. My name passing from throat to throat.

Wolfe. Not of the Stonefang Pack. But of the *Hollow*.

I let the silence stretch as we walked away, my wolf pacing just beneath the surface. Restless. Like me.

"Call a meeting," I told Killian. "At dawn. Elders, sentries, warriors. I want to know who's loyal, who's lazy, and who's going to cause problems."

"And Rowen?"

I didn't answer right away. "She's smart," I said. "But she's not ready for this yet. She needs time to let go."

Killian arched a brow. "You gonna make her?"

"No," I said flatly. "I'm going to give her space to grieve. And while she's losing herself in it—I'll be molding this pack with my hands."

Killian murmured something that sounded a lot like approval.

I spent the night in the pack hall, in the alpha's quarters, learning as much as I could about this pack from Malric's files and my memory. I had no intention of taking up residence in this hall. I believed that the alpha should be approachable, but I also believed that the alpha needed space. There was no space from the pack when you slept where they ate.

Housing myself here wouldn't accomplish what I needed. When Killian came back after delivering the message about the upcoming meeting, *my* message, I told him I needed to find somewhere to stay. He left again, and a few hours later, he returned, telling me to follow him.

Blueridge Hollow homes were single-story, cut into rock or immersed between and beneath trees. Killian had found a house that looked long empty, and as I stared at it, I thought back to my time here. As far as I could recall, it had lain empty then too.

"It has two bedrooms," he said in the quiet of the night. "It's more spacious than it looks. Needs a shitload of work done in it." He shrugged. "We've got pack back at Stonefang that can fix that easily." He jerked his head to a nearby home, smaller. "That one's mine."

"You'd live here?" I looked at him in surprise. "Stonefang has always been your home."

Killian glared at me, his tongue swiped his top teeth, and his words were sharp through the mindlink. *If this is where you tell me that I'm not your full beta, for however many packs you want to lead, then this is where I tell you to bite my ass.*

"Two packs," I grumbled out loud. "Two is more than enough." I folded my arms across my chest. "So you're saying…I have no choice?" I asked with a raised eyebrow. "I have no choice, I'm stuck with you?"

He grinned at me. "Of course not, you're my alph— leader. I'm saying to my *leader* that this isn't even a conversation we need to have."

I sniffed as I looked at the two houses. "I forget how needy you can be."

"Suck it, Wolfe," he said as he walked past me, shoulder blocking me on the way. "You need me here." He looked back at me with a gleam in his eye. "Because…well, because your *wife* is likely going to kill you. Someone has to watch your back."

I wasn't sure he was wrong about that either. "Another of your manifestations," I grumbled at him, seeing his feigned look of innocence. "Do me a favor, stop tempting fate, eh? What was it you said about no one expected me to marry her?"

"I'm completely innocent," he mumbled.

I kept my mouth shut, whether that was alpha wisdom or just good sense, I decided not to examine it too closely.

He swiftly changed the subject. "You know there are a lot more houses empty than I thought there would be."

"Yeah, I noticed that too," I told him. "There's a lot of work that needs to be done here." We exchanged a look. "Good thing I sent for help, right?"

He grunted in agreement. "We're going to need all the help we can bring."

By dawn, the air smelled of pine, old smoke, and expectation.

Killian had already gathered them. Elders, guards, even those who hadn't been on rotation in a while but showed up anyway. Which was good. That meant curiosity was doing its job. Or fear.

It didn't matter which, as long as they were here.

I stood in front of the old training ring where my predecessor had once met with this same assembly. It looked pitiful, much like some of the ones in front of me. There were twenty gathered. Maybe more. Some still waking up, some trying to hide their scowls. I could smell the tension in the air.

I let it sit. Let it stew a little longer. Let them get the

measure of me, or think they had at least, while getting the measure of *them.*

Then I stepped forward. "I'm not Malric," I said.

No greeting. No nod. Just the truth. Some flinched. A few straightened. One of the younger warriors blinked like he was waiting for the real speech to begin.

It didn't.

"I won't run this pack the way he did. I won't walk his path. I won't ask for permission to lead the pack already under my protection." A beat of silence. "The druid's rite bound me. But I was leader the moment I stepped over your border and smelled blood in your woods."

No one spoke. Good. I wasn't in the mood for interruptions.

"There are rogues pushing in from the east. Pack scent markers tampered with. Messages clawed into trees. I saw it. I tracked it. And I hunted it."

"Did you kill it?" someone asked—sharp and doubting. An older wolf. Not Council, not warrior. The kind who survived too long on stories and too little on service.

I let my gaze cut to him. I remembered him from when I was younger. Ezra. Surly but he'd been sharp in his younger years.

"No," I said. "Not yet. But I'll know him when I see him. And when I do?" I stepped toward him. "You'll smell the death on me before you have the breath to ask stupid questions."

Killian let out a single low chuckle behind me. A few shifters shifted uneasily. Ezra looked away.

I turned back to the group.

"You've had peace too long. And peace makes wolves fat

and soft. That ends today." Now they were listening. "By tonight, I want border rotations set, scouts mapped, and every shifter and elder briefed on emergency protocols. If you have questions, speak now. If you have doubts, take them to the Goddess."

Nothing. Not even a twitch. I let the silence stretch until it strained. "No questions? Then go," I said. "You have a pack to protect. A territory to defend. I'll be watching."

They dispersed quickly. Good instincts. I didn't need them to like me. I needed them sharp.

Killian sidled up beside me, arms folded. "You sure know how to say good morning," he said.

I grunted. "You think they'll listen?"

"They heard you," he said. "Doesn't mean they'll follow like you want. Not yet."

"I don't need their faith."

"No," he said. "But you'll need hers."

My eyes snapped to him. I hadn't seen her since last night. Hadn't sought her out either. Because this wasn't about her. It was about the packland. It was about fighting a war, one I *knew* was coming.

But even I couldn't pretend that everything hinged on dominance and planning. She was the Hollow's heart. And if I wanted to lead it? Eventually…I'd have to gain her faith, too.

I watched the pack scatter like dry leaves in a storm— pack wolves pretending they were ready for war when most had never even seen a proper skirmish, let alone bled for their territory.

Malric had kept them safe, sure. But safety made wolves complacent…and the complacent died fast.

I walked the inner path of the Hollow—low pine branches brushing my shoulders, the dirt beneath my boots soft with old needles and silence. I didn't need a guide here. I remembered these woods better than I remembered some of my own pack's names. This place had shaped me once.

I wouldn't let it do it again.

From the slope behind the training ring, I saw warriors starting drills. A few glanced my way. Their stances straightened. One dropped his fist mid-swing and his opponent promptly laid him flat on his ass.

Better. Still not good enough. I clocked each one—names Killian fed me earlier, assessments filed in the back of my mind. He'd been watching them for days, and they hadn't suspected a thing.

I turned toward the old forge—disused now, just a soot-stained skeleton with tools rusting on the pegs. That's where I found Lewis. Malric's second. Loyal to this land. Loyal to her. Smart enough not to speak first.

"Lewis," I greeted.

He watched me approach, jaw set, arms crossed. "You're moving fast."

"Rogues don't wait," I said.

"And neither do kings, right?" he asked dryly.

"I'm not a king."

"You are sure as hell acting like one."

I stepped into his space. Not threatening. Just closer than he liked. "You've got doubts, Lewis, I hear them. But if you ever voice them in front of this pack? I'll break you."

His eyes flared—offended, angry, and maybe just impressed enough to listen.

"I don't need your loyalty," I said. "I need your discipline. This pack doesn't survive without it."

"And Rowen?"

"Has no problem speaking for herself."

He huffed. "True."

I looked him over and saw what he was trying to hide: a man grieving his alpha. His friend. "I'm sorry for your loss," I told him, my tone shifting slightly. "I know how hard it is to lose someone, and you knew Malric a lot longer than most here."

Lewis sniffed as he looked away. "He was my closest friend."

"He will most definitely be missed," I said to him. "Your plan? Or have you not thought that far ahead?"

Lewis blew out a breath, looking away from me. "I don't know. I thought I would be better prepared." He glanced at me. "It wasn't unexpected, but still…"

"The death of a loved one is always unexpected, no matter how well we prepare for it." We stood in silence for a moment. Lewis turned to look at me, and I raised a brow in question. "What?"

"Do you want me to leave?"

I stared at him, genuinely confused. "Leave? Leave this conversation or Blueridge Hollow?"

He flushed. "Leave the pack."

My face must have shown my surprise because his ears got redder. "Lewis, you knew me when I was a scrawny kid sleeping in the pack hall; why would you ask if I wanted you to leave? For fuck's sake, this is your *home*." I hesitated. "Isn't it?"

"Yes," he mumbled.

And that pissed me off. "You think so low of me that I would kick you out?" I demanded softly.

Lewis shrugged. "You hear that new leaders want to clean the slate…and you *did* just say you'd break me."

"*If* you disrespect me in front of others." I pushed my hand through my hair. "Fuck, I was going to ask you to be an advisor…"

Lewis looked surprised by my admission and hopeful, if only slightly, but it was something. "You would ask that of me?" he asked carefully.

I shook my head ruefully. "You've been a beta, an advisor to Malric for *years*. Who else knows this pack's history, the factions, the allies, the adversaries, as well as you?"

He dipped his head slightly. "Well, all that's true…" He looked back up at me. "Rowen does."

"Does she?" I challenged him softly. "Does she *really*, or does she *think* she does?" I held up a hand when I saw his eyes harden. "I'm not saying she doesn't know her shit, but does she know *everything* you do?"

He rubbed the back of his neck. "She may not know it all," he admitted grudgingly.

Why would she? Half the shit would have been done before she was even born. I didn't say that, I simply nodded. "Think about it. Killian, my second, chats a lot. You'd be a welcome balance, if you chose to take the position, that is."

I turned and left him there. A small test. A bigger message.

Back near the central clearing, Killian was waiting with a rough-cut list of pack assignments in hand. He raised it like a peace offering. "They're trying to adjust. You know that, right?"

"Adjustment is for children," I muttered, taking the list. "This is survival." I ran over his list and glanced at him. "This reads more like a cry for help."

"They need a lot of work. I need help." Killian hesitated, then said, "She still hasn't come out of her rooms."

"She will."

"Because she wants to or because you're making it impossible to ignore you?"

I gave him a look that made him laugh.

"Fair enough," he muttered, then handed me another note—this one with the druid's sigil pressed into the wax. *Wax.* Fuck me, I hated theatrics.

"They want a word."

Of course they did. Old ways and older politics. Couldn't burn one without invoking the other.

"Fine," I said, tucking the parchment into my back pocket. "But if they start preaching fate again, I'm going to ask if the Goddess left us a manual—because right now, it feels like I'm writing one blind." I cast a casual glance across the pack, seeing no one was close to us, but I still opted for safety.

I asked Lewis, the old beta, to be an advisor.

Killian nodded, his look one of appreciation. *Nice. Clever. Keep them close.*

Yeah, and plus, he knows this pack better than us. Which was a true and valid point.

And he doesn't say much, Killian added.

"It'll be a welcome change," I said and saw Killian's fake outrage, but I left him, tapping my back pocket because a druid was waiting for me, and while I wasn't rushing, I sure as shit wasn't getting on their bad side. Not yet.

Brand, Cody, and Axel are on their way, I told him. *They'll need somewhere to stay while they're here.*

Already found something, he told me smugly.

The druid waited in their tent, where the walls were covered with old glyphs and the air smelled of crushed herbs and smoldering ash. They sat like they'd been there forever, cross-legged before the flame bowl in the center of the room, smoke curling around them like it answered only to their breath.

"*Alpha* Wolfe," they greeted me without looking up. "You arrived with blood on your boots, temper in your veins. Now you sit with bone on your shoulders. Do you understand the weight you've taken?"

I stepped forward, ignoring the seating cushion across from them. I stood. I wanted them to look up. "Better than most," I said. "You've got questions for me?"

"No," the druid replied, lifting their gaze. "You already know the answers—and you're hoping I'll say them first."

Clever bastard.

They reached for the fire bowl, fingers hovering over the smoke, drawing symbols I couldn't read. "Rowen is the daughter of this pack. You've taken her in bond. Claimed a place that was never yours by birth."

"No one is more surprised than me," I said dryly. "You were there when it happened."

The druid gave a small, knowing smile. "You came here because you think the Hollow will bleed. You haven't even seen it wounded."

"I've seen enough."

"You've seen enough to know the pack is fractured. Split down the spine between old ways and survival. Your presence is a blade in both directions."

"I'm not here to please everyone," I said flatly. "Being popular isn't my goal."

"No," they murmured. "You're here for something else."

They finally gestured to the seat across from them. I didn't take it. "Rowen will need more than bloodlines and fire to survive what's coming," the druid said. "She will need you to be more than the wolf with the sharpest bite."

"She doesn't need me at all," I said, eyes narrowing. "What she needed was for everyone outside of this pack to stop seeing her as something more than a birthing canal. I give her that."

"Ah," the druid said, sitting back, looking strangely satisfied. "And what do *you* need from *her*, Alpha?"

I didn't answer. Because that question had more claws than thorns. Instead, I turned toward the smoke bowl, watching the curl of ash rise and scatter. "What I need is Blueridge Hollow prepared," I told them, "for whatever's coming next."

The druid gave a low hum. Approval? Warning? I didn't care.

They reached for a clay jar at their side and tossed a pinch of dark powder into the flames. The smoke flared green, then gold. The scent was sharp and ancient. It clung to my tongue.

"You've lit the hearth," they said. "Now keep it burning. Or everything you've claimed will turn to cinder."

I stared at the flame. "I don't plan to burn," I said. "I *will* consume if I need." I held their stare. "Remember that, and next time, call me for more than riddles and light shows. I'm busy."

I walked out, not waiting for permission to leave, because I had no time for their crap and vague warnings.

The druid was a powerful figure, but they didn't run a pack. They didn't *build* a pack. I would make something real here—with claw, strategy, and a pack who knew where their loyalty belonged.

With me.

Chapter 19

Rowen

I HADN'T MEANT TO GO LOOKING FOR HIM.

Honestly, I'd meant to avoid him entirely. Let the silence stretch long enough for both of us to forget the truce after the wedding and the fact that I'd kept to my rooms for almost two days.

But the Hollow was buzzing with activity.

People whispering. People moving. Lines being drawn, redrawn, *shifted*. And when I followed the sound of booted feet and sharp commands…I found him.

Wolfe stood in the training ring with five of our scouts. Not barking orders. Not dominating them like some conqueror staking ground. No. He was moving among them like he belonged. Asking questions. Testing reflexes. Correcting stances.

And they were *listening*.

Killian stood nearby, arms crossed, watching like a guard dog with a vendetta. Three other males flanked him, clearly Stonefang Pack, because they were strangers to me. When the heck did they get here? I pushed that aside for the moment, looking at the other shifters around Wolfe.

They were of my pack. Blueridge Hollow wolves, and they were turning toward him like sunflowers to the sun.

I hated how efficient it all looked. How smoothly he inserted himself. Like he'd been here all along, just waiting for this to fall into his lap. I stayed at the far end of the clearing, watching. He corrected Marla's stance with a low word and a nod, then clapped another on the shoulder and moved on to the next.

Not arrogant. Not overbearing. Worse. Much worse. *Capable.*

I clenched my jaw, decided enough was enough, and began to walk to the practice ring.

He spotted me, of course. Eyes like a storm system— sharp, tracking every shift in the wind, monitoring for threats. He didn't smile. He didn't nod. Just watched me patiently.

"How are you?" he asked when I stopped in front of him. He was being nice; I wasn't ready for nice.

"Training?" I asked flatly.

"Assessment," he replied coolly. "You've got strong fighters, but their patrol patterns are outdated, and our eastern flank is soft."

"Oh, forgive me for running an *outdated patrol pattern*," I said, voice low.

Wolfe didn't flinch. "You've been keeping them alive. Now I make them dangerous."

I folded my arms. "And they weren't dangerous before?"

He stepped closer, lowering his voice so only I could hear. "You were the leader this pack needed to survive a failing alpha, and now you need time to grieve. I'm the one they need right now to survive whatever comes next."

It wasn't arrogance. It wasn't posturing. It was truth.

I hated him for it.

"I can still help," I reminded him, every word laced with conviction. "Remember, this is *my* home."

"Okay." His stare was hard, unwavering. "Let's start *helping* by remembering, I'm not your enemy." His voice was a low rumble, eyes locked on mine, ignoring my snort of disagreement. "If you focus your energy on not fighting me every fucking day, then maybe we have a shot at keeping this place from going under when the attack comes, because trust me, Rowen, it's coming."

I didn't reply. I turned to look at the training ring, an *actual* fighting ring. "Where'd this come from?"

"Ikea."

I was going to kill him. Goddess help me, I was. Instead, I smiled. Fake. For the benefit of anyone watching, and I knew they were *all* watching while they pretended to be *very* interested in their chores and their training.

"Ah, I remember," I said, keeping my voice light, "you tell jokes the same way as you kiss…" I shot him a look of malice with a sweet, saccharine smile. "Sloppily."

Wolfe smiled, but it didn't reach his eyes. Several of those nearby laughed, averting their heads so he wouldn't see them appreciate the joke. Killian had no qualms about laughing out loud. Feeling slightly vindicated, I looked around and decided to park this until I could discuss it with him later. He *had* said I could help after all.

"I need to check the kitchens," I told him, calm and controlled. "I'll speak to you later."

"I can't wait," he murmured.

I had walked a few steps away from him when he moved fast. Too fast. Fingers wrapped tight around my wrist, not enough to hurt, but enough to drag me backward in one unyielding motion. My breath caught as I stumbled into the solid wall of his chest. Heat radiated from him, wild and consuming, and before I could open my mouth to protest, his mouth was already on mine.

It wasn't gentle.

It was a *claiming*. A challenge. A dare wrapped in fire and frustration.

I tried to speak, but he didn't give me the chance. His hand slid from my wrist to the back of my neck, fingers tangled in my loose hair, holding me there, angled perfectly for him to deepen the kiss. His tongue swept in with ruthless precision, tasting, teasing, taking.

My thoughts shattered.

Because dammit, I was *reacting*. My fingers fisted in the front of his shirt, not to push him away—but to hold on. My knees buckled under the weight of the kiss, molten and merciless, my body arching toward him despite every single logical reason not to, feeling his hand press against my lower back.

Wolfe broke the kiss just enough to speak, his breath hot against my lips. "What were you saying, princess?"

I hated the smug twist of his mouth. Hated the sound of hooting and hollering from the pack. Hated that he had regained the upper hand so effortlessly.

Hated how much I wanted him to do it again.

"Say something now," he murmured, voice thick with heat, lips brushing over mine once more, tongue tasting my bottom lip, "and I'll make you forget your name. Right here."

Wolfe let me go, the gleam in his eyes victorious as the pack reacted to his *show*.

"I'm going to spit in your soup," I told him under my breath as I fixed my shirt. I looked up at him as the bastard tilted his head back and let out a roar of laughter.

"Adds to the flavor," he said when he looked back at me, grinning widely. He walked past, slapping me on the ass as he did so, making me jump, much to my pack's delight. "I'll see you at dinner, *wife*," he called over his shoulder. "Save me a seat."

I made my way to the kitchens, forcing a laugh out as people called out to me, commenting on our *playfulness*, and halfway across the clearing, I realized with bittersweet clarity that my pack was *laughing*.

Happy.

Wolfe wanted to show them a united front, wanted them to *want* to fight what may be coming for them, and what better way to do that than to show a leader and his wife as *united*. The worst part wasn't that he was right. It was that part of me—deep down, clawing at my ribcage—*wanted* him to be.

I'd intended to go to the kitchens. My mourning period was over, and while it pained me that I seemed to be the only one who mourned, I knew I needed to get it together, because Wolfe wasn't hanging about. Threats didn't wait until it was convenient for you, and Wolfe knew that.

Wolfe.

What the heck was that kiss? I knew I'd provoked him, but…I could still taste him. I had to stop myself from looking back over my shoulder like a lovesick pup. With a slight shake of my head, I knew the kitchens could wait; I needed a moment. I'd only been out of my rooms for twenty minutes max, and my world was spinning.

I didn't go far. Just to the outer path, where the trees gave a sense of peace, and the wind through the branches sounded like voices from a time when my world wasn't getting more and more out of control.

I couldn't breathe inside the Hollow anymore. I couldn't settle knowing my father was no longer here with me. Seeing his memory being erased in front of me was so hard.

Everywhere I looked, Wolfe's fingerprints were etched into the bones of my home—subtle, sure, spreading like frost under the door.

And the worst part? The pack *welcomed* it.

How could I blame them? This is what packs did. An alpha died or was replaced and the pack moved on. That's what we were meant to do. *Evolve*.

Wolfe looked like an actual alpha. Spoke like one. Moved like one. The kind that brought order out of chaos. The kind they'd follow into fire...and I resented him so much for it.

Not because he was unworthy—but because he *was*. He was who my father chose, and he was every bit the leader my dad had seen in him.

And it hurt.

It hurt so much that my dad didn't get to see him meet the challenge my dad had given him. It hurt that my dad would never see his pack laughing again, free from the burden of sorrow.

I sat on a moss-covered boulder and pulled my knees to

my chest, fists clenched in the fabric of my pants as I fought back my tears. I missed him so much. It wasn't fair.

Life was seldom fair.

I wiped my eyes with the back of my hand. I could still smell the smoke from the Binding rite in my hair, even though I'd washed it three times. Still feel the weight of it—of expectation, of grief, of the Goddess's unseen hand pressing on my back.

I was known as the daughter of the Hollow. But now? Now I was the wife of a pack leader. I needed more time to make the transition, but time seemed to be the one thing Wolfe wouldn't give me as he started to mold the pack to his way.

A branch snapped nearby, and I didn't look up.

"I said I needed space," I muttered, not looking up, not wanting to let him see my tears. "You had your fun," I added irritably. "Stop following me."

"It's a forest," Adair's voice replied gently. "You don't own it."

A laugh tried to rise. Failed. Relief filled me instead that it wasn't him. "Don't tempt me to try."

She sat beside me, her presence calm as always. Adair never asked questions unless she already knew the answer. Today, she just waited.

"I thought I was ready," I said after a minute. "I really did. I thought I could…keep going. Step up. Do what needed to be done."

"You will," she said quietly.

"Then why does it feel like I've already lost?"

"Because your dad died," she said gently. Adair tilted her head. "And because you thought you would fight alone."

I looked at her, bitter and tired. "It was supposed to be that way."

"But now it's not." She nudged me with her shoulder. "And that terrifies you more than any trouble coming, doesn't it?"

I didn't answer. We sat in silence for a few more moments, and then she stood, brushing off her knees. "You can resent him all you want, Rowen. But don't forget—you're still *you*. No one gets to take that. Not even Wolfe."

When she left, I stayed in the trees, watching the light fade. When I finally stood, the ash clinging to my pants fell like dust to the earth.

I might've married Wolfe, but he married *me*.

I smiled as I straightened my shoulders. We'd see who'd be laughing when this was over.

***

I HADN'T spat in his soup, and he hadn't kissed me again.

We were operating a truce—fragile, I was sure of it—but for the pack, we looked like we were settling into our new marriage.

Wolfe and some of the others were out on a perimeter run, and I had been busy all day with pack duties. I was halfway back to the main grounds from the stream that ran down the mountain before I felt it—the tension.

Not grief. Not respect.

Challenge.

It rolled over the air like a low growl. Subtle. Dangerous.

Some of the pack circled near the training ring again, but this time they weren't sparring. They were watching.

Confused, I moved closer. I'd heard Wolfe tell the others they'd be gone most of the day.

Standing in the center, arms crossed, wearing a self-satisfied smirk that made my blood simmer, was not Wolfe, but Kirk. He was older than me by a few years. Son of a warrior. Full of the kind of brittle, inherited pride that never learned to bow. The fact that he wasn't with the others was no surprise to me.

Kirk turned when he saw me. Loud enough for everyone to hear, he greeted me with scorn. "I thought pack leaders chose wives based on strength. Not sympathy."

My boots hit the dirt harder than I intended as I walked closer. I heard someone murmur something behind him, but he didn't flinch.

"You've got something to say?" I asked, coming to a stop just outside the ring.

Kirk smiled, and it was all teeth. "Just wondering how long the Council's puppet plans to sit as leader of this pack."

"Careful," I said, stepping closer. "You're starting to sound like a traitor."

"I'm just saying…" Kirk shrugged. "We buried Malric. The pack is ready to move on. But how can we? With two pretend leaders—one supposedly sanctioned by blood and the other by a ceremony that was so rushed it left a bad taste in my mouth."

The pack that had gathered shifted around us. Uneasy. Curious. Waiting.

"I didn't realize I needed an audience to prove my worth," I said, voice low. "Or that a *named successor* did." I cocked my head slightly. "Are you offering to challenge Wolfe?"

Kirk barked a laugh. "He's not my problem. You are."

There it was. Years of animosity reared their head. There was silence as I stepped into the ring.

"I'm not the one you need to fight, Kirk," I said. "But you're damn right I'm your problem now."

"Yeah?" he sneered. "You are." He looked me up and down. "You tried to take over this pack when your father was dying, and failed." His scorn was ugly. "So now you're fucking your way into position of leader." He spat at the ground, and I looked down, seeing his spittle on my boot.

Oh, he was going to pay for that.

I grinned because I didn't intend to hold back. I closed the distance fast. My palm struck his chest—just enough to force him to stumble back a step.

Dominance. Raw. Earned.

"You're right," I said, stepping into his space again, raising my elbow and catching him on the jaw. "I didn't take the mantle."

My fist drove into his gut, and I shoved him again. Harder.

"I'm *just* a female shifter." I punched him. "Who has *held* this pack together while my father wasted away. It's *me* who got ready to bury the man who raised me, and *still* showed up *every day* to lead this grieving pack."

Kirk growled, shoulders tensing, ready to strike, but I was already circling him.

"You think I haven't earned your respect?" My fist struck out, clipping him on the chin, but it lacked power when he moved at the last moment. "I didn't run from my responsibilities in this pack either." I dropped, swept my leg, and the idiot landed flat on his back when I took his legs from under him.

I rested my boot on his chest, message delivered.

"You want to lead Blueridge Hollow, Kirk? Challenge *Wolfe*. He is your pack leader." I looked around at everyone gathered, letting them see me. I looked back down at Kirk. "Or shut the hell up, never speak of this again, and remember who kept you alive when you were stupid enough to run your mouth." I wiped my boot across his chest. "Remember who I am," I spoke to more than just Kirk. "Remember who kept this pack together while you were shivering in corners, worrying about who was going to organize food orders, planting seasons, supply runs." I tossed my hair off my shoulder. "Remember who kept this pack together while you got ready to fall apart."

Silence.

Kirk stood up. He seemed ready to lunge—but he held back because he saw what he had forgotten, not a girl mourning her father, but someone ready to fight, someone who didn't care if she got bloody.

I turned and walked out of the ring; the crowd parted for me like mist. I didn't look back. Let them whisper their doubts. Let them weigh me with their eyes.

I knew they'd remember this.

I went to my rooms to wash the dust and sweat from my face, changed clothes, and went to the kitchen to find something to eat. I was halfway through peeling an apple when I felt him.

Not footsteps. Not sound.

Wolfe's presence surrounded me. I didn't turn. The air

shifted when he entered a room—dense, electric, *laced with judgment.*

"You put Kirk on his back," he said flatly.

"Tongues wag a lot faster when they're telling tales." I sliced the apple clean through, not looking up. I'd told the idiot to keep his mouth shut. "It was nothing you need to get excited about. He just needed someone to put him in his place."

Silence. Then the door clicked shut behind him. His boots hit the floor once. Twice.

I turned slowly to find him standing behind me, arms crossed, jaw tight. Not with rage. Or disappointment. But… possessiveness?

The kitchen was empty, and I hadn't heard anyone leave.

"Why didn't you tell me?"

I blinked. "Told you what? That I punched a packmate? Not the first time," I scoffed. "I didn't even know you were back."

"That someone challenged you *at all* is enough," he growled. "I'm pack leader here. They want to challenge anyone, they challenge *me.*"

My brows lifted. "So this is about your pride, then?"

"No," he snapped impatiently. "This is about the fact that while I was dealing with routine practices to keep this fucking pack safe, one of these *fuckers* thought he could take a run at what's *mi*—"

He stopped himself, but it was too late. The tension snapped between us like a live wire.

"Your what?" I asked, voice like ice. "Your *little* wife?"

His jaw clenched. "Is that what he called you?"

"It doesn't even matter," I said with a sigh. "You came in here throwing words around like you've earned the right."

"I've earned more than you give me credit for."

"And I've bled more than *you* know," I snapped in irritation. "For Luna's sake, Wolfe, you think Kirk's the first shifter to start shit with me because of who I am?"

Wolfe shook his head, looking away in frustration.

Finally, he took a slow breath and stepped closer, voice dropping low. "You handled it. I'm glad you did," he said slowly, as if he was choosing the right words. "I'm not angry at *you*. I'm angry that anyone thought they had the *right* to."

I swallowed hard. Because Goddess help me, I believed him.

"What are you going to do?" I asked him, concern blooming in my chest when I saw the raw fury in his eyes. "Wolfe? Don't hurt him. It was nothing, it's forgotten."

He looked at me for a long moment, gaze dark and unreadable.

"Don't hurt him?" His voice was a low, dangerous thing. "Is that what you want?" he asked me. When I nodded, his temper flared brighter. "Fine. But I will make sure no one ever forgets who the fuck my *little wife* is."

Stupidly, I poked the beast. "Careful, *husband*, it sounds like you care."

He froze, his eyes fixed on mine, the fire within him shifting to a different heat. He reached past me slowly, brushing against my arm and causing goose bumps, as he picked up half the apple. He remained still, our faces so close. Too close. His breath was warm on my lips, his gaze locked on mine, testing me as he moved an inch closer. I dared not move in case I did something stupid, like kiss him, which was exactly what he wanted, I realized when I saw the satisfied gleam in his eyes at my breathless reaction to his nearness.

He turned and left the same way he came—silent, controlled, a storm barely caged. Luna help me...I didn't hate the way he was making me feel, and that just wouldn't do at all.

Chapter 20

Wolfe

Killian had been told as soon as we got back.

"She laid him flat on his ass, apparently." Killian had the decency to wait until we were out of earshot of the others, voice low, like saying it too loud would set me off.

It did anyway.

"Kirk challenged her," I repeated, slow and measured. Like I hadn't heard it right the first time. "I remember him. He was a fucking dipshit back then. Age hasn't improved him."

Killian nodded. "He said she wasn't strong enough. Something like because she was female, she was weak."

"And the pack let it happen?" I glanced at him. "Say shit like that in Stonefang, a female will serve you your balls for supper."

Killian nodded in agreement. "The only redeeming thing this pack has so far is that they let her handle it," he said with a shrug. "They didn't intervene. She put him down fast. Clean. No hesitation."

That didn't settle the fury burning in my gut. She

shouldn't have had to handle this kind of bullshit at all. Not because she couldn't—but because someone should've made damn sure she never needed to.

"Spread the word, I want everyone in the clearing now," I told him. He didn't say anything, just peeled away from my side to do as I bade as I went to find Rowen.

Speaking with her hadn't helped. In fact, it made me worse. My blood was hot for her, and I had no idea how to resist the pull to her. It was making me irritable and rash. And while I would never be described as fluffy, I was never reckless.

I stalked across the dining room, ignoring greetings, nods, and submissive eyes cast down. I didn't care. My temper was too hot, too sharp, laced with the knowledge that someone had tried to fuck with her—while she was grieving—and tried to exploit that crack in her armor, and thought I'd do nothing.

They were wrong.

She'd been cool and collected when I spoke to her in the kitchen, but the fuse to my anger was already lit.

It was time to remind this pack who they now answered to.

I found Kirk in the shadows outside the pack hall, bruised and sulking, his jaw tight with a resentment he hadn't earned. He hadn't shifted to heal his bruise, which meant he *wanted* people to see it. He straightened when he saw me coming, and I knew he was thinking of running.

"I heard you had an opinion," I said casually as I walked forward, loud enough to be heard by anyone who was listening.

He swallowed hard. "Pack Leader Wolfe—"

"Don't," I snapped. "You don't get to speak." I looked him over. "I'm still envisioning ripping your tongue out with my bare hands, so hearing your voice is not in your best interests."

Kirk's hands curled at his sides. "She's not—"

"I said, *don't*," I cut in. I didn't take my eyes off him for a long moment until he got the message. He paled, but I wasn't finished. I looked around, seeing there were a handful of pack scattered around us.

I knew Killian would be rounding up more, but I had no patience to wait.

"I am going to make one thing very clear to you, *all* of you," I said, turning slowly to see the pack avidly watching. "Rowen is my wife. She is the wife of your *leader*, and as such, she gets the respect that *I* get." I met each stare. "She has fought for this pack. She has bled for this pack. She has *sacrificed* for each and every one of you." I'd turned full circle and was back to looking at Kirk. "What she has done for this pack, you wouldn't even know, *that's* how much her life has been *serving* Blueridge Hollow."

I let that settle.

"Alpha Malric was ill and failing for a long time, a *long* time," I reminded them. "Who do you think kept this pack going? Who do you think ensured that this pack wasn't at the attention of the Pack Council?" I took a breath. "Who do *any* of you think was bartering, trading, and buying your stock and supplies for the winter while Malric was bedridden?"

Most heads were down, and I hoped it was because they were hanging their heads in shame. The clearing was filling with more of the pack.

"You think the druid left this pack to make the journey to the human towns to get your fucking food?" My temper was rising again. "You think Malric's betas were going to be tolerated by nearby packs when they had to scavenge and *beg* to get you grain for your planting ground?" I snorted with disgust. "Did you see anyone else ready to marry a fucking stranger so your pack could continue?" My temper was flying high. "Tradition states only a male can be a pack leader," I said, my voice firm, as I tried to contain my anger. "But you fucking idiots have had your leader in front of you for years." I knew my voice was louder. "*Years.*"

I let that settle too as more shifters arrived.

"You never needed an alpha or a male," I reminded them all. "Rowen's been leading this pack without help, even though every fucking one of you have told her at one time or another that she isn't good enough, and she's still been fighting for you *all* for a *long* time."

The clearing was deadly silent.

I turned back to Kirk. "She kicked your ass today," I told him frankly. "And then she *asked* me not to tear your spine from your body for the disrespect you showed her. She *asked* me not to hurt you." The scorn in my voice was heavy. "Because let me make one thing very, *very* fucking clear to you all. This shit doesn't fly in my pack. Had you done this at Stonefang Pack, you'd already be dead." I swept my glare at the ones gathered. "Because members in my pack *respect* their leaders and the *females* in the pack as much as the males."

I rolled my head on my shoulders. "You've disappointed me. You've disrespected me. You disrespected my wife and this pack." I let that sit with them. "I am your leader. You don't like it, challenge *me*."

Kirk looked like he was going to faint at the thought of challenging me. I looked him over and dismissed him with a grunt of disgust, but I wasn't finished.

"I will let you grieve," I told them all coldly, "out of respect for Alpha Malric. But your mourning period is soon to be over. Tonight, you have a choice to make. You stay? You follow me, and you *follow* Rowen." I gestured to where Killian stood. "And you listen to what the fuck my second tells you to. You don't want to follow, you know what to do."

Stunned silence met my words. Killian came and stood beside me.

"Wh-what do you mean?" an older shifter said at the back. "You want us to leave?"

"If you don't like my leadership, then why the fuck would you stay?"

"This is my home," he spluttered in outrage.

"Yeah?" I nodded as I looked at the others. "Well, now it's mine."

A murmur of surprise rippled through the crowd.

"You don't even live together!" Kirk shouted, and I thanked Luna for the gift of his stupidity.

I turned, every muscle in my body coiling in anticipation. "What the fuck did you just say to me?" I asked him softly.

He stumbled back a step. "We all know you took the house, and that your man's with you. We know she's in the pack hall." He seemed to grow braver the more a hush settled over the pack. "You want us to respect her, but you can't even bring yourself to fuck her."

"She just lost her father, you fucking idiot," I snarled at him.

"Yeah, and what will your excuse be next week?" he sneered.

My movement was a blur of speed, and the deadly silence that followed as I stood in front of his crumpling body with his throat torn out made it so I didn't have to raise my voice.

"Rowen?" I knew she was there.

"Yes?" Rowen's voice was low but steady as she emerged from the shadows.

"I never promised you I wouldn't hurt him." I stooped and tore the shirt off him, using it to wipe my hands. "But I *did* intend not to, as per your request."

Rowen was paler than I had ever seen her, but she played her part well. "I know." It was a whisper, but I had no doubt everyone heard her.

A roar of rage crossed the clearing, and an older male was racing towards me. He didn't get far. Killian had him immobilized in a headlock in seconds.

I shared a look with Killian.

Let him challenge, Killian said through the mindlink.

He doesn't want my place; he wants to avenge his son.

"Let him go," I told Killian. I watched as the male seemed frozen between the two of us, his emotional outburst suddenly warring with common sense. He knew he couldn't fight us both. "You lost a son tonight," I told him flatly. "One death in your family is enough." I jerked my head to the two younger males who Axel and Cody were holding back. "Take your family, and make your decision to stay or go."

He hesitated, but both my pack let his sons go, and they came hurrying to their father, their hands circling his upper arms and pulling him gently back. Neither of them looked at their fallen brother or me.

"You have tonight," I told the pack. "When the dawn breaks, any who intend to leave should be gone."

"Is this how you will rule us?" Someone else's voice cut through the darkness. "With fear?"

I turned towards them. "I don't *rule*, I lead. I lead those who want to follow. This? This isn't to scare you." I gestured to Kirk's dead body. "This is what happens to those who insult what's mine. That includes my wife and members of my pack." I considered my next words carefully as I spoke to the pack. "This is the kind of leader I am. You accept me, or you don't. I don't care about the ones who choose to go, but I will fight till my dying breath for the ones who stay."

I turned away before I said something worse. Or did something I wouldn't regret. Like tear some more throats out. I didn't need the pack to fear me. But they would learn to respect what I stood for. Killian fell into step beside me as we walked away, and I could feel his approval through the link.

And Rowen? I turned back to her, seeing her still rooted to the spot, as I walked closer. "Pack your bags, princess, you move tonight."

"Move?" she asked, her eyes widening. "I am *not* leaving my pack."

"No, but you *are* leaving the pack hall." I didn't look around to know we were alone. "I just made a very big fucking statement for you. I'm not saying your mourning period is over, but you staying at the hall is. I'll send someone to help you move into our house."

I could feel her seething behind me, but she said nothing. She knew what I'd done here, more than her father ever had done for her when it came to establishing her authority in this pack.

She'd never need to fight for her place here amongst them again. That was my vow; that's what I'd given her tonight with strong words and one dead shifter. She knew it, and she'd accept it, even if she'd snarl in my face for making it happen.

You sure you want to sleep beside her? Killian asked with amusement. *I'm still not convinced she won't stab you.*

But think of how exciting bedtime will be.

He chuckled out loud as Axel, Cody and Brand fell into step behind me. I knew exactly what we looked like as we left the clearing.

A conquering leader and his betas.

They'd thought I was here at the behest of the Pack Council. They'd thought I was *controllable*. They thought I was *just* a pack leader.

They'd thought wrong.

SHE DROPPED her bag like she was daring me to flinch.

I didn't.

Not when she glared at me. Not when she spun back around and acted like this was her idea. Not when the scent of her hit me all over again—wildness laced with vanilla and orchid—seeping under my skin.

She was fire and resistance and a tempest I hadn't asked for. But I'd take it. I'd take her. Because that's what alphas did. We didn't wait for comfort. We made order from chaos. And Rowen was both.

"You're late."

"Hard to say goodbye to my solitude." She turned her head, just enough to meet my gaze over her shoulder.

"No one said you had to talk."

"Good," she barked. "Because I have nothing nice to say."

"I don't need nice." I stepped forward. "I need you where I can see you. Where I can protect you from the remaining idiots in this pack."

"I don't *need* your protection."

"Doesn't mean you won't *get* it."

Silence stretched taut between us. My blood pulsed, and I felt a whisper under my skin, under my ribs. I didn't know what it was, but I knew I didn't like it.

I leaned against the far wall, arms folded, watching her explore the space like it might bite her.

"You expected velvet pillows and flower petals?" I asked quietly. I crossed the room, slow and deliberate, until the space between us crackled. "This isn't about comfort," I told her. "It's about *claim*."

"So Kirk was right, you want a trophy?" She lifted her chin, the challenge in her eyes. "You want to pin me to your wall with the rest of your victories?"

I grinned at her insolence. "No. I want the shifters in this Hollow to understand *who stands beside you*."

"Well, they got the message," she retorted.

"They did," I agreed. "And I'll do it again until even the dumbest gets the message."

I saw her flinch, knowing that she would hate that. Rowen was angry, I knew it, and I *welcomed* it. It was about time she showed something more than *compliance*.

"Do you want to control me?"

"No." I stepped toward her, slow and deliberate. "I want you close because you're mine."

The words hung between us like a match about to catch flame. Her lips parted. Whether to argue or breathe, I didn't know. Didn't care.

"I married you. That's all." She held my stare with a steady gaze. "I don't belong to you."

"No?" My voice was low. "We'll see, princess."

She looked away from me, her breath halting as she absorbed what I'd said. With a sigh, she looked between the rough-made bed and me. "There's only one bed."

"Mm-hmm."

She stared at me in expectation. "I thought..."

"You thought I was sleeping somewhere where my wife wasn't?" I asked her, loving her trying to mask her features. "You still a virgin?"

Rowen glared at me like I'd just slapped her. "Not that it's your business, but no."

"Oh, it's definitely my business," I corrected her. "But you can drop the affronted maiden look," I said as I sat on the bed, enjoying her discomfort while I made myself comfortable physically and with the topic of conversation. "You're not a stranger to sleeping with a male."

"I'm not a whore," she spat with venom.

"Princess," I tsked. "No one implied you were."

"I don't want to sleep in the same bed as you," Rowen told me through a clenched jaw.

I shrugged, leaning back, putting my hands behind my head as I watched her. "Fine. Sleep on the floor."

She faced me then, and her eyes—Goddess, her eyes—were sharp enough to flay a lesser man.

"I am not sleeping on the floor!"

I grinned. "These are your options," I said, my voice smooth. "Your only options. You sleep in this bed with me, or you sleep on the floor in the same room as me. You will wear my scent, *wife*, so the backward fuckers in this pack know you're my wife in more than name." I held her furious glare. "The alternative is I throw you on this bed and fuck you right now until you're swimming in my scent. Your choice."

"That isn't even a choice," she hissed at me, her body practically vibrating with anger. "You disgusting pig."

I got to my feet smoothly. "I sleep on the left," I told her as I walked to the door. When I was beside her, I inhaled deeply, scenting her temper but also a hint of something soft, spicier. "Mm-hmm, princess," I murmured, my lips at her ear. "Someone isn't as outraged as they pretend." I dipped my head into the crook of her neck, feeling her stiffen at the movement. "Was it someone in this pack that took what was mine?" I asked her softly.

"Wh-what?" Rowen asked, her body humming with confusion.

"The lucky bastard that fucked you first." My lips skimmed over the column of her throat. "Who was it?"

Rowen's chest was rising and falling faster, her scent a

mix of fury and the tanginess of her arousal, an arousal she was fighting. "It's none of your fucking business."

She flinched when my hand ran down her back, over the curve of her hip, until I cupped her ass. "It was always my business," I murmured, desire pulsing through me, much to my ire. "I tasted you first, princess, remember?"

Her whole body was rigid, but her voice was calm. "I don't remember much about you at all, Wolfe."

Pretty little liar.

"Well, I'll need to change that," I promised her as I stepped back. "I changed my mind," I told her, seeing the flare of hope in her eyes. "No choices, you sleep with me in the bed."

The speed with which she schooled her features should have had her pack groveling on their bellies for thinking she was anything less than a fucking leader.

"Fine," she said coolly, turning her back to me. "But don't expect civility."

"I never do," I said, closing the distance until I was pressed against her. "But I always enjoy earning it."

"Don't hold your breath," she whispered lowly. "Actually, do. You'll suffocate before you have it."

I wanted to laugh with delight as she fought me. But instead I said, "Dinner in thirty. You'll sit beside me."

"Another warning?"

I met her gaze. "Another promise."

Then I left her standing there—angry, beautiful, burning in my room—because if I didn't, I was going to forget this wasn't real and kiss her like she'd already claimed my soul. But I wouldn't. I gave her my heart years ago, and she'd just reminded me I meant nothing to her then.

I'd be the one to break her this time. Mark my words.

247

Chapter 21

Rowen

My head was reeling.

My heart was thumping, and I felt like I hadn't had time to breathe since I'd been made to pack my things. I'd done as he directed because he had just stood up for me in front of everyone in a way no one ever had. Not even my dad, and it pained me to admit it.

So I had come to my rooms and began to pack my things. I'd shoved the majority of my clothes into a leather pack and cinched the tie hard enough to snap it. I'd stepped out of my rooms into the corridor, bag over my shoulder. Pack lingered in corners. Whispered. Watched. Their eyes weren't fearful, not anymore. They were *curious*.

I had crossed the clearing with long strides, ensuring those watching saw there was no doubt I was standing with my husband.

No doubt. Goddess, there was plenty of doubt. Piles and piles of doubt.

I hadn't looked at any of them as I walked here. I hadn't looked at the bloodstained grass where Kirk had fallen, even though I could still see the gaping mouths of those who'd watched Wolfe make an example of Kirk.

I left the pack hall, where I'd lived since the day my mother put a braid in my hair and told me this was where leaders lived. I made my way to share a room with the new pack leader. An *executioner*.

Not that he was wrong. Kirk had stepped out of line. Had tried to make a stand against the wrong person. *Me.*

Still. I couldn't shake the sight of seeing it. Wolfe had moved so fast. He hadn't even used a weapon, just his hands.

My pulse was still pounding from the fallout. From the way the pack had *watched* me after he'd done it. Because now I was part of the man who had declared himself as both protector and punishment.

No one questioned it.

Because Wolfe had just shown everyone, including me, that he didn't leave space for questions. He gave orders and executed judgments. And now...now he was offering me *proximity* like it was a favor instead of a prison sentence.

Goddess, what had I done agreeing to marry him?

I'd lied to his face. I remembered every little thing about Wolfe when we were younger.

I remembered the giddiness I used to feel at the thought of seeing him, of knowing I was going to sneak out of my room and race to our secret meeting spot and spend hours talking to him, sharing our dreams, letting him steal kisses under the moonlight. Until kisses became more, and his touch had been all I could feel the next day. We hadn't had sex, but we'd done everything *but* sex. He was my first kiss, my first touch, my first orgasm.

We'd been eager to take it to the next level, but then he went and ruined it all when he told me he wanted us to be married.

Ruined it. What a fool I had been at seventeen.

I let out a low breath, slow and controlled, as I tried to pull myself together. What a night. I wanted nothing more than to lie down, close my eyes, and pretend today was over. But I still had to go to dinner, and with another sigh, I knew I needed to change because *everyone* would be watching, and I needed to let them know that while everything was different, *I* was still the same.

Dinner was served in the pack hall. Same place it had always been. Same creaking benches, same carved beams, same air thick with herbs and meat and the heat of too many bodies packed in too close.

I walked in as I always did, no longer just the alpha's daughter, now I was the leader's *wife*.

And apparently, that came with new seating arrangements. Before, we all sat mixed, wherever we wanted, but I hesitated when I saw a long table set apart and barely made it two steps before I heard his voice.

"Rowen."

One word. Calm. Deep. *Commanding.*

Every head turned. I saw the flicker of discomfort in Lewis's expression, the slight frown from one of the pack elders. But no one stopped me when I shifted course toward the table's head.

Wolfe didn't look up when I sat beside him. Didn't smile. Didn't smirk. Just poured me a drink like we were any other husband and wife. My skin buzzed with the tension. I could *feel* the stares. Hear the whispers behind hands.

"Did you see her move?"

"She didn't argue."

"Do you think it's real—"

"She didn't even *flinch* when he called her."

The noise settled just enough for one brave—or stupid—voice to rise above it.

"So…Rowen," someone called from farther down the table. I didn't even bother to check who, wondering how, even after what happened with Kirk, an equally idiotic packmate thought this was a game.

"How's married life treating you?" A chuckle followed. "Wolfe going to be keeping you…busy?"

Beside me, Wolfe set down his mug.

Very slowly.

I was almost scared to look at him. The silence that followed was a full-body thing; it reminded me of the feeling you got when you held your breath for too long.

Then Wolfe smiled.

Goddess, it was the *worst* kind of smile—lazy, lethal, polite enough to be terrifying.

"I'm keeping her where she belongs," he said, his voice smooth as ice sliding across a blade. "Right beside me."

I could *feel* my face heating. Rage or embarrassment—I wasn't sure which. Probably both.

"She's not yours to keep," Tyler said. *Why the hell was he still here?* Stupid. So stupid. "You married her, not marked her."

Wolfe didn't move. But the shadows seemed to stretch a little farther under the table.

"Fuck, I forgot all about you," he said with a slow drawl, and I winced in sympathy at how totally emasculating that would be for someone as proud as Tyler. "Is that a challenge?" Wolfe asked, his voice lazy and bored.

Tyler blanched.

"I didn't mean—"

"Because, if it is," Wolfe cut in, lifting his mug again, "we can settle it right now." He looked over the other shifter with total disdain. "Are you still here because you can't go back to your father and tell him you couldn't even secure a marriage contract?" He tilted his head, arrogance pouring from him as he spoke to Tyler. "Would killing you do you a favor?"

The room held its breath.

I wanted to scream. Throw something. Crawl under the table—or maybe set it on fire. Instead, I reached for my knife, casually slicing into the venison on my plate.

"I've already married you, Wolfe," I said, forcing a warmth into my voice that I didn't feel. "You can stop posturing to impress me." I smiled up at him, seeing that he understood what I was doing, and he smiled back. It was as empty as mine, but it broke the tension.

A ripple of laughter sounded throughout the hall.

Wolfe didn't laugh. He leaned toward me, his voice a whisper only I could hear.

"Your knife's dull."

"What can I say?" I murmured back. "I like a little resistance."

He chuckled, a dark, soft sound. "You'll get it."

Luna help me, part of me already knew he was right. "Are you done threatening everyone?" I asked, my voice still low.

Wolfe sniffed as he leaned back. "They seem to react better to demonstrative action more than pretty speeches."

I didn't comment and concentrated on the food on my plate. I didn't touch the mug of wine placed in front of me. Not because I was being difficult, but because I didn't trust what might spill out of my mouth if I let even one drop loosen my tongue.

Wolfe, of course, was relaxed. Elbow on the table, long fingers wrapped around his cup, like this was any other night in any other pack.

"Eat," he said softly, as if the command were meant for my benefit alone.

"I am eating," I muttered.

He turned his head lazily, stormy blue eyes catching mine. "No. You're picking."

I pressed my lips together to stop the snappy retort; instead, I forced a lightness into my voice that I wasn't feeling. "Maybe I'm savoring."

He leaned in, voice just above the clatter of cutlery and low conversation, his voice thick with something I hadn't heard from him before. "You do that with everything, princess? Or just when you know I'm watching?"

My fork stopped mid-air as a pulse of warmth spread through me.

Focus.

"Stop calling me that."

His gaze was pure sin as he watched me. "Make me."

I inhaled sharply, turning back to my plate. *Don't rise to it. He wants you to react.* But he wasn't done. He shifted his leg under the table—just enough that his thigh brushed against mine.

I froze. He didn't move away.

"Tell me," he murmured, low and rough in that gravel-and-smoke voice. "Is it easier when they look at you like that? Like you're a symbol instead of a woman?"

I turned slowly, meeting his eyes. "You think I care how they look at me?"

He tilted his head. "No. I think you hate that they don't see you clearly."

"Unlike you?" I said, voice tight. "You think you're the only one who knows me?"

"No," he said. "But I'm the only one who remembers how heartless you are."

A dig for my earlier remark when I said I remembered nothing about him. Fine. I blinked once, slowly. "So this is the game we're playing, then? Nostalgia, bruised pride, and thigh contact?"

"Maybe." He smirked, while his hand lay on my thigh, squeezing, inching higher than was right given where we were. "Or, maybe I'm only just getting started."

His hand brushed the back of my chair, fingers grazing the top of my spine like it was nothing. Like we weren't surrounded by people who'd gossip about this for a month.

I sat up straighter, forcing an easy smile on my face as I turned to face him, knocking his hand away. "Quit it, or I will stab you with my blunt knife."

Wolfe's grin widened. "Use the sharpest one. I'll show you where it tickles."

I choked on a laugh—damn him—and shoved back from the table. "I'm done."

"Mm-hmm, good call." Wolfe rose with me, not a

second's hesitation. "We're done for the night," he said to Killian.

Now everyone was watching. Pack members paused mid-bite, eyes flicking between us like they weren't sure if they were about to witness a lovers' spat or a political coup.

I didn't care right now. Let them whisper. Let them wonder what we were. Allies? Rivals? Married in name only?

They'd find out soon enough. Because this thing between us? It wasn't cooling down. It was just beginning to blister.

Someone called for Wolfe's attention, and I took the opportunity to leave without him. The second I left the hall, I felt the tension leave me. Or it tried to.

The cool night air wasn't cool enough. Not after the inferno Wolfe had just lit beneath my skin. I stalked away from the hall, past the fire pit, heading for the edge of the tree line like it might give me clarity.

Boots walking steadily fell behind me. Confident. No rush.

I didn't stop walking. "Do you get bored following me, Wolfe?"

"I do love watching that ass when you walk away," he taunted.

I spun, fast, hands clenched. "Do you ever listen?"

Wolfe was already too close. Arms at his sides, head tilted, like I was amusing, not dangerous.

"I listen when it matters."

"To who? Certainly not to me."

"To you most of all," he said. "Which is why I'm out here. You walked away."

"Because if I stayed, I'd have broken a plate. Possibly over your head." He stepped closer. I didn't back up. "You enjoyed that," I accused. "You're enjoying *all* of this too much."

"The dinner or your anger?"

I gave him a long, seething glare. "You really don't care, do you?"

"I care," he said, voice low. "But not about the things you think I do."

"Enlighten me," I said, tossing my hands up. "What does the great *Pack Leader* Wolfe care about, then?"

"Fairness," he said simply. My breath caught. He took another step forward. "Respect. Strength. I would have bled for this pack once—and will again, if needed."

"Then why this charade?" I said in exasperation.

A calmness settled over him that made me want to back up a step. "Is that what you think this is?" he asked. "A performance? Something where I'd put on a show to stake my claim, just to say that I got you?"

"No," I whispered. "I know you didn't want this marriage," I admitted grudgingly. "But I think you like reminding me I'll never be free of you."

He was silent, and then he murmured softly, almost cruelly. "You're right. You will never be free of me, Rowen."

My spine straightened. "And you will never be the alpha this pack lost."

He moved so close I could feel the heat of him again. "But you're going to accept me one day, *wife.*"

"I'm not afraid of you."

"You should be."

We stared at each other. Two storms, no eye between us.

This pull between us wasn't tugging anymore—it was dragging. Tearing at old wounds and twisting new ones open.

The tension was building between us, and I needed to walk away, and quickly. "You're in my way," I said.

He smiled, eyes dark with challenge, and he gave me a slow smile. The smile of a predator that knows its prey has nowhere left to run. "Am I?"

I shoved him. *Hard.* He didn't move an inch—not one inch. I stepped back. Enough for my palm to slam into his chest, for my pulse to spike, and for the tension between us to crack.

"Don't you dare," I breathed. "Don't you dare stand there and play games with me."

"Play?" he growled, closing the distance I'd tried to put between us. "Do you want to play, princess?"

"We have bigger problems," I snapped at him. "You killed someone tonight, there's rogues out there you said, killing, and you want to stand here in the woods with me to, what, *toy* with me?"

His hand rose slowly and deliberately, brushing a strand of hair behind my ear. His fingers trailed down, grazing my jaw. "Toy with you." He said it as if it were a new idea to him. "What does *toying* with you look like, hmm?"

"Wolfe," I whispered—but my voice broke as I struggled to fight the sheer raw animal magnetism of him, and I knew exactly how cliché that sounded coming from a shifter. Was it because he was so much *more* than he had been before? I'd never felt a pull like this to him when we were younger.

"What if I want just a little taste?" he asked, reaching out and pulling me into his hard body, and Goddess help me, I went. "You used to be my favorite flavor."

He was going to kiss me, and I was going to let him.

I let him close the distance. His mouth crashed into mine, all teeth and heat and vengeance. There was no gentleness, no soft, tentative searching. This was the kiss of a man who took what he wanted and didn't care about the consequences.

And me? I kissed him back just as hard.

My hands fisted in his shirt, dragging him closer. His arms wrapped around me, one hand at my lower back, the other threading into my hair as he backed me into the nearest tree.

Bark dug into my spine. I didn't care.

He kissed like he was trying to erase the last ten years and every inch of distance we'd fought to put between us. I bit his bottom lip, and he growled—actually growled—into my mouth. The sound went straight to my core.

Then his thigh slipped between mine. A hiss escaped me as he pressed upward, and delicious heat filled my body at the contact.

"Rowen," he rasped, forehead pressed to mine, eyes locked on mine as I pushed down against him.

I didn't stop. I couldn't. I should have.

His hand slid down my side, slow and claiming, fingers tightening around the curve of my ass before pulling me flush against the hard line of his cock. I gasped, the pressure sparking deep in my belly as he ground against me—deliberate, punishing, perfect. His other hand moved with ruthless precision, unfastening my pants, dragging them low enough for cool air to kiss my thighs before his hands covered them—hot, rough, and unbearably skilled. He cupped my pussy like it belonged to him, then stroked through the slickness he found there, dragging a moan from my throat as one finger slid deep inside me.

I clung to his shoulders as he pushed in a second finger, nails biting into muscle, chasing the friction as we moved together—our rhythm instinctive, filthy, maddening. Every breath was a gasp. Every thrust of his hand sent pleasure tearing through me, high and sharp, building toward that edge I could already feel trembling beneath me.

So close. So close I could taste it as I rode his hand, chasing my release.

And then—I froze.

My heart thudded in my ears.

What the hell was I doing?

His breath hitched. And slowly, painfully, he pulled back. We stared at each other. Breathing like we'd run miles. His hands still on me. My body still trembling.

"Shit," I said, voice barely a whisper. "This wasn't supposed to happen."

"No," he agreed, eyes dark and wild. "But now it has."

He stepped back first. Hand withdrawing slowly, trailing over my body. He let me go. Just like that. I hated how cold I felt without him.

"I'll see you at home," he said—home, like we'd already built one together—and turned to leave, jaw clenched, body tense.

I didn't stop him this time.

But my fingers were still curled like they were holding onto him, and my heart was still racing like it was running toward something I couldn't name.

That couldn't happen again. Ever.

I walked the long way back to the house, but the packlands were surprisingly *full* tonight. Was it because of Wolfe in general or what happened earlier?

I could still feel every eye on me, every conversation that didn't *quite* continue once I passed.

Adair was up ahead and I made my way to her. She broke off her conversation and smiled at me in welcome.

"Why does it feel like everyone's talking about me?"

"Probably because they are."

I blinked. "What?"

She grinned at me. "You and Wolfe."

My stomach dropped.

Adair gave me a sweet, too-innocent smile. "Apparently, pine trees carry sound really, *really* well."

I blinked again, leaning forward to whisper at her. "No one *saw*—"

"Oh, I don't think so," she said lightly. "They may have *heard*." She made a not-so-subtle gesture to sniff me. "You definitely smell like him."

Someone walking nearby coughed. The kind of cough that carried snickering undertones. Further down the path, two older she-wolves were whispering behind their hands and *not even pretending* it wasn't about me.

My ears burned.

Adair leaned in. "For what it's worth," she murmured, "you got them talking. The pack was starting to wonder if the mating was just for politics. Now?"

"Now they think I threw myself at him in the forest?" I hissed at her.

"They think it's *real*." She looked me over, a small smile on her face. "And, Rowen? Most of them are happy about it. Look how quick he is to defend you; they love him for it."

I stood frozen for too long. Up ahead, Wolfe walked into view a second later, licking his fingers like they were his favorite candy. I felt everything go *still*.

He didn't look at me, but the heat that bloomed low in my gut at the sight of him was completely, utterly *inappropriate*. Because the entire pack was watching like we were the headlining act in their favorite drama.

And me?

I'd been caught kissing the hero of the show—only to me, he was the villain.

Chapter 22

Wolfe

She slammed the front door behind her like she meant to break something with it.

Honestly? I almost wished she had. Would've saved us both a conversation.

I leaned back against the kitchen counter, arms crossed, heart still pounding from the feel of her in my arms in the trees, the taste of her on my tongue. Every shifter in the Hollow now believed this marriage had teeth—and Rowen? Seemed like she just figured it out, and she was *livid*.

I watched her, the smirk playing about my mouth as her glare narrowed in on me with laser focus.

There she was—this was the girl I remembered. The one with fire in her belly and rage in her soul. She needed to stop pretending she could lead this pack with polite nods and strategic silences.

Unrest didn't wait for consensus. Neither did I.

She stood there in the hall, furious, wrapped in a too-thin tank and loose drawstring pants that clung to her hips like temptation carved in cotton. Her scent hit me first—sharper now, laced with something raw and resentful.

"You *scented* me," she said flatly.

I said nothing.

"You—" She took a single step forward. "Just now. In the forest. You *scent*ed me. You *marked* me like you had the *right* to."

Still, I didn't speak. Because yes. I had. Not with teeth. Not with blood. But with instinct. Because it wasn't *just* about dominance, it was *need*.

"Say it," she hissed, stepping closer. "Say that this isn't all some twisted ploy to get me into your bed."

My nostrils flared. "You're not in my bed. Yet."

Her chin lifted. "Never."

I moved. Fast enough that her breath caught as I crowded her back against the wall. I didn't touch her.

"I didn't scent you to manipulate you, princess." My voice was low. Dangerous. "I scented you because every shifter in that hall had eyes on you, and my wolf wanted to rip half their throats out."

"Are you serious?" Her eyes narrowed. "So this is about jealousy?"

"No," I said, stepping even closer, "I told you, this is about *claim*."

Her breath stuttered. I caught the flicker of heat behind her glare. And I hated how much I wanted to chase it.

She shoved me. Hard. Not enough to move me—but enough to make her feel in control. I gave her the space she craved. She walked away from me, crossing to the far end of the living space, arms folded tight.

"I was right, this is a game to you."

"No," I said quietly. "You're not listening. Your pack needs to see us united. This is how we do that."

She turned. Slowly. "What's that supposed to mean?"

"It means what I already said. If I have to bleed to make them believe you are mine, I will. If I have to."

She stared at me like she wasn't sure whether she wanted to slap me or kiss me. Hell, I wasn't sure either.

"Do I have to?" I asked her in a low voice. "You didn't seem to mind too much…" I turned toward the back of the house that led to the bedroom. "Don't even think about sleeping on that couch. You sleep beside me, in *our* bed, or you don't sleep—that's the only choice you get."

Her voice followed me, brittle and biting: "You're full of shit, Wolfe. You're not doing this for the pack. You're doing it because you're a controlling bastard."

I paused at the threshold, glancing back just once. "Control is earned. Being a bastard was a bonus."

I left the bedroom door open. I went to the bathroom and started the shower. In the two days since Killian had found this house, the pack had worked tirelessly to make it habitable. Killian had been correct; the bones of the house were fine, the rest was cosmetic.

The pipes had needed minor repairs, the wiring had taken a little longer, and the cleaning had been made light due to the amount of pack that helped. It wasn't fully restored, but the bathroom, the bedroom and the kitchen were in order. The rest would follow.

As I stepped under the spray of hot water, I felt the pull of her—through the wall, across the silence, beyond the damn void that was created between us all those years ago.

I *was* being a bastard, making her sleep beside me, but

this pack needed to smell my scent all over her. They may not have followed her as their sole leader, but that didn't mean she wasn't their precious princess of the pack. I could toy with her, as she called it, but I think she'd be surprised at how quickly most of this pack would rise to defend her if they thought she wasn't willing.

She *was* willing, she proved that in the forest. But…that didn't mean I *couldn't* play with her, just not *break* her. Plus, it would be fun. I remembered how eager she was in my arms, and bit back my groan.

This was going to be a long night.

When I came out of the shower, a towel around my waist, she was already lying on the top of the covers, in the thinnest, sexiest black satin nightgown I'd ever seen.

"What is that?" I asked before I could stop myself.

She looked down. "My nightdress…why?"

Temptress wrapped in satin and lace. "What happened to the flannel bottoms and inspiring slogan shirts?" I asked, forcing myself to sound casual.

"Um…I'm not seventeen anymore?" Rowen arched an eyebrow. "Anyway, it's too warm for that. Those are winter sleepwear." She looked down at her chest, a finger running along the curve of the lace, and I knew she knew *exactly* what she was doing. "Problem?"

Sneaky wife.

"Wear whatever you want," I told her, holding her eye. "Wear less if it makes you more comfortable."

"We'll see how I feel," she said easily, returning to her book. "I have shorts and camis, but I didn't pack everything."

She called my bluff and I was fucking speechless at the

thought of her in tiny sleep shorts. I could feel her smugness as she read her book, and I forced myself to move and get ready for bed.

She wasn't as immune as she appeared, I noticed, pretending not to catch glimpses of me as I moved around the room.

But I wasn't sure which one of us won the silent contest, because I was having difficulty keeping my eyes off her, so to call her on sneaking peeks at me would make me a hypocrite.

I would not bite, I told myself. The control was mine. Not hers. I usually slept nude, but with her lying there in hardly anything, and the taste of her lingering in my mouth, I knew I wouldn't be able to hide my hard-on. I was glad I'd pulled on sleep shorts after my shower.

They wouldn't help. This night would be torture, and I was going to suffer through every second of it.

THE SCENT of bacon hit me before I stepped into the kitchen—smoky, familiar, and definitely not expected. I hadn't stocked the fridge since I moved in because I hadn't really moved in yet. Plus, I wasn't a breakfast guy. I was an "eat on the move" kind of guy.

Which meant that not only was Rowen up, she'd made herself comfortable. I stopped in the doorway and leaned against the frame, arms crossed.

She didn't glance up. "Kitchen's neutral ground," she muttered, flipping a strip of bacon with more aggression than necessary.

"Didn't say a word."

"You're thinking loudly." She turned and pinned me with a glare. "Relax. I'll replace whatever I eat."

"I'm not worried about food," I said, not bothering to tell her I didn't know where it came from.

"Then what?"

"I'm worried about the way you're manhandling that frying pan. You trying to seduce me with violence?"

A flicker of amusement passed over her face. Not a smile. Not quite. But close. "Trust me," she said, "if I wanted to seduce you, I'd use better weapons."

I barked a short laugh and stepped farther into the room. She was barefoot and I ignored the rumble of approval my wolf gave. That damn tank top was back. And my shirt—*my* shirt—was tied around her waist like she didn't even know what it was doing to me.

She did. I had no doubt she was using her *weapons* with alarming accuracy.

I grabbed a mug, poured myself coffee. Watched her over the rim. "You always cook like you're preparing for war?"

"I always live like I'm preparing for war."

We stood there a beat too long. The only sounds were bacon crackling, the drip of coffee, and my heartbeat banging like it wanted out of my damn chest.

Her arm brushed mine as she reached for a plate. Just a touch. Nothing, really.

But it felt like fire.

She stilled. So did I.

I turned my head slowly and met her eyes. Her pupils were blown wide. Her breathing had changed.

She felt it too.

"Rowen…" I warned.

"No," she snapped, eyes blazing. "Don't you dare."

I grinned at her ferocity. "Don't I dare what?"

"Act like this means something. Like we're just…falling into place."

I didn't say anything because my body had already betrayed me.

So had hers.

The tension crackled. One move towards each other, and we were going to burn. I stepped back first because I had to. Because if I didn't, I was going to pin her to that counter and give the pack something real to gossip about.

And this game? This war of wills between us? It wasn't over yet.

"I need to go on perimeter runs," I muttered, turning for the door.

"Great," she said too brightly. "Use the time to check your ego."

"Will do, princess," I said with a laugh as I headed to the door.

"Wait, Wolfe!"

I turned, and she handed me a breakfast sandwich. "Breakfast." She didn't look at me, and I said nothing as I took it from her.

We hovered there, two people unsure of what to do next. Rowen's eyes flicked up at mine and looked quickly away again. That one look broke the spell.

"You don't need to cook for me," I said quietly.

"I know." She turned back to her plate and started making her own sandwich.

I didn't reply. I left before I did something stupid. I left the silence behind, because that silence? It was starting to sound a lot like want.

The door slammed behind me with more force than necessary. I told myself it was the frame sticking again and made a mental note to look at it later.

I knew it wasn't.

The morning air hit like a slap, but it did nothing to clear my head as I ate my breakfast sandwich in three bites. Damn, even the way she cooked bacon was fucking delicious. Goddess, this wouldn't do at all. I needed to get my head back in the game.

We didn't even like each other, why were we both fighting this insane attraction? An attraction that shouldn't exist.

I stalked toward the woodpile at the edge of the tree line, hands clenched, breathing unevenly. This wasn't how it was supposed to go. She was supposed to be distant. Distrustful. Cold, maybe. But manageable.

Instead? She smelled like temptation and need, like every instinct I'd buried years ago was clawing its way to the surface, howling for her, and that shouldn't have been possible.

There was a constant *pull* towards her—a tugging in my gut—that shouldn't be there. It felt more like *want* than lust, and fuck knows I didn't need an excuse to lust after her. She felt perfect in my arms.

"Fuck."

We were faking it. *Pretending*. Going through the motions for the sake of a pack and a legacy and a dead man's last wish. But my wolf didn't give a damn about any of that. Not when she touched me. Not when she looked at me with fire in her eyes and defiance in her soul.

I saw a woodpile, and in an act of desperation to clear my mind, I decided to chop wood and get this *aggression* out of my body. I gripped the axe beside the chopping block and slammed it down into the first log. It splintered instantly.

Yes, this is what I needed.

I lifted the axe and went through the methodical routine of chopping wood as my heart pounded. Not from the swing but from *her*. From the whisper of her scent on my clothes. From the way my wolf had gone still the second she brushed against me, like he'd just come home.

From something deeper. Something ancient. Something I didn't recognize but *my wolf did*.

"You look like you're going to punch the forest in the face," Killian drawled from behind me, arms folded like he hadn't just materialized out of thin air like some smug little specter. "Want to tell me what she said that made you go full lumberjack rage?"

I didn't answer. Just yanked another log into place and shattered it with one clean strike.

Killian whistled low. "I'm going to assume this is less about firewood and more about that look on your face. You okay?"

"I'm fine." Classic lie. Weak.

Killian snorted. "You're sweating through your shirt, and your wolf's pacing like he's about to jump out of your skin, because your eyes are fucking glowing. Try again."

I set the axe down, jaw locked. "It's not her. It's not—" But the words burned on the way out.

Killian stepped closer, gaze sharpening, his mouth drop-ping open. "Oh, shit." I didn't say anything, my silence was enough. He blinked like he couldn't believe it. "You're feeling it?"

Silence.

He dropped his voice. "Holy shit, are you feeling"—he looked around quickly, ensuring we were alone—"a *mate* bond?"

I turned my face away. The wind shifted, and I caught the faintest thread of her scent on it—like warm skin and coming rain. And fuck me, my chest ached.

"It can't be," I muttered. "We're just faking it, it's just… it's nothing."

"Unless it was never fake," Killian said, carefully step-ping closer. "Unless this—her—it's real."

I hated how much I wanted to agree. How much that possibility made my wolf settle.

"It makes so much sense." Killian exhaled, rubbing a hand over his jaw. "But, not going to lie, that complicates things."

I snorted. "Understatement of the year."

"If she's your mate…" He hesitated. "You sure you want to keep playing house like this is temporary? And um…the *other*, other thing you haven't told her yet."

"I don't know what I want." Another log. Another swing. Splinters everywhere. "But I know what my wolf wants."

I didn't want this. I didn't trust this. Mates were sacred, yes—but they were rare. Rare and *permanent*. An alpha didn't choose his mate. The Goddess did, and fuck, I wasn't ready to be chosen. Not by Rowen. Not when she hated me. Not when I still carried the wound of her turning me away all those years past.

But the way she smelled…the way her skin had warmed when I got too close…the way my wolf was pacing now, circling the scent she'd left behind like it was already ours… because it *was*.

She was my destined mate.

Fuck. Me.

I dropped the axe, breath ragged, avoiding Killian's wide-eyed stare. This was more than strategy. More than duty. This was Luna's claim…and my instincts had already answered.

Killian watched me quietly. Then, with the exasperated patience of a man who knew me too well, he said, "What do you do now? Stop treating her like the enemy and start figuring out what this actually is before you screw it all up?"

I let out a slow, bitter laugh. "Too late for that."

I pressed my hand to the bark of the nearest tree, trying to ground myself. Because I could handle enemies. I could handle war. But Rowen, with a mating bond starting to bloom in her blood?

That was a battle I had no idea how to win.

Chapter 23

Rowen

I couldn't sit still. Not for long.

I finished breakfast, unpacked the food delivered to the house from pack well-wishers, and then reorganized everything in the kitchen pantry—twice, like I ran a grocery store. Then I moved through the house he had chosen, noting what needed to be done and what could be improved. I found myself in the bedroom, staring at the bed as it sat there in silent accusation. I straightened the sheets and left again, trying not to remember how I had woken up curled into his side this morning.

I folded a blanket on the back of the couch. Made tea I didn't drink.

Something was off. Not wrong. Just...*off*.

I could *feel* him. Even from outside, even across the grounds. Wolfe's presence settled in my bones like an itch I couldn't reach. I told myself it was just because we were sharing a house now. Sharing air. Sharing walls.

But I'd spent years pretending I didn't feel anything at

all. And now, every time he came close, it was like my skin remembered him before my brain could catch up.

I hated it.

I hated that I *noticed*.

A breeze pushed through the open window, and I caught the scent of woodsmoke and something…warmer. Something male. Dominant. Familiar in a way I didn't want to unpack. I shut the window hard enough to make the frame rattle.

"Rowen? You okay?" I turned to the voice that came from the hall behind me. Adair was there, a basket of herbs in her arms. "I've been watching you from outside. You've been pacing for twenty minutes. Either you're plotting a murder or trying to calculate how many steps it takes to walk off sexual frustration."

I laughed at her crudeness. "Shut up. I am not…frustrated." I was, I really was. I saw more of the pack milling about outside, waiting patiently. "What's happening?"

"We're fixing the pack leader's house up for him," Adair said easily. She grinned at me again. "Just saying, you're twitchier than a pup with her first heat."

"Because I'm trying to survive sharing a space with a man who thinks growling directions at me is foreplay," I snapped waspishly.

Her eyebrows went up. "You think it's foreplay?"

"I think he *thinks* it is."

I didn't tell her about the look in his eyes earlier. The way his voice had dipped. The way my name had sounded in his mouth—dark, ruined, reverent. I didn't tell her about the need to climb his body like a tree.

I sat down on the edge of the couch, pinched the bridge of my nose. "He's up to something."

Adair nodded slowly. "Of course he is. He's a male. They're *always* up to something."

"No." I looked at her. "This feels different. Like he's—maneuvering. But not just politically. Personally."

"Well, you did marry him."

"It isn't real."

Her smile was soft. Pitying. And a little infuriating. "No, but the way he looks at you? It could be if you wanted it to be."

I shook my head, rising again, pacing the floor. "No. No, no. This is a game to him. Power consolidation. Territory gain. This is about the pack. About the Pack Council. About his *ego*."

"Or maybe," she said, voice quiet, "it's about you."

I hated the lump in my throat that rose at that. I hated that it *wasn't* rage I felt anymore. That it was *confusion*. That maybe, just maybe, under all the fighting, I was starting to wonder if Wolfe was the only one who had ever seen me for who I was—and liked what he saw anyway.

"I can't be here," I said to her, striding for the door. I stopped and looked back. "Do you…do you need me here?"

She shook her head, fighting a smile. "Nope, we're pretty much ready to go, and hopefully we'll be finished today."

I nodded, my eyes scanning the group of workers waiting for me to leave. There were two or three women, and I knew I was frowning as I took in their lithe figures and pretty, arranged hair.

I turned back to Adair. "Only you in the bedroom." I

spoke fast under my breath, in a rush to get the traitorous words out. "Only if you have to."

I would die if she laughed, and thankfully, she merely nodded, and I practically ran out the door before the sound of her amusement followed me. What was happening to me? I was becoming territorial over who was allowed in our bedroom.

Our?

Goddess Luna, what have you done to me? I demanded as I made my way to the pack hall.

I shrugged off the crazy feelings and sense of *wrong*, and by the time I got to the hall, I was determined to start the morning with purpose. Spine straight, lists to conquer, and orders ready.

Routine was my armor. Always had been. I started in my rooms, packing up what I thought I would need, having a clearer idea of what I was heading into. I should have been proud of how quickly the pack had transformed an old, unused house into a functional one; instead, I only resented their competence.

When I was done with my final packing, I made the rounds—checked in with Lewis about the border shifts, only to be told Wolfe had them in hand. I smiled and bit my tongue. Then, when I went to update the rotation for the hunting patrols, one of the younger pack told me that Killian had taken care of that this morning. I nodded, brushing it aside. It was fine, it was part of the change. But when they started talking excitedly about training rotations with the males from Stonefang Pack, I put my politeness aside and left them without another word.

In the kitchens, I discussed the weekly menus with the

ones who prepared and did all the cooking. Ordering and checking supplies for the food halls was the same as ever. My voice held the same weight as always.

Feeling better, I went outside and saw three of the scouts at the far end of the clearing. I made my way over, like I had done many times before. They chatted easily and were like they always were. Respectful but reserved. Or so I thought. At first…they listened. They participated. Heads dipped. Nods were given.

But then came the looks. Small at first. A glance over my shoulder. A subtle pause after I made a suggestion or gave an instruction. I caught it from the corner of my eye —one of the scouts hesitating before moving, eyes scanning the ridge behind me like he was waiting for confirmation.

"What are you looking at?" I asked, looking over my shoulder. I saw Wolfe and Killian just beyond the tree line, and I knew the answer to my question.

They were waiting for Wolfe.

I turned back and saw three very bashful faces. "Really?" I asked, my voice low. "I've run this pack for almost a year. Is there something different you think he—" I hesitated. I could not show scorn for their leader; I needed to be more diplomatic. "Is there something you think that he'll suggest to you that I haven't?"

They all shook their heads, and I didn't show the grace I should have. I simply gave a curt nod, a grunt of agreement, and walked away. I wanted to keep walking right to the edge of the ridge and scream into the void.

I didn't. We were supposed to harvest our small crop of corn in a week, and I needed to make sure we had everything ready. But it happened again—Wolfe had already taken stock of what was needed and changed the schedule.

Fine. It was earlier than I would have harvested, but it wouldn't make too much difference. All morning, it happened again and again. He'd already either done something or they were looking past me *for* him.

Even Lewis, steady as stone, hesitated to answer one of my directives until Wolfe emerged from the trail nearby. Not to correct me—just to exist. Breathe in the same damn space. That was all it took.

The moment he was in view, the pack settled. Like the gravity of him reset their instincts. It burned. Hot and heavy and familiar. This was what had always been denied to me —instinctual trust. They trusted him before he even opened his mouth. They trusted me only if I proved myself first.

And I was tired of proving myself to wolves that had been raised alongside me, grown on the same land, and learned the same rites.

I clenched my teeth and moved on. I knew that my pack would follow my orders. But their ears…their hearts…were already open to him.

Wolfe hadn't even looked at me. He was talking with Killian, his shirt slung over his shoulder, abs on display, broad shoulders catching the morning sun, nodding at something one of the guards said, the ash mark of our marriage bond clearly displayed on his shoulder. My eyes narrowed on the three males who were not from Blueridge Hollow; it was time they were introduced to me.

All five of them turned to me in unison in a strange synchronized move that I doubted they even knew they'd done—it was so automatic and smooth. Somehow, the four of them positioned themselves in front of Wolfe as if he needed protection. It should have been amusing because he stood taller and broader than any of them, and the glint in his eye looked much more dangerous than any of the group on a good day. And every single one of them looked dangerous, but none of them looked like Wolfe.

"Wife." Wolfe growled the word like it insulted him, causing Killian to give him a sharp look and a not-so-subtle nudge.

What the hell was that?

I ignored the way the word *wife* curled from his lips like a curse. I pretended to ignore Killian's side-eye and sharp elbow, though I tucked that little moment of friction between them into my pocket. I'd dissect that later.

Right now, I had shifters in my territory—*my* territory—who hadn't so much as bowed their damn heads to me. The three strangers—Wolfe's entourage, no doubt—stood like they were forming a shield wall. Instinct or training, I wasn't sure. But it rubbed my wolf all the wrong ways that they were keeping him from me.

I smiled. The kind of smile that made warriors shift on their feet.

"How nice," I said, voice saccharine and just sharp enough to cut. "To see Stonefang Pack sends his finest. Though I wasn't aware *we* were hosting a parade."

One of them—broad shoulders, shaved head, the type who probably did a thousand push-ups before breakfast just to feel something—had the audacity to snort.

Wolfe didn't move.

Didn't say a word.

So I stepped forward.

"Is there a reason you're in my territory, in the patrol quadrant, without informing Lewis or myself?" I asked, voice clipped.

"You mean *our* patrol quadrant?" another said. Dark-haired, bright-eyed. "Wolfe told us to scout the perimeter."

I let that settle between us like a gauntlet on the dirt. Then I looked at Wolfe. Really looked. "Is that so?"

He didn't flinch, but I noticed a flicker of irritation—or maybe amusement. "I said they could assist," he said smoothly. "They have eyes. And teeth. They know how to use them."

"They don't know this terrain," I argued, feeling my frustration bubble over. "And they sure as hell don't know our scent trails. Which makes them a liability *not* an asset."

One of the Stonefang wolves growled low. Just enough to stir the air. Wolfe's head turned so fast I barely saw it. "Stand down," he ordered.

The growl vanished.

"I'm sure they meant no offense," Wolfe added, voice thick with irony. "After all…you're my wife."

The air changed. Even Killian stiffened. The others looked at me like I was a puzzle that had just grown fangs.

I took a step closer until Wolfe and I were toe-to-toe. "If you think calling me your wife *repeatedly* makes me yours—"

"I don't think it," he said, low and deadly. "I *know* you're mine."

I refused to react, even though my blood was singing at his words of possessiveness. Wolfe leaned down, just enough that only those standing next to him could hear his next words.

"Remember your place, Rowen. You wanted the pack to see you lead? Then act like you belong at the top."

He stepped past me without another word, and damn him—I *couldn't* stop myself from watching him walk away.

I spent the rest of the day going through my usual routine, and then I'd come back to the house on the pretense of adding my own touches to it. I hadn't meant to linger. I hadn't meant to miss dinner at the pack hall.

I'd eventually told myself I was going to bed, that I was done overthinking everything.

But the house was too quiet.

And Wolfe wasn't inside.

I spotted movement through the back window and instinctively pulled the curtain back a finger's width—just enough to see him by the tree line. The scent of him sneaked through the open window, and my fingers curled into fists as I took a greedy gulp of air.

He was alone, shirtless, and splitting logs. No aggression. No fire. Just precise, controlled motions that spoke of routine, not rage. Every muscle flexed under his skin. His back moved with clean, lethal power, the kind that didn't need to be loud to command attention.

I should've looked away. I meant to.

But then he paused, leaning on the axe handle, and tipped his head to the side like he was listening. Not to the woods. To something in him.

And then, slowly, like it cost him something to admit it even in private, he whispered, "Rowen."

My heart jumped. I didn't move.

He looked toward the house—toward me—eyes

narrowed, as if he sensed me behind the curtain. As if the air had shifted around us, even with walls between us.

"I don't know what this is," he murmured, barely audible. "But it's not going away."

He dragged a hand down his face, then raked it through his hair, frustration and something more painful written in every motion.

Not lust. Not power. *Longing.*

I stumbled back from the window like I'd been burned. That wasn't strategy. That wasn't control.

He stormed into the house about ten minutes later, and I jumped like I hadn't been preparing for him. I was on the couch, and Wolfe stopped short when he saw me, growled something under his breath, and then strode down the hall to the bedroom.

The door slammed behind him, and I sat there for a moment, reeling from the sheer *energy* coming off of him. Did I follow?

Well, if I was going to share this space with him, then I better go see what was wrong with my husband. It could be something that I could fix for him if it was pack related.

I raised my hand to knock on the door and caught myself in time. This was where *I* lived too, so I opened the door with a confidence that I wasn't feeling.

"Wolfe? I—"

He was naked.

Naked.

Not one stitch of clothing on. Nothing. Everything was...bare. We were shifters, and clothes didn't shift with you when you changed forms. I'd seen plenty of naked people in my life. Lots. Tons.

None looked like him.

I swallowed. I stared. I may have forgotten how to breathe. My gaze traced over every inch of him. *Every* inch of him.

"My eyes are up here," he growled, and my eyes moved up to his.

"I—" I turned abruptly, giving him my back. "I didn't know you'd be naked." I sounded so stupid.

"It's fine. I'm sure I'm not the first naked male you've seen."

He sounded furious at the very thought. "Um, no. Of course not. The first one was my dad."

Wow.

That sounded…wrong. So wrong.

"I mean, obviously in a non-sexual way, and of course it wasn't even anything like that, you know that, and oh my Goddess, why am I making this worse?"

Warm hands curled over my arms. He was behind me, solid, present, warm, *and naked*. "I don't think I've ever seen you rattled," he said, his voice low, amused.

"You're still naked," I whispered, my body unnaturally still as he seemed to press closer and I felt his thick cock press against me.

"I'm going for a run," he said, still close, still there. "You want to come?"

"*Yes.*"

"I mean on a run with me," he murmured, his voice laced with laughter.

"Oh my Goddess." I was going to die of embarrassment. "I'm okay here, you go." *Please.*

"I'll see you later." He stepped away, walked past me,

and I heard furniture move aside as he changed form to his wolf.

He was outside before I had a proper look at him, realizing I hadn't seen his wolf since he returned, but he was already gone.

As my heart slowed down from its racing, I knew I had a new problem. The fact that he was taking over wasn't the immediate threat; it was the fact that I was insanely attracted to him.

I had no idea which one was more dangerous.

Chapter 24

Rowen

It hit like a punch to the ribs.

One second, I was marching down the eastern trail, barking orders at Lewis about rotating border patrols—despite what Wolfe said—and the next, I was doubled over behind a supply shed, breath locked in my lungs, my wolf clawing to the surface with a howl that didn't quite make it out of my throat.

No. Not now.

My heat hit me unawares. It couldn't be this soon. It had never been this close to one that had just passed. A heat was not the same as a monthly cycle, it was a *need* to mate.

I clutched my stomach; it was nerves. That was it—I'd been under a lot of stress. I lost my father, my alpha. I was married to the male I rejected when I was seventeen; there was a *lot* going on in my life. Of course I was stressed. The only way I wouldn't have been feeling the stress was if I were dead, and I was very much alive.

I straightened slowly. It was stress. That was all.

A flare of pain, sharp, sudden, and wrong, stabbed

through me. My skin prickled, *burned*, and my mouth went dry.

Oh Goddess, it was my heat. I almost sobbed.

My thoughts were scrambled, but not about Lewis, or the patrol schedule, or the farce with the suitors.

No. It was *him*.

Wolfe.

I reached out and grabbed the corner of the shed, using it to pull myself upright as I shoved the thought away, but it was already too late. The moment I inhaled, the moment I caught the faintest trace of oakmoss and black pepper, and whatever damn scent he carried like a brand, I knew.

My body knew. And worse…so did his.

Because before I could move, before I could straighten up and force myself back into control, I felt him. Not just his presence—but that unmistakable ripple that shouldn't exist, tugging at the very center of me.

"Please, Luna, please no," I whispered fervently as I leaned against the shed just for a moment. This couldn't be happening. Not after everything. "I can't go into heat with him here," I begged the Goddess softly.

But she wasn't listening to a mere shifter like me.

I turned—and there he was. Still as a stone. Watching me like a man facing a fight he'd long ago resigned himself to losing.

"Rowen," he said softly.

The way my name sounded in his mouth, like it belonged there, burned me.

I stepped back. "Don't."

The tic in his jaw pulsed. "You're in heat."

"No shit, Wolfe."

His eyes were dark. Torn. Hunger and fury and something that looked a little too much like pain warred across his face.

"I didn't know this would happen," he said, his jaw clamped like it was carved from marble. "What do you need?" he asked me, his hands in fists at his side. "Do you have—" He looked ready to kill someone. "Do you have someone who…" He stopped. He looked like he was in physical pain, which would have been funny if I hadn't been the one in *actual* pain. "Do you have someone who *helps* you with…this?"

"*You're* in pain?" I laughed, but it cracked halfway out of my throat. That was unnecessary, I scolded myself. He was trying to be helpful. "I need my rooms," I told him, my hand pressed into my lower abdomen as the heat built. "My old rooms," I added. "I have—" Fire licked along my veins, and I let out a whimper. "Goddess, please…" I begged softly. "I need to get to my rooms."

"I can help."

That did it. "Well, fucking help!"

I shoved past him, but he followed, silent until he was beside me. His steps matched mine, as if we were being dragged by the same current. Which we were. And no matter how fast I ran, his wolf kept pulling back.

I wanted to scream.

Instead, I almost doubled over as another surge swept through me. "Why now?" I asked, not expecting an answer.

His voice was rough. "Because whatever we are, whatever this is—it never died. It waited."

I couldn't breathe. *What did he mean?*

He stepped closer, eyes on mine. "You feel it too. The pull to me?"

I did. Goddess help me, I did. But I wasn't ready to say it. Not to him. Not when everything between us was raw and broken and laced with too many wounds that hadn't healed.

"It's nothing," I whispered. "It's nothing," I repeated frantically, avoiding looking at him.

He stepped closer. I could feel the heat radiating off him.

"It's not nothing, princess." His voice was like gravel, but there was no malice in it. Just need. Just restraint wrapped in barbed wire. "You think I like knowing that every cell in my body is screaming to claim you and I can't fucking move because I know you'll hate me for it if I do?"

I looked up at him, seeing the tightness around his eyes, the way his nostrils flared, the way his hands kept jerking like he was restraining himself from grabbing me.

Goddess, he looked like he meant it.

Neither of us moved. Neither of us touched. But the throbbing was there, thick as blood and just as dangerous.

When I finally spoke, my voice was barely a breath. "It changes nothing."

His eyes locked on mine. "It changes everything."

A fiercer stab of pain, want, and need had me on my knees. "For fuck's sake, Wolfe, *help me*. Get me to my rooms." My head was almost on the gravel as my body curled in on itself. "They can't see me like this," I whispered, tears running down my face.

"Who?" he sounded confused, but he inched closer.

"The pack," I told him, my fists pressed into my belly as

if I could punch the need from my body. "They've never seen me in heat."

"Ever?" He sounded surprised.

I didn't give a damn if he was surprised. I needed to move, but my legs were no longer strong enough to support me.

"Wolfe, I need you to help me," I told him again. "Get me to my old rooms."

"I can't."

For one moment, fury overrode the pain, and I glared at him. "What do you mean you *can't?*"

"I gave them to my pack to use."

I stared at him. I was going to kill him.

"My rooms are warded," I snarled at him. "My scent is contained in my fucking rooms, so when I go into heat—" I gasped as my body clenched. "I can be *alone* and ride the fucking thing out."

"I'll take you home," he murmured. He stepped forward and stopped. "*Fuck.*" He sounded as bruised as I felt. "I don't think I can touch you," he said with so much disgust I recognized it for what it was.

Self-loathing.

"Yes, you can," I told him, willing myself to stand, settling for a bent-over crouch. "You're the strongest, stubbornest asshole I ever met." I was panting. "Take your wife home." His eyes flared a pale silver, and I almost fell over in surprise. "What the—"

I didn't get the chance to speak; I was grabbed and thrown over his shoulder, then he was *running* through the forest. I couldn't focus on what hurt more: the way my body bounced off his shoulder or the burning pain in my stomach.

Too soon, I was offloaded and dropped on a bed. I didn't know where I was, and I didn't care. My wolf was clawing at my insides to get out, but I fought with every fiber of my being. I had the sense of being lifted again, and then I was screaming in fury as I was dumped under the ice-cold spray of a shower.

"Wolfe!"

"Stay under," he growled, pinning me to the wall. "Stay under," he muttered frantically, pressing in behind me, "or I *will* fuck you over every inch of this house."

I heard him. He didn't want to take me like this; it was our shifter instincts trying to rule us. For both our sakes, I pressed my head against the tile, and I sobbed. His body curled over mine and he clung to me as I fought to hold onto my control.

We ended up curled up on the floor, damp and miserable. The first wave ebbed, and I could breathe a little easier. I pulled away from him, but strong arms pulled me back.

"No," he murmured, nose buried in my wet hair.

"It's okay," I told him tiredly. "The first wave has passed." I reached behind me, catching his hand, giving it a slight squeeze. "I have time before the next one."

Slowly, I got to my feet, and my body felt like I'd rolled down an entire mountain.

Wolfe stood, and the two of us exchanged a wary look. He handed me a towel, then strode past me. I heard the front door open and close, and I knew he had left.

I sagged onto the bed, not caring that I was wet, not caring about anything other than I needed to refuel before the next phase. With a sigh, I got up and headed to the kitchen.

I didn't eat.

I tried, Goddess, I tried. I sat in the chair in the living room of the house I now lived in with Wolfe—my husband in name, my rival in truth—and stared at the food on my plate while I waited anxiously for my heat to rise again.

I couldn't move past one simple fact. Wolfe was as affected as I was. I could feel it in my bones. In my blood. In every heartbeat that came too fast when he was near.

Why?

Wolfe had barely spoken since the encounter by the shed. But what would he have said? His presence alone was louder than any words. The way he had stayed with me, resisted the need to touch me, fuck me, that took enormous restraint. Huge control. *Huge.*

I knew his wolf was pacing beneath his skin. I had seen it. I had seen his eyes change, meaning his wolf was too close to the shift. But he hadn't acted. I wouldn't have believed it if I hadn't been there to see it. Or feel it, because I'd spent most of the night with my eyes squeezed shut.

And my wolf? Mine was curled up and waiting for him.

Betrayer.

The room felt too quiet. Too aware of its occupants. Me, alone. For now. I knew he'd be back. Where was he? Was he with someone else?

The sheer fury of my snarl at the thought of it scared even me. I set the plate down with a shaky hand. I stared at the window in front of me, jaw tight, breath shallow. I could see my reflection in the pane. Pale skin, hair a mess, wide eyes, a sheen of sweat across my brow.

He would never. I knew it with more certainty than anything else. He would come back. I didn't know when, didn't know how long he'd give me, but Wolfe would come.

And sure enough—I heard his heavy, deliberate footsteps.

I didn't look up as he entered the house.

"You okay?" he asked, voice low. Controlled.

"My heats usually last three days," I told him quickly. "The first bit is usually the worst. If you could ask your friends to leave the rooms, I can go—"

"No," he said. "You stay here." He looked at the untouched food on my plate. "You didn't eat?"

"I wasn't hungry."

A long silence followed.

"I was," he murmured finally, "but I didn't eat either."

I glared at him, fists clenched. "Is that supposed to mean something?"

He stepped closer, anger flashing in his eyes. "It means you're not the only one whose wolf is crawling under their skin."

I stared at him. At the broad frame, the bulge of his biceps under his T-shirt, the heat radiating from him like a threat and a promise all in one.

"You don't get to act like this is hard for you," I snapped.

"Trust me, princess, it is *very* hard for me." His lip was curled into a sneer. His voice was sharp now. "Don't mistake my kindness for weakness."

I pushed myself to my feet and walked past him, or tried to. His arm shot out and caught mine. Not hard. Not rough. But firm. A reminder of who he was. Of who we were.

I turned on him, my anger flaring like wildfire. "You don't get to touch me."

His jaw tightened. "And yet here you are—shaking with anticipation."

"I'm not—"

"Don't lie." His voice dropped. "You feel it. You know you do."

I did. My body betrayed me in every way it could—heat pooling low, breath catching, heart thundering.

We were nose to nose now. One move. That's all it would take.

I hated him. I *craved* him.

"It's never been like this," I whispered, the words scraping out of me. "Why? What changed?"

"You've been through a lot." His voice was tight with control.

The power in his voice hit like a gut punch.

"I know what this is now," he said. "I feel it."

"Feel it?" My voice broke on the edge of a whisper. His scent was all around me, tempting me. "You…" I couldn't believe I was going to say it. "You can do it," I whispered, need coating my tongue. "You can ease it…"

"No," he said, and that single word stole the air from my lungs.

"No?"

"I want you to *choose* me because you want *me*, not just my cock."

He let go of my arm. Stepped back. Because he could. Because he wasn't going to take what his wolf wanted.

And Goddess help me—that was worse.

"Go to bed, Rowen," he said. "I'll sleep here tonight." Then he walked past me like his whole body wasn't on fire.

And I let him go.

Because if I didn't, I wasn't sure who I'd be when the morning came.

I hurried to the bedroom and wished the door locked. I wished I could chain myself to the wall. My body was crawling with lust once more.

I couldn't breathe. It wasn't panic. It wasn't even my heat.

It was *him.*

His scent lingered in the air like smoke after lightning struck—wild, electric, undeniably his. My legs wobbled under me, the heat rolling low and sharp in my belly, an ache starting to spiral.

No.

No, no, no.

I gripped the windowsill tighter, knuckles bone-white as I stared out over the small yard, where Wolfe was shirtless again, *of course*, and driving a post into the ground like it had personally insulted his ancestors.

My wolf was no longer curled up quietly. It was pacing now, tail high, ears twitching. Waiting.

Pining.

It was sickening.

I shoved the window open and gulped fresh mountain air, but it didn't help. Not when the breeze carried his scent straight to me—tangy pepper, the deep richness of oakmoss, and something deeper. Something dark and *mine.*

Heat.

Real heat. Spiked through me.

This wasn't like last time. Last time I'd survived it. Just me, locked in my quarters, teeth gritted, body wracked, refusing to let instinct win. But this? This was different.

This was him. His scent. His voice. His *dominance.*

A firm tug in my core felt like nothing else, and I stayed bent over as a sense of certainty settled over me.

He had resisted the need to claim me. His will had been so strong.

Will.

"No." My denial was a whisper of horror, and I felt what he'd so carefully hidden from me since his return.

The power of an alpha.

I stumbled back from the window, chest heaving, skin damp.

My wolf *knew.* It knew what I'd been denying. What I'd *refused* to consider. And now, cornered by biology and fate and the cruel twist of whatever cosmic joke Luna was playing on me…I finally saw the truth.

Wolfe wasn't just a pack leader.

He was an *alpha.*

And worse? He was *my* alpha.

My *mate.*

I dropped to the floor, shaking, lips parted on a gasp. He'd known.

He'd known.

He'd scented it, felt the tether, *walked back into this Hollow knowing exactly what he was*—and said *nothing.*

Rage rose fast and hot, clashing hard with the pulse of desire thudding low in my belly. My body wanted him. My wolf *craved* him.

But *I?* I wanted to rip him apart. I staggered to my feet. My wolf howled in my chest, a mix of grief and euphoria.

I wasn't sure if I was going to kiss him—or kill him.

But I was going to find out.

Chapter 25

Wolfe

FEET POUNDED ACROSS THE DIRT, FURY LACED IN EVERY STEP.

I didn't turn. That energy—untamed, sharp as a blade, and twice as personal—could only belong to one wolf.

She didn't call my name. That wasn't her way. She stormed into view like the Goddess herself had set her alight. Eyes blazing. Cheeks flushed. Breathing ragged.

And fuck, she smelled like—

Mine.

Every step she took forward, my wolf howled in triumph. But I stood still. Grounded. Steady. Because one of us had to be.

"You knew," she spat. Not a question. An accusation.

I met her gaze without flinching. "Knew what?"

"You knew." Her body was shaking with adrenaline. "You knew you were an alpha, and you said nothing?"

The tic in my jaw jumped. "What would you have done if I had?"

She froze. Her hands clenched at her sides. "That's not your choice to make."

"You're wrong," I said softly. "It was no one else's choice *but* mine."

She stepped closer, chest rising and falling. Her scent hit me like a hammer to the chest—heat and pain and everything primal between.

"You came here knowing you were an alpha," she hissed. "You came here and—what? Stood back. Watched. Played games."

"I came here to make sure that a girl I once knew wasn't treated like a hunk of meat at a trading market," I said, voice low. Controlled. "I stayed because an alpha named me his successor." I fixed her with a hard glare. "You know?"

"Yes," she hissed. "I feel it," she spat with rage. "You did this?" she demanded, like I had summoned it from thin air.

"No," I said, stepping closer. "Neither of us gets to make this choice, you know that."

That stopped her. Just for a second. But her eyes still burned.

"You kept it from me."

"I didn't owe you an explanation," I growled, stepping into her space. "Not when you looked at me like I was the mistake that ruined your life."

She shoved me. Hard. Hands flat to my chest. I didn't move. I let her rage crash over me like a wave hitting stone. Let her spit the fire that had been burning her alive.

"I hate you," she said. "I hate you for this. I wish I never met you. That I'd never let myself—" Her voice cracked.

And my wolf snapped from my control. I grabbed her wrists—not to hurt, just to stop the shaking. "Say it." She shook her head, tears spilling over. "*Say* it, Rowen."

"You left me!" she roared, eyes shining. "You left and

you never came back! You said I meant something—then vanished like I was nothing!"

Silence.

When I spoke, there was nothing but truth in my voice. "I left because you told me to go."

She blinked. Trembled.

"I left because you looked me in the eye and said you'd rather die than be with someone like me," I reminded her. "And I believed you."

Her lip quivered. But she didn't back down. "You're my mate," she whispered.

"Yes."

She breathed out, slow and shaky. "I don't want this."

"No," I said. "You do. You would want to be an alpha's wife. You just don't want to be mine." I leaned in, voice just for her. "But your wolf does."

Her breath caught.

"And mine?" I said. "Would raze this mountain for you."

I let go of her wrists. Didn't touch her again. Because I could see it now—in her eyes, in the way her body fought itself, in the war she waged between fury and instinct. The pull between us was real. It was more than physical attraction. It was destiny. The mate bond was active. Triggered into play with her heat, and we were both losing ground.

"Go back inside," I told her, low and calm. "Before I make good on every promise your scent is begging me to keep."

"I won't sleep beside you." She pulled herself to her full height, her head held high like a queen.

"Then you won't sleep. Your choice." It was the second time I'd said this to her, only this time it was heavier because need was riding both of us too hard. "Get in the fucking house, Rowen," I said quietly, my voice tight with anger. "If I touch you again tonight, I won't stop until I've fucked the heat out of you. Understand?"

"This isn't over," she hissed before she turned and practically ran to the house.

I looked up at the sky through the heavy canopy above me. "I don't know what you're thinking, but you have time to change your mind."

The Goddess didn't answer.

"So…that's intense."

I looked across at Killian, who was leaning against the side of his house. "How much did you hear?" I asked with a sigh.

"Did *I* hear?" He shook his head. "All of it. But it's not me you need to worry about."

I closed my eyes in resignation. "Shit," I groaned. I opened my eyes and saw him watching me. "Gather them in the hall for me?"

"On it." He gave me a sympathetic smile and turned to round up the pack.

The pack who now knew I was their alpha and hadn't told them. The pack who now knew I was mated—and married—to their former alpha's daughter.

This was not how I wanted this to go, but you played the hand Luna dealt you. Or you cleaned up the mess you made, and I'd made a mess of this.

I looked at the bedroom window, seeing the shadow of Rowen as she paced. I couldn't leave her here. Could I? I couldn't take her with me; I was likely to spread her out on a dining table and feast on her.

With a growl, I headed into the house and made my way to the bedroom. Fury and judgment met me when I opened the door and entered the room.

"The pack knows," I told her with no tact at all. "I have to go address them in the pack hall. Will you be okay here?"

"I want to come."

"You're in heat, Rowen. You come with me, I either bend you over a dining room table or kill every male in the room who so much as looks at you. What would you prefer?" I pulled on a clean shirt.

She looked resigned when she spoke. "I'll stay here."

I nodded curtly. "Good girl." I walked out of the room. "Three of my pack are outside. Don't try to get past them; they have orders to chain you to the bed if they have to."

"You've changed so much I no longer recognize you," she whispered as I started to close the door.

"I didn't change, Rowen," I told her. "I grew up."

I walked to the pack hall alone. I passed few of the pack along the way, and I hoped that was because they were already gathering in the pack hall. I stepped into the clearing just as the sun dipped low, the last rays slicing through the pines and casting long shadows across the space. The pack hall was already cast in shadow, and I had a fleeting thought about how fitting that was.

When I walked into the hall, the pack was waiting. They always were. Watching. Weighing. They stood clustered in loose groups—guards, hunters, elders. Some curious. Some tense. Some suspicious.

It was good they were here. They deserved answers.

I didn't raise my voice.

"Let's get this over with," I said, stepping into the center. "You've got questions. So here's the truth."

The silence that followed was so tense it felt sharp enough to cut skin. Killian moved to the back of the hall, and I knew it was so I could see him and so he could see *everything*.

"I didn't lie to you," I said. "But I didn't offer the whole truth either. When I returned to Blueridge Hollow, I didn't want to come as the alpha of *my* pack. There are those of you who know me from when I called this pack home. I wasn't sure what reception I would get when I came back, and I knew Malric was dying. So I came here as a representative of my pack. Not as someone looking to become alpha of yours."

A few confused murmurs rose. I lifted a hand to stop the whispering.

"Alphas are born, we don't get to make the choice." I saw a few of the elders, those who knew me when I was young, exchange looks. "An alpha's power comes later. Are there signs I was one? I don't know; I never even thought it was possible. Malric was kind enough to let me stay in this pack during my younger years. Everyone here who knew me back then knows I wasn't groomed for the title. When circumstances"—I almost choked on the term—"made it that it was time to move on, I did. I left this pack when I was eighteen. Not an adult yet. I found a new pack. Alpha Lars of Stonefang Pack was a good alpha. He saw something in me, and when I hit the age of change, he trained me and recognized the changes when I didn't. He knew I was an alpha, and he led me through it. Guided me. So that when he passed, he had already named me the successor to Stonefang Pack. There was no real fight for it, the pack accepted. I was challenged, but they weren't serious."

"Is the challenger dead?" someone asked, and I didn't need to look to know it was one of Kirk's kin.

"No," Killian spoke before I could. "There were three challengers in all. One is still telling the tale of how his alpha landed him flat on his ass with one punch, another sits on Alpha Wolfe's council, and the third is here, as his beta."

"You?" a female to the back asked.

"Brand," Killian said easily. "He is currently guarding your alpha's wife during her heat."

Lewis looked at me. "You let someone who challenged you for your position become a beta?"

"Brand was always a beta," I explained easily. "He's got a good head on his shoulders, calm and capable. I didn't want to lose that just because he wanted to test my commitment to my pack." I shrugged. "Pretty much like when I asked you to be an advisor for here, I don't believe in letting knowledge and wisdom go to waste."

"The point is," Killian said. "Wolfe helped lead the Stonefang Pack without being the alpha for years. He did the damn job without needing the rank. Alpha Lars didn't hide from us that Wolfe was his successor. His sons weren't born alphas, but they still serve in our pack alongside Wolfe, like they served their father before him."

I let that settle. Some of them shifted uneasily.

"I didn't hide it from Malric. He knew." I let out a small smile. "Well, I tried to hide it from him," I admitted, "but he was too clever for me, even at the end." I heard a few chuckles in the crowd. "The druid knew too. When your alpha named me his successor, I didn't take it lightly." I turned slowly, meeting eyes. Letting them feel the weight of it. "I never intended to rule two packs. I didn't come here for this."

"But you accepted it," Elder Murrow said, sharp-eyed.

"I accepted it," I echoed. "Because your alpha asked. Because this Hollow matters. Because I saw the threats gathering on your borders, and I knew what it would mean if you fell."

"And the mating?" someone asked. "The daughter of the alpha? Our Rowen?"

That tic in my jaw was back.

"That was not part of any plan," I said. "But if you're worried about manipulation, stop. Rowen chose her path long before I returned. You think she bends to anyone?" That got a few huffs. A few grudging smirks.

Someone stood up, someone I didn't know, and they looked at me with nervousness. "I heard you, heard both of you while you argued earlier." She swallowed. "She is your bonded mate?"

The noise level rose as people clamored to be heard over each other, some in outrage, some with joy.

"Quiet, everyone!" I commanded. I looked for the female who had spoken. "It seems she is," I admitted, the words feeling like lead. "I only suspected it…recently; her heat came upon her earlier today, and the mate bond is in place." I didn't add that she hated it, or me. I didn't add she hadn't accepted it nor had we sealed it. They didn't need to know *all* the details of my life.

"Praise be to Luna," I heard several say as they thanked the Goddess. I kept my thoughts on that to myself. Personally, I wanted to have a very long conversation with the

Goddess and ask her what I ever did to piss her off so much.

"Mate bond aside," I said as I crossed my arms, bringing their attention back to me, "you want to question my right to be here? That's your prerogative. It's like I already told you when you thought I was your pack leader. I didn't take this title from anyone. I was given it by Malric, who knew exactly who and what I was. And now that I have it, I will defend this land, this pack, and every shifter in it with my life." I hesitated and saw Killian's subtle nod. "As your alpha, and I am sorry that I kept that from you."

I stepped forward, slow and deliberate.

"I don't need blind loyalty. I don't need you to even like me. I just need you to follow when it counts. And if you can't do that?" I let the quiet stretch. "Then I'll make the same offer I made before: you've got until sundown tomorrow to leave the Hollow."

Silence.

Then Lewis stepped forward and gave a short nod. "You're not Malric. And...I get why you kept your true nature of who you are secret from us, though you shouldn't have." I could see by the look in his eye that he had a good idea that Rowen was involved in the why, but he didn't voice it. "But you're here, and Malric was happy"—he paused as a flicker of pain passed over his face—"really happy when he named you his heir." Lewis met my gaze. "We'll see what you do with it."

The druid stepped out of the shadows, and I saw Killian glaring at them. He obviously had no idea they were here either.

Their robes whispered over the floor as they walked

towards me, ash-stained and heavy with the scent of sage and pine needles. A hush swept through the pack like wind through dry leaves. Even the pups at the back stilled.

"I would speak," the druid said, voice carrying with no effort.

Permission wasn't asked. It never was, with them. They turned, slowly, to face the gathered wolves. Their one pale eye caught the dying light.

"Many of you wonder how this happened. How the Hollow now bows to an alpha who returned without fanfare, who stood beside you not as a conqueror but as a wolf among wolves."

The tension built. I said nothing. Let them speak.

"I knew," the druid continued. "As did your late alpha, Malric. Wolfe speaks the truth, Alpha Malric knew exactly who he was leaving his beloved pack with. The Goddess does not always announce her plans with thunder and flame. Sometimes, she moves quietly. Through bloodlines. Through loyalty. Through pain."

They paused, letting that settle.

"We have long followed tradition," the druid said, eyes sweeping across them all. "But even tradition must bend when the winds change. Wolfe did not steal this title. He did not posture, or challenge, or burn his way into this pack. He did not return to this territory with this intent."

They turned, eyes locking on mine.

"He was chosen."

A murmur rolled through the crowd like the distant rumble of a storm.

"I have walked this land for generations. I have marked alphas in blood and bone. And I tell you now—this one carries the weight of leadership. The Hollow will not fall under his watch."

They turned again, voice rising.

"But it is not just he who must rise. It is you. *All* of you. The pack must rise with its alpha—or risk losing the legacy we have bled to preserve." A pause. Then, they raised one hand, fingers curled in a symbol only the oldest among them recognized. "This is not the end of the old ways," they said. "This is their evolution."

They lowered their hand.

"The Goddess watches."

Then they turned their back on the crowd, signaling that the words had been spoken—and the judgment was final.

That was enough. For now.

"Alright, I think we've had enough excitement," I said to the pack and was pleased I heard a few light laughs. "Now, I have a mate to calm down and hopefully keep my head while doing it." That got even more laughs. It had been a long time since Blueridge Hollow had a mated pair leading them. "You can always ask me anything," I added. "I will utilize Malric's rooms in this hall as my office, but my home is my home," I said with a little more firmness.

"How do you plan to run both packs?" someone asked at the very back.

I let out a sigh and answered with the truth. "I haven't quite figured that out yet." I looked to the door where the pull to Rowen was tugging me. "But don't worry," I added with a wink. "I know exactly who's going to offer me advice."

I gestured to Killian. "Killian is my beta, my second. In both packs. Brand is another beta, and I have one more at

Stonefang, Diesel, who is leading in my absence. The other two here right now are Axel and Cody. I want both packs to get to know each other, but if you want to wait for that, I understand." I walked to the door. "This is your home, your pack, but I am alpha of this territory…remember that."

I unmasked my alpha scent, and the room breathed in a collective breath. I wanted them to know I hadn't used my Will on them—I hadn't manipulated them—but I also wanted them to feel it.

I was their alpha, and they could accept it or leave.

I turned my attention deeper into the forest, where it seemed my three guards were having difficulty containing my mate.

Chapter 26

———

Rowen

I didn't bother with shoes. Didn't bother with a coat. The damn house was too warm anyway—too full of his scent, his presence, his claim. I just needed air. Trees. Space. Something that wasn't this suffocating heat crawling under my skin like wildfire.

Two steps down the stairs, and I felt it.

Eyes.

"Don't," I warned before I even saw them.

The guards stepped from the shadows near the front entrance like obedient ghosts. Three males. Not pack, not truly. Stonefang shifters sent by him to ensure I didn't tear off into the woods and embarrass us both.

"I'm going out," I said, brushing past them.

One of them stepped in front of me, the one who Wolfe had told to *stand down* earlier. "The alpha said—"

"I don't give a shit what your alpha said," I snapped. "I'm not a prisoner. And unless you're about to physically stop me, I suggest you move."

He hesitated. The wrong move.

The low growl that came out of me wasn't polite. Wasn't civil. It was feral. I didn't even recognize my own voice anymore.

"You going to challenge me?" I asked sweetly. "Right here, right now, on the front steps of your alpha's house?"

He looked at one of the others and then stepped back.

I walked out.

The warm air wrapped around me, but it wasn't what I needed. Nothing was. My skin itched, my blood simmered, and my wolf was restless in a way that made me want to tear out of my own body. Granted, this heat wasn't as painful as others, and I was reluctant to think it was because I was Wolfe's *fated mate*. I wasn't convinced the primal part of me gave a shit who was the male to sate my need, just that there was a need that needed sating. I also knew that was bullshit. There would only be one male who could sate my need.

Thinking about it hurt my head. Not thinking about it made me focus on the constant pull of my body that seemed to be *searching* for him.

I didn't know where I was going. I just knew I couldn't stay still. Couldn't stay inside. Not when everything about that house smelled like Wolfe. Not when the bond was pulling so tight I swore I could feel his heartbeat in my chest.

Somewhere between the edge of the forest and the clearing where we held the bonfire rites, I stopped. Wind tangled in my hair, the scent of pine and ash barely cutting through the haze of him.

Stupid, stupid girl.

What was I doing? Running through the Hollow with nothing but rage and heat in my bones like I was still seventeen and thought freedom was something you could steal under moonlight.

A twig snapped behind me. Slow and deliberate, letting me know he was there.

"I told them not to stop you," Wolfe said, quietly, steadily. "Figured if you were reckless enough to run, you were stubborn enough to need to be chased."

I turned slowly. "Is that why you followed?"

"No," he said. "I followed because I knew where you were headed."

"You don't know anything about me anymore."

He stepped closer. Just one step. Enough that I felt the bond shiver between us. "I know you're in heat," he said, almost gently. "And I know you're scared."

My spine straightened. "I'm not scared."

His eyes flashed. "Then why are you running?"

I didn't have an answer. Not one I could say out loud. "I'm not scared," I said again, sharper this time, like volume could make it true.

"You should be." Wolfe's voice didn't rise; he already had my attention and it was because he wasn't wrong.

My fingers curled into fists. "You think I'm afraid of *you?*"

"I think you're afraid of *what this means*." He took another step. Close now. Too close. "You feel it, Rowen. You're not that good a liar."

I shook my head. "You don't get to do this. You don't get to come back, don't get to be an alpha, and—"

"I didn't choose this," he cut in, tone flat, controlled. "I *wasn't* supposed to stay. I wasn't supposed to *want* to. But then I saw what they were planning for you. Heard how they talked about you like you were nothing more than someone to warm their bed." He stepped closer again. Just a breath between us now. He gave a rough laugh. "I came to *check* on you. I never planned to stay. Your father did that," he added, and I caught the hint of resentment. "And now…" He looked away with a sigh. "The Goddess has made damn sure I'll stay."

"It must be so hard for you, having everything delivered to you on a plate," I lashed out.

"Tell me you don't feel it," he murmured, ignoring my anger. I could smell the truth on him. Taste the storm building in his chest, and I was tired. Tired of running, tired of fighting against an invisible might. I felt my shoulders droop as some of the tension left my body.

"I felt it the second you walked back into this Hollow," I admitted quietly, voice tight. "I just didn't know what it was."

His eyes searched mine, and I hated how steady he looked. How *in control* he always was when I was falling apart.

"The mating bond must have always been there," he said carefully. "What we had when we were younger was maybe more than either of us knew." He licked his bottom lip as he considered his next words. "I thought your rejection had killed anything left in me to care about you. But…" He looked up at the sky in defeat. "I come back here and all I want to do is smother you in my scent, so…shows you what little I know."

I stared up at him. "Why didn't you say anything?"

"About what?" he asked tiredly.

"Being an alpha."

"Because I don't trust you," he said bluntly. "Your father never knew either until the morning he asked for a hug." His lips twisted with bitterness. "And I, like a fool, still seeking his approval, gave him one. The next thing I know, I'm named his successor, and it's decided that the best thing for you is to be my wife *if you want it*. And you said yes." Wolfe pushed his hair back as he looked at me. "I blame you just as much as you blame me," he added softly.

I looked down at the ground, my heat rumbling through my blood but not painful, not yet. "Do you think he knew I was your mate?"

"I think he didn't care about that," Wolfe said, his resentment easy to hear.

"You married me," I said slowly. "You're saying that… you're saying you married me, knowing you're an alpha and a mate could be out there, waiting for you."

He held my look with a steady gaze. "I did."

"Why?"

"Because it's like I said, Rowen, you needed someone who could let you lead this pack, who would stand beside you, not in front of you." He didn't look away. "You never needed to hide who you were. Not from me. I always knew exactly who you were." He didn't say it in a complimentary tone.

I should've slapped him.

I kissed him instead.

Fury and heat and need collided as I yanked him to me —mouth crashing into his with all the desperation I had bottled inside me. His groan was low, rough, and it lit something dangerous in me. His hands came to my hips, gripping hard enough to bruise, pinning me in place like he could anchor us both.

I hated how right it felt. How easy it was to burn in his hands. I shoved him back a step, breath ragged. "I didn't mean…" I gulped down a breath. "This doesn't change anything."

"No," he agreed, his gaze dark and hungry. "It just makes everything worse."

And then he kissed me. Harder. Meaner. Like punishment. Like a promise.

I didn't want anything more from him, not out here, not yet. But if the mate bond had been a thread before, now it was tightening around us like a noose. And as Wolfe kissed me again, I wasn't sure who it was meant to hang.

His hand was still on my hip. My breath still tangled in the space between us. And I hated that for a second—just one fucking second—I leaned into it.

Into him.

I shoved him again. Not hard. Just enough to remind us both that I could. He let me. Smirking like he liked the fight. Like he missed it.

"You really think I'm going to be the one who loses control?" I demanded.

Wolfe's jaw tightened, but he didn't break. "You already did. You just don't want to admit it."

I laughed—sharp and bitter. "I've spent years mastering my control. Do you know what that's like, Wolfe? Do you have any idea what it costs to keep yourself in check when every damn person is waiting for you to fail?"

He didn't flinch. "I know exactly what that feels like."

And damn him—he said it softly. Honest. Like he meant

it. I hated him more for it. Because he was the only one who could understand.

"You think this mate bond makes a difference?" I whispered, stepping closer, chest brushing his. "You think I'm yours now?"

"No." The word was low. Final. "I think you're mine *still*."

The air crackled between us. Something deep inside me bucked against the truth of it, against the part of me that had never really let go of the way he said *mine*.

I turned my head. "You've gotten good at pretending you're not the one breaking."

He moved fast—grabbing my wrist, not to restrain but to feel. His thumb skimmed the inside like he could map the wild beneath my skin.

"You think this is me breaking?" His voice was low, dangerous. "This is me holding back."

I stared at him. My lips parted on a breath I hadn't meant to give. That's when I knew it—knew what the Goddess had done. Not a punishment. Not a gift.

A challenge.

Because if he was my mate…then she was testing me. Maybe she didn't want us to fall in love. Maybe she wanted us to survive it.

"You need to get back to the house," Wolfe murmured. "Your scent is intoxicating," he said, his voice tight with need. "I just told the pack who and what I am, so let's not give them more to handle tonight with the scent of your heat making them crazy."

"If you just let me go to my old rooms—"

"I had them cleansed and purified," he told me, his grip on my wrist firm. "You belong at the house, where I am."

"Why would you purify them?" I asked him in disbelief.

"Because the only place that should smell like you and the sweet scent of your pussy is in our house."

I stopped walking, too stunned to respond to his crassness or my reaction to it. Wolfe didn't stop walking, and his hold on my wrist yanked me forward to walk beside him.

"I can walk, unaided," I snapped, yanking my arm free for the third time as he stalked beside me, one hand always hovering like he expected me to bolt. "I won't run away," I added like a petulant child.

"You're right," he growled. "You won't. You're not going anywhere." His voice was rough, command woven through every word, and my wolf *liked it*. Worse—*I* liked it, and I hated that most of all. "There's nowhere you can go now, that I won't find you."

The house loomed ahead, the same one I'd sworn wouldn't be my prison, and yet now…it didn't feel like a cage. Too many eyes on me. Too many truths gnawing at the edges of the bond pulling taut between us. His three men hovered nearby, and I chose not to look at them, convinced I would see smug satisfaction on at least one of their faces as their alpha returned me to the house like I was a rebellious pet being returned to their master.

Wolfe pushed open the door and waited for me to walk inside.

I didn't.

He didn't say a word. Just stepped behind me, one hand grazing the small of my back—a touch so light it felt like fire

—and waited. I swallowed my pride and walked in, spine stiff, fury barely banked.

He followed. "You can go," he told his pack. "I won't be leaving again tonight." The door shut with a soft *click*.

I whirled on him. "You don't get to keep me here like I'm some feral—"

"You're in heat." His voice was steel. "You're drawing attention. We haven't fucked. To males out there, you can still be *taken*. I'm protecting the pack—*and* you."

My laugh was sharp. Bitter. Even though I knew what he was saying made sense. I just didn't care. I felt wild. *Reckless.* So I pushed him. I wanted to see how *mighty* this alpha was. "Protecting me? Or hiding me?"

"I don't *hide* what's mine," he growled, stepping closer, jaw tight. "But I'm not going to parade you around when you're vulnerable either."

"You don't get to make these decisions!"

His gaze burned. "*Yes*, I do. I am your mate, and I am your husband. Your heat needs to pass. Be grateful we are already married and the pack knows you are already claimed, but you don't smell like me yet, and until you do, there is the possibility that we'll have another problem on our hands." His gaze fixed on mine like he was made of stone.

My heart slammed against my ribs. Before I could find a reply—before I could tear into him—there was a knock at the door.

Wolfe opened it without looking.

The druid stepped inside, calm and composed, as though none of this heat-laced chaos touched them. Their robes swept the floor, their bare feet silent on the wood. They looked between us with unreadable eyes.

"I thought it best to speak now," the druid said, eyes settling on me. "Before choices are made that can't be unmade."

"Then speak fast," I muttered. "Because apparently, I'm under house arrest."

Wolfe didn't react, but the druid's mouth twitched. "You are not a prisoner," they said. "You're a torch held too close to dry tinder."

That wasn't comforting. I folded my arms. "You want to talk about Wolfe?" I challenged them. "You want to talk about how you knew he was an alpha but you bound us in ceremony anyway?"

"I want to talk about the Goddess."

I didn't flinch—but it was close.

"The mate bond between Alpha Wolfe and yourself…" the druid continued, stepping farther into the room, "is an interesting development, do you not think?"

"Interesting development?" Wolfe mumbled. "Not the phrase I'm using."

"Did you do this?" I asked the druid suspiciously.

They smiled with what looked like genuine mirth. It would have been unsettling if I wasn't feeling so crazy in my own skin.

"Your heat rides your good sense, Rowen," they murmured. "A mate bond cannot be *made*. It is born as the shifters who complete it are born. I have thought on this— when Wolfe was with us before, your bond would have recognized you both, but you were too young. Wolfe was not yet into his alpha power, and you…" They watched me with a gleam in their eyes that made me cautious about what was coming next. "You were already fighting for your place in this pack. A place you were so scared that was going to be *given* to you, not earned by you." The latter was said with a hint of a sneer. "Wolfe left, and the mate bond was left to cool. Untouched. Unclaimed."

"So?" I was not behaving my best, and I knew it, but it didn't stop me.

"So," they said, voice soft and maddeningly patient, "if you are truly mates, as it now appears, then this is not merely a union of strategy. It is a union of sacred design. The Goddess does not pair lightly."

I scoffed. "Or maybe she's just got a sick sense of humor."

"She's given you strength. A pack. A chance." The druid's eyes gleamed. "And a male who matches you, soul for soul."

Wolfe didn't say a word. But I *felt* him watching me. Breathing me in. The heat between us climbing, scorching, and I didn't know whether to rage or run.

Or stay.

"What do you want from me?" I asked the druid.

He looked at Wolfe. Then back at me. "I want you to decide. Not out of fear. Not out of heat. But with clarity. Either claim him…or find a way to end this now. For your pack's sake and for your own."

I felt the weight of Wolfe's silence behind me. Heavy. Steady. Waiting. But I wasn't ready to speak. Not yet.

The druid dipped their chin once to Wolfe and left the room, their footsteps vanishing like smoke.

And I was still burning.

"Go to bed, Rowen," Wolfe said quietly. "Try not to climb out the damn window," he added as he headed to the kitchen.

"What will you do?" I asked, knowing he was giving me time. Time I desperately needed.

"Don't worry about me," he told me, opening the fridge. "Just get through this. No doubt there will be something else to dodge when it's past."

He sounded tired. No, he sounded *exhausted*, and it was because of that, that I kept my head down and slipped into the bedroom, closing the door firmly behind me.

I lay on the bed, still damp from us from earlier in the night, and closed my eyes. I had a lot to think about, and I didn't know where to start.

Chapter 27

Wolfe

I DIDN'T LIKE FEELING WATCHED.

I liked it even less when I was right about it.

The druid's words still clung to me like smoke. I'd left Rowen in that room with her jaw set and her eyes wild, and every part of me had screamed to turn back. To drag her out of the Hollow and keep her somewhere safe. Somewhere *mine*.

But that wasn't how this worked. Not with her. Not with this pack. Not with the rumors circling like vultures on the wind.

It had been a long night, and though she'd done everything I asked, eventually, I could still taste her need on my tongue. I'd dealt with it the only way I knew how: I'd gotten up off the too-small couch, closed the door behind me, shifted to my wolf form, and run as far away from her scent as I could.

In the small hours of the morning, Killian had tracked me, and together we had done a wide sweep of the territory.

Something had pulled at me, tugging me back to the Hollow, and it wasn't my wife's heat.

We'd come back to the pack, and the pack hall already had elders gathering in it. I'd sent Killian and Brand in to investigate while I followed the sense of "offness."

I stood on the ridge just beyond the Hollow's main perimeter, staring down at the pine-split valley that had been quiet only a day ago. Now, the birds were silent. The air trembled with a warning only wolves knew how to hear.

The wind was wrong. It came from the north, thick with smoke, ash, and something fouler—panic.

"They hit Deep Hollows," Killian said as he came up behind me, his voice tight. "Middle of the night. A lot of casualties. Survivors are saying they were a pack of rogues," he sighed. "But they were organized, Wolfe. It's too clean for a random strike."

I didn't speak. He knew what I was thinking.

"Deep Hollows?" I turned and looked at him. "One of the males who came for her hand was from there, right?" He nodded. "We need more information," I said eventually. "Is someone feeding them our movements?"

Killian shrugged. "I don't know, but your new *elders* are getting jumpy. They're questioning the mating pact. Wondering if this union made Blueridge Hollow more of a target."

A low growl scraped up my throat. "The union didn't make us a target. Leaving Stonefang without an alpha present might have made my *other* pack vulnerable. Malric's dying made *this* pack a target."

"Your elders don't see it that way."

Of course they didn't. The moment they didn't control

something, they turned on it. Like a rabid dog too far gone to remember who fed it.

I turned my eyes back to the ridge. "Send a scout team, I'll send Brand with them. They need to be quiet. I want to know what's left of Deep Hollows before anyone else does."

Killian hesitated. "Brand's on Rowen."

My jaw flexed. "Switch it out to Cody. He's…likeable."

Killian snorted. "Cody is *not* likable." Killian looked around us. "Cody might actually just kill her and ask you for forgiveness afterwards. Maybe."

Rowen had barely looked at me since the heat snapped between us and nearly brought us to our knees. She'd been turning inside out from it, and still somehow fought it to fight *me*. She was still running from everything it meant. Still resisting what we both knew now couldn't be denied.

She was mine, and every instinct in me howled to protect her.

"Tell Cody to keep her close," I said. "Tighter patrols. And get ready to move her out of the Hollow to Stonefang if there's even a whisper of a breach."

Killian looked at me with surprise. "Really?" When I nodded, he whistled low. "You going to tell her any of that?"

"No," I said flatly. "She's not ready."

"She's going to hate you for it."

"She already hates me."

Killian gave a low chuckle. "That's got to be some kind of record. Married a few days and already at war."

I didn't answer because he wasn't wrong. And because a part of me—one I didn't like admitting even to myself— *liked* it.

Rowen didn't kneel. Didn't flinch. She challenged,

clawed, snapped at the bit, even when her body was against her and the bond between us was thrumming like a live wire. She was still fighting.

And I was falling. Too fast. Too deep. Too fucking sure of her.

I turned from the ridge. "You coming?" I asked Killian as I started to walk back to the pack.

"Where we going?" he asked carefully as we left.

Time to get the pack to accept the alpha bond. I saw his look of surprise. *What, you think I was going to* not *claim my pack?*

I thought you'd maybe wait… His tone was careful.

The quicker I have this pack under my Will, the quicker I know if there's a traitor in our midst.

Killian sniffed. "Well, when you put it like that…"

"Exactly," I growled.

As I got closer to the Hollow, I didn't need Killian to deliver any message to Brand; I was close enough for the mindlink to work. I would never judge my betas, but the speed with which he agreed to scout and stop shadowing my mate would have been amusing if it wasn't so fucking depressing.

My guys were loyal to me, fiercely, and also the most outspoken, contrary bastards I'd ever met. If they disliked Rowen, then the rest of the Stonefang Pack would be even more unwelcoming towards her. I didn't want that.

I'd need to talk to her. Talk to her about fitting in. I may as well discuss the possibility with that tree over there.

Rowen was exactly what this pack needed her to be. *Respected but distanced.* She was a living relic of pack tradition and a threat to anyone who underestimated her. She was the one who was never meant to lead but everyone still looked to when things fell apart.

I respected the hell out of that, knowing that the very thing I respected her for was what she resented most about her life. There had always been a quiet rage in her—the kind that comes from a life of being told "you can't" and deciding to prove them wrong in *everything* that she did.

She believed in loyalty above law. Honor above hierarchy. But I knew never to mistake that for softness—she'd protect what's hers with teeth.

I knew all this and still had absolutely no idea how to introduce her to my pack. The Goddess better be enjoying this clusterfuck she put me in, I thought.

At the edge of the packlands, I stopped. Killian paused with one eyebrow raised. "Shifting?" he asked.

"Quickest way I know to get them all," I told him grimly, pulling off my shirt and handing it to him. "Try not to drop them in a puddle this time." Because that's what he did when I did this at Stonefang, he "accidentally" dropped my clothes in the muddiest puddle he could find, and then when I shifted to get dressed, the pack had laughed at the look on my face as he handed me muddy dripping clothes.

"You never know, Wolfe," he murmured as he stooped to pick up my boots. "You may welcome the icebreaker."

They don't want the ice broken, Killian…they want it smashed.

My wolf was big. I knew it, everyone who saw it knew it. I would not blend in a pack of ordinary wolves. Hell, I didn't even blend in a pack of shifters. The size of my wolf had been described to me as *monstrous*.

My fur was deep charcoal gray, like a shadow under moonlight, and I needed no introduction as I walked the land of the Hollow. I moved silently over the ground, but not unnoticed. My eyes shone pale silver and I opened myself up to the pack of Blueridge Hollow.

I am your alpha, submit.

The mindlink snapped open.

It was like a door blowing off its hinges.

Multiple presences bloomed into my mind—familiar and unfamiliar—startled wolves blinking into awareness as the connection surged through them. Some reached back instantly, relief thick in the bond. Others hesitated, testing the waters.

But they all *felt* me.

I walked the worn paths to the pack hall, paws silent, head high, the ancient roots beneath me thrumming with recognition. The land had accepted me. The wolves were beginning to.

It wasn't love that poured into me; it was their gratitude. Raw. Fierce. Laced with a quiet desperation they hadn't dared voice—not until now.

They hadn't needed a ruler. They needed an *anchor*. A protector. And whether I'd planned for it or not, I'd just become the mountain they leaned on.

I see you. I sent it through the link, low and sure, my voice a tether of steel across the pack's collective pulse. *I claim you. I will bleed for you. And I expect the same.*

Wolves responded. Some with a hum of acknowledgment. Others with a mental bow of their heads. Even a few howls cracked across the mindlink like sparks catching fire.

Not all had submitted. Not yet. But enough had. I was no longer a visitor in Blueridge Hollow.

I was its *recognized* alpha.

I shifted back as I reached the rise before the pack hall, the ground slick with morning dew under bare feet. My skin steamed in the cold air, muscles humming with the power still riding my spine.

Killian handed me my clothes. He didn't say a word. He'd felt it too.

"Let's hope they know what they just invited in," I muttered, pushing open the doors.

Because being alpha wasn't about dominance. Not really. It was about burden, and I'd just agreed to carry theirs.

"How many didn't accept?" he asked, low enough that only I would hear.

"Enough," I murmured back. My eyes fell on the chestnut braid of the female with her back to me. "I'll fix that."

"I hear Cody—" Killian was already gone before he finished.

Chickenshit, I sent to his retreating back.

I headed to Rowen, letting my Will precede me. The three pack who were with her instantly accepted the bond, and almost as quickly as Killian, they made their excuses and left my wife looking around in confusion.

Our eyes met and I saw her realize what was happening at the same time. I closed my Will off.

"Bullying into obedience?" she asked with a sweet smile. "That's new. Or is it?"

"It's called submission," I said lightly. "You should try it. I would love to see you on your knees…again."

Do you remember the last time you were on your knees in front of me, princess?

Her eyes flared at my taunt, and I felt her presence across the bond like a hot ember in a fire gone cold. Not acceptance, not quite. She didn't bend that easily.

But she felt me and she didn't shut me out. That mattered more than I wanted to admit.

Her grief was raw. Her rage was louder. But she was still part of the link—and I felt her in the same way I felt every wolf that had trusted me to be their alpha.

What I felt from her was *not* love. I wasn't sure I would ever earn that from her. But there was something solid. Something dangerous.

I welcomed her, and she didn't meet me with silence.

My mate, she purred, *the alpha with the adolescent brain.*

She'd accepted me as her alpha, and that meant everything. I didn't hide my reaction—my smile was wide and full of relief. I saw her answering smile at my reaction before she turned away, pretending to look at something else.

I entered her space, placing my finger under her chin and tilting her head back. "Thank you," I murmured before I brushed her lips with mine. She didn't pull back, her fingers curled around my wrist, not to pull away but to hold on.

"Alpha?"

I turned to one of the pack, who looked like they wanted to be somewhere else rather than interrupt us right now.

"What is it?"

"The druid asked for you, sir."

I blanched. "Goddess, do not ever call me *sir* again," I muttered, stepping back from Rowen. "Alpha or Wolfe will do just fine."

"Um...sorry, sir." The boy gulped. "They said you were to come no matter the reason you gave not to, sir."

I shot him a quizzical look, and his face reddened all the way to the tips of his ears.

"Alright, let's walk and talk," I said, slinging my arm over his shoulder. "What's your name? Mine is Wolfe, not sir."

"I'm He-Henry. Si—Wolfe. Alpha... Wolfe."

I heard Rowen's titter of laughter behind me and turned to look at her, her fingers pressed over her lips like she was trying not to grin.

"I'll see you at supper?" I asked, already walking away with Henry.

You will.

Her voice in my head made me hard as stone, and not for the first time, I cursed the damn druid and their impeccable sense of terrible timing.

THERE WAS a pause in the wind.

A stillness so unnatural it made my skin crawl. Even the trees held their breath, the forest around me suddenly absent of birdsong, no rustle, no shift—just silence so thick it rang in my ears.

I scanned the path again, every instinct screaming without a source. My wolf pushed beneath my skin, agitated, teeth bared and pacing, the primal version of myself sensing danger I couldn't yet see.

I turned toward Killian as we walked. He had been waiting for me outside the druid's tent. "You feel that?"

He paused. Head tilted. Then slowly, carefully, nodded.

"Something's wrong," I said.

"Wrong how?"

"I don't know," I answered tightly. "But it's here."

My hands dropped to my sides. I didn't move. I didn't blink. I just *listened*.

Then the birds fled.

Dozens of wings exploded from the canopy ahead, a mass exodus of fear ripping through the sky like a warning.

The howl came mid-thought. Sharp. Distorted. *Wrong*.

Rogues. Too close. Too many.

I was moving before Killian even turned. "Move!" I barked. "Rowen's in the pack hall!"

Everyone get to the clearing, I commanded as we ran.

We tore through the trees, heartbeats pounding like war drums. The Hollow's outer perimeter blurred past in green streaks and brown shadows. Voices rose, screams sounded, and the clearing was in chaos.

And in the center—Rowen. Katana in hand. Face pale, but eyes lit with fury. Blood at her temple. Two rogues down at her feet. Three still circling. I leapt the last barricade just as one lunged.

She didn't see me coming.

My wolf roared from beneath my skin, and I tackled the rogue mid-air, shifting in the process, claws slashing, bones cracking beneath the impact. I didn't stop until the ground was red and the threat was ash in my mouth. Killian charged at the other.

Another rogue came at her blind side. She didn't miss. Wood met flesh in a clean, perfect arc, and he fell with a wet grunt.

She shifted. Her wolf was small, but I remembered her speed. We kept close together now, breath labored, blood slicking our paws.

And then it hit. The mate bond. Not a flicker. Not a whisper.

A *detonation*.

It snapped into place between us like a lightning strike straight through my ribs, and from the way she staggered, it hit her just as hard.

It forced the shift on us both, and I turned slowly, chest heaving, meeting her wild eyes.

"You feel that?" I rasped.

She didn't answer. She looked like I felt—raw, broken open, torn between fight and surrender.

I reached for her, just once, hand cupping the back of her neck as the world spun around us.

"You're mine," I whispered, kissing her fiercely, knowing this wasn't the time but needing to taste her anyway.

She didn't deny it. But she didn't accept it either.

And as I drew back, the part of me that still remembered how this started—how she rejected me—wasn't going to beg her for it. I'd told her and she was still not ready to accept this, so I made my decision.

I wouldn't stay here, frozen in want. Not when my pack needed me bleeding and brutal. Rowen had made her choice—her pack, not me.

I turned back to the fight. Shifting back to my wolf, I surged forward into the fray.

Chapter 28

———

Rowen

I couldn't move.

Couldn't breathe.

The heat of his mouth was still seared into mine, and the words—*You're mine*—still echoed in my ears like a death knell. And maybe it was. Maybe that was the end of who I thought I was. Because when Wolfe kissed me, the bond didn't just flare.

It *claimed* me.

Every instinct in my body—my *wolf*—howled in recognition. And then he turned his back and left me gasping in the dirt.

The bastard.

The sound of bone breaking jarred me out of my trance, and I spun to see a pack member thrown against a tree. Blood slicked the earth. Screams rang out. Someone shifted mid-lunge, the snap of spine and muscle twisting the air as they clawed toward a rogue trying to tear through the line.

I blinked once, twice, and *moved*.

My limbs felt foreign—too fast, too strong—but I didn't stop to question it. My feet pounded across the forest floor, and I launched myself toward the nearest threat. One of the rogues had taken down a young Hollow wolf and was going for the throat.

Not on my damn watch.

I hit him like a landslide, dragging him off the pup and rolling into a snarl. My claws extended mid-motion, raking deep across his back as he twisted, jaws snapping. He was strong.

But I was *furious*.

The bond was still burning under my skin, and I used it—channeled the rage and betrayal and *power* into every strike.

He'd kissed me like I was oxygen—and left like I was smoke. He'd branded me as his—and walked away before I could decide if I'd accept *all* of him.

And Goddess help me, it made me fight harder.

I took down the rogue. Heard the sickening crunch as his skull cracked under my final blow. My lungs were heaving, my legs shaking, but I didn't stop. I turned—just in time to see Wolfe's giant wolf tear through the clearing like vengeance made flesh.

He was *huge*.

Beautiful.

Terrifying.

When he passed me, brushing against my side with a growl that *felt like a command*, my wolf whimpered—and obeyed. Not out of fear. Out of *recognition*.

But I wasn't done yet. I wasn't going to let the pack see me cower, not even under the weight of fate.

Wolfe might be alpha.

He might be my mate.

But I was still *the daughter of the Hollow*, and I'd earn my place at his side with blood and fury—not because the mate bond demanded it.

I heard a pained shriek and turned to see the last of the intruders being taken down by Wolfe's mighty strike.

The fight was over as quickly as it began, and the clearing stank of blood, piss, and wet fur.

Bodies littered the ground—some breathing, some not. The rogue pack had been relentless, vicious in a way that wasn't about hunger or territory. This had been a message —and not one we could afford to ignore.

Injured wolves whimpered and snarled as our people moved through the wreckage. Wolves shifted to heal their injuries, but some were too broken to force the shift; they'd need their alpha's help. Every nerve in my body screamed, but I kept moving, jaw tight, claws still half-shifted at my sides.

Not because I was afraid.

Because I was angry.

I came to a stop in the middle of it all, panting, sweat cooling on my spine. My vision was still sharpened. His presence hadn't faded. If anything, it had settled—low and steady—like a drumbeat behind my ribs.

Wolfe.

His name was a pulse.

I could feel him at my back without turning. The scrape of his presence against my senses was too specific to mistake. Not just pack. Not just alpha. Mine.

I hated that it comforted me. Hated even more that it thrilled me.

A Hollow wolf limped past, dragging a wounded brother toward the pack hall. My legs felt like iron, but I moved, forcing one foot in front of the other. I was still in command. Still needed. And I couldn't break down. Not yet.

"Rowen."

I froze. His voice wasn't gentle. It was gravel. Roughened by battle and smoke, by too many truths left unsaid. I didn't turn.

"Are you hurt?" Wolfe asked, closer now.

"No." The lie slid too easily from my throat. I was hurt. Just not in ways a healer could fix.

He stepped beside me, his arm brushing mine. The contact sent a jolt through my system so sharp I had to clench my fists.

"We weren't prepared," I whispered.

"I know."

I finally looked at him. "This is what you've been saying all along?"

"No. Not all along." His gaze held mine, clear and unflinching. "But this is why we came here," he said, looking away. "One of the reasons."

My throat tightened. "And what does that change?"

He didn't answer.

Silence stretched between us. Heavy. Charged. Until he moved away, walking amongst the fallen, helping the injured.

We'd been caught off guard. The perimeter had been weak. Wolfe had told us that, and I was too busy *raging* against an injustice, so busy *moping* that *I* left my pack fragile.

Was it just our perimeter that was weak? Or had someone known how to slip past the wards? I turned back toward the heart of the field—and stopped.

Wolfe stood at the center of it. Towering. He had a pair of shorts on but was still shirtless, bloodied, his eyes lit up silver-white, gleaming like twin moons under the midday sun. Not a drop of hesitation in him. Not a flinch. Not a flicker of doubt.

Around him, pack bowed their heads.

Even mine.

Even *mine*.

The rogues were dead or gone, the threat neutralized—but the real reckoning had just begun. I could feel it in the way the pack shifted their weight, looking to him. Their alpha.

And he hadn't needed to raise his voice once.

Lewis appeared beside me, grim. "He's something," he said quietly, handing me a dress, and I didn't ask where it came from as I slipped it on. "Look how easily they follow."

"I noticed," I ground out. My wolf bristled. Not in fear. In fury at what had happened here today.

Wolfe raised his head. His voice poured through the Hollow, steady and calm—but soaked in something deeper. *Power.* Authority. A command that didn't demand submission. It *invited* it—and the pack ran to give it.

It is over, for now. But they'll be back, and we need to be prepared.

The effect was immediate. Chests lifted. Shoulders squared. The panic subsided. It shouldn't have surprised me. But it did. Because I knew this pack better than anyone —and they were ready to follow him without question. And worse? Part of me understood why.

Wolfe didn't try to soothe. He didn't sugarcoat. He *stood*, and right now, that was what we needed.

I watched Wolfe, his Stonefang Pack coming to stand beside him, their eyes watching the pack gathered. I saw what they were thinking; this wasn't a random attack.

Wolfe glanced my way, and I held his gaze across the blood-slick grass.

He didn't smile. Didn't soften. But he dipped his chin—just once—and the raw heat of his acknowledgment sent a tremor through me.

Not as his mate. As someone who knew exactly what it cost to lead. I turned before he could call for me. We had dead to bury and possibly a traitor to find.

———

THE ADRENALINE WAS STARTING to fade, leaving behind the ache of bruises and the sting of failure, but my mind wouldn't settle. The rogues hadn't just stumbled onto our land. Not with the way they'd moved. Strategic. Surgical. Like someone had drawn them a goddamn map.

I knew this territory like I knew my own bones—every ridge, every fault line, every hidden passage through the dense Appalachian pine. They hadn't guessed their way in.

They'd been *led*.

I moved through the camp in the hours after, checking on packmates, murmuring comfort I didn't feel, eyes constantly scanning. Not for more attackers. But for cracks.

Lewis joined me near the creek, his face pale, blood drying in streaks across his jaw.

"Most of them were loners," he said softly. "But they knew what to hit. Fast, clean."

"Too clean," I muttered. "Like they knew exactly where to aim."

He met my eyes. "You think it was someone from the inside?"

I didn't answer. Because I could *feel* it. There was rot somewhere in the Hollow. A whisper in the wrong ear. A slip of information that had led shifters to their deaths.

"I need the patrol records. Every single one," I said. "The schedule, the names, who was where—day and night."

Lewis hesitated. "That's going to ruffle feathers."

I turned to him, hard. "Then let them be ruffled."

He nodded and moved off. I didn't thank him. I couldn't afford to.

I stood alone by the tree line, arms crossed over my chest, mind spinning. There were only a few wolves with that kind of access—ones who had reason to move freely, to be trusted implicitly, and that narrowed the list far more than I liked.

Somewhere behind me, I heard Wolfe's voice again. Low, commanding. The pack still buzzing in his orbit.

I clenched my fists.

He was the alpha. But I still knew *my* pack.

I would find the traitor. And when I did? They'd pray Wolfe got to them first. Because if I found out who sold out my pack, I wouldn't need claws.

Just rope. And time.

I turned, intending to head back to the war room—what was left of it—when I saw him behind me. That damned tether tugging at the base of my spine, warm and steady and impossible to ignore.

"You're still bleeding," he said, voice too calm for the aftermath we were wading through.

"Must've missed a spot," I said, brushing past him.

"Rowen."

I stopped. Turned just enough to let him see the set of my jaw.

"You're not going to like what I have to say," he told me.

"Then don't say it."

He crossed his arms. His voice dropped. "I'm bringing in more from the Stonefang Pack."

I stared at him, unblinking. "Excuse me?"

"We need more boots on the ground," he said. "This attack showed how exposed the Hollow is. We need structure, reinforcements, a pack that's trained for—"

"No."

His head tilted slightly. "No?" He took a deep breath. "We need more eyes on the perimeter," he said. "More teeth. That ambush was coordinated, and we both know it. I won't risk this pack again."

I laughed once, sharp and humorless. "So your answer is to replace them?"

He frowned. "Reinforce them."

"Same thing."

"No," he said, voice hardening. "It's not. This pack is vulnerable, Rowen. They need training, backup—"

"They don't need strangers," I snapped. "Not outsiders. Not a babysitting unit from a pack that thinks we're feral and backward."

He stepped closer. "They need to survive."

"You don't get to treat my pack like it's some wounded animal that needs your wolves to carry it." My voice shook with restrained fury. "We are not broken. We are *not weak.*"

"You were *breached*, Rowen," he said, voice rising just enough. "They got through your perimeter like it was made of leaves. How many more need to bleed before you stop pretending this place is untouchable?"

I took a step forward, heat flashing down my spine. "This *place* is my home. This pack is *mine*. You want to help? Fine. But you do not override me."

He was silent for a breath too long. Then—softly, frustratingly calm—he said, "I'm not overriding you. I'm protecting you."

I flinched at that. Not because I believed it—but because some terrible part of me *wanted* to.

"Your Stonefang shifters," I said, stepping back. "They don't belong here."

"Maybe not yet," he agreed. "But they will. Because you and I both know this isn't the end. And I won't risk another ambush without backup. *Trained* backup."

The silence between us stretched taut. "Is this your decision as alpha?" I asked bitterly.

"It's my decision as a male who nearly lost his mate today," he said.

I hated the way that affected me. Like it slid right past my defenses and curled somewhere dangerous behind my ribs. So I did what I always did—I struck.

"Then next time, lead from the front. And *ask*, not dictate." I turned before I could see the impact of my words. But I felt him watching me as I left.

Let him. I'd fight with him, against him, beside him. But I'd *never* fall in line behind him.

The quiet hush of footsteps over pine needles got my attention. I knew who it was without looking. The druid. Always arriving like mist. Never when you wanted them.

They didn't speak at first, just studied me as they fell into step beside me. Their pale robes were smudged with ash.

"Fate," they said softly, "always asks for something in return."

I stiffened. "What's that supposed to mean?"

"You are bound now. And bonds, like borders, shift under pressure. Be wary of what you sacrifice—just to feel safe."

My expression turned to stone. "Is that a threat?"

"It's a truth," the druid said. "One he should remember before he fills this land with shifters who owe *him* loyalty, but not the Hollow."

Then they turned and walked away, robes trailing through the bloodied grass like a specter.

I didn't look for Wolfe. I couldn't shout across the forest that finally, *finally*, after all these years, the druid agreed with me. So I turned around and headed back to the pack hall.

The walk to the pack hall felt too quiet.

Blood hadn't even dried on the grass, and already it was like the pack was trying to forget. Like pretending things were normal could erase the scorch marks.

I wasn't in the mood for pretending. Is this why Wolfe thought he needed to bring in strangers?

I took some detours, checking in with pack, my legs aching from exertion, adrenaline still skittering under my skin. I wasn't sure where I was going until I stopped outside Adair's house.

I knocked once. Lightly. Then pushed the door open.

She was sitting cross-legged on the floor, drying damp hair with a towel, with that same quiet focus she always wore.

Her eyes flicked up. "You're bleeding."

I looked down. There was a gash on my forearm, raw and ugly, and I hadn't shifted to heal it yet.

"I'm fine," I said.

"Uh-huh." She stood, crossed the room, glared at the gash in my arm, and leaned back. "Shift."

I quickly undressed, shifted, healed and shifted back, because she wouldn't let me leave if I didn't.

I got dressed again and noticed the bruises forming under her collarbone. The shadow in her eyes.

"You alright?"

Her jaw flexed. "I wasn't the one covered in claw marks."

"Adair."

She looked up and there it was—that flicker of fear she kept buried under thoughtfulness and usefulness. "We lost three tonight," she said. "One was seventeen. One was a father."

"I know."

Her voice dropped to a whisper. "I thought we were safe. That with Wolfe…we were going to be okay."

I didn't answer because I'd thought the same damn thing.

"Do you trust him?" she asked suddenly.

"Wolfe?"

She nodded. I stared at the wall across from us. "I trust him to protect the pack."

"That's not what I asked."

"No," I said, "it's not."

Adair dropped the towel, then sat beside me. "You used to be so sure of who he was."

"I used to be a lot of things."

Silence fell again, but it was heavier now. Shared. Tired.

"I'm not ready to let go," I admitted. "Of this place. Of my father's legacy. Of me in it."

Adair didn't argue. She just leaned her head against my shoulder. "I think you're still in it," she murmured. "You've just got company now."

I didn't cry. I wanted to. But instead, I reached for her hand, held it tight, and stayed there a little longer—because tomorrow, I might not get the chance.

And tonight? Tonight, I needed to remember those we had lost.

Chapter 29

Wolfe

THE PACK WAS ALREADY ASSEMBLED WHEN I STEPPED outside.

They knew I was coming. They always did now. The druid had checked that all the rites were met, just me and them under the Heartwood, and I was very much the alpha of this pack as much as Stonefang.

Rowen stood to the side, arms crossed, chin high. Watching. Calculating. That sharp mind of hers hadn't dulled, and good—because it was about to be tested.

I stopped at the top of the steps leading to the communal clearing, the morning sun cutting sharp across the tree line. I let the silence hang. Let them wait for it.

"Members of Stonefang Pack arrive by dusk." That was all I said.

A murmur rippled through the gathered crowd. Unease from some. But not all.

A gray-haired female near the front—one of the elders, if I remembered right—nodded slowly. "Extra eyes. Good. We're stretched thin."

Gratitude. That was new. Others looked at her, surprised she'd spoken. I let her words sink in for the crowd.

"We were ambushed," I said. "They knew the terrain. They knew our weaknesses. That wasn't a rogue op. That was precision."

Lewis stepped forward. "You think we've been compromised?"

"I think we'd be fools not to act like we have."

No one argued. I looked at each of them in turn. Not challengingly. Just with the kind of calm weight that said: I see you. You see me. This is happening.

"The shifters from Stonefang are not here to replace Blueridge Hollow. They're here to reinforce it. Until we find who's feeding our enemies information, members of *both* packs will walk your borders, train beside your young, and bleed if needed."

A sharp whistle cut the air. Not disrespect. Approval.

Someone behind the crowd murmured, "About damn time."

Lewis gave a stiff nod, then turned to the others. "We hold Blueridge Hollow, but we don't hold it alone. Not anymore."

The message was sinking in.

Blueridge Hollow and Stonefang were no longer two separate packs. They were uneasy allies—and that was enough for now. I didn't wait for questions. I turned, walked down the steps, and out toward the ridge trail.

And that's when the wind changed.

A howl broke the silence—low, long, unmistakably Stonefang. Not warning. Not aggression.

Arrival.

They came through the trees like shadows, powerful and lean, fanned in formation across the trail. Some of my top fighters. Scouts. Enforcers. Trained in Stonefang's ways, loyal to their alpha's word.

Twenty of them in total. Not a show of power—a show of readiness.

Rowen's people watched in tense silence. It was all very well saying it was good to have reinforcements, but seeing them as they walked over your land was something quite different.

From somewhere deep in the crowd behind me, I heard a low growl cutting through the air—followed by a sharp voice.

"You bring wolves we don't know onto Blueridge Hollow and expect us to trust them?"

I turned to the pack behind me, voice flat. "You trust me. Or you don't."

Silence.

Killian, appearing at my side like the smug bastard he was, added helpfully, "You could always challenge the alpha for your chance to take the pack."

No one moved. I think half of them stopped breathing. *Exactly.*

Some of the Stonefang shifters dispersed without needing any command. They took up silent sentry positions around the perimeter, scanning, scenting, and ready. Three others came to stand beside me, ready for whatever I needed.

They did exactly what I wanted. I didn't need them to blend in; I needed them to be seen. Because a message was being sent today—loud and clear.

This pack was not alone anymore.

"Alright," I said to them all. "Let's start. Get comfortable, we have a lot to discuss."

I shouldn't have been surprised by the predictability of both packs. Blueridge Hollow shifters on one side, Stonefang on the other. There was tension, of course there was. But they were here and that's all that mattered.

I didn't stand above them. I walked among them.

Listened.

An older hunter from the Hollow was leaning forward, arms braced on his knees, talking to Brand. "That southern trail's too exposed. No decent coverage past the ridge—if they're coming through there, we won't see it until they're on us."

Brand nodded. "We can fix that. We'll triple patrols, rotate in the younger ones as part of their training, and use elevation to our advantage."

"How long before the younger ones are ready?" I asked.

Brand looked up at me, then dipped his head. "By the next full moon."

"Then do it," I said, looking back to the Blueridge pack male. "Work on the rotation with him, help select the names on the duty schedule."

"Really?" the old man grunted. "Didn't think you'd ask us. Figured you'd just replace us."

"I'm not here to replace anyone," I said simply. "If I was, I wouldn't be asking."

That settled something.

A female from the Hollow's outer sector stepped next to me. She looked exhausted, but her eyes were sharp. "I lost my husband late last year. I've got three under ten, and I haven't slept in days."

I didn't offer sympathy; she wasn't looking for that.

"There are rooms in the pack hall you can use. I'm making space for anyone who doesn't want to be separated from the pack right now. There will be guards that will rotate shifts there until further notice; there will be plenty on hand to ensure you get some sleep." She bowed her head, and I wasn't sure if it was because she was grateful or just too exhausted to keep standing straight. She went to move away, but I caught her elbow and lowered my voice. "And if any of your young need tutors or food, speak to Axel." I gestured over to him. "I've assigned him to logistics along with Lewis; they've got resources," I said. "Please don't be afraid to ask."

She looked up at me, blinked, and looked a little stunned. "It's that easy?" she asked dubiously.

"This is a pack," I said. "Pack help each other."

I watched her as she walked away and wondered what had changed in the Hollow that a widowed shifter would find it hard to ask for help. Why hadn't she gone to Rowen? I'd need to make sure my pack was asking the right questions. I saw several of the elders watching me, faces grim, saying nothing.

I watched them back. This was not how trust was built—it wasn't by orders, but by outcomes. Solutions.

I felt Killian watching from the edge of the clearing, arms crossed, a ghost of a smirk on his face. He knew what this was. This wasn't domination. This was integration.

It wasn't loud. It wasn't flashy. But it *was* working.

And as more voices spoke up—Blueridge, then Stonefang—something rare happened. They started speaking to *each other*, not just to me.

Shifters from two sides, bonded by circumstance, slowly stitching together what years of pack politics had kept apart. And I let it happen. Stepped back. Watched. Intervened only when needed. Guided when it mattered.

Because being alpha didn't mean I had to own every moment. It meant I had to shepherd them.

My gaze drifted toward the tree line where I knew Rowen lingered. She hadn't joined us. Not yet. But her presence pulsed like a thread just out of reach.

Let her watch. Let her see. This wasn't her pack or mine anymore.

It was theirs, and I was going to build it right.

By the time I pushed open the heavy door to the house, dusk had settled deep into the Hollow. The kind of dark that crept between trees like it had a vendetta. I welcomed it.

Silence greeted me as I walked through the door. The living room was empty. No clatter of her in the kitchen. Just the steady hum of a house that hadn't decided who it belonged to yet.

I closed the door behind me and took off my boots. The shirt I was wearing wasn't mine and was stained from the day's work. I pulled it off and left it near the door as a reminder to return it to the pack hall tomorrow. I rolled my shoulders once, then twice—the weight of command had settled on me like a second skin, and I was eager to shed it in the privacy of my home.

I looked up and saw her leaning against the doorway between the hall and the sitting room, arms crossed, hair loose over one shoulder, as if she hadn't realized how lethal she looked like that.

Or maybe she had.

"What now?" I asked, voice low, even, not attempting to hide my fatigue.

She didn't move. "You made a lot of decisions today."

"I made necessary ones."

"Without talking all of them through with me."

I shrugged. "You weren't there. Too busy sulking in the shadows."

Her eyes narrowed. "I wasn't sulking. You didn't ask for me to join you."

I yawned as I walked past her, heading for the shower. "I didn't need to. If you wanted to be part of it, we both know you would have been."

She followed me. "That's not how this is supposed to work."

"No," I said, stopping and looking over my shoulder. "But it's how you're making it. If you want to change it, make more effort."

The space between us pulsed like it always did—charged, unspoken, unfinished. And her eyes, Goddess, her eyes…they weren't angry. Not really. They were wary. Watching. Measuring.

"You're good at it," she said quietly, changing tactics, becoming softer.

"Being alpha?"

"Taking control." Her voice remained low. "The pack listens to you."

"So they should," I told her, finding a clean towel. "That's the point."

"And where does that leave me?"

I turned back to her then. "You tell me." I shook my head slightly. "I can't keep having this conversation with you, Rowen."

I saw the flicker of uncertainty in her gaze. Maybe even hurt.

"I never came here to inherit a pack, Rowen," I said, voice lower now. "But they *are* my pack now, and I'm not going to let them fall apart because you're still pissed at me. You want to lead? Lead. But you lead *with* me. Not against me."

A breath passed between us. Her expression shifted—less war, more weathered steel. "I don't want you to be the one who fixes this."

"Tough," I said bluntly. "It's my duty as alpha, and I don't care anymore if you like it or not, but you can't keep resenting me for doing it."

She stepped back, not retreating, just…choosing space.

"You smell like pine and politics," she muttered.

"I smell like your pack."

"You mean ours," she corrected sharply and walked away before I could reply, disappearing down the hall toward the front of the house. I didn't know if she was staying or leaving.

I didn't hear the door open, so I assumed she was staying. That was progress. Maybe. Plus, I was fed up with chasing her; it didn't make a difference when I caught her anyway.

In the bathroom, I shed my shorts and stepped under

the spray of water, closing my eyes as warm water cascaded over me, and I let out a sigh.

When I was finished, I dressed in loose sweatpants and walked down the hallway. I didn't stomp. I didn't puff out my chest like some walking testosterone parade. I just walked. Quietly. Like the predator I was.

I leaned against the wall, much like she had done when I came home, and watched her as she sat on the couch, arms wrapped around herself as she stared out at the night like it had answers she couldn't find in me.

"You always lurk like this?" she asked without looking at me.

"Only when I'm invited."

"You weren't."

"Wasn't I?"

She turned then, arms falling to her sides, expression unreadable. "You trying to be funny?"

"No," I said honestly. "But I think this is our home, and we live together. So you tell me how we're supposed to do this without tearing each other apart."

Rowen shrugged and then got up and walked to the window. "Maybe tearing each other apart is all we're good at."

"Or maybe it's how we started," I said, walking over to where she stood now, only a breath between us. "But does it need to be how we end?"

"I don't know," she whispered. "I don't want you to be soft."

"Good," I said. "Because I'm not built for gentle." My hand lifted, not touching her, just hovering near her jaw. "But I am built for you."

Her breath caught, barely. Just enough to betray her. "You're not supposed to say things like that," she said, voice quieter now, more a warning to herself than to me.

"Why not?"

"Because then I have to choose whether or not to believe you."

"Then believe this," I said, finally letting my fingers brush down her arm, circling her wrist. Her pulse thudded hard under my touch. "We're mates—it's not going to go away. Not tonight. Not tomorrow. You don't have to want it yet. You don't have to like me. But stop pretending like you don't feel it."

"I never asked for a mate," she said, chin lifting.

"I never said you did." I laughed. "I never thought I'd have one, but here we are."

"What do you want, Wolfe?"

I stepped in, close enough to steal her air. "I want this house not to feel like a battlefield every time I walk in. I want my pack whole. And I want you to stop treating me like I'm your enemy every time I make a decision that saves this place."

Rowen stared at me. "And if I can't?"

"Then I'll keep doing it anyway. Because I'm the alpha, whether you like it or not."

She didn't respond, but when she finally looked away, it wasn't with fury. It was with something far more dangerous.

Acceptance.

Maybe not of me. But of the situation we were in.

I left her at the window, standing in the soft hush of twilight, and for the first time since stepping back into the Hollow, I didn't feel like an intruder.

Not completely.

Later, I was lying on the bed, Rowen asleep beside me, both of us very careful not to touch each other. I envied her ability to sleep so soundly. She was mere inches from me, and she wasn't close enough.

Stupid mate bond, making me want something that she wasn't willing to give. I'd be damned if I took it. Rowen would either submit to me willingly or not at all; if not at all, well…I'd need to consult an alpha whose mate rejected him after the mating bond had clicked into place to find out how to survive not being able to touch her.

Goddess knows where I would find one; my understanding was that mates meant happiness.

Not this fucking misery I was in.

You awake?

No, Killian, I'm sleeping, I told my beta, smiling in the dark despite myself.

Well, I knew you weren't getting hot and heavy with the missus… Never seen a woman so cold before.

I lost my smile. *Careful, Beta, that's your alpha's mate you're talking about.*

Well, Alpha, *I need you front and center,* he said, all humor lost from his voice.

I sat up slowly, careful not to disturb her. *What the fuck is it now?*

Stonefang, he said, and I could hear the strain in his voice.

What about them? I was already walking to the front door. I opened it, and my second was waiting for me.

"Killian?"

"Stonefang is here," he told me. "*All* of them."

Epilogue

Wolfe

Two weeks later

THE HOLLOW WAS QUIET.

For the first time in weeks, no one was arguing. No one was bleeding. And I wasn't holding Rowen back from tearing someone's throat out.

It should have felt like peace.

It didn't.

The moon was high overhead as I stepped out of the house. My head ached from the day's work, my back from too many hours mediating between two packs still learning how to share a space. Stonefang had arrived in force. They brought strength. Loyalty. And a handful of wolves I didn't trust as far as I could throw them.

Killian joined me without a word. We stood in silence, side by side, watching the pines shift under a breeze that smelled too still.

"Something's wrong," I muttered, walking away from the house.

Killian snorted as he joined me. "Just now noticing?"

I gave him a look. "One of ours intercepted a message," I said. "Encrypted. Complex enough to not be rogue. Not entirely."

He straightened. "From the Hollow?"

"From someone *in* the Hollow," I corrected. "Using an old coding system that I had to search for someone to know it."

Killian swore under his breath. "What did it say?"

I tried to curb my anger. "Stonefang reinforcements have arrived. Blueridge Hollow is unstable. Wait until the power shifts."

His jaw tightened. "Unstable? They're trying to turn the packs against each other?"

"Or against me." My voice was low. Flat.

"Any idea who?"

I shook my head. "Not yet."

But I would find them.

Before, they proved Rowen right that a bigger pack didn't mean a *better* pack. We'd been arguing for days, ever since Stonefang Pack had turned up unannounced, and I was tired of it.

Footsteps crunched behind us. I didn't turn. I knew the scent.

"You have something to say, say it."

One of my trusted men, one who'd been here from the start—Axel—cleared his throat. "Hearing too many rumblings," he said quietly, but his displeasure was clear. "Some of the younger wolves…they're asking questions. About the bond with this Hollow. Your loyalty to Stonefang Pack." He looked apologetic as he spoke. "Why Blueridge

Hollow has your favor." He let out a sigh. "It's not just Stonefang, Blueridge is asking the same questions about *them*."

"Do they need reminding who their alpha is?" Killian asked, voice hard like steel.

I shook my head, slow and deliberate. "They don't need reminding," I said. "They need watching."

Axel nodded, but his eyes didn't meet mine. That alone told me what I needed to know.

Dissent in the packs was taking root and growing.

By morning, I'd have names. A list of who still walked beside me—and who was looking for a way to cut me down.

Because I hadn't clawed my way back into this place, mated with the only female who ever made me forget myself, just to watch it crumble all around me.

No. Let them whisper. Let them wait. I'd already bled for one pack. I'd burn for this one too. I knew what they were saying; I'd heard the murmurs myself. Heard enough whispers to know I'd find the source.

I would not fail my pack.

Even if I suspected it was my mate who plotted against me.

About the Author

Eve L. Mitchell is a USA Today Bestselling author of Contemporary Romance, New Adult Romance, and Paranormal Romance. If you love morally gray alpha-holes, there's a good chance Eve has your next book boyfriend ready and waiting to be claimed.

A lifelong book lover, Eve still considers herself a reader first. She believes there's nothing quite like the thrill of getting a new book, whether on her e-reader or in her hands. Sharing that sense of excitement with fellow readers is one of her greatest joys. Writing under a pen name helps preserve her "Secret Agent" status (because who doesn't love a little mystery?).

Eve lives in the North East of Scotland with her three coffee machines (one is never enough) and her significant other, Mr. M. When she's not writing, she can usually be found watching NFL football (or complaining that it's not football season yet), playing music loudly, or having long conversations with the voices in her head—conversations that often turn into her next story.

THE BLACKRIDGE PEAK SERIES

The Blackridge Peak Series is a wolf shifter series about rival packs, hidden secrets, a little bit of magic, and a girl who's trying to find her way amongst a pack that doesn't want her. Kezia is an outsider, and when given the chance she leaves the pack that never truly accepted her. But trouble follows Kezia and she soon learns that only an alpha can protect her.

An alpha who may be her mate.

The series includes **Wolf's Gambit, Wolf's Betrayal, and Wolf's Endgame.**

THE SHADOWRIDGE PEAK SERIES

Dive into the enthralling world of the Shadowridge Peak Series that draws you into the mysterious realm of wolf shifters.

Join Willow Harper as she navigates life in the quiet town of Whispering Pines, where solitude has always been her refuge. That is, until Caleb Foster appears, bringing with him an undeniable allure and a secret that could unravel everything.

As curiosity turns into an obsession, Willow is thrust into a web of supernatural threats and urban legends that blur the lines between reality and myth.

The series includes **Wolf's Chance, Wolf's Fate, and Wolf's Providence.**

GET THE SERIES
WWW.EVELMITCHELL.COM

THE WATCHER SERIES

The Watcher Series is a paranormal romance trilogy that will take you on a journey where you will get lost in a world that will hold you in its depths. With a blend of steam, humour and angst, be ready to buckle up for the ride.
With demons, devils and one sassy, clueless witch, what more could you ask for? Join Star as she gets a crash course in what not to do when you get involved with the Watchers.
An enemies-to-lovers story that has all the emotions packed between the pages as the heroine deals with love, betrayal, loss and so much more.
This series is a trilogy and must be read in order. If you love cliffhangers, this series is for you. If you hate cliffhangers, don't worry, the next book's already written.
The series includes **A Glow of Stars & Dust**, **A Flame of Stars & Midnight** and **A Blaze of Stars & Dawn**.

GET THE SERIES
WWW.EVELMITCHELL.COM

THE AKRHYN SERIES

Creatures of evil roam the shadows - the Drakhyn. They may look like humans, but their taloned hands and razor-sharp teeth serve one purpose only; killing.

A Sentinel's purpose is to patrol and protect. They are highly trained soldiers with superior skills and abilities. Whether they be Vampyres, Lycan, Castors or gifted Akrhyn, their purpose is the same; hunt the Drakhyn and rid the world of their evil presence.

This fantasy trilogy covers tropes of chosen one, fated mates, good vs evil.

The series includes **Into Darkness**, **Lost in Darkness** and **From the Darkness**.

Fractured Loyalties – A forbidden, high-stakes romance packed with irresistible tension, criminal underworld intrigue, and the kind of love that ruins and rebuilds you.

The series includes **Her Ruin and His Fury.**

The Torn & Broken duet is a duet with a twist. You can read either book as a standalone. *Torn by Grace* was written first and one of the female side characters in that book is the main character in *Broken by Faith*, however, you don't need to know what happened in *Torn by Grace* to enjoy *Broken by Faith*. There is a little bit of crossover, but no spoilers.

Torn by Grace is a second chance, enemies-to-lovers, brothers-best-friend romance.
Broken by Faith is an enemies-to-lovers, forced proximity, fake relationship romance.
The series includes **Torn by Grace and Broken by Faith.**

THE RUTHLESS DEVILS SERIES

A college sports romance series following twin brothers and their cousin. Three football stars who have it all: looks, money, talent and the world at their feet. No one messes with the Devils. Each book deals with a different Devil and their love interest who will either make them or break them. The series covers tropes of enemies-to-lovers, second-chance romance and forced proximity.

This is interconnected three-book series with an underlying story arc that carries through from book one to book three, and therefore the series must be read in order. The series deals with some elements that sensitive readers may find triggering.

This series includes **Ruthless Heart**, **Ruthless Desire** and **Ruthless Charm**.

GET THE SERIES
WWW.EVELMITCHELL.COM

THE ORDER OF THE RAVENS SERIES
writing as Ava Speirs

The Order of the Ravens Series is a traditional epic fantasy series where the focus is on action and adventure.

Bastian dal'Leif is a Knight of the Order, an Order that has fallen into distrust. The Order of the Conclave which were once seen as warriors of the Gods and a beacon of hope, are now cast in shadow.

Bastian and his men remain true to their Order but are forced to become mercenaries, selling their swords for coin.

In the halls of his Order, Bastian is entrusted with a mission. A mission he is reluctant to accept.

The mission is so dangerous and deadly only a fool would take it…and only a coward would reject it.

The series includes **Knight of Sword & Shadow, Knight of Sacrifice & Shade, Knight of Dagger & Darkness, and Knight of Trials and Twilight.**